I0689698

PRAISE FOR

The Seller of Secrets

"Drawing upon the infamous Medici family as inspiration, Yutzy creates a magical world. The story is loaded with intrigue and full of deception, secrets, and a touch of romance, and readers will be drawn in by Bell's search for the truth. A combination of mystery, burgeoning love, and strong worldbuilding makes for a tempting read."
—*KIRKUS REVIEWS*

"*The Seller of Secrets* is a luscious tale of whimsical magic, deadly secrets, and how using one's gift can either better the world or bring destruction. Yutzy weaves themes of sisterhood, sacrifice, and friendship while also giving us a magnetic romance with the best emotional whiplash. The worldbuilding is intricate and persuasive, making it feel as if we could step right into its pages. Perfect for readers of Stephanie Garber!"
—**EMILY BARNETT**, author of *Thread of Dreams*

"*The Seller of Secrets* will sweep you away to a magic-infused Renaissance Italy full of intrigue, enchantments, and romance. If you love historical fantasy, humble heroines discovering their bravery and untapped talents, charmingly mischievous suitors, and settings so vibrant you can almost smell the magical flowers, this book is sure to become one of your new favorites."
—**CARRIE ANNE NOBLE**, award-winning author
of *The Mermaid's Sister*

"A spellbinding tale rife with intrigue, intricate magic, and finely-drawn characters. You will want to revisit Bardia over and over again!"
—LAURA WEYMOUTH, author of *The Light Between Worlds* and *The Castle & the Cloister*

"Sheri Yutzy's *The Seller of Secrets* is an immersive cross between *Caraval* and *Flowerheart*. It's a beautiful adventure with complex worldbuilding and a slow-burn romance, lushly told."
—EMILY BAIN MURPHY, *USA Today* bestselling author of *The Ivory City*

SHERI YUTZY

The Seller of Secrets

KEYLIGHT
BOOKS
AN IMPRINT
OF TURNER
PUBLISHING

KEYLIGHT BOOKS
AN IMPRINT OF TURNER PUBLISHING COMPANY
Nashville, Tennessee
www.turnerpublishing.com

Cover design by Audrey Puente
"Bell's Cottage" on hardcover case by Mira Byler
Book design by Ashlyn Inman

Library of Congress Cataloging-in-Publication Data
Names: Yutzy, Sheri author
Title: The seller of secrets / by Sheri Yutzy.
Description: First edition. | Nashville, Tennessee: Keylight Books, 2026.
Identifiers: LCCN 2025025331 (print) | LCCN 2025025332 (ebook) | ISBN 9798887981697 hardcover | ISBN 9798887981703 paperback | ISBN 9798887981710 epub
Subjects: CYAC: Magic—Fiction | Ability | Romance stories | Fantasy | LCGFT: Romance fiction | Fantasy fiction | Novels
Classification: LCC PZ7.1.Y977 Se 2026 (print) | LCC PZ7.1.Y977 (ebook)
LC record available at https://lccn.loc.gov/2025025331
LC ebook record available at https://lccn.loc.gov/2025025332

Printed in the United States of America

To Dan
I love you more with each mask you remove.

We should not mind so small a flower
Except it quiet bring
Our little garden that we lost
Back to the Lawn again -

So spicy her Carnations nod -
So drunken, reel her Bees -
So silver, steal a hundred flutes
From out a hundred trees -

That whoso sees this little flower
By faith, may clear behold
The Bobolinks around the throne
And Dandelions gold.

—Emily Dickinson

Isle of Bardia

Agnella's Cabin

Abandoned Tower

House Medoro

Santo Spirito

Brick Factory

Santa Maria Novella

House Asbury

Night Bazaar

Bell's Garden

Piazza

Palazzo Vecchio Hotel

San Giovanni

Rotunda

Santa Croce

Aless's House

Attuale Current

Attuale Current

Attuale Current

Glossary

The Maestris' Consiglio
Maestra of Metal – Lux
Maestra of Carpets – Anna
Maestra of Scents – Agnella
Maestro of Wood – Carlo
Maestra of Water – Piccarda
Maestro of Fire – Bruciare
Maestro of Stone – Calcione

The Houses

House Medoro – the most powerful Bardian family
Pater Cosimo of Medoro
Matrona Contessina of Medoro
Garam of Medoro
Piero of Medoro
The Merchant Medoros
Alessandro of Medoro

House Asbury
Pater Antonio of Asbury
Matrona Francesca of Asbury
Roza of Asbury
Goldenbell (Bell) of Asbury
Bethesda – their maid
Elena – their maid

House Salviati
Grigor of Salviati
Isa of Salviati

Makers
Carasti – woodmaker, friend of Bell

The Night Bazaar
The Seller of Secrets
Guardia de' Lanzi – the Seller's personal guards
Arabia – firemaker
Florian (Rian) – stonemaker

The Fioré
Aronil for truthtelling
Sciver for clarity
Common Elder for fabrication
Blue Hertes for beauty
Princess Seed for calm
Myrtle Leaf for comfort
Jonga Lily for illusion

The Magia
Jonquil lifts the mood. Addictive.
Insidio deceives the mind.
Taiga creates pain.
Smemor induces forgetfulness.

Elixirs
permanenza – makes any elixir permanent. Highly illegal.
truthtelling – a truth serum
protezi – protects against other elixirs
mindmeld – makes the victim's mind pliable

Places

San Giovanni – nobles' quarter

Santa Croce – merchants' quarter

Santa Maria Novella – commoners' quarter

Santo Spirito – farmers' quarter

Night Bazaar – the underground magic market. The entrance is on the edge of the Piazza

Sotto – the lower level of the Night Bazaar where deadly black market goods are sold

Vasari Corridor – the passageway that leads below all the noble houses and ends in the Seller's stall

Palazzo Vecchio Hotel – the luxury hotel owned by the Medoros

Piazza della Signoria – the central plaza of Bardia

Rotunda – where the Consiglio meets

Midnight Garden – the Seller's underground prison, filled with dark makings

Other terms

attuale – the magical current surrounding the island, a gift from the patron saint of Bardia, San Giovanni.

La Festa di San Giovanni – the festival celebrating San Giovanni and the renewal of the attuale power, held at Summer Solstice. Every year, a thunderstorm marks the renewal of the gift.

Infiorata – the centerpiece of La Festa di San Giovanni. Flower carpets cover the main road of Bardia and the Maestris walk it just before the Solstice storm begins.

Infioratore – artists who create the flower carpets.

Prologue

THE SPY

H E HAD WATCHED THE SCENTMAKER FOR years now, but this was the first time he'd seen her with blood on her golden dress.

When she pushed her way across the Piazza to where the foreigner lay writhing near the edge of the Bazaar, he stepped out from behind the pillar to see what she would do. Creamy linden blossoms tangled in her hazelnut brown hair and curled around her waist. She looked like she belonged in a flower garden, not kneeling by the side of a dying man.

He slid into a space at the edge of the circle of spectators as she touched the man's neck. The foreigner opened his mouth to speak and instead coughed a spray of blood across her sleeve.

She flinched, then set to work arranging a vial and mixing an elixir. Her jaw clenched as she spoke to the man's companion without looking at her.

Her movements were sure and certain. Even the silvery flame that whooshed from the vial was a subtle reminder to those watching that she was a person with power. Magic. The reason they were all here.

The Spy watched her with wonder.

Her work complete, the scentmaker rose gracefully, petals drifting down around her. Before her gaze reached the place where he stood, the Spy melted away from the circle like a shadow blown by a sultry summer breeze.

1

One

ON THE ISLAND OF BARDIA, THE *ATTUALE* magic stirred.

Bell of Asbury couldn't help but stare at the mainlanders smothering the Piazza della Signoria's brilliant ocher and orange cobbles with their ornamented skirts and puffed sleeves.

From where she perched on the low stone wall edging the Piazza, they looked like overfertilized wildflowers, too reedy to support their own flamboyant heads.

Every summer Bell swore she would hide in her bedroom high on the hill above the Piazza until the opening night was over. Yet every summer found her here, watching the swarm of hungry-eyed tourists. What made them risk the voyage, risk the *magic*? Was there nothing in their luxurious, normal lives on the mainland that could compare?

She didn't blame them. How could she, when the *attuale* thrummed inside her blood like too much oxygen? She knew the pull to the Night Bazaar—where the magic pooled—was nearly irresistible.

Nearly.

Her foolishness usually faded around now, after she'd watched them disappear by scores into the Bazaar entrance, and her fingers all but crackled with pent-up power. In those moments, it seemed inevitable Mother was right: One step into the Bazaar would shatter Bell's control, and her gift would lash out like a lightning storm.

That was how Mother made it sound, anyway.

And so she sat on the edge of things, tucked beneath the blooming

3

linden trees lining the Piazza's low walls. The cream-colored flowers hung in bunches, nudging her back and face and arms as they sensed the restless *attuale* within her. Their warm, familiar scent soothed like cool hands on humid skin.

She closed her eyes, tucked her fingers around a clump of blossoms, and let her power leak out as if from a dropper.

It was like a favorite aunt had come to call. The linden shimmered with expectancy, petals cascading as flowers wove themselves into her hazelnut hair, tucked behind her ears, wrapped the waist of her loose golden overdress. She laughed at the open-hearted delight radiating from the tree.

A fake cotton smell intruded, and Bell stiffened. A clutch of foreign women with jeweled necks and stenciled eyebrows pulled aside the branches and peered into her cocoon, murmuring to each other.

"It's her." The whisper scattered like spilled soil.

Bell straightened. She considered brushing the blossoms away with her hands, but that would steal the linden's delight, and for what? They'd already seen.

"Yes?" She resisted wincing at how rude she sounded. These were likely noblewomen, but how was she to know how to address them when all they'd done so far was stare?

"We're looking for a scentmaker." The closest woman moved forward, chin lifted. Her heavy brocade skirt massed around her like a solid thing.

For one breath, Bell considered lying, but the foreigner's gaze was too sharp. She wasn't only looking for a scentmaker; she was looking for the one who commanded trees. She would have seen the linden trees bending in the still, sultry air.

"I'm not working tonight," she said.

The woman teetered forward eagerly. "I can pay quite well."

"Bell of Asbury." A boy with frazzled brown hair burst around the women, sending them faltering back. "Is Miss Asbury here—?" His breath whooshed out as he caught sight of her. "Miss Asbury, you're needed."

4

"It *is* her," the tight-skirted one said smugly to the others.

Bell sighed. "What is it?"

The boy gulped. "A—a foreigner, Miss Asbury. He's collapsed outside the Bazaar."

The Night Bazaar. These wealthy mainlanders swarmed the island like brash summer weeds, celebrating the saint who brought the *attuale* to Bardia. They came to wear the youth-bringing perfume, sleep on the dream carpets, devour the waist-shrinking pastries. They came to be enchanted, and it all began tonight when the Night Bazaar opened for the first time, marking the beginning of La Festa di San Giovanni.

Sweat trickled down her back as she wove through the crowd, keeping her gaze on the boy's linen shirt. The smells on the summer air thickened as they crossed the Piazza and neared the Bazaar's entrance into the hill. Perfumes, both cheap and expensive, mingled until they knocked about in Bell's head. The stone archway to the Bazaar, hung with multicolored lamps that glimmered off the metal leaves sculpted along the arch, filled her with wary curiosity. The alchemy worked within the underground market made the air into a brewing thunderstorm—and it would only get stronger as Solstice drew nearer.

"Miss?" The boy's eyes were wide with anxiety.

Bell pulled her gaze from the lamps and took in the cleared cobblestones before her. A ring of foreigners stared at the linden flowers still wound in her hair.

A man writhed on the ground before her. His long face dripped with sweat, and he gripped his stomach. A woman in a wrinkled velvet purple dress crouched next to him, wringing her hands. She sobbed softly as tears made her violet eye shadow run in streaks down her face like an uneasy dusk. Bell knelt on his other side. She touched her fingers to his chin, and he opened his mouth and coughed. A fine spray of blood spattered her arm and sleeve. She picked up the empty vial lying beside him and sniffed it. Its sweet, plummy scent turned sickly as she realized what he'd done.

"He drank it?" Bell's glare prompted the woman to swallow her sobs.

5

The woman nodded. "He bought it in the Bazaar. It was supposed to make him beautiful, but—"

"Give me some room." Bell unlatched her kit. She jerked on her ivory scentmaking gloves and set out a squat, wide-mouthed mixing vial. "Blue Hertes is meant to be used one drop at a time—on the wrist. Not ingested. Didn't the scentmaker explain?"

"I dared him to drink it." Her breath hitched. "I didn't think he would actually do it."

"This was your idea?" *People like this shouldn't be allowed within a mile of the Bazaar.*

"It was a...a joke. I think he was upset because I said I wished I'd come with Angelico instead, and—will he be all right?"

"His brain is trying to remake his intestines," Bell said acidly, gathering three slender vials of scent from her black velvet kit. Into the mixing vial, she poured a drop of Princess Seed, two drops of Myrtle Leaf, and the smallest speck of Aronil.

Did they think their wealth excused them from the rules of Bardia's magic? Did they not *feel* the undercurrent of danger running through the whole Bazaar, touching everything in the stalls? In two weeks, the Summer Solstice would unleash a storm of magic through the *attuale* current circling the island city-state. Bardia would shimmer and swell as its makers—those with affinity for magic—strove to shape their strengthened power into jewels and wine and potions that would enchant.

When Solstice arrived and La Festa finished with a great parade, the visitors would return to the docks of Santa Croce where their ships awaited and sail away, enchantments left behind. The *attuale* gave Bardia magic, but also held it in. To carry any Bardian wares across the current was to risk being sucked into a whirlpool as the *attuale* drew the magic back into itself, along with whoever and whatever was nearby. Had greedy mainlanders attempted this? Of course they had. Enough had perished that fellow passengers were now as vigilant as the guards on the Santa Croce docks. Now they all accepted the ephemeral nature of Bardia and its beguiling goods.

6

Blending the elixir, Bell called her scentmaking gift to the surface too quickly, feeling it rush hot along her arms. A silver flame whooshed from the mouth of the mixing vial. She bit back a curse as the crowd gasped. This was only the second overdose of the season, but this was the first time she was forced to work in front of spectators. Now they would hound her incessantly until Solstice.

She poured the steaming elixir into the man's mouth, and his convulsions eased immediately. Packing her kit, she rose and turned to go, cream-colored linden petals drifting to the ground around her.

"Wait, miss, don't you want payment?"

She looked down at the woman's tear-swollen face. "Keep him away from the Bazaar." The spectators parted for her, but their gazes felt as heavy as the scents floating in the air.

As she headed back toward the south end of the Piazza, a slender girl fell in stride beside her.

"Second time this year, huh?" Her best friend Carasti's enormous blue eyes peered out of a curly halo. Her cinnamon brown hair sprang in all directions, making her head seem large. On someone else it might have been grotesque, but with her delicate chin and round eyes it had the same effect as a baby.

Bell grimaced. "My mother's going to find out, isn't she?"

Carasti nodded slowly. She ducked to the other side of a passing cart of peaches, and when she rejoined Bell, she had juice dripping down her chin and a half-eaten peach in her hand.

"Did you steal that?" Bell scowled.

Carasti turned away and looked behind her as if Bell was talking to someone else. When she turned back, the peach was gone. She had that magnetic yet innocent gaze all blue-eyed people had. "Steal what?"

Bell shook her head. Ordinarily she'd be fighting a smile, but she was still rattled. "You get away with far too much."

"It's because I don't go around with my forehead permanently wrinkled. No one suspects me." Carasti brushed a silky petal from Bell's shoulder. "You might want to take those flowers off if you're trying not to attract more idiotic foreigners."

7

Bell tugged the blooms out of her hair. A young Bardian couple wandered through the crowd. The girl's pretty eyes sparkled at the sight of the Piazza while the boy hardly looked away from her face. What would it be like to be simply in love?

Using the blossoms from her hair, Bell shaped a bouquet. As they passed, she pressed it into the boy's hands. He looked confused until Bell motioned at the girl.

In the next moment, they passed each other, and the couple disappeared into the crowd.

"Perhaps that will pay for your peach," she said in response to Carasti's wrinkled nose.

Carasti glanced toward the gleaming structure to the south of the Piazza. "The Maestra of Scents sent me to find you. She wants you to meet her at the Palazzo."

The Palazzo Vecchio Hotel was the only building taller than the Consiglio's Rotunda beside it. It dripped with iridescent Bardian metal and waterfalls that disappeared into thin air—a paradise for anyone who wanted to experience Bardian magic without venturing into the Bazaar. Now, it teemed with foreigners in gleaming oiled beards and stiff lace collars.

Bell's stomach tightened with dread. "Maestra Agnella? Did she say why?"

"Her words were, 'Tell that girl I'm going to name Piero my assistant if she doesn't come.'"

She snorted. "I've beaten him a dozen times."

Carasti cocked a brow and bent to pick up a pebble. "But were rich foreigners ever watching?"

Bell's fingers twitched. "I can't imagine a more disgusting scenario."

"Okay. I'll tell her you give in to Piero. I'm sure she'll be disappointed, but—"

"I'll come." Bell took one step toward the hotel to prove her commitment. It felt too close, looming over her, like a giant eye that saw through her skin.

Carasti's incongruous smirk bloomed. "At least this will make your mother happy, right?"

Bell tightened her lips as they approached the front steps of the Palazzo Vecchio. Stringed music spilled from the open doors of the lobby. "I'm not sure if even the approval of wealthy foreigners would win her over."

"But it's in the Medoros' hotel. That's who she's trying to impress, right?"

Bell stared miserably at the golden wood doors. The maroon-suited doorman watched them approach. "It's a fine line with Mother."

To Bell's disgust, Carasti darted away before the doorman even had a chance to frown at her plain blue cotton overdress.

"I'm here to see Maestra Agnella," Bell said reluctantly. Her best friend would climb the tallest tree just for a good view of the sea, but she fled at the sight of bejeweled women.

The doorman bowed and led her through the high-ceilinged lobby. A man with a white oiled moustache that curled in perfect spirals stood in the center of the velvet-lined back lounge, his fingers steepled. Two dark-haired women flanked him. One was a younger copy of the other. Their gowns were heavy and richly dyed, and their powder-white faces were stark against their dark hair.

Agnella, the Maestra of Scents, waited by a gold embossed table covered with buckets of fioré blooms. Agnella's crown of white-streaked braids was perfectly neat, and her black eyes were implacable, as always. Piero of Medoro stood by her side. His perfectly cut burgundy coat marked him as a noble's second son.

Bell's stomach stirred uneasily. This could not be good.

"Only two of them?" The man's accent swept over the words like syrup.

Agnella cleared her throat. "Signor Strozzi, few Bardians are born with gifts strong enough to train as apprentices."

"This is especially true among scentmakers, is it not?" a voice said from the door behind her.

9

Bell forced herself not to whirl, but her mouth twisted into a sour knot. Of course Piero's older brother Garam would be here poking his nose into this—as if he had any stake in a Bardian gift.

The gift manifested in one family member of each generation, and Piero had received it.

"It seems so," Agnella said.

"And this one is your fiancée's sister?" The younger woman pursed her full lips and eyed Bell with a spark of envy, as if Bell were the one lucky enough to be engaged to the heir to House Medoro. Bell restrained herself from returning the scowl. When Garam moved to join the mainlanders, his broad shoulders and statuesque face contrasted sharply with their curved features.

He wore the short burgundy cape marking him as the Medoro heir, and gold earrings peeked out from beneath his dark, curly hair. He was nearly too perfect to look at, exactly her sister Roza's type.

Being near him made her skin crawl.

He'd always been clear about what he thought of makers—and of Bell herself. Now here he was to watch, control, critique.

Piero shifted beside Agnella, and Bell dragged her gaze from his brother. Piero's fitted coat looked somber against the backdrop of lurid mainland colors, but the rancor in his dark gaze felt like a rotted log she was about to step onto.

"Feeling nervous, Bell?" Piero said with a sneer.

"I'm feeling fine, thank you." She moved to stand beside Agnella, taking in the heaps of fioré blooms piled before them. The animosity between her and Piero—her greatest scentmaking rival—was familiar enough that it reassured her.

"What's going on?" she whispered to Agnella.

"Our guests are friends of the Medoros. They require a demonstration. Fuse whatever you like." She tilted her head in a way that said both *cooperate* and *make it impressive*.

All seven first-level species of the magical fioré had been supplied for this demonstration. Aronil for truthtelling. Sciver for clarity.

Common Elder for fabrication. Blue Hertes for beauty. Princess Seed for calm. Myrtle Leaf for comfort. Jonga Lily for illusion.

Signor Strozzi was watching her. If he was so eager for an impressive show, why wouldn't he visit the Bazaar? Half a dozen scentmakers would be fusing elixirs at dizzying rates this very night. Agnella, for that matter, could perform with more—

"Bell, are you ready?" Agnella said.

Fighting a scowl, Bell pulled on her gloves. She was ready to weave an unforgettably enchanting elixir and to leave Piero tidily in the dust, but she didn't like Signor Strozzi's eyes.

"Begin." Agnella snapped her fingers, and Bell jolted into motion.

She took two stalks of Common Elder, snatched a small bloom of Blue Hertes, and surrounded the bouquet with Jonga Lilies. One stalk of lacy Common Elder drooped too far to the right, and she tucked it back in. With her free hand, she picked up an empty vial.

Bell eased her gift through her chest, her arms, her fingers. She *pulled*. The bouquet shriveled. The essence of the flowers dripped down the stems, and the multicolored droplets flowed into the empty vial. Delight shivered through her at the release. The tangy scent of the elixir rose into a scent cloud only a scentmaker could see. It looked like a pale blue blossom floating beneath a gold-white arch, a soft brown square surrounding it all. The cloud faded as it drifted toward the ceiling. She dropped the bouquet and fit a cork into the neck of the vial. The liquid glowed dark gold, bands of blue twisting within it.

The young woman gave a startled hum and stepped closer. Piero tossed aside his shriveled bouquet and lifted his umber-filled vial. Bell's skin prickled as she eyed his vial. His elixirs always looked so predatory. Had he slipped in a second-level fioré? He'd corked it too quickly for her to see its scent cloud.

"Let me hold it." The young woman held out her hand to Bell imperiously. Bell glanced at Agnella before reluctantly handing it over. Bell held her breath as the girl lifted the vial, colors turning inside, to the light. Her fingers caressed the cork.

11

Bell had been working on this elixir for weeks, but now under Garam's scrutinizing gaze, it looked petty and useless.

A misuse of her gift, he would call it.

"I've named it 'Wings.' I will test it for you, Miss," Bell murmured. The girl pouted, but her father nodded. Taking back the vial, Bell dabbed a tiny drop to her wrist. The girl squealed and clapped her hands as sparkling silver wings rose from Bell's shoulders. Their tips brushed the ground.

"Fabulous," the woman exclaimed.

Signor Strozzi nodded, grudgingly pleased at his daughter's reaction. "Surely they don't fly?"

Bell swallowed. *If you use the whole bottle.* She'd tested it at night a week ago, and she'd turned luminescent and flown around her garden from tree to tree, light as the wind. She'd lost track of time, and an hour later, the elixir faded, dropping her into a flower bed without much warning. Luckily, she had only dared to hover a few feet from the ground.

Neither Signor Strozzi nor Garam would approve of Miss Strozzi flying around the Piazza.

"No, sir. The wings will last for an hour if you apply three drops to each wrist."

The girl's face fell, but she smiled as she took the vial back. "You haven't made this to sell before? No one else will have it?"

Bell's lips curved. "No one else."

She tucked it into her purse. "Then I'll save it for La Festa. And yours?" She gestured to Piero's dark vial.

Piero tilted his head, his eyes hooded with careless confidence. He dabbed a droplet onto his own wrist.

Bell's neck prickled when fangs sprang from his mouth and his gaze turned predatory yellow. Claws extended from his fingers, so sharp and lethal looking she had no doubt they would cut skin easily.

"Ooh," the girl squealed.

Her mother frowned. "That doesn't seem appropriate."

Garam cleared his throat. "Perhaps a gift for her chosen companion?"

The girl's grin widened, and she snatched the vial before her mother could protest further. Garam murmured something that made the girl's laugh ring out. She touched his arm as she whispered back.

"What do we owe you?" Signor Strozzi turned to Maestra Agnella.

"Nothing at all. Please accept these as a gift in honor of your support of Bardian crafts." Agnella's smile was proud.

With the demonstration over, Bell quickly turned to go. Signor Strozzi watched her steadily.

Garam called after her as Bell descended the Palazzo Vecchio's front steps. She pretended not to hear him, but he caught up quickly.

"Miss Asbury, I think it would be best if—"

She glared at him and kept walking. "Why are you here, Garam?"

"Matrona Asbury asked me to escort you home."

"You're marrying my sister. Why don't you find her and escort her home? Or do you have plans with Miss Strozzi?"

He cocked a brow. "Miss Strozzi is a family friend. What makes you think your sister is away from home?"

Bell scoffed. "It's two weeks until Solstice. Roza would never sit dutifully at home when she could be dazzling tourists in the Bazaar."

Something dark shifted in his gaze. "Regardless, you're the one your mother asked me to escort."

Bell lengthened her stride as they joined Via dei Calzaiuoli, the main street that climbed up to Santa Maria Novella, the nobles' quarter. "We've left the Piazza. You can consider me escorted."

His boots thudded beside her until she wanted to howl. "I heard you fused an elixir, right next to the Night Bazaar's entrance, for a foreigner."

"I didn't have a choice. The man would have died."

He stepped in front of her, the setting sun glowing in his eyes. "You should be more careful." His voice lowered. "People are watching you, Bell. People who want to use your gift."

She scoffed and sidestepped him. "Use my gift? Like Signor Strozzi? As far as I can tell, *you're* the one watching me."

"I'm merely the one you can see."

13

Bell folded her arms, ignoring sudden goose bumps. The street steepened as it reached the edge of the nobles' quarter. The arched gate to House Asbury finally came into sight, and a guard stepped forward to unlatch it as they approached. Garam fell behind her and stopped. "Good evening then, Miss Asbury."

Frowning, Bell walked through the gates of her home.

As the sun dipped below the horizon, the dusk shadows felt suddenly heavy. She couldn't stop herself from looking back. Her gaze skittered over the darkest corners of the street. As the gate swung shut behind her, a sharp breath of relief escaped her lips.

Two

THE SUMMER BELL TURNED ELEVEN, SHE and Roza were inseparable.

That summer was like sweet Bardian wine—warm, golden, effervescent. Bell had always loved the walled garden behind House Asbury, but that season the soil eagerly produced glorious blooms for her. When she wasn't tying new climbing roses to her trellis, she and Roza would sneak out through a hidden door in the walls. They roamed Grenwood, the forest outside, finding hidden burrows and paths, and collecting strange nuts and leaving them in piles for the squirrels.

One day in late August, Roza got bored with the garden and wandered off into Grenwood. Bell didn't follow. As beautiful as the wild wood was, the garden held her heart, and she spent every morning tending it.

When the evening heat closed in like a sticky hand, Roza didn't return for dinner. Calling her name, Bell roamed in the direction Roza had disappeared. Perhaps she had forgotten the time?

Bell found Roza in a thicket near the Piazza della Signoria. Her pale face peered through the branches like a wildling. Leaves stuck out from her hair, her skirt was torn at the knees, and her eyes glowed feverishly.

"Roza. Where have you been?"

Roza smiled widely and held out her hands. A bouquet of strange gray blooms filled her fingers. There was nothing beautiful about

15

them, but their scent grew until Bell felt dizzy. Her blood stirred, and her hands rose to take the blooms. Sparks flashed against her palms as she seized the stems, her fingers brushing Roza's. Her vision clouded as a gray, iridescent mist rose in a foggy circle around them. Multicolored droplets ran down her wrists. Mind hazy, Bell reached for the sparkling fog with her hands, somehow sending her thoughts with them. The mist swirled when her thoughts touched them, spreading foggy tendrils away from Bell—and straight into Roza.

Bell laughed with a wild elation as the sparkling mist vanished into Roza's head.

Roza slumped onto the ground. Her eyes rolled back as she convulsed.

Bell's joy evaporated. The misty circle faded as the droplets spattered the ground. Fueled by panic, Bell dragged her writhing sister up the path toward the garden. When Mother found them, Bell still clutched the withered bouquet.

By the time the rider Father sent returned with the Maestra of Scents, Roza lay on the couch in the parlor, pale and still. Grim-lipped, Maestra Agnella dropped to her knees and felt Roza's forehead. Her gaze swept the room, eyes sharp with accusation. She focused on the withered bouquet in Bell's hands—and cursed. Maestra Agnella turned back and mixed an elixir with sure, steady hands.

Bell trembled beside her. She didn't speak a word, even as the color returned to Roza's cheeks. Maestra Agnella stood and pointed one knobby finger at Bell.

"She will begin an apprenticeship under me."

Mother protested fiercely.

"She fused Magia completely unprotected," Maestra Agnella said, implacable. "She nearly wiped her sister's mind clean. They'll likely both contract Lymbodia from the exposure. Without training, it's bound to happen again."

Mother's lips were pale and tight. "We'll make certain she never touches a magical blossom again."

Maestra Agnella shook her head. "Do you think she can live her

16

life like that, here on Bardia? She must be trained so she can at least protect herself."

Father held Roza's clammy hand and smoothed her hair. His stricken gaze lifted to Mother's. She shook her head, but Father looked back at Maestra Agnella. "She will be trained."

Bell shifted under the weight of their gazes. Her breath fluttered in and out, never enough to ease the panic gripping her chest. She'd almost erased Roza's mind? Guilt sickened her.

Maestra Agnella frowned down at Roza as she stirred weakly. "There is nothing more I can do for her."

Mother grabbed Maestra Agnella's sleeve with desperate fingers. "When will we know if they're sick? How long will they have to live?"

"I don't know." The Maestra turned to go. "Send the girl to me in three days." Bell watched the Maestra's stiff figure disappear out the front door without a backward glance, her mind full of a deep, insistent dread.

Roza would never be the same.

And it was Bell's fault.

That summer was like the dark and tangled root system of Bell's gift— from it came her fierce determination to master her power and use it for good. To heal.

But underneath, the ugly roots lurked. She felt them even now, years later. The possibility of the damage they could do.

Another ship arrived from the mainland the next evening, and the Piazza's orange cobbles could hardly be seen beneath the churn of feet.

At the table in Maestra Agnella's open workshop along the west wall, Bell curled her hands around a bouquet of luscious blue and cream Hertes blossoms and let the *attuale* unfurl through her fingers. Warmth swept along her arms, flowing through her veins. The multicolored drops she'd pulled from the stems trickled into a glass vial.

17

She closed her eyes and breathed in the plummy fragrance. It was full and sweet on her tongue. A warm night breeze swept across the crowded Piazza and through the booth, tickling her skin and scattering the remnants of the scent into the air. Murmurs rose from the four apprentices surrounding the scentmaking table. She corked the vial, forehead creased.

Why were they staring at her, and not at the elixir?

Standing at the end of the table, Maestra Agnella suppressed a smile. Her crown of white-streaked braids caught lamplight when she dipped her head.

"Drat," Bell muttered. A sliver of skin showed through a tiny slit in her right glove. It was below the wrist where her veins were most vulnerable to the magic. She yanked off the glove and scrubbed her wrist with an alcohol wipe until her skin burned. The Hertes scent would take an hour to wear off. Until it did, her honey skin would be smooth as glass, her eyelashes long and lush, her pink lips impossibly full. She would be a walking portrait of unnatural beauty. Bell's head felt swollen, and the sweet, dusty aroma of scentmaking took on a sour edge. Why hadn't she checked her gloves before fusing? She'd let the tourists distract her from her usual careful routine.

Piero snickered from across the workshop. He dropped his crumpled bouquet and lounged against the table, watching her.

Bell flinched. It was mortifying that everyone could tell she'd made a mistake.

Agnella's hand, bony but warm, rested on her shoulder. "A fine demonstration, as usual."

"Can we be finished with Hertes now?"

"Afraid of a little magic, Bell?" Piero taunted.

Agnella picked up the vial holding the distilled scent. "If you want to make a living, you'll have to sell Hertes. Is it such a burden to be stunningly beautiful for an hour?" She picked up Bell's glove. "You'll need new gloves."

She groaned. "But everyone knows it's not real."

"In Bardia, that doesn't matter."

"It matters to me." Bell turned away, pretending to watch the crowd outside the workshop. A pair of farmers' girls in neat linen dresses clutched each other and whispered. Their eyes were fixed on her. Bell's elixirs were becoming more potent lately, strong enough to affect those a dozen yards away.

Agnella's flinty face softened. "And that is why you will soon take my place as Maestra of Scents."

That again? Piero was still watching. Why was he here, anyway? He usually made some excuse not to help teach at Agnella's midweek classes, despite it being required for two years after graduation.

Bell pulled her silky hair from its tie and let it cloak half her face. "I'm not meant for that, Agnella."

Agnella motioned the other apprentices closer. "The first scent-maker, Firinacci, taught that to fuse any elixir of value, a scentmaker must give to her gift as much as she receives." Her finger stabbed at their bouquets, half of which were unfused. "Most of you are giving nothing. If I see no progress when next I look, perhaps you should find another Maestra to follow." She turned back to Bell, ignoring the others' stricken faces. "I will speak to the Consiglio when we meet tomorrow."

Bell gripped the table. "Maestra Agnella, I am honored, but—"

"Look around the Piazza, Bell. None of the other Maestris have four apprentices. I have so few because the *attuale* is gathering in preparation for my succession ceremony."

The Maestris' training workshops and their thrifty customers, eager for magical wares at apprentice-made discounts, lined two opposite sides of the square. Agnella was right. The other booths each held ten or more apprentices.

Bell's gaze refocused as a young, familiar blonde noblewoman strode toward the scentmaking booth. She took a deep breath. "Am I finished here?"

Agnella glanced out at the throng, her nimble gaze missing nothing. "You may go."

Bell's older sister halted across the booth's sales counter, ignoring

19

the stares and whispers following her. Her rich blonde hair hung in an artful curtain down her back, and her scarlet silk overdress swirled around her, suspiciously thin. Was she even wearing a chemise?

Roza was two years older, and she had a way of making Bell feel like a child in her own loose lemon-colored dress.

Bell's eyebrows arched as she peered over the counter at Roza's matching four-inch heels. "How can you walk the cobblestones in those, Roza?"

"Practice."

Roza had once persuaded Bell to wear heels to a party at House Salviati. Her blistered toes hurt for a week.

Roza tilted her head, and a velvety white rose peeped from behind her ear. "Hertes suits you. Why you don't wear it more often?"

Bell frowned. "Is that one of my roses?"

Roza wiggled her fingers on the counter. "You have plenty, don't you?"

Irritation wormed beneath Bell's skin. "Yes. But I'd prefer...never mind. Where's your fiancé?"

"Hard to keep track of." Roza popped a licorice candy in her mouth. She rested her elbows on the counter, her neckline dropping low.

"La Bella." Piero moved close and Bell edged away. "What a pleasure. Allow us to serve you."

Bell glared at his ear. "She's not here to be served."

"Oh, you'd be surprised." Piero didn't take his gaze from Roza.

"Back to your work, Mr. Medoro," Agnella called.

As he slunk away, Roza whispered, "Have any Insidio scent?"

Bell stiffened. "Why would you ask for a Magia scent?" she said through her teeth. "Are you wishing to die?"

Roza flashed a smile. Her blue eyes told Bell to trust her, and everything would be *magical*. "A deceptive scent could be very useful, in certain situations. Besides, I might as well enjoy life a little, while I can."

Bell hid a pang of sadness with a frown. When Lymbodia failed to kill Roza within the first year after her diagnosis, she treated it as a joke, a game she was playing with a deadly disease.

20

The gray flowers Bell had fused as a child had been Magia—second-level fiorés—and were strictly forbidden by the Consiglio. Not only were the elixirs Magia created treacherous, but inhaling the droplets of their scent cloud exposed you to Lymbodia, or the Burning Blood, as some called it.

Lymbodia was a cancer that originated deep within and eventually revealed itself in bruises on the torso. It was a disease peculiar to Bardia; no mainlander had ever reported catching it. Fanatics of San Giovanni shouted that it was the judgement of God on Bardia for monetizing the Bardian gifts. The Consiglio had banned Magia use decades ago when research showed it was the source of the disease, but they kept their findings quiet, for fear its deadly reputation would besmirch the rest of Bardia's magic.

A week after Bell had fused the gray flowers in the garden, Roza had been struck with the painful, wasting, and unpredictable disease. Sometimes death came slowly and painfully, and other times it was mercifully swift.

Bell saw the shadow of it within her sister now, though she hid it behind a sultry mask. Why it had happened to infect Roza and not Bell that horrible afternoon six years ago haunted Bell every single day.

Bell's glare softened slowly. "Magia are banned. You won't find any here."

"Can I help you, Miss Asbury?" Agnella said over Bell's shoulder, her voice acerbic.

"Apparently not." Roza stuck out her lower lip in a pretty pout. "Bell's finished, right?"

Agnella nodded, but she studied Roza for a moment before she turned to rearrange Avrile's bouquet for the fifth time.

Roza took Bell's arm, tugging her around to the booth's opening. "I need a shopping partner. Come with me."

"Into the Night Bazaar? This close to Solstice?" At the Piazza's north end, multicolored lamps marked the entrance to the underground magical market.

Roza tugged a silver pocket mirror from her pocket and dabbed at the edges of her eye shadow. "This close to Solstice is when you can find the best enchanted clothes." She snapped the mirror closed, her face lit triumphantly. "I know a lacemaker with a new kind of gloves for scentmaking...."

Bell's stomach flipped. In all the years since Roza's accident, she'd hardly stepped inside the Bazaar over the two weeks of La Festa. It was then the *attuale* was strongest and all the wares were magical. During the rest of the year, she would explore the outer streets with Carasti—the ones that sold spiced strawberries and gelato and chocolate cannoli—but even then, she didn't venture far into the magic market.

Last year, Carasti had convinced her to go inside on the first day of La Festa. The attempt had ended in an explosion of greenery when she tripped over someone's train and lost hold of her gift, pulling living cotton threads from the lady's dress and festooning the stalls around her in delicate puffs.

The poor woman was left wearing a silk chemise—thankfully not as vulnerable to Bell's *attuale* as the rest of her ensemble.

So, no. It hadn't gone well.

Roza smirked. "Are you still thinking about the incident from last year?"

"I practically stripped her naked. Of course I'm thinking about it," Bell hissed.

Roza laughed, drawing a fresh round of admiring stares from passersby.

How did she stand it, being looked at like a piece of art they could frame and take home? Bell supposed her sister had been painted often enough by artists—Bardian and foreign—that perhaps they thought they *could*.

But Roza didn't seem to care. If Lymbodia didn't kill her soon, she would be married into the formidable Medoro family, next in line to be Matrona of the whole clan. None of it seemed to matter to her though. She still had that searching hunger in her eyes.

The hunger had been there since Bell poisoned her with Magia.

Roza softened, her smile fading. She touched Bell's hand and leaned closer. "Please, Bell. This is my last year free. I want to enjoy it. With you."

Bell's mind clamped down on *last year*, rolling the words over and over as if their bitter taste would fade with friction. She glanced over her shoulder at the Bazaar entrance across the Piazza. She had more control now, didn't she? She'd fused multiple bouquets, and her *attuale* gift was lying quiet.

Agnella was watching from the far end of the table with an unfathomable expression on her face.

Garam would be a hulk of disapproval if he ever found out. But who would tell?

Roza took hold of her arm. "Come on. Mother will never know."

"All right. But not too far inside."

Piero leaned toward them. "Hope you don't disappear," he called.

"What does that mean?" Bell whispered.

"Forget him. Stay close." Roza pulled her through the crowd.

Three

THE SCENTS OF THE NIGHT BAZAAR swelled as Bell followed her sister toward the entrance into the hill. She twisted open the goldenbell-shaped vial hanging around her neck for a whiff of her *protezi* elixir. Without it, she'd have an immediate headache as her gift tried to discern the intense fragrances. Each breath of elixir she took lasted a few minutes, but she kept it closed in between so as not to affect those around her—a mistake she'd made and learned from last year.

Keeping up with Roza's long strides helped Bell silence the disapproving voice in her head. As they passed the last of the Maestris' booths, the lanterns lining the Bazaar's archway dulled the stars.

Descending into the magic market, Roza finally slowed her steps. The first street flowed like an underground river, and lights twinkled in the darkness, illuminating bubbling cider and fine dyes sold in orange- and red-curtained booths on both sides of long aisles. The stalls closest to the front held sellers wearing velvet robes, ink-purple turbans, crimson pants, and feathery capes. They hovered over their wares, beckoning the masses. Behind them, artisans performed alchemy, weaving glittering silk, melting metal into intricate shapes, or squeezing potent wine from fruit. Warm air filled her nose with intricate scents.

A turbaned man proffered a tray of tiny crystal glasses. "Powerful Myrtle wine, Miss, eases the worst pain."

Bell's tight stomach loosened at the familiar fioré name, but when

24

she leaned close, the smell of sour wheatgrass mingled with mossy Myrtle wrinkled her nose. "That's not *pure* Myrtle."

His dark gaze narrowed. "If it does not please you, Miss, perhaps…"

Roza yanked Bell along.

"How can he sell it as Myrtle?"

"This isn't your garden, golden girl." Roza tapped Bell's nose and Bell scowled back. "You can't control the Night Bazaar. It's *wild* magic. Trust your instincts."

"My *instincts* are telling me this—"

Roza hurtled herself back into the crowd, and Bell had no choice but to follow.

The river swept them into a current of color and fragrance. At a dream-carpet stall, the carpetmaker wore an orange wraparound skirt and several pounds of gold jewelry, a half-finished rug on her lap. Bell fingered a small rug made with a simple golden weave. Its latent magic warmed her arm and soothed the muscles in her neck.

"It would give you beautiful dreams." The maker's eyes prickled on Bell's skin.

"How much?"

The woman looked at Bell's vial. "Depends on what you have to offer."

"Gold florins?"

"Not from you, Scentmaker."

Brows raised, Bell turned toward Roza.

"Of course she won't," Roza whispered. "Not when you have something else to trade."

"I can't trade this. It hasn't been certified yet." Bell curled her hand around the flower-shaped vial. "Why can't I pay?"

Roza shrugged. "You'll have to barter."

Bell stroked the rug with one finger. "Let's go."

"What's the point of *attuale* if you won't use it?"

Bell frowned. "I use it every day. Properly."

Roza made a disgusted sound. "What *they* say is proper," she muttered.

"What?"

"Better luck next time, Anna." Roza strode further down the street.

"You know her?" Bell quickstepped after her.

"Of course. She's the Maestra of Carpets."

Bell glanced back, and her gaze collided with Maestra Anna's. She'd thought the Maestris officially disapproved of the Night Bazaar since it was too big and secretive for them to control. It had been started by the Seller of Secrets, after all, someone who flouted the Consiglio's authority simply by existing.

They passed several more streets, twisting alleys, and dark stairways. Bell kept close to the lantern light and brilliant booths. A stall on the left held bowls of sparkling gems. One, a creamy, opaque gem, was as big as her head.

Roza glanced back to see her staring at the giant gem. "You can't afford that. Not if you're a *proper* scentmaker who sells what's been *certified*."

Bell tilted her head, watching the lamplight play on the gem's multifaceted surface. "Doesn't mean I can't look."

Roza tugged Bell away. "Come on. Maybe we can get you some decent shoes." She grimaced at Bell's brown work shoes.

They reached the crowded main thoroughfare and passed a fountain filling the center. The water rose up and formed a blood-orange dragon, its roar scattering droplets of flame. After her heart slowed, Bell reached out and brushed a finger against its swaying tail, smiling at its coolness. It was formed from water droplets, part illusion, part fabrication.

Everything in the Bazaar was both wild and easy at once, as if none of the makers doubted themselves. If only the *attuale* always felt that way to her. Her gift thrummed within her, eager for release, but she eased it down.

She turned to ask Roza what it would cost to have a watermaker transform her own garden fountain.

Roza was gone.

Bell scanned for Roza's crimson dress, but the colors of the crowd swirled together. Royal blue, magenta, smoky black, and carmine red blurred, changing in the lamplight.

The intoxicating smells became suffocating. She broke from the throng and found room to breathe in front of a shoemaker's stall. The maker reached for a pair of golden slippers. "Make your feet light…"

Bell spun away before the maker could finish, straight into someone's well-tailored chest.

"Why hello, Miss Asbury." Grigor of Salviati smirked crookedly down at her. His sister was already tugging at his arm. The two of them made a predictable pair: Grigor, perpetually half-drunk and disheveled, and Isa, scowling with disapproval at everything he did. The Salviatis were one of the oldest families on Bardia, and as the youngest members, perhaps they felt the weight of it more than most.

Bell's face flushed scarlet, even through the Hertes. "Excuse me." She fluttered a curtsy, ignoring Isa's disdainful mouth. Of course they would shop the Bazaar like all the wealthy Bardians, but fraternizing with a maker like Bell was not something the Salviatis approved of.

"Oh Goldenbell, won't you come and have a drink with me?" Grigor slurred. "You're looking so—"

Isa yanked him half off his feet, muttering fiercely into his ear. Bell darted away, letting the crowd swallow her. Perhaps they could have shown her the way out, but she'd rather spend the night here than suffer through that much leering. She stumbled out of the stalls next to a shadowed alcove holding a small arched fountain.

She needed to get higher to look for Roza. Clambering onto the bench behind the fountain, she peered around the street. The lamplight flickered through the colors of the rainbow. People moved everywhere in every direction. Roza could have gone anywhere.

Surely she wouldn't have left me here on purpose.

"Why is a sunbeam like you standing in shadows?" said a voice beside her. His profile was covered by a half mask encircled by thick, black hair spilling across his forehead, and his lips curved up.

27

Bell lurched away and would have toppled had the man not grabbed her wrist and helped her down.

Bell's heart gave one painful thud, and then her ears rang.

No one wore a mask in Bardia unless they had something to hide. And only a Spy for the Seller of Secrets, the most powerful man in Bardia, would wear an amaranth-colored mask in the Night Bazaar.

She should have begged Grigor for help.

"You are looking for your sister." His voice was coaxing and much younger than she'd expected.

She clutched her vial with stiff fingers. How did he know she would be here, looking for Roza? *Say nothing.*

"I've seen her. And others whom you know."

He'll twist anything you say.

She edged toward the street, but his warm fingers touched her bare elbow. "Do you want the truth, Bell?" His eyes, rimmed in kohl as if they leaked shadows, were inky as a starless sky behind the mask.

"Let me go," she whispered.

"I could tell you so many secrets." He was close enough she felt his breath on her ear. "About your future brother-in-law, for instance."

She froze, tensing against his grip. *He's trying to draw me in.*

"He acts so righteous, does he not? But underneath, he is a web of deception."

"Why should I believe you?" she whispered.

"You don't need to. Hear it from his own mouth." His finger touched her chin, turning her to face the street.

Across the way, a tall dark-haired man in a burgundy cape bent in conversation with the lace seller. He straightened and held lace gloves up to the light. When he turned to scan the throng, his gold earrings glistened. Garam.

Strange. He looked…anxious wasn't the right word. He was waiting for something, and he wasn't sure he wanted to be.

She turned, her skin tingling where the Spy had touched. He was gone, but a lingering scent of hot stone remained.

When she looked back, Garam was striding deeper into the Bazaar, the sea of people parting for his broad frame. Bell hurried after him, but she was halfway across when he vanished. She burst out of the crowd into view of a narrow stairwell that led below street level. The back of Garam's descending head was visible.

Bell was gathering her nerve to follow when a hooded, thick-shouldered man in a gray camouflage cloak brushed past her and strode down the stairs. The undulating folds of the indistinct gray made him vanish into the shadows. Her forehead creased. Wasn't that a Guardia de' Lanzi, one of the Seller of Secrets' enforcers? First a Spy, and now an enforcer? What was happening?

The Lanzi reached Garam quickly, and they disappeared into an arched tunnel on the right.

It was as if Garam had been expecting him.

Bell pressed against the stone wall of the stairway as people streamed by outside. Cool, damp air from below prickled her bare arms.

She shouldn't be here.

What kind of game was the Spy playing? His inky gaze filled her mind, deep and unfathomable.

Untrustworthy.

She should go home before Mother sent for her and found her missing from the Piazza.

Bell frowned and shoved away images of Mother's icy disapproval. Garam was involved in something, and Roza needed to know.

Heavy, unfamiliar scents slid over her mind as she descended. Did this lead to the Sotto? Were those Magia scents slithering through the air toward her? She shoved her vial up to her nose. Keeping to the wall, she tiptoed into the arched passageway. Lamps flickered on either side. The slippery scents faded slightly, and she relaxed her lungs. A murmur came from an alcove several yards into the passage. Bell retreated back to the stairwell and peered around the corner.

"—the girl?" Garam said.

"Soon I'll have the proof." The Lanzi's voice was gruff.

"And her family? Her sister?"

"Just her. Her sister is a loose thread."

Garam nodded. "I'll take care of the girl and bring in her sister. Do you have the Insidio?"

The Lanzi handed him a bundle. "Straight from the Seller of Secrets. Why don't you break the engagement? I can get the proof without you."

Garam was silent for a moment. "I can never let her go," he finally said. "The Consiglio are watching both of us," he added quickly. "Strozzi has set it all in motion."

Bell heard Garam's heavy booted footsteps leaving the alcove, and she whirled and dashed back up, her chest burning as though her heart pumped acid instead of blood.

Garam was going to use Insidio from the Seller of Secrets on her and Roza.

He was going to brainwash them both.

Four

THE COLORFUL CROWD BLURRED AS BELL collected her thoughts.

She had to move before Garam saw her. Her knees trembled, and she stumbled against a stonemaker's stall. He frowned as his wares jostled. She tried to straighten, but nausea swept over her.

What was happening?

A scent slammed her from behind, coiling like poison in her belly. Jonquil, in the middle of the street? The addictive, mood-lifting Magia was illegal, but like most prohibited things, it could be purchased in the Sotto. But users generally kept it to the back rooms of mansions and underbellies of taverns.

The stonemaker asked something. Her gorge rose, and she stuffed her *protezi* vial into one nostril. The queasiness eased, floating in the background.

"Hey, Goldenbell." Piero leaned next to her, a vial hung on a silver chain slipping from the open collar of his black silk shirt. It had the same sort of cork as hers did, allowing him to twist it open without danger of spilling the Jonquil or releasing the elixir's scent cloud. Which was a small relief, since an accident would put everyone nearby at risk of contracting Lymbodia.

The stonemaker laughed and sat down, beaming at them. This was the menace of Magia—it deeply affected everyone within smelling distance, not only the wearer. Unlike the first-level fioré Blue Hertes that

31

changed the exterior of the wearer, Magia changed what they felt and thought inside.

"Why are you wearing that?" Bell asked tightly.

He gasped and put a hand to his lips. "Doesn't the happy scent work for you?"

"Obviously not."

He grinned at Avrile, who hovered on the other side of Bell. "Our prize scentmaker is too sensitive for our scent choices, Avrile. What shall we do?"

Avrile laughed too loudly.

"Leave me alone." She hissed, dizziness swelling as Piero leaned closer.

"I guess your *protezi* elixir can't always protect." He tapped her hand clutching the vial, his fingers cold. "I ought to take it from you, to clarify the lesson."

Fury enveloped her, steadying her vision for a moment. She jerked her vial away, unlocking it from the chain and dousing his neck in one motion. He staggered back, cursing. Bell remembered the first time she'd used it directly on her own skin—it burned like hot pepper oil. He reached for her neck, his fingertips grazing her skin as she danced back.

"What the hell is going on?" Garam's irate voice sent mingled warmth and ice through her. He hurled Piero into the throng, then Avrile. Dirty looks from passersby soon turned to confused smiles as the mingled scents rising from Piero reached them.

Garam grabbed Bell's arms and half carried her to the next corner. The dizziness disappeared, and she struggled to get free.

"What were you thinking? That Jonquil could have killed you." His dark gaze bore into hers.

How dare he talk about the dangers of Magia? She glared, but the effect seemed lost since she had to lean back to see his face. Had the Hertes worn off yet? "I was handling it. How did you know I'm allergic?"

He grunted. "This isn't the first time he's used Jonquil, obviously. Why did you let him get close enough?"

She gaped at him. "I didn't see him coming. It's not my fault your brother is a bully. And a criminal. You knew he uses Jonquil?"

He frowned. "He's not the only one who would take advantage of an allergy like yours."

"He was taunting me. No one else knows about my allergy anyway."

He scanned behind her. Piero and Avrile had gone without so much as a glare in Garam's direction. The Jonquil had made the rest of the observers forget the altercation mattered. "Not likely. It's impossible to keep secrets in this place. Did you speak to anyone else?"

She lifted her chin. "It's none of your business if I did."

When he straightened, he loomed even bigger, but she stood firm. "Your mother has made it my business."

"Why, is she paying you to bodyguard me?"

He ignored that. "You should never have come here alone."

"I came with Roza, but she lost me."

A strange mixture of emotion creased his brow. Pain and irritation and…something wistful.

"Show me the way out, and I'll go home."

He nodded and took her elbow tightly. His touch made her skin crawl, but she didn't pull away until the Bazaar entrance came into sight.

The air cleared as they stepped through the archway into the Piazza. Garam led her across the Piazza, and she followed because the crowd parted so easily for him. He finally slowed as they reached the sweeping marble steps of the Consiglio's Rotunda. Legs weary, Bell leaned against the crystalline barrier at the foot of the steps. The moss streaking it stirred at her touch. Created by a fusion of all seven Maestris' gifts, the barrier was a twelve-foot wall of clear gemstones girded by stone and metal ribs every five feet. The barrier encircled the Rotunda, its only entrance through the gate at Bell's back. The Maestris alone could open the gate using their *attuale* gift. The Rotunda was so guarded because it housed the Solstice Spring, which flowed from the Inchio Sea surrounding the island, bringing a current of Bardian magic, *attuale*, for the Maestris with it every year at Midsummer Solstice. This was usually her favorite time of year, but it was also wedding season, and Roza and Garam's was set for the day after the Solstice.

The hot fragrances of the Bazaar still brewed in Bell's body. She avoided his gaze, but Garam's presence crawled along her mind.

He smelled like treachery.

"*There* you are." Roza burst out of the mass of people with half a chocolate cannolo in one hand. "Where in Bardia did you go?" She scowled at Bell, then took a bite of the cream-filled pastry.

"Where did *I* go? You left me in the middle of the Bazaar."

"I told you to keep up."

Garam took a step towards her. "You shouldn't have taken her in there, Roza."

Roza smirked and tossed a pebble toward the barrier. The pebble tinkled against the gems. A young stonemaker gazing at the Rotunda scowled at Roza, and she smiled devastatingly at him until his cheeks pinked and he darted away. "You're as much a child as she is." She finished the cannolo and brushed her fingers on her skirt.

"Piero was wearing Jonquil. She could have been injured."

Bell straightened. "Who even told you about that?"

Garam flicked a hand. "Everyone knows."

Bell huffed. "That is not—"

Stepping between them, Roza stretched her arms overhead and spiraled to some unheard melody. Her hair spun, a golden enchantment, and a kind of effortless energy poured off her body. Bell couldn't look away when she did things like this, and neither could anyone standing close by. Garam's lips were parted around some word he was going to say, but he remained frozen like a statue. What fire burned within her sister that gave her this wild courage? She lost herself in something Bell couldn't reach and yet remained aware she was being watched. Admired.

Roza's hands came to a graceful stop, a laugh ringing from her. "If you want to know where I've been, I got trapped at a music stall—they wouldn't let me stop dancing. Now, children, where were we?"

"We were leaving." Bell started toward the adjacent carriage park, biting her tongue when Garam followed.

Roza spun along behind, pausing in the row of pine trees between the carriage park and the Piazza to stare back at a hot chocolate stand.

"Roza, come on. Mother's going to be furious." Bell was seventeen, but even so, Mother was implacable when it came to rules during the Solstice. She remembered the years before her gift had been uncovered. Back then, they'd come to the Piazza della Signoria as a family, and Father would give Roza and Bell three florins each. They'd wander the booths buying arancini rice balls and cannoli, taking bites out of each while they watched the apprentices working in the Maestris' workshops and studied the people entering the Bazaar. The *attuale* magic swirling through Bardia's air and the sugar on Bell's tongue kept her from resisting when Roza whirled her in a blissful, childish dance.

Life was simple then.

As Garam handed her into the carriage, Bell glanced back toward the Piazza. A lithe shadow of a figure leaned on a lamppost between the carriage park and the trees. With his hood thrown back, his mask was outlined by the light.

Dozens of yards away, Bell shivered.

Five

"**D**ID YOU KNOW THAT SPY, BELL?" GA-ram held the curtain aside and stared at the now-empty space beneath the lamppost. "I've never seen one show himself like that."

"I don't know." She didn't know for sure it was the same one that spoke to her, but he'd thrown back his hood so she could see him. What had he meant, sending her to eavesdrop on Garam? Was the Seller drawing her into one of his schemes?

Roza lounged against Garam's shoulder with one bare foot propped up on the green velvet carriage seat and her hair tumbling down his arm. Now that she was still, Bell couldn't look away from her sister's sharp cheekbones. Was she thinner than a month ago? She ate more, if anything, but none of it stuck to her. The disease devoured it whole, like a parasite in her blood.

"You haven't seen him before?"

Bell shrugged. "Maybe he was watching *you*. Or Roza." Maybe he was trying to protect them from Garam. She pushed away the thought. Spies had their own reasons for everything, none of them honest.

Roza's gaze moved lazily across the window, but she said nothing.

Garam grunted and dropped the curtain. "I warned you about this, Bell. If a Spy is watching you, the Seller is planning something."

She studied her hands twisted in her yellow skirt to hide her scowl. "I'm not stupid, Garam. I know what spies do."

"They're not so bad." Roza smiled a tiny smile.

36

"They're professional secret thieves. Of course they're bad."

Roza sighed. "You are a bore, fiancé. I should have chosen Piero."

"Roza," Bell hissed.

Garam scoffed. "Piero wouldn't have lasted a week."

Roza laughed deep in her throat and kissed the edge of his jaw.

Bell flushed at the heat in Garam's gaze as he stared at the top of Roza's head. Was it anger or desire? Either one made her want to leap from the moving carriage.

He pulled a white paper package from his pocket. "I bought something for you, Bell."

She stared at it.

"They're for scentmaking." He tossed the package onto her lap.

Cloth. Not a vial of Insidio scent. Her fingers shivered as she slowly tore the paper. Tawny brown lace and suede gloves spilled out. Were these the ones he'd been looking at?

"Specially warded. You can fuse through the lace, but it protects you from contact."

Bell frowned. "How did you know I needed new gloves?"

"You always need gloves, don't you?"

A coincidence? The carriage clattered onto their street. House Asbury's lower windows still glowed. The familiar shapes of the fruit trees arching above the back garden walls soothed the last of Bell's nausea.

"Thank you."

She slipped the gloves into her pocket and climbed out onto the courtyard. Garam said good night and mounted his horse, which he'd left to ride with Roza, and Bell finally released her vial.

Mother waited rigidly in the hall at the foot of the stairs with her chin raised and back spine-straight as if she were an ice sculpture. Her purple silk overdress closed neatly with lace at her wrists and throat, and her golden hair was sleeked back under a lace cap. "You are an entire hour late, Goldenbell."

"I'm sorry, Mother."

"What kept you?"

"I took her to meet some friends, Mother." Roza breezed past, through the dining room, and into the kitchen. "Garam had a cousin visiting."

Bell gazed longingly at the carved wooden stairs leading up to their bedrooms, but Mother followed Roza, and Bell reluctantly followed Mother. They walked into the kitchen, where the housekeeper had left platters of leftovers from dinner on the counter. Embers still glowed in the hearth.

"What side of the family?"

"Medoro, of course." Roza hid a wink at Bell by bending over a plate of pastries on the kitchen counter.

Bell's mouth dried. She could never tell Mother the whole truth. Every imagined scenario ended with Bell banished from scentmaking and forbidden to go near the Piazza again. She wandered across the kitchen to the window overlooking the garden. Her fingers found the potted herbs on the sun bench, coaxing a sprig of lavender into a bracelet. Its ordinary aroma soothed her pounding heart.

"He'll inherit a good chunk. Not as much as Garam, of course." Roza selected a cream cheese pastry and bit into it. "Mmm, starving."

Mother's chin lowered an inch. "Well, then. You must uphold House Asbury at all times if this cousin is going to look at you twice."

As if the Medoros had impeccable reputations. Apparently, wealth and power kept your slate neat and clean. "Yes, Mother."

Mother swept her gaze over Bell's lemon-yellow overdress. "You'll need something proper the next time you see this cousin. Tomorrow, we'll send for a dressmaker."

Bell looked out the window to hide her wrinkled nose.

Mother turned away. "Stop eating those, Roza. You have a wedding to prepare for. And get your hands out of the dirt, Bell."

Bell jerked, severing the sprig. It coiled close as if it liked her warm skin. Roza stuck out her tongue at Mother's back and stuffed another pastry in her mouth as Mother glided up the stairs.

"Don't look so glum, Goldenbell," Roza said when Mother was out of earshot.

"What am I going to do?"

"You'll wear a spectacular—" She gestured at Bell's dress. "Non-yellow gown, make Mother happy, and impress Garam's cousin."

Bell smoothed her skirt. "Why can't I wear yellow? Wait, there actually *is* a cousin?"

"I knew she'd pounce on it."

Bell shook her head. "Roza..."

Roza lifted her chin. "I'll leave you in the lurch next time, how about that? See what Mother says when she catches her favorite daughter disobeying orders." She strode toward the stairs, heels dangling from her hand, a stack of pastries in the other.

"I'm not her favorite."

Roza stumbled on the first step but threw her shoulders back and rushed on. Bell hurried to catch up. When they reached Roza's bedroom door, Roza blocked her. "Mother didn't care if *I* went into the Bazaar when I was seventeen. If I disappeared in the Sotto forever or perished from the Burning Blood, the first thing she'd think about is our lost alliance with Medoro. *You*, on the other hand...you're the golden one." She slammed the door in Bell's face.

"Roza, wait." The lock clicked. Bell laid a hand on the wood. "I need to tell you something."

Silence.

Mother's door at the far end of the hall was closed, but there was no way Bell could shout about Garam's betrayal through a solid piece of wood. She'd have to wait until Roza came out of her sulk.

Bell padded the other way, past the stairs, and into her corner bedroom. Roza complained that Bell had the bigger bedroom, but Roza's only looked smaller because it was strewn with clothes and food and stuffed with three dressers and an enormous four-poster bed.

Bell's room felt quiet. Linen curtains surrounded her bed and hung over the wall of windows facing the balcony. Her wardrobe held all her clothes, neatly organized, and its doors were never left open. Her desk on the right side held a row of leather-covered journals, each one full of meticulous notes about her craft. Bell crossed the room, straightened her inkwell, and ran a finger along the leather spines.

Here she could breathe, but a part of her still danced at the memory of the Bazaar. The *attuale* current had filled the very air with possibility.

Garam's conversation with the Lanzi ran slowly through her head, over and over. Did the Consiglio suspect what he was doing? What was Strozzi setting in motion, and what could it have to do with Bell and Roza?

I can never let her go, he'd said. Was this all driven by an obsession with Roza? Why would Bell need to be involved at all? *He* was the one who'd warned her about people using her gift. Did he plan to brainwash her into doing something for him?

She shuddered, the air constricting.

Bell slipped out onto the narrow wooden balcony. The smell of loam and living things rose from her garden. She mounted the low railing, found footholds in the lattices, and picked her way down. Creamy roses bobbed aside as she brushed past.

Father and Mother's bedroom was dark. Roza's window blazed. Bell hurried down the main hedged path to the fountain at the center of her triangular garden. A glass sculpture rose from it, and moonflowers basked in the mist, their melon-sized faces glowing. Iridescent water lilies floated in the pool, clusters of pink and purple flowers in their centers.

Eight beds circled the fountain patio, each holding carefully tended fioré. Father had given her an Aronil plant start this year, completing the collection she'd begun when her gift first manifested at eleven. Princess Seed, the silver-blossomed calming fioré he'd given her first, crowded its bed now.

Grown in certain patches of Bardian soil, fioré were delicate and demanding. As was their right, the Consiglio laid heavy taxes on the nobles who owned the land that could grow the blossoms, as well as strict standards about the fioré's quality. Much to Mother's dismay, Father had indulged Bell as much as he could, but she'd often gone without new clothes and jewelry so he could buy her another species.

Bell walked the circle of fioré, stroking blossoms and pulling weeds. The fioré stirred as she passed. A few pushed out new leaves as she touched them. Their colors shone in the darkness, their fragrances seeming to fill the air with a bright haze. She gathered Princess Seed and Aronil and carried them to her workshop at the north tip of the triangle. Her workshop was a simple wooden frame and a roof, built against the courtyard wall and draped in a weaving vine that she'd coaxed into place. It was covered in so much greenery that it was hard to spot between two ornamental trees. The vine rustled at her approach, and a white-flowered tendril caressed her hand as she reached for where a doorknob would be. A thick, Bell-sized curtain of vine crawled aside. "Thank you," she whispered.

Inside, she closed her eyes and breathed in the essence of soil and tender shoots. Dense walls of leaves blocked the breeze, leaving the inside a perfect temperature. She blew on a glow gem mounted on the ceiling and cool sapphire light swelled until she could see the labels on the vials along the back wall. The workshop was large enough to hold a bench filled with three neat rows of vials and a basket of corks, and a small wooden stool. Dried fioré and herbs hung in bunches along the ceiling, and buckets for discarded leaves and stems were tucked in the corners. Her stomach tightened as she laid Garam's gift on the bench. Was he trying to win her trust?

But he'd bought the gloves before she'd overheard his planned crime. The slit in her other pair must have been an accident. No one had access to those—unless they'd crept into her room. She carried them with her during the day and laid them on her desk while she slept.

She shuddered and put the thought out of her mind as she pulled on the gloves. The tawny fabric, soft and buttery suede, molded to her skin.

The first thing to do was make Roza a protective elixir. It wouldn't negate Insidio completely, but it might help long enough for her to escape. She arranged the fioré into a bouquet as her gift warmed within her veins.

Someone cleared their throat.

Six

"KNOCK, KNOCK," ROZA SAID FROM OUTSIDE. Bell's shoulders relaxed. "What are you doing out here?"

"I won't touch anything."

Bell stroked the vines behind her, and they folded aside.

"Ooh, magic." Roza hunched through the doorway. Her head nearly brushed the ceiling. "A little late-night scentmaking?"

"Are you feeling better?"

Roza took in a deep breath and seemed smaller afterward. Wet grass coated the hem of her silk bathrobe. "I need your help, Bell."

"Okay."

"I've been using that Aronil scent you gave me on Garam, but it wears off so fast."

"Roza, I think you should know—"

"Is there a way to make it last longer? So he can't hide anything from me before the wedding? I feel like he's hiding something." She turned toward the workbench and bent to read a label.

"I wanted to tell you earlier. I saw him take Insidio from a Lanzi. He's going to use it on you."

Roza's gaze flashed as she straightened. "Insidio? Where did you see this?"

"In the Night Bazaar, in an alley. A Lanzi told him about a girl working for someone, and Garam said he'd take care of it."

Roza frowned. "It's probably some girl causing trouble for their family."

"The Lanzi asked if he'll break the engagement. Garam said he won't, that he can never let her go. Who else could it be?"

Roza twisted a curl around her finger. "Bell...I can't do anything about it now. We have a week to go until our betrothal."

"Tell Father you can't marry him. Anyone who uses Magia can't be trusted." Bell gripped the bench with her fingertips as Roza's face shuttered. "You could tell Garam about the Lymbodia."

"No," Roza said. "We need this alliance with House Medoro. Garam will take Pater Medoro's place one day. It's my chance to make a difference in Bardia. Before the end."

Bell's heart squeezed. "We don't need it this desperately. Not enough to risk accelerating your Lymbodia."

"There's too much at stake." Roza pinched a vine tendril, and it shriveled back until released. "Garam is the heir. To break it off now... he would be humiliated."

Bell sank into the wooden stool behind her. "Better he be humiliated than you brainwashed."

Roza's eyes glimmered dark blue in the light, their depths seeming far away. "Please make me a permanent Aronil. If I must marry him, I want to know where he stands."

"You can't be serious." Bell gestured toward the house. "Tell Father. He'll find a way—"

Roza hissed through her teeth. "You don't understand, Bell. We cannot alienate House Medoro. Accusing their son of using Insidio, right before we're married? We'd never recover our good name."

Bell's stomach twisted. "Since when do you care about our good name?"

Roza said nothing.

Bell shook her head. "What matters is that you're safe. If he uses Insidio, you won't remember why you can't trust him. And the Spy said—"

Roza's face twitched. "What Spy?"

Bell stilled. "I—"

"What. Spy."

Bell scuffed her shoes on the mossy floor. "When I was looking for you in the Bazaar, a Spy appeared from an alcove. He pointed out Garam and said he has a lot of secrets, that he can't be trusted. If he wants to use Insidio, what else could he be planning?"

Roza's eyes glowed icy blue now. "This Spy, what did he look like?"

"He was dark-skinned. Kohl around his eyes. Dark hair about this long." She held her fingers up to her ears.

Roza cursed. "You can't trust him, Bell."

Bell scoffed. "I don't trust *any* Spy who works for the Seller."

"That's the trouble—even the Seller doesn't control this one. He's working for himself."

"And the Seller isn't?"

Roza's gaze flashed. "The Seller works for the common people. Everyone in power tells you not to trust him because he's a threat to *their* control." She slashed her hands down. "We need to move faster," she muttered.

"Faster to do what?" Bell frowned. "Why won't you tell me what's going on?"

"I can't tell you yet." Roza leaned forward and put her hands on Bell's shoulders. "I need you to trust me, Bell. Make me an elixir. If I get the Aronil working first, I'll be able to see through the Insidio. Then we won't have to worry about Garam or the Spy at all."

Roza's words took on the weight of a magic spell. *Won't have to worry* echoed in Bell's head. She bit her lip. "*Permanenza* elixirs are illegal. Even a lengthening elixir would have to go through the Maestris' Consiglio." She could be disciplined for even asking.

"No time for that. Come on, Bell, you know I'd use it on Garam."

A week ago, she would have protested this, but knowing Garam had plans and the means to accelerate Roza's illness changed everything. "I could be banned from scentmaking."

"If you get caught. And you won't."

Bell looked beyond Roza at the line of vials along the wall. The elixirs within them glimmered in the glow gem light. "I'd have to use Magias. A *permanenza* elixir would require something potent. I don't—I don't know if I—"

"Please. Everyone knows you're the strongest scentmaker in Bardia. You're not at risk if you're careful."

Bell softened before she flushed with irritation. After all these years, she should be immune to Roza's flattery. *But is it flattery if it's true?*

She silenced the voice inside. "It's too dangerous. You of all people should know." She regathered her bouquet. "Besides, the only place to get Magias is the Sotto."

"Please," Roza whispered. "I trust you. I can't ask one of the other scentmakers—Garam would find out."

Bell let the bouquet fall.

Roza pulled a package from her pocket. "Supply won't be a problem. Dried samples of every Magia. Tell me when you need more."

Bell flinched back from the package. "You shouldn't be—"

"Trust me, Bell." Roza's pleading eyes caught her. "I'll be careful. But I need you. Don't abandon me."

Something in Bell's gut twisted. This was her chance to right the past. To help Roza instead of hurting her.

Bell hesitated, then nodded.

Roza smiled. "You can be so much more than a scentmaker, Bell. Do this for me, and I'll get you everything you dream of." She pulled a pair of ink blue velvet shoes from her pocket and dropped them onto the counter. "Oh, and Bell? Stay away from the Spy. He'll try to seduce you."

Bell grimaced. "I'm not that naïve."

"Don't say I didn't warn you." The vines scurried apart for Roza as if they were glad to see her go, and Bell watched her glide between the hedges. The opening closed, and she turned the flat velvet shoes in her hands and stared at the black package on the counter.

All she wanted was to be a proper scentmaker, to heal people, and to make the world right. This could cost her that dream, no matter what Roza said.

Part of her knew that whatever trouble Roza was miring herself in, it had begun the day she'd burst out of Grenwood with wild eyes and a Magia bouquet.

It had begun when Bell accidentally fused a darkly powerful Smemor elixir that changed something inside her sister. Hardened her. That penchant for darkness would not disappear even if Roza broke off her engagement to Garam. It would haunt her to the end of her days.

Bell's gift had first manifested itself in violence against Roza, but she would now use it to protect her.

Seven

BELL JERKED AWAKE, PIECES OF A FORE-boding dream floating along the edges of her mind like leaves in brackish water.

She pushed aside the bedspread, swung her feet onto the rug, and stretched. Her dreams had been filled with deadly wines and telling glances. She wanted to forget them all.

The early morning sun spilled across the wooden floor. A gentle knock came at her door as the clock struck eight.

"Come in." Bell yawned.

"Good morning, miss." Elena bustled in, tea tray balanced on one hand. She set the tray on the bedside table.

"Mmm…you're the best, Elena." Bell poured cream into a cup of mint tea and stirred. Steam coiled above the cup.

Elena smiled and opened Bell's wardrobe. Her dresses were arranged in a rainbow of tawny color—from palest cream to deepest gold. The carefully arranged shades soothed Bell's unease.

"Which dress would you like today?"

Bell took a sip. "One with short sleeves." Her room was already pleasantly warm. The air hung heavy, a sign of the building Solstice storm.

Elena held up two summer dresses, one a pale butter linen, the other an ochre knit. Bell chose the knit, and Elena brushed the sleep tangles from her dark hair while Bell finished her tea. She formed Bell's usual low, loose tail and secured it with a Bardian crystal rose clip Roza

47

had given her—tossed into her lap at breakfast—for her last birthday. Its petals opened wider when it touched her hair.

The velvet shoes had looked big, but now they molded to her feet. Her first Bardian-made pair. Had Garam given Roza the money?

Where *had* Roza gotten the money for all the Bardian wares she'd dropped in Bell's lap over the years? Her goldenbell vial. A satin wrist bag that could hold twice what it should. The rose clip that moved at her touch. Now these velvet shoes.

Their lives were easy, but they lived nothing like the Medoros with their ancient, endless wealth. That wealth had pardoned their crimes, enabled their magic abuse, and sanctioned their abiding control of Bardia's economy. That wealth was the reason Mother's shoulders straightened with pride whenever she talked about Roza's wedding.

The vial had come when she first started apprenticing, years before Garam and Roza started courting, so it couldn't have been from the Medoros.

A thread of relief loosened in her stomach. Mother and Roza might accept being under the Medoros' sway, but she could not.

She finished her tea and turned to set the cup on the tray. Elena stood by the window with her eyes closed.

"Elena? Is something wrong?"

She jumped and cleared her throat. "I'm sorry, miss."

Bell moved toward her. "What is it?"

Elena smoothed a strand of chocolate-colored hair back under its cap. She met Bell's eyes with tight lips.

"Is it Eduard?"

"He's in such pain this week." Desolation sharpened her face.

"And he's still working at the Medoros' brickyard?"

Elena made a frustrated noise that ended as a sob.

Bell reached out and pulled the maid close. Elena's arms came up slowly to complete the hug. She rested her chin on Bell's shoulder, and gradually her tension eased.

Elena's brother had developed Lymbodia earlier in the year. Elena had never said he was exposed at his workplace, but Bell had heard tales of others contracting Lymbodia while working for the Medoros. Another reason to despise that family. They obviously had no concern for the protection of their workers.

"I'll come to see him with you today," Bell murmured. "I have a new elixir I can try."

Elena sniffed hard and pulled away. "Thank you. It is so hard for my mother to watch him like this."

"Let me talk to Father, and then I'll be ready."

With a refilled scentmaking kit in hand, Bell slipped downstairs to find Father's study door ajar.

No matter what Roza said, she couldn't keep this secret from Father. The sooner she told him, the sooner something could be done about Garam.

Paper crinkled inside the study as she pushed the door open. Mother stood at Father's desk, staring out the window into the garden with both hands clenched.

Where was Father?

Bell turned to go, but her shoe whispered on the wood floor, and Mother whirled.

"Bell. What are you doing here?"

Bell blinked. "Looking for Father. Is something wrong?"

Mother cleared her throat and loosened her fists. "No. Your father is on a business trip. He won't return for several days."

"Business trip where? He never said anything."

Mother strode for the door, her silver-heeled boots clicking. "Santa Croce. It was a last-minute arrangement. He's visiting the Medoro holdings at the docks, solidifying our relationship with them." She paused. "What did you need to see your father about?"

Bell opened her mouth. "I—" Would Mother even listen to her concerns without proof? Doubtful. "It's nothing."

Mother's gaze narrowed on Bell's kit on her wrist. "Are you going somewhere?"

"I'm going home with Elena. Her brother is ill."

She raised a brow. "Ill?"

49

"Lymbodia." Bell said. "I think it's the final stages."

Mother hesitated, then nodded crisply. She laid her hand on Bell's shoulder. "That is kind of you, my dear. Take care not to be seen."

Bell closed her eyes for a second in relief as Mother left. Thankfully, Mother had always had a soft heart toward her staff. She was the one who sent Bell with flowers and baskets of bread and cheese every day for a week when Elena's father died two years ago.

She moved to the window, scrutinizing the blooming row of giant fire chrysanthemums she'd planted outside the study. Uneasiness stirred. With Father in Santa Croce, it was up to Bell to keep an eye on Roza.

A crumple of cream paper lay in the wastebasket, out of place in the immaculate study. She picked it up and smoothed it out, remembering the sound she'd heard before entering. Had Mother thrown this away?

Dear Francesca,

I have been thinking of you lately. Every waking moment, it seems, and sometimes in my dreams. Do you dream of me?

I think it is time we met again. Do you not think so? I can hear your protests, but remember, I know the truth about your daughter.

I regard you always,

Salieri

Bell's hand closed around the note. Who was Salieri? And what did he know about Mother's daughter? *Which* daughter?

Bell had no real secrets. It must be Roza.

She dropped the note back into the basket. Why was Mother receiving letters from a strange man? What would Father say if he saw this?

Elena was waiting in the courtyard when Bell slipped out with a bouquet of roses and ferns in hand. "We ought to be taking the carriage, miss."

"And miss this walk?" The day was warm but the mugginess from the morning had eased. A soft breeze caressed her skin as they stepped out onto Via dei Calzaiuoli. Behind them, the road curved beyond House Asbury to where dark stone House Medoro loomed at the very peak of the hill. Its abandoned tower was visible from most places on the island. On the other side of the peak lay farmlands.

Bardia was divided into four quarters of roughly equal size, the Via leading down the middle of them. House Asbury sat at the border of Santa Maria Novella, the nobles' quarter. Between Santa Maria Novella and the northern sea lay the farmlands of San Giovanni. The Piazza della Signoria was considered outside of any quarter, and south of it was Santa Croce, with its terraced merchants' homes, shipyards, and docks.

Today they walked the Via to Santo Spirito, home of the common people and Bardia's industrial area. The ochre cobblestones of the street glowed in the sun. Via dei Calzaiuoli was always clean, but down the alleys Bell glimpsed lines of bright but tattered laundry hung between upper stories, smudged children kicking balls, and gray-haired *nonnos* tucked in the shade of crooked awnings. The breeze brought the smell of savory tomato sauce simmering.

They turned into a side street that crooked itself out of sight. The *trullos*—low, stuccoed houses with terra-cotta roofs—sat close together. The roofs slanted toward the street, in some places close enough to touch. Packs of children burst through the alleys accompanied by scuffling and shouting as they played. Sometimes they caught sight of Bell and stopped to stare and ask for sweets. When they spoke to her, she pulled pink roses from her bouquet and used her gift to coax out bracelets and necklaces for them, making the blooms stretch as far as they could. Seeing their wild dark heads festooned in her flowers made her chest hurt.

Elena clucked her tongue. "Now they'll always expect something from you."

"I don't mind." Giving her gift freely felt like flying. It was one way to silence the voice inside that judged her useless.

Beyond the houses of Santo Spirito lay Bardia's industrial district. Pinned between the commoners' dwellings and the Inchio Sea cliffs, the brickyard was flanked by a textile mill and a lumberyard. These were some of the raw materials the makers used to create their enchanted Bardian goods. The *attuale* current's roots laced Bardia with magic, but in between lay ordinary clay.

As they stepped into the brickyard, the smells of fresh sawdust, sun-baked mud, and hot fibers rattled around Bell's head. Eduard was nowhere to be found, but they followed directions to a shambling apartment sandwiched between the yard and the mill. They found Eduard lying on a bare straw cot in the first open dorm, his face pale. Bruises edged out from his sleeves, his frame gaunt within the loose fabric.

His jaw set as his agonized eyes recognized them. "What are you doing here, Elena?"

"Why won't you come home, Eduard?"

He scoffed, but it turned into a gasp. "The Medoros cut my pay in half as soon as I got ill. If I can work a few hours every day, I'll still make a few florins. Mother can't feed the little ones on your *salario* alone, can she?" He cut Bell with his gaze as if she were solely responsible for Elena's poverty. Guilt stirred within her. Could they be paying Elena more? Could they afford it?

He tried to push up on his elbows but only made it halfway. "Go home. I'm fine."

"I brought you an elixir I've been working on," Bell said softly, kneeling beside him. "It will help with the pain." She'd fused countless elixirs over the years, hoping to discover the one to cure Roza.

"I said I was fine." He looked at Elena instead. "Why did you bring her here?" His voice sounded hoarse.

"Give her your arm," Elena hissed.

Eduard glared back. The stuffy air closed in around Bell's shoulders.

A sharp voice rose within. Soon she might have to watch Roza go through this.

Frustration snatched the gentleness from her. She took Eduard's arm, ignoring his gasp. He was too weak to jerk free. She popped the vial open in a smooth motion and dabbed four drops onto his wrist. As soon as they sunk into his skin, she stepped back.

His breathing slowly evened, though he was still glaring at her. She held out the stoppered vial, but he made no attempt to take it.

Elena grabbed the vial from Bell and tucked it in her pocket. "Thank you, miss. I'll see he takes it later."

An aching lump of hopelessness filled her throat. Bell retreated back the way they had come.

Mother called her into the little parlor beside Father's study when Bell arrived home. Ornate furniture perfectly filled the silver-papered room, and heavy brocade curtains the color of champagne blocked half the light from the narrow windows opening on the orchard. Still, Bell loved the way the champagne warmed the light, softening the silver's glimmer. On windy days as a small child, she used to sneak in before Mother was awake and lie on the thick rug, watching the shadows of the fruit trees' leaves dance on the ceiling.

That was before her soul rooted itself in the garden outside.

Mother sat at her walnut desk, writing a neat list with a gleaming silver quill. "How was your time with Elena's family?"

"He—her brother is very ill. And he didn't want to take my elixir." Bell hoped the champagne light hid her wan face.

Her quill paused. "How unfortunate. I hope you're not too upset."

"I wish there was something more I could do."

Mother hmmed and turned to take Bell's hands. "It is hard for those less fortunate to accept the gifts of others, no matter how graciously offered."

Mother's skin always felt cool as if it was as reserved as the heart it held inside. Perhaps Bell's imagination tangled with her longings, but this touch felt warm. Warmth from her mother—such an ordinary thing—had the potency of Bardian wine, but it wasn't strong enough to drown the questions rising to her lips.

"Do you know how they feel?" she asked softly. *Eduard is suffering because the Medoros care nothing for his safety,* she wanted to say.

She met Bell's gaze, unguarded for a moment. *Always,* her gaze said.

Then she pulled away, cool again. "I want your opinion." She held up two swatches of glimmering Bardian fabric, one the color of ripe strawberries, the other indigo purple. "The trimming on my dress for the wedding. Which one?"

Bell pushed her longing down and pointed to the red. "Roza likes this color."

Mother tsked. "But Roza won't be wearing it. It doesn't matter anyway. I'm sure Matrona Medoro will be wearing an entire gown of Bardian fabric." She dropped the samples and faced Bell. "Perhaps it's best you don't try to do more healing, Bell." She reached up to smooth Bell's hair, but this time the gesture felt...unsure. "This scentmaking of yours could be seen as charming, perhaps, in the right light. If people know it isn't too serious, merely a pastime growing flowers and elixirs to charm the mainlanders, it could be an asset rather than an eccentricity."

"The *attuale* isn't a pastime."

She waved a hand. "Pastimes, gifts, whatever you want to call it. Don't let it show too much. You could help with the roses for the wedding—Roza has all sorts of plans. Then everyone will see it's frivolous and pretty."

Frivolous and pretty. Was that all she was? Like the goldenbell she was named for—pretty, useless, ordinary. Too weak to handle real power. Her fingers twitched, aching for soil, and she fisted them.

Mother's full lips turned down, her face its usual icy mask, but something strange flickered in her gaze. "It's important we maintain decorum, Bell. I've explained this many times."

Bell stared at her. Normally she'd be hurt, frustrated by Mother's reprimands. Instead, she found herself studying her eyes, trying to read them. Mother turned away, dropping her gaze and drawing back into herself. What was she hiding? Bell muttered an excuse and stepped back into the hall.

"The dressmaker will be arriving shortly," Mother called.

So she hadn't forgotten. Bell scowled as she left the room.

She wandered through the hall and out the garden door that lay between the little parlor and Father's study. She walked toward her workshop, her feet crunching on the gravel. When she looked back, squinting in the noonday sun, the windows of the two small rooms were like symmetrical leaves on a house-shaped plant—or eyes.

Her arms prickled with the feeling of being watched.

"Relax," she muttered. "This isn't the Night Bazaar." The Spy couldn't come here.

Bell ambled between the towering hedges along the path, the last of the lilies growing at their base nestling beneath her trailing fingers. She breathed in their spicy scent. Before the fountain patio, leafy vines arched over the path. The canopy filtered the sun and blocked her completely from the house's sight. She knelt to smell the sweet alyssum growing in great patches on either side, digging her fingers into the soil.

Wet soil.

At the very edge of the patio was a large muddy footprint. Bell jerked to her feet, heart pounding. None of the servants were allowed beyond the vegetable garden flanking the house. The only reason a stranger would be here, so close to her fioré…

She stumbled onto the patio and into sight of her workshop. Crushed Aronil and Princess Seed petals littered the ground. Bardian soil lay in heaps beside the ransacked raised beds. The fountain misted on plucked moonflowers. The weaving vine making up the walls of her workshop was still intact, but cuts from shears bled sap and broken leaves, and stems were scattered around the base.

Bell staggered toward her workshop, stumbling through the carnage. Every step on the ruined petals stabbed her heart. She fell to her knees. A groan ripped from her soul.

Eight

THE WEAVING VINE HAD FOUGHT AND won. Bright new growth marked places where shears had cut through, only to have the spot refilled.

Bell parted the vines and stepped inside. Everything was as she'd left it—the package of Magia, rows of vials, even the glow gem. She stroked a tendril hanging from the ceiling.

"Thank you," she whispered. The tendril slid over her shoulder, leaving petals on her dress.

"Bell? The dressmaker is here. Why is there dirt everywhere?" Mother's heeled boots crunched on the path outside.

Bell patted her face and stepped out, closing the vines behind her. "Someone has destroyed my fioré. We need to tell Father."

"Destroyed—but why?"

Should she tell her about Garam? "I found a footprint."

Mother followed to the edge of the sweet alyssum. Bell was so focused on the footprint that she didn't notice Elena standing further along the path.

"Miss." Her voice shook as she stared, aghast.

"Elena." Mother pointed. "Do you recognize this footprint?"

Elena stared beyond them, her cheekbones sharpening as her face sagged with horror.

"Elena," Mother snapped.

The maid's eyes jerked to the footprint. "It—it seems to come

56

from a nobleman's boot, Matrona. The tread is too fine for a servant's shoe…" Her words faded to a hoarse whisper.

Mother traced two fingers down her own forehead to the end of her nose, a calming motion. "Bell, follow me to the study."

Bell moved slowly after her. It felt like she was walking in a dark cloud. Any minute she'd step out of the mist, and this would all be a dream.

"Bell." Elena grabbed her arm as she passed. "I'm so sorry."

Bell tried to smile. "It wasn't your fault, Elena."

Elena's mouth opened and closed. There was something sharp in her gaze, but it seemed to be turned inward. She dipped her head. "Still, I mourn with you."

"Thank you."

In Father's study, Bell paced before the windows, her skirt clutched in her fists.

Mother sat on the black velvet half-sofa across from Father's desk with her legs crossed and fingers laced elegantly over her knees. "Please understand, Bell, if this involves a nobleman, the investigation must be discreet."

"What do you mean?" It had to be Garam, trying to destroy Roza's last defense. Who else would have a motive?

"In fact—if we discover it to be someone of a certain—stature—"

Bell blinked. "Stature?"

Mother straightened her lace cuffs, avoiding Bell's gaze. "If it's someone from House Medoro, we won't investigate."

The numbness slowed her thoughts. "But—"

"Scentmaking has already eroded your reputation, and now it's become dangerous. This is a sign it's time for you to move on. We can't let it make enemies of powerful houses as well."

"If a nobleman is destroying fioré, that's a danger to every—"

"That is the end of it, Goldenbell. Once this alliance is complete, we can fill the empty beds with normal flowers—roses perhaps. We can afford it then, and you can spend your days tending them if you like." Her cold words rang crisp and clear like falling midwinter icicles.

Bell blinked to stop her eyes stinging. "I *will* talk to Father about this."

Mother slammed her palm against Father's desk. "Your father is doing everything he can to ensure this family's future. You will *not* undo it all with your stubbornness. I'm sorry, Bell." Mother lifted a hand as if to touch her, and Bell shied back.

There was nothing to say.

The strange expression flickered through Mother's eyes again; then she straightened. "The dressmaker is waiting in your room. I've selected a few fabrics, but I'm leaving the final choice to you." She gestured sharply, and Bell drifted into the hall.

Her scentmaking was worth nothing to Mother, but was Roza's happiness and safety also worthless?

She imagined telling Mother everything. The response would be icy fury, polished nails digging into her arm as she was warned never to speak of Garam's guilt again.

No.

She ran her hand along the carved banister as she climbed the main stairs. They had more than enough, but Mother would never be satisfied until their position among the Bardian Houses was secure.

Perhaps not even then.

Would Bell be the next to be married to a nobleman she didn't love? It didn't matter now. She had to find a way to keep Roza safe without her fioré.

When Bell reached her room, Mistress Materia waited before the full-length mirror hanging on Bell's bedroom wall with swaths of fabric over her arms. "How about this lovely sky-blue cashmere, Miss Bell?"

Bell frowned. An airy-looking peach silk and a bright coral cambric hung from Mistress Materia's other arm.

"You don't have anything...yellow?" Yellow was warm, comforting, familiar.

Mistress Materia's mouth softened. She was the finest non-Bardian dressmaker Mother could find, and she couldn't have earned that reputation without knowing who to listen to. "Matrona Asbury was quite clear. How about the peach? It's close to yellow. Let's try it on."

At least Mother hadn't made her wear red. Bell followed the dressmaker's directions in a fog.

"I wish you always held this still, Miss Asbury." Mistress Materia pinned another crease in the peach silk around her shoulders. Bell stared into the mirror.

The shadows under her eyes appeared deep enough to fall into.

The silk might bring out her skin's honey tones, but it looked foreign. Mistress Materia seemed to sense her mood and finished her measurements quickly.

"Marvelous. You will look lovely, Miss Bell."

Bell nodded absently as the dressmaker excused herself. How could she and Mother think so differently? Her fioré lay in ruins because of a nobleman, and all Mother could think about was Bell's appearance.

A rap at the glass balcony door made Bell jump.

"Can I come in?" Carasti leaned around the door. Half of her pine green woodmaking tunic was tucked into her leggings.

"Mother will banish you if she catches you climbing the lattice."

"Bah." She dropped the small piece of auburn-colored wood she'd been carrying on the bed and sprawled next to it, nearly yanking down the linen bed-curtains. "She'll never catch me."

"If she ever figures out I can climb it too…"

Carasti's eyebrow disappeared into her hair. "You?"

Bell made a dismissive noise. "It's not that hard."

"Still, I'm impressed at anyone who can do it in a dress."

Bell lifted her chin. "Mother says a lady should be able to do everything in a dress."

Carasti cackled, sounding like a child who'd dropped a handful of leaves on someone's head. "But she wasn't thinking of climbing lattices, was she?"

Bell sighed and flopped on her belly next to Carasti. This was the Carasti most people missed, taken in by her guileless eyes. "Something about comportment, I think."

"Comporwhat? Never mind. I brought you something." Grabbing the wood piece, she rolled off the bed and knelt by the row of windows showing the balcony and the garden beyond.

Bell propped her head up to watch her work.

Carasti placed the wood parallel to the windows and stroked its length. It glowed golden, swelling and stretching until another board appeared. Using swift strokes that raised sparks, she fastened their ends together so the first was twice as long. Carasti repeated this until she'd made a rectangular frame big enough for Bell to lie down in. She nudged it tight along the wall below the windows. Sweeping her sparking fingers along its whole length, she doubled the frame's height.

Bell propped her chin on her hands. The warm smell of sawdust felt like an arm around her shoulders. "Is that a raised bed?"

Carasti grinned over her shoulder, her small teeth white like pearls. "You say being near the plants gives you more energy. So why not have them while you sleep?"

Bell pressed fingers to her forehead, the emptiness a cave within her. How long before she collapsed?

"It's not working, is it?" Carasti's slight weight nudged the bed, and her curls brushed Bell's cheek.

"You saw?"

"I was hoping to make you forget for a few minutes. Who did it, and where can I find them?"

Bell cracked an eye at Carasti's soft words, but all she saw was a cluster of curly hair. She blew out a long stream of air. "We found a nobleman's boot print. I think it was Garam."

Carasti jerked upright. "Garam of Medoro, destroying your fioré? But he's marrying your sister."

"But who else has a motive?"

"Come on." Her friend wiggled off the bed and pulled Bell with her. "Let's examine the damage."

Ghosts haunted the gutted fioré beds. Bell kept her gaze unfocused while Carasti scowled over one heap of topsoil and prodded another with a stick she'd found.

Finally, Carasti led her down a path that opened on the goldenbell arbor along the right wall of the garden's triangle. The devastation was hidden here. The faint honey scent of goldenbell was a shelter from it. They sank onto the wooden bench Carasti had made when they met as children. Bell had found out years later Agnella had arranged for Carasti to work with Bell, knowing Bell needed someone who was also a maker but wouldn't see her as a rival. From the moment she witnessed Carasti trying—and nearly succeeding—to convince the current head gardener they needed to build a three-story tower in the center of the Asburys' garden, Bell had known they would be friends. Carasti's impetuosity should have driven her crazy, but instead, it made her feel alive.

Though they did argue—a lot.

"You think Garam would have come in here during the night and ripped up your garden with his own hands?" Carasti gazed back out at the path as if she were imagining it happening this instant.

"I..." Garam, who was never seen without his burgundy cape marking him as a first son? Whose fingernails were *always* clean and buffed? "Or he hired someone. But who else would have a reason to do it?"

"Piero?"

Bell let out a sharp breath. "But he's a scentmaker. No matter how much he hates me, could he stoop so low as to destroy fioré?"

"You're willing to believe it of Garam, who can actually speak civilly to you in public," Carasti pointed out.

She shook her head. "I don't know. Maybe it wasn't him, but something *is* wrong about him. I followed him in the Night Bazaar—"

"What? You went in *without me*?"

"Let me finish."

Carasti visibly restrained her outrage while Bell relayed the conversation she'd heard between Garam and the Lanzi.

Carasti tugged a curl and let it bounce back. "He does look like a man with secrets. I just wouldn't have thought..." Her eyes narrowed to dramatic slits.

Bell shuddered. "And then he came upon me while I was having an allergic reaction in the Bazaar, and it was so——"

"You what?"

Bell spilled the story of the Spy, Piero and the Jonquil, and ended with the creepy gift of gloves.

"Weirder and weirder. Have you told your parents?"

"Mother wouldn't listen. Father's in Santa Croce, and I don't know when he's coming home."

"I can't believe a Spy actually talked to you." Carasti slapped her legs. "You get all the excitement."

"I'd take less, thank you."

Carasti stood and paced—or bounced, rather—in front of the arbor. "What if we go to Santa Croce and find your father?"

Bell grimaced. "He's at the Medoro estate there. Garam might use the Insidio even sooner if he found out."

"But it would wear off eventually, wouldn't it?"

Bell shook her head. "Magia imprints itself on the victim with the first dose. Each one afterward takes hold easier."

"It sounds like Roza's determined to stick with him even without the Insidio. Why is he bothering with it?"

Frustration rose slowly, sticking to her insides like mud. "There's something going on that I can't see. Maybe he's afraid she'll uncover something else he's doing."

Carasti grunted. "What if we found out what that is? What if it was enough to bring down the whole Medoro family? Then you wouldn't have to worry about crossing them anymore. No one would."

Bell dropped her chin into her hands. "Would anyone believe us? I doubt Mother would."

"What you need is concrete proof, and coming from someone else, so they have no reason to doubt."

"But who could——" Bell's eyes widened as Carasti froze mid-bounce. "The Seller of Secrets," they said over each other.

"Everyone would believe him."

"I almost think he wants to help, if he sent the Spy to point me to

Garam and the Lanzi." The Spy's dark-rimmed gaze played in her mind.

Carasti gasped. "Do you think he's trying to pull you in?"

Bell frowned, taking a long sprig of goldenbell and weaving it into a crown. "But why would he?"

"He manipulates people. His spies can get in anywhere, and they're masters of disguise." Carasti's voice turned grand as it always did when she was about to tell a story. "They use tunnels to move through Bardia, some of them right into your house. Anyone could be a Spy— the maid, the seamstress, your best friend."

Bell's scoff turned to a giggle. "I'm not worried about you being a Spy."

She gave Bell a dusty look. "You should be. Perhaps I was put in position all those years ago."

Carasti slinking behind curtains and listening at doorways? Her hair would stick out. "I doubt it."

"Am I not mysterious enough?"

"You tell too many stories. I doubt spies tell stories."

"Of course they do. They know everyone's secrets so they're the best storytellers."

Bell handed her the crown, and she settled it into her curls. "You want to be one, don't you?"

Carasti grinned impishly. "You're right, I'm not sneaky enough. But I do want to meet one." Her grin dropped away, but her eyes sparkled. "If we do this, we'll have to search for his stall in the Sotto."

"We? I don't know if you should—"

Carasti made an interrupting noise. "You don't get all the excitement. What better way to meet a Spy?"

Bell shivered. Would she see the Spy at the Seller's stall? Surely he'd be out...spying...or something. Disappointment and relief tangled within her at the thought. The numbing despair was eroding, and in its place lay determination.

Mother wouldn't listen, so it was up to her to find a way to defend Roza from Garam.

Nine

THE CLOUDS HAD CONSUMED THE MOON like a seed, and silver streaks grew from it. Bell crept down the lattice, scanning the garden below for strange shadows. The Asbury guards watched the front gate, and the driver slept in the driver's cottage at the front.

Her garden should be unwatched. In the bright sunlight, she'd laughed at Carasti's story about the spies, but this dappled darkness could hide anyone.

Mother had demanded she stay on the grounds until the fioré thief was found, but she had to see Agnella. She would know what to do.

Under the goldenbell arbor, Bell brushed aside the vines and revealed a door set in the wall. This was the door she and Roza had slipped through to explore Grenwood years ago. Once she'd learned how to fuse, she'd installed a scentlock a glassmaker had fixed to open to her elixirs alone.

Uncorking the goldenbell vial at her neck, she poured a drop of her *protezi* elixir into the scentlock vial on the doorknob. The scentlock hissed, and the knob turned under her hand.

Grenwood waited on the other side, its trees looming shadows. Bell tucked her tan cloak close around her.

Why didn't I borrow Roza's black cloak? I look like a spirit.

At the edge of the wood, oak and black poplar trees grew in loose formation, and city lights below the hill peeked through. The faded

64

path from the garden door led all the way down to the Piazza, but Bell followed a branch to the right, picking up speed as her vision adjusted to the moonlight. Her blue velvet slippers rustled, and the night breeze lifted her hair. The wild growth stirred at the gift in her veins, but she stayed on the path. It felt foreign, nothing like her garden she had raised from shoots.

It hadn't felt safe since she was eleven years old.

Bell's hands were clammy when she left the cover of the trees at the edge of the first Bardian farm. This far past the nobles' houses, the cobblestones of the Via turned to white gravel, crunching loudly beneath her feet. Her chest squeezed every time a night bird called. The darkness seemed to be watching her.

She followed the road east along the edge of Grenwood. The farmers' fields on the other side held slumped outbuildings and sleeping cows. The forest was a murky shadow on the horizon. Beyond it, the Inchio Sea murmured. Agnella often muttered about the difficulty of getting a permit to clear trees from the Maestro of Wood. He had to examine each tree before it could be cut, and there was one of him and dozens of farmers looking to spread toward the coast.

Two crumbling stone pillars and a row of ancient cypress trees guarded the lane to Agnella's farm. Bell darted across, breathing easier when the trees' shadow enveloped her.

Agnella's stone farmhouse loomed pale. A candle shone in the window, beckoning her closer. Bell knocked gently, and after a moment the door creaked open a few inches to reveal the Maestra's weary face.

Ten minutes later, Bell sat by the hearth cupping a mug of hot broth, asking Agnella to help her find the Seller of Secrets.

Agnella stiffened, her eyes glinting like black stones. "No. Do not go near him."

"But if he gave me proof, everyone would have to believe it."

"Once he knows your deepest secret, he can make you do anything. He'll destroy you."

Bell shuddered. "But Mother won't even investigate—"

"Listen to me, Goldenbell." Broth sloshed from Agnella's mug as her grip tightened. She pointed a bony finger at Bell. "If a scentmaker like you walks into his clutches, he will never let you go."

"What do you mean?"

Agnella looked away for a moment as if deciding something. "We were apprentices together."

"He—he's a scentmaker?"

"His gift wasn't strong to begin with, but he's delved for power where he should not. He's the most dangerous manipulator Bardia has ever known. He'd take over the mainland if he could."

"A *scentmaker*. How can he maintain his gift without refreshing at Solstice? Surely the Consiglio wouldn't allow him..." Bell frowned into the fire, trying to envision the Seller of Secrets showing his face on the Piazza during Summer Solstice. Would he wear a mask like his spies?

Agnella grimaced. "Not the Consiglio, no. As I said, there are no depths he's not willing to go to increase his power. His control over the city."

"But if he's a maker himself—"

"He's nothing like you, Bell. I've avoided him for years, kept my secrets closer than my skin. He's threatened me, offered me everything to make me work for him. Makers are tools to him. If he knew how strong you are..." She stood and poured her broth back into the pot hanging over the fire. "Firinacci claimed that a gift like his own comes once in centuries. No one after him could match it. The Seller has been looking for such a gift."

Bell made a disbelieving sound. "I'm not that strong."

"Growing things know you as one of their own, like Firinacci." She stood and took a burning lantern from a hook by the back door. "Come."

Bell set down her broth and followed Agnella out the door and toward the long, low workshop behind the farmhouse. The workshop was fifty feet long, its roof made entirely of glass panes glimmering in the deep night. The thorny vine covering the door and streaking the walls and roof responded only to Agnella's touch, and Bell entered behind her slowly. Agnella's protective vine had given Bell the idea to grow her own version when she first started collecting vials of elixirs.

"My thorny vine has never been tested like yours." Blossoms bobbed at Agnella's voice as the long beds full of fioré plants came sleepily to life. The Consiglio's gift of a workshop full of Bardian soil and fioré to a Maestra of Scents was the singular thing that made Bell long for the station. Someday she would have a safe space for her fioré and the elixirs she drew from them, even if she had to forsake Santa Maria Novella and live apart from her family.

Then she could use her *attuale* gift to *do* something.

"It's like my own skin has been cut." Skin wasn't the right word, but she hurt.

"Come. You must fuse to heal your mind." Agnella plucked a handful of fuzzy striped Myrtle leaves, then handed the bouquet and a vial to Bell. The green leached into the air, filling Bell's nose until she tasted moss.

She arranged her fingers in a fusing position. Heat eased down her arms and out her fingers, warming the fioré. Bell closed her eyes as the dusty smell of scentmaking rose. Her surface emotions smoothed when she let a few drops of healing Myrtle touch her wrists. The rest slid into the vial, a scent cloud rising and opening like green leaves. The pain remained, but it lay beneath a new calm.

"It is so easy for you, Bell," Agnella whispered.

Bell looked down. The vial was already full. "Because you taught me well."

"I have taught you how to use the gift you have. I knew from the beginning yours would be stronger than mine."

"My gift can't be stronger. I don't have enough control."

Agnella set aside the withered bouquet Bell had fused and gathered a new one. "Do you know what happens when I try to fuse Princess Seed?" She put her fingers in position and paused, her brow furrowed. "Nothing, Bell. I'm losing the fioré one at a time."

"What's happened?"

"It's a balance of power, so you can take my place. This is why you must stay away from the Seller of Secrets. My gift is weakening, and Bardia has fewer scentmakers, to make room for yours."

Bell pushed away a chill. "That can't be true. You need your gift."

"I want you to present yourself at the Summer Solstice, and the *attuale* will choose you as it chose me long ago."

"That will be too late. Roza's wedding is the day after. Even if it wasn't, you know I don't have the control to be Maestra."

Agnella snorted. "Who else could take my place, hmm? Piero?"

Bell flushed. "I—I need more time."

"You already have your own elixir. It took me ten years to fuse my own. The Consiglio accepted me as Maestra because Maestro Alphonse's gift was fading. As mine is."

Bell shook her head. "Yours will return when you refresh it at Solstice."

"Pshaw." Agnella tossed the withered fioré into a mulch bucket. "You're afraid. In your mind, you'll always be eleven years old, ruined by your first mistake."

Bell scooped a handful of water from another bucket and poured it into a pot of wilted Myrtle. She stroked the fioré's stem, and the leaves straightened, hanging eager and full, larger than the others. The current of power sliding out her fingers soothed the anxiety prickling her neck. "I almost lost my sister, Agnella, because I had no control. She's never been the same." Roza's Lymbodia was a family secret, but Agnella had been there to tend to her several times after the incident. She knew the signs.

"She handed you Magia before you knew what it was. What did she expect?"

"She didn't know what it was either."

Agnella narrowed her eyes. "Are you sure about that?" she said quietly.

"Why would she give me something so dangerous if she knew?" Bell scoffed. "You didn't know her then. Yes, she loved adventure, but she wouldn't risk her mind like that. Or her health."

Crickets sang from the far corner in the long silence. "Whoever gave her the Magia knew what it was. They must have suspected your gift."

"*I* didn't even suspect my gift." Bell slipped her fingers into another pot. She needed to feel the life of the soil, its constant, efficient humming.

"But the Seller of Secrets would." Agnella leaned toward her. "He knows the signs, and there's very little he doesn't know about the people he's watching."

"What are you saying?"

"I think he set you up, Bell. He wanted you to fuse the Magia. He wanted to know if you could."

Bell scoffed, shaking her head. "Why? What possible reason—and then he left me alone for six years? Why wouldn't he approach me when I was younger?"

Agnella cut a sharp glance at the window. "Stay away from him."

The Myrtle plant she was touching shot up too fast, drooping on its too-thin stem. "I have to protect Roza."

Agnella snatched the Myrtle away. The thorny vine threading over the glass roof stirred, creaking against the glass. "You won't accept the Maestra's gift, but you'll try to fuse *permanenza* for Roza?"

Bell met Agnella's hard gaze. "Who told you that?"

"I may not know everyone's secrets, but elixirs are my domain. I've heard disturbing rumors these past few days." Her set face said there was no point in denying it.

Bell's forehead pinched with pleading. "Roza needs something to protect her. Will you let me use your fioré?"

Agnella's lips flattened. "No. It's too dangerous. Not to mention illegal."

"Then I have no choice but to do it on my own."

"Nonsense."

Bell gestured with both hands. "I know Garam has Insidio. He could use it on Roza at any time. If I can't convince her to leave him before he does, she won't be able to resist him. He'll make her a slave, Agnella. I'm afraid he already has."

69

"And what happens if the wrong person gets hold of a *permanenza* elixir? Hmm? He could use it with the Insidio, and she'd never be free."

"Which is why I need to fuse it and use it on *him* as soon as possible. Please, Agnella. I need your help."

Agnella snatched a waving strand of thorny vines, and the creaking stopped. "There is much you don't understand, Bell."

"Then help me understand."

She shook her head sharply. "I need to tie some things together, and then I'll tell you everything."

Bell stared at her. The crickets were quiet now, silenced by their raised voices. The humming of this many fioré kneaded her gift, begging her to use it.

It was unbearable. She turned to go.

"Promise you won't go near the Seller, Bell. Or try to fuse *permanenza* on your own."

Bell paused. "I can't, Agnella."

Ten

"WHAT ABOUT A LATTICE THAT LETS the sun in, but keeps anyone from touching it?" Carasti stroked her delicate chin, pacing along one of Bell's empty fioré beds. The undergardener that came twice a week to help with heavy tasks had meticulously swept up the Bardian soil and refilled the beds, leaving the courtyard stones clean. Bell had saved a single Princess Seed root and had potted it in her room, but some of the fioré needed more sunlight than her windows could give.

"I would need to touch it. Could the lattice have hinges?"

"The hinges would have to be Bardian made, if you want it secure."

Bell squeezed her vial. Bardian metal, Bardian wood. "I don't think we can afford it. Not if we're replacing my fioré too."

Carasti made a sympathetic noise. "What about Maestra Agnella? Doesn't she have some extra?"

Bell winced. "She needs it for fusing new elixirs and teaching apprentices." And she wasn't likely to let them leave her workshop, knowing what Bell would use them for.

Carasti nodded as if expecting her response. "Let me look around, see what I can find."

Elena tiptoed out from the hedged path, scanning the clean beds nervously. "Miss Bell, the Matrona is asking for you."

Bell brushed her hand along the bed's edge as if that could smooth the crawling feeling in her stomach. It was like spiders had been unleashed inside her, their tiny feet always moving. "What does she want?"

Elena hesitated. "She didn't say, but miss...she is upset."

71

The spiders suddenly stilled. "I'll come in a moment."

Elena nodded and tiptoed back.

Bell squinted up at the sun. "She probably wants me for lunch. Sneak around the front when you're done."

"Her majesty will never know I was here."

"Her what?"

Carasti waved her hand. "Go eat."

Bell opened her mouth, then spun away. No time for one of Carasti's dramatic mainland stories.

Mother appraised her from the dining room when she stepped in the door, somehow spotting the soil under Bell's nails. In an imperial purple overgown with a fringe brushing the floor, she looked prepared to ascend a throne. Her golden hair was pulled back, sleek and sure, exposing high cheekbones and lips painted to match her dress.

Bell swallowed, her throat dry. Something dreadful had happened.

"Go get your sister, quickly. We have a visitor." Mother's voice was low but indomitable.

"Who?" Bell's feet seemed rooted to the wooden floor.

"Matrona Medoro."

All the way up the stairs, Bell considered various reasons why she couldn't be present at lunch. A headache, nerves, her nails were stained. Matrona Medoro, Garam and Piero's mother, was darkness to Mother's sun. No one made Mother colder, sharper, more menacing. Even Father and Pater Medoro sensed this, and any interactions between the families had never left the two women alone.

Now it was up to Bell and Roza.

Why was Matrona Medoro here now, without warning? Coming from the position of power in the match, she had no need to eclipse the doors of House Asbury. Was she trying to reassert her authority?

Bell shuddered and paused in the hall. If Roza married Garam, she'd be enfolded into this family, submerged within their sway like a bulb buried too deeply to sprout.

Roza would vanish.

Bell rapped on Roza's door.

"Roza, are you in there?"

Something chafed in her throat. She leaned forward, bending toward the crack beneath the door. A pungent scent burned her eyes: Princess Seed and a slippery, unfamiliar fragrance. She stumbled back, lifting her goldenbell vial. With her hand cupped over her nose, she opened the door. Lying on the floor, a pair of shoes and legs in a white servant's skirt stuck out from behind the bed.

Elena.

Bell darted inside. Holding her breath, she grabbed Elena's ankles and dragged her out into the hall. She gulped fresh air, then ran back in. The room was empty. The bed was a rumple of sheets and dirty silk stockings. Something glinted beneath the half-open window—an empty glass vial. A fading, muddy green scent cloud twisted in the air above it, looking like a rotten, leafless tree. Lungs burning, Bell slammed the door on her way out.

"Mother!"

Elena's lips were blue. Bell hooked her under the arms and staggered down the hall to her own bedroom. Mother's heels clicked as she strode up the stairs.

"What is the meaning—" Mother burst into Bell's room and gasped as Bell gently lowered Elena's head to the rug. Bell crossed the room and rummaged through the cabinet by her bed.

"How did this happen?"

"I don't know." Bell yanked open her kit and sent three vials scattering before she found one of pure Princess Seed. She pulled out the stopper as she knelt on the rug and sloshed some onto each of Elena's wrists. "I found her like this, in Roza's room."

Mother spun toward the hall. Bethesda, the housekeeper who'd followed Bell's call, hurried out of the way.

"Mother, no. The poison is still too strong."

"Then get me a mask. Where is Roza?"

Elena's lips pinked. Bell left the vial open and pulled a mask from a drawer below the cabinet. She dabbed five *protezi* drops into the silk and held it up. Mother's lips compressed, but she tied it on.

73

Bell donned her own mask and followed, leaving Bethesda to watch Elena. The scent in the hall had faded, but Bell could still sense it. They burst into the room. Mother's movement grew more and more rigid as she flicked aside lingerie and jerked up the sheets. Bell peered out the open window Elena had been facing. The rose-covered lattice below the window was undisturbed. Had the poisoner come through the house, taken Roza, and left Elena behind?

She should have detected this before it happened. And Agnella thought she could be Maestra of Scents?

"Hello?" A deep voice came from the stairs. Bell bolted upright.

Mother smoothed her skirt and stepped into the hall. "Garam, thank San Giovanni you're here." She moved closer to him, and the rest of their conversation was too quiet for Bell to hear.

The spiral bedpost felt crooked as Bell clutched it, trying to breathe normally. Why would Garam be here if Roza wasn't? Had he taken Roza away somehow?

"Bell, are you all right?" Garam's shoulders filled the doorway.

She blinked. If Elena had stumbled on him kidnapping Roza...

Mother beckoned to Bell. "Come out of there, dear." She turned to Garam. "It's her maid, so she's in shock, I think."

Garam barely moved aside for Bell to slip past. His gaze prickled her neck, but she kept her face turned away. Her mask couldn't hide her horror. "I'm going to check on Elena."

She helped Bethesda lift Elena onto her bed, and her chest loosened at Elena's improved color. She might not wake for an hour or two, but pure Princess Seed was the best antidote for the poison in her lungs.

Garam had followed Mother downstairs into the parlor, and the rumble of his words from downstairs made her fist her hands. How dare he act as if he'd done nothing? Matrona Medoro's smoky voice rose after his, bringing silence.

"Her breathing is still shallow, miss." Bethesda adjusted Elena's pillow.

Bell held the vial beneath Elena's nose. "Keep this close to her. Tell me if it gets worse." She strode toward the door. This had gone too far.

Bell burst into the parlor, hands tight on her hips to hide her shaking knees. "Where is she?"

Garam stood slowly, setting down his teacup. "She?"

"Where is my sister?"

Matrona Medoro's thick dark hair was a braided mass over her head, and her deep burgundy gown was cut wide to reveal a necklace of white Bardian jewels around her thin, pale neck. Her face looked made of perfect marble as she studied Bell.

Mother stepped toward her. "Bell, calm yourself."

"Elena was poisoned in Roza's room." Bell stabbed a finger toward the stairs. "She could have died."

Garam frowned. "Roza and I went for a ride, and she wanted to check if the Maestro of Fire had finished her fireworks order for the party. I came here to see if Pater Asbury had returned yet."

Bell crossed her arms. "And we're to take your word for it?"

"Goldenbell, be silent." Mother's hand clamped around Bell's forearm.

Bell tried to yank away. "Roza isn't safe with him, Mother. Can't you see?"

Garam took a step forward. "I would never hurt Roza. I'm as concerned as you are about her safety."

She braced herself. "But you'd use Insidio on her?"

He flinched, then his eyes turned stormy.

Mother dragged Bell into the hall. "Go to your room and stay there," she hissed. She closed the parlor door in Bell's face.

"Mr. Medoro, Matrona, I do apologize. My daughter is upset due to a recent event..." Her voice faded as Bell staggered toward a garden door, rubbing her arm where Mother's nails had dug in. She left the house and hurried down the path, glancing back once before she stepped through the hidden arbor door.

Garam's flinch was proof enough. He was guilty, and angry she knew it. Bell had uncovered the game he was playing. She had to find Roza before it was too late.

Eleven

THE PIAZZA'S PULSE SLOWED IN THE SULtry afternoon.

The Maestris' workshops sat mostly empty with the odd apprentice present to answer tourists' questions and watch the sales tables. Cafes and bars and food stalls created most of the traffic, selling pastries and caffè and iced desserts all afternoon.

On the patio outside the largest bar, Roza held court. Surrounded by men with white teeth and girls with luminous hair, Roza had her head tilted back in infectious laughter as Bell approached. The relief spooling through Bell's stomach made her actually skip a step.

Roza looked as she always did with her admirers—brilliant as the sun, like a goddess who graced the isle with her gossamer beauty. She reached for a plate of croissants likely bought for her by a passing nobleman. When she wasn't sitting where all the passing tourists could see her, she was tucked away in some artists' gallery, posing while draped in something white and sheer.

Under normal circumstances, Bell would have given her a wide berth. When she was like this, her words and gestures had a way of twisting under Bell's skin that Bell couldn't forget later when they were alone. She said beautiful things, some of them speckled with poison not everyone could see. But now, full of relief that she was not lying sallow skinned in the dungeon below House Medoro, Bell approached.

"Roza," she said.

Roza looked up, her lips already curved into a smile that froze and

76

thawed so quickly Bell almost missed it. "Goldenbell," she purred, all delighted surprise. "What brings you out this afternoon?"

Bell stepped closer, focusing on the glaze-latticed croissants rather than the considering eyes of the dark-haired boy beside Roza. "I need to talk to you," she murmured.

"Right now?"

All the gazes at the table burned into her, searing her blue velvet shoes, her loose knit overdress, and her unadorned brown hair.

"Yes," she said. "Right now."

Roza stood slowly, looking like she wanted to laugh at Bell's discomfort. She strode away without a word to her court, and Bell followed, smoothing her hair down and feeling their collective gaze on her back like a fire's heat.

Roza sank into a chair at the next bar. A waiter hurried their way, but he jerked to a halt when Roza flicked a hand at him. "What is it? I was busy." Roza's bemusement was gone.

"Matrona Medoro came for lunch, and Mother didn't know where you were."

Roza cursed. "That hag. She's trying to catch me off guard." She snatched a napkin off the table and worried it between her fingers. She grinned. "Did you keep Mother from drawing her sword?"

"I don't know. We didn't have lunch."

Roza paused, an eyebrow raised.

"Someone tried to poison you, Roza. They got Elena instead." Bell took a shaky breath.

"What do you mean, poison?"

"They left a vial of poison in your room. She went in to look for you and passed out. She's all right th—"

Another curse burst from Roza's lips, sounding like a weapon she could use to cut down the recipient. "The *fool*. I will make her regret this."

Bell went rigid. "*What*? You think it's Elena's fault—"

Roza flicked a hand. "Not her. Someone else."

"I think it was Garam."

Roza's blue eyes flashed up to Bell's, suddenly bright and full of fear. "Why?"

"He was there, right after I found Elena, as if he was waiting to find you unconscious."

"Garam…" she whispered.

"Who did *you* think did it?"

She shook her head slowly, dropping the wrinkled napkin on the table. She looked so desolate for a moment, her perfect face like a window looking in on a roomful of broken glass. Sharp and empty.

Bell's heart twisted, and she took her sister's hand. "Please, Roza. Break off the engagement. It's not worth this."

Roza jerked free as her face closed. "You don't know how it is, Bell. You're the golden girl who's never had to give up anything."

Bell opened her mouth and shut it. What could she say to reach Roza's heart? "I'm trying to protect you."

"I don't need your protection. All I need is the *permanenza* elixir."

"And if I can't do it? What will you do then? Marry Garam, who tried to poison you? What kind of life—"

"Better than what I have now," she bit out.

Stunned, Bell waited for Roza to laugh or wave her hand to say her words meant nothing. Her gaze was icy, daring Bell to argue and already scornful of what she would say. Hurt welled up from Bell's chest, tightening her lungs. She closed stinging eyes. "Is it so bad? Would it be so much better at House Medoro, with…with him?"

Roza didn't soften. "There are many things you don't know, golden girl."

"Stop calling me that." She wanted the words to come out angry, to cut like Roza's did, but they stayed soft.

"I'll stop when you stop being naïve, Bell. You know nothing of the pressure I'm under. Everyone wants something from me. Even you."

"I want you to be safe."

"No. You want me under control, like everything else in your life." Roza stepped out into the Piazza. "Let go of me, Bell."

Bell sat long after the growing crowd had absorbed her sister. The waiter glanced her way several times but didn't approach. The thunderstorm raging in her mind must have been visible on her face.

Roza was dying, slowly but surely. The Medoros couldn't offer healing, merely the illusory safety of wealth and power. What would make Roza see that?

If Garam *had* tried to poison Roza, would he try again now that he'd failed? Had he been trying to kill her or knock her unconscious?

Would he have the skill to do it? How had he made it up to her room unseen? *Could* he have done it? Did he hate her so much? She tried to imagine him throwing the vial onto the floor, malice twisting his face, but all that came to mind was the intense longing in his face when he looked at Roza.

Perhaps he hadn't done it. Did Roza have another enemy? Who was the *her* she had mentioned?

A skilled scentmaker could design a poison trap to be tripped when someone entered the room. Bell pulled the empty vial from her bodice where she'd tucked it. The sinister red glass glittered, and it still smelled faintly of poison. An uncorked vial tossed on the floor seemed more like an attacker who had fled moments before Bell saw Elena.

She shuddered.

The lattice outside Roza's room would hardly have supported someone of Garam's weight, at least not silently. She and Carasti had to choose their path carefully so as not to pull any slats loose. To escape out the window in broad daylight had to be the work of a Spy. Mother would have seen Garam or anyone else if they'd used the stairs.

Was Garam working with a Spy—or had a Spy tried to cast the blame on him?

When the waiter approached with irritated regret on his face, Bell shoved herself up and turned to go.

The sun had lowered over the now busy Piazza, but the heat would take an hour to fade. She drifted through the crush of people, her gaze unfocused. A tingling sense of wrongness came over her. Her neck prickled as she reached the corner where Grenwood brushed the stone walls of the square. She turned slowly, trying to look casual. Tourists, bright and noisy, swept toward the Night Bazaar in a leisurely current. Bell edged toward the break in the wall, and then her gaze caught on a shadow at the edge of the first Maestro's stall.

The shadow was staring at her. They pushed back their cloak enough for her to see their amaranth mask. Bell's half-smile collapsed as her breath stopped.

Eyes glittered out of the hood, cold and malevolent, and red lips spread in a beautiful snarl.

This was not her Spy.

The shadow vanished while Bell was blinking.

Fear twisted its grip and she darted into the forest, desperate to be out of sight of those cold eyes. The malice in them—even Piero's hatred hadn't looked so deep.

The path through Grenwood was perceptible once she was on it. As far as she knew, she was the only user, and so it remained overgrown. The lengthening afternoon shadows darkened the green canopy, and she moved quickly, her legs burning at the incline. The farthest corner of House Asbury appeared, the mossy stone wall looming. She slowed as she rounded the huge oak marking the arbor entrance. A trilling whistle floated toward her, and she froze.

Twelve

A FIGURE PEELED AWAY FROM THE WALL and pushed back his hood, revealing a half mask. His black cloak rippled, seeming to suck in sunlight, and revealed a crisp, fitted white shirt beneath.

Her Spy. He knew the secret entrance to her garden. Carasti was right.

She felt a moment of relief it was him, and not the malevolent watcher from the Piazza, but then it was like a choking vine wrapped around her lungs. She stepped back.

He leaned a shoulder against the oak tree, his flawless lips turning up in a smile. His lean legs looked relaxed, but she was wearing a dress and slippers. He could probably walk faster than she could run. And what if the other Spy was waiting for her?

"What have you been looking for, Bell?"

Were the spies working together? Had she been herded here? She glanced back down the empty path, then stared at him, thoughts tangling. She wanted him to sink back into the shadows and never reappear. She wanted him to unearth Garam's secrets and save Roza.

She wanted him to come closer so she could see his eyes.

Bewildering desire twisted around her tongue. Carasti would be furious to have missed this—that thought finally cleared her mind enough to speak. "Why are you here?" she forced out.

"I want to help you."

81

She frowned. "Roza told me not to trust you." *Not to let you seduce me, actually.*

His smile spread and he glided closer. "She's right. You shouldn't trust anyone. Even your sister."

Furious, she lifted her chin as her heartbeat pulsed in her wrists.

He glanced away, muttering something under his breath. "I came to warn you," he said.

She huffed a laugh. "That's ironic. Everyone else has already warned me away from *you*."

He swept toward her, so close his cloak brushed her skirt. She flinched, swallowing a scream—deeply aware no one would hear her anyway.

"And yet you're still here." His eyes were still as the starless sky, rimmed in kohl. She could not look away.

"I need to get to the Seller of Secrets. I assume you know how to find him," she said.

His gaze flickered. "I wouldn't advise going near him."

"I didn't ask for advice. I asked you to take me to him." She stepped forward. "You said you would help me."

He studied her. "It will cost you."

"And what is the cost?"

One side of his mouth tipped up, and he pressed a folded paper into her hand. "Nothing you can't part with."

At his touch, she forced herself still as a breezeless morning. Her heart was racing, but she wasn't exactly afraid. The feeling tingling through her reminded her of how it felt to test a new elixir for the first time. "What is it?"

"Open it and see, Sunbeam."

Her breath caught as she stared at his smile. He was so unlike what she expected him to be. Her forehead creased in a frown. What did he want? She unfolded the paper and tore her gaze away from him. It was an elegant map of the Night Bazaar. Every booth was labeled according to what was sold there. Below the Night Bazaar, connected by dozens of stairways, lay the Sotto.

"I was here?" Bell touched the stairway next to the silkmaker close to the Sotto.

The Spy placed his finger next to hers and traced a path from the stairway into a labyrinth of side streets and alleyways, ending at an amaranth smudged circle labeled *The Seller of Secrets*.

She looked up to see him watching her.

"It's best if I'm not seen with you yet, but I will be watching." He closed her fingers around the map and leaned close. She resisted the urge to snatch the mask off his face.

"Be certain this is what you want. The Seller of Secrets will demand far more than I will." He pulled up his hood. "Until we meet again." He walked past her, vanishing into the trees. She shoved the map into her pocket. He might ask for something, but she hadn't promised him anything.

As far as she was concerned, she didn't owe him. So why did she feel like something inevitable had begun?

"Goldenbell, where have you been?" Mother's voice cut across the fountain like a spear of ice.

"In the garden." The lie tasted sour, but Bell swallowed it.

"Have you found her?" a man called.

Bell dashed around the fountain and past Mother. "Father!"

Father strode toward her from the house, his tan skin glowing in the last rays of the sun. When his arms closed around her, Bell took a deep breath.

Her relief faded when he tensely asked her into his study.

"Sit down, Bell." He sat in his own chair before the desk, and she sank into the half sofa across from him. Mother stood by the window, her face backlit by the sunset. "We thought you'd gone out to look for Roza," Father said.

"I needed some time to think."

"I was ready to send the guards to the Piazza." Mother's back was rigid. She considered involving the guards in their personal troubles to be low behavior, of course. "Next time you hide in the garden, tell us first."

"Did you think to look for Roza too?"

"Garam told us where she was."

Bell tightened her face to keep from scowling or shouting the words boiling within her throat. *Why does Roza hate her life with us? Why do you not care about her like I do?*

Mother stepped closer. "This suspicious attitude must stop. I had no choice but to send a messenger to call your father home when you disappeared. I shouldn't have to tell you we can't afford to offend House Medoro."

Bell slapped her knees. "You'll let her marry a poi—"

"Silence!" Mother's control slipped and her voice came out shrill.

"Francesca..." Father moved between them.

Bell glared at Mother. "A lot of things happened while you were gone, Father."

"I'm beginning to see that."

Mother touched fingers to her forehead, appearing to steady herself. "Antonio, our daughter is easily excited. This—conspiracy—she's imagined could damage our future forever."

Father studied Bell, then turned and met his wife's gaze. "Give us a moment, my dear." He took her hand and kissed it, and she swept from the room with a sharp glance at Bell.

Father let the silence settle, then stood and held out his hand. "Come. Show me the damage."

Bell took his hand and fell in step beside him as they made their way to the garden. The rays of sunset painted the tips of the hedges scarlet orange. They passed full beds of alyssum and blooming lilies, but Bell barely saw them. Father's forehead creases deepened as they stepped onto the fountain square, and he took in the empty beds.

"All gone?" He squeezed her hand.

Bell nodded, pursing her lips. He pulled her close. "I'm so sorry, Blossom."

84

She took a deep breath of air, empty without her fioré. Garam, or whoever it was, would pay for this.

"They left your other flowers untouched. That's good."

Bell stiffened and pulled out of his grip. Right now, she didn't care about ordinary flowers. "Mother's glad. She never approved of my fioré anyway."

Father's forehead found its familiar creases. "Your mother means well, Bell. She loves you."

"In her own way, I suppose," Bell grumbled. "And Roza? Does she love her?"

He brushed his fingers along the stone edges of the fountain. "Of course."

Bell studied him for a moment. She took a deep breath. "If you and mother truly love Roza, you won't make her marry Garam. Father, I saw Garam take Insidio from a Lanzi."

Father frowned. "Where did you see this?"

Bell stared at the hedges, guilt squirming in her belly. "It...it doesn't matter. They talked about Garam's engagement, and Garam said he wouldn't break it off, he couldn't let her go, and he'd use the Insidio to take care of the problem."

"That is a serious accusation." He let out a long breath and placed his warm hand on her shoulder. "Bell, we're not forcing Roza to do anything. Her courtship and her marriage were her own decisions. She knows what's best for the family. Even if you think you heard that, Garam is the first son of House Medoro. I would need solid proof before I did anything. You endanger our alliance by making wild claims like this—"

Bell clenched fistfuls of her dress. "A nobleman broke into my garden and destroyed my fioré, and then Elena was poisoned in *Roza's* room this morning. What if Roza wants to break it off, and Garam got the Insidio in order to keep her from leaving him? What if someone destroyed my fioré so I couldn't use it to protect Roza? What if Garam had someone poison Roza to—"

Father squeezed her shoulder. "Please, Bell. We need to think this

85

through. I can't imagine Garam could do anything to hurt Roza."

She checked rising hysteria. Would Father brush off everything like Mother had? "There was a footprint. The boot print was too fine to be a commoner's. I'm certain a nobleman destroyed my fioré."

"Why couldn't a guard, or even a maid, have stolen fine boots? The destruction could have been motivated by greed. They could be selling what's left of valuable fioré in the Sotto." Father frowned. "The servants must be questioned."

"What about Garam? What about Roza?"

Father took her hand in both of his. His palms felt rough, capable. They used to make her feel safe, but now she sensed he was patronizing her. "Bell, my dear, the world of Bardia is convoluted and often ugly. It can't be controlled. To investigate House Medoro without proof is impossible. We would lose their support, and our future—*your* future—depends on it." He kissed her hand. Had new wrinkles crept across his skin? She imagined him pacing late last night, his face crumpled in worry. "Do you understand?"

She wanted to. "No."

He took a deep breath. "I will ask Roza again to be certain she is willing to go through with the marriage. I will double the night watch. I won't let anything happen to the two of you—and I'll look into Garam's background privately." He squeezed her hand. "If you promise not to do anything rash."

Bell sighed. "I'll do my best."

He gave a bemused smile and bid her goodnight.

Bell sank onto a bench. Long after he'd returned to the house, Bell stared at the empty beds where her fioré used to be. Her hand drifted to her pocket, and the map of the Night Bazaar crinkled.

Thirteen

THE CARRIAGE JOSTLED OVER A POTHOLE, and Bell clutched the green velvet seat. Her silky brown hair was rolled into a complicated bun at the nape of her neck, and a pin was already digging into her scalp.

"You can't go to my engagement party looking like you bit your tongue," Roza said from behind her silver pocket mirror. Her golden hair mounted her head like a crown. Her cardinal red silk overgown, gathered in the front, faded into her blood-orange petticoat as if she'd stepped into a melted sunset. Her sharp plunging neckline made the skin of Bell's own chest crawl. What would it be like to be so comfortable with her own body?

"You expect me to smile when I'm in his house?"

She dropped the mirror. "Still mad about Garam? I thought this was about you having to wear peach."

"Well, it's not." Bell glared out the window, fingering the golden-bell blossom she'd woven into her hair behind her ear. They passed House Salviati as Grigor handed his sister Isa into their carriage. Isa's sapphire blue gown glittered like it was made of actual sapphires. The evening stretched before Bell like eternity. She pictured all the beautiful people jostling for a better spot in the Medoros' sphere. Their eager courting of the most powerful family in Bardia reminded Bell every moment of Roza's precarious position.

Roza sighed. "I'm sorry for what I said before. I was upset." She popped a caramel into her mouth and hummed.

87

"Are you unhappy about the marriage? Are you frightened?" Bell asked quietly.

Roza looked at Bell through her lashes. "The world is a happy place for you, Bell. I'd like it to stay that way."

"You can tell me anything." Bell leaned forward to touch Roza's knee.

Roza looked away. "Make me a *permanenza* elixir, and I can take care of myself."

"If you are unhappy, tell Father you refuse to marry. He said he considers your opinion. I'm begging you—"

Roza's hand tightened on the velvet curtain. "It's happening, Bell. They have money, power, everything we need to survive Bardia."

The carriage slowed as it turned into the Medoros' hedge-lined lane. Blood-red roses entwined the hedges, stirring as the carriage passed.

"Roza, please—"

"You're wearing Garam's gloves, I see." Bell clenched her fingers. "Try to look happy. Garam's cousin is here." She frowned and tugged Bell's neckline down.

"What does he look like?" Bell said as she slapped Roza's hand away. The peach silk gown was tailored perfectly, and it felt like she was wearing a breath of air rather than actual clothing. The feeling of exposure added to her anxiety.

"He's a Medoro. They all look like gods. Dark hair."

Bell stared out the window at the glowing front doors of House Medoro. They'd wrapped the pillars and bushes in gold glow gem garlands and covered the doors with glimmering paint. The crumbling tower behind loomed like a monster from Carasti's stories. It brought Eduard's desperate, agonized eyes to mind. The carriage came to a stop, and Roza threw open the door without waiting for the footman.

"Make me a crown, would you?" Roza said as she stepped down. "I'm past the humiliation of their footing the party bill, but I at least need to make a good entrance."

Bell followed her, fists clenched. Her fury crackled within her—at her parents, Garam, and most of all Roza for refusing to save herself.

88

Her gift sparked and burned from her fingers before she reached out, fingertips brushing the hedges. A hundred red roses, a thousand, rustled toward Roza. Stems lengthened and broke off as they wove into her skirt and hair. The roses took on the hues of her gown, lightening to orange at the bottom.

Roza laughed and spun. Velvet petals fluttered behind her. She grabbed Bell's face and kissed both cheeks. "They'll all be staring." Then she spun toward the entrance hall.

Bell stalked after Roza, trampling the endlessly falling petals. The gown was the last thing Roza should be thinking about.

In the dim entrance hall, Garam and Piero waited to escort them in. Enormous amber glow gems hung in chandeliers from the ceiling, making the Medoro sons' eyes dark and mysterious and leaving the ceiling and corners in shadow. Garam took Roza's arm and murmured something she laughed at. Father and Mother had come earlier to meet with the groom's parents. Bell would have refused Roza's plea to join her, but riding under Mother's icy gaze would have been even worse.

"Miss Asbury." Piero smirked and bowed.

She pretended he was someone else. She envisioned dark kohl-rimmed eyes, a gaze that saw to the end of her.

"Mr. Medoro." Bell took his arm.

"I didn't know this was an exotics party." He was looking at the demure neckline and capped sleeves of her new peach dress. The silk clung in different places than she was used to, but at least she was covered.

She scoffed. "Exotic?" The ballroom lay to the left, white roses tangled in an arch as an entrance. Bell churned with a longing to unleash her gift again and spread the roses out like a cloudburst, covering all the darkness with velvet light.

"I've never seen you in anything but yellow." He said as they stepped under the arch. "Peach does become you, I must say. As do the gloves." She pulled away, and he grabbed her arm. "Not so fast. We're the witnesses for the betrothal ceremony."

89

The words coated Bell's heart with black frost. The engagement would be legally binding after the contract was signed and witnessed. She had little time to find proof. She wrenched free and dashed up to Roza.

"Roza, last chance," she whispered.

Garam's black eyes glared down at her from the other side. She glared back.

Roza leaned close. "You know what you have to do to keep me safe." Then she strode ahead with Garam. Bell crossed her arms tightly until Piero's fingers dug into the soft skin of her inner elbow.

"Let's not make a scene," he said. "Father hates scenes."

The Pater and Matrona of House Medoro stood inside the ballroom, greeting guests. Matrona Medoro's black gaze was a weight on Bell's shoulders. Her dark hair was pulled up in ringlets hanging around her face, revealing a slender, marble neck. She wore a heavy necklace of white jewels and a shimmering golden gown.

A labyrinth of maroon- and gold-curtained stalls filled the far half of the enormous ballroom. Great swaths of fabric studded with twinkling stars blocked out the glowing chandeliers above the stalls. A marble dance floor, filled with murmuring nobles, took up the remaining space. Somewhere a chamber orchestra of Bardian instruments filled the air with their music.

Mother, dazzling in a muted version of Roza's sunset, gaped at Roza's skirt. Father smiled comfortingly as Bell caught his gaze. Pater and Matrona Salviati stood beyond them, and the Matrona's eyes narrowed as she scanned Roza's explosion of a dress.

A low stage rested in the middle of the dance floor, and the Medoros led Garam and Roza onto it. The nobles turned to face them.

Bell stood on the floor beside Piero, palms sweating. How could Roza have so much faith in her scentmaking skills? If Agnella didn't let Bell use her fioré, it would be months before Bell could even begin to fuse a *permanenza* elixir. What if she couldn't fuse it before Garam brainwashed Roza?

Chatter and music quieted as Pater Medoro produced a document of heavy ivory paper and laid it on an elaborately carved table. Roza picked up a quill. Bell focused on the table, picking out roses and ivy.

When she looked up, Roza had already straightened, and Garam was signing the document. They stood with their hands clasped, and the guests cheered as Garam bent to kiss Roza.

Bell felt sick, and her heart beat so fast that black spots edged her vision. She took a slow breath and closed her eyes. She hated this family. Their selfish power, their endless wealth, the way their fingers reached all the way around Bardia and squeezed. When she opened them, Pater Medoro stood before her. He had the same proud forehead and thick hair as Garam, but his lips were heavier, and his locks were streaked with silver. He was patron of the arts, supporter of makers, friend to the most powerful mainlanders, and the singular nobleman the Consiglio deferred to. Garam and Roza's engagement had been his idea, quickly made reality.

His good looks hadn't faded with age, but they barely concealed an uncomfortable watchfulness in his gaze. It was as if every time she twitched, he catalogued it for his future use.

"Miss Asbury, what do you think of our little Night Bazaar?"

She curtseyed to hide her surprise. Where had Piero gone? "I find it astonishing, sir."

His handsome smile pooled in her stomach like grease. She almost recoiled when he held out his arm. "Join me."

He led her beyond the stage and into the mock Bazaar, stopping at an alcove between stalls. It held a seating booth, a table, and a beaded opening in the wall. A maid pushed the beads aside and asked what they'd like. The Pater ordered two cream teas without looking at her.

"Our families will soon be indelibly connected, Miss Asbury."

Bell followed his gaze across the path. Piero lounged against the carpetmaker's stall, staring at them.

"I would like to further this connection, if possible. You are unengaged?"

Bell stiffened. "Seventeen is too young for engagement, Pater Medoro."

"But when you come of age, would you consider a mutually beneficial arrangement?"

Piero was still staring. "If you're talking about Piero, no. We are—"

Bell cleared her throat. "—ill-suited for one another."

To say the least.

"We shall see."

The maid set Bell's tea before her, but her hip caught on the table as she moved toward the Pater. His cup tipped on its saucer and tea splattered onto the table. His face remained unchanged as the maid gasped and wiped the mess with her apron.

"Consider yourself dismissed," he said as she curtseyed silently and backed away.

Bell suppressed inappropriate words at the horror on the maid's face. Had he *fired* her for spilling tea? She wanted nothing more than to be far away.

"Is that all you wanted?" she asked shortly.

"Not at all. I have heard you're to become Maestra of Scents at the Summer Solstice."

The black spots returned. "Who told you this, Pater?"

He shrugged. "It's not secret."

"It's not common for a noble to become Maestra."

"Precisely why we need you to do it. Think of it, Bell." He leaned forward. "One of us, on the Maestri's Consiglio. We'd finally have a say in the makers' gifts. We could accomplish so much."

Bell stared. "I was under the impression you already have a say."

He smiled. She supposed he was used to being seen as handsome, but his proud features made her ill. "One can always further secure one's position, Bell. Something you would be wise to consider."

"What do you hope to accomplish?"

He took a sip of a new cup a different maid had brought and looked at Bell through the steam. "The makers live by our patronage, but some of them entertain ideas that would be damaging to our homeland. Bardian goods belong in Bardia. As a maker yourself, you must see the danger of taking pieces of Bardia to the mainland."

92

Bell frowned. "That isn't something I worry about because it isn't possible."

He made a dismissive gesture. "If trade is opened, Bardian wares will pass from our control. Mainlanders will take advantage of us. Makers will be able to come and go as they please, taking their wares with them and stripping Bardia bare. There are those in the Consiglio who don't see it that way. In fact, there are several prominent members of your community actively seeking a way to cross the current with Bardian wares. Is that enough cause for worry?"

Unease stirred in Bell's gut. "If that's true, there isn't much you can do to stop them."

"I'm afraid the Consiglio would need to bring more extreme measures against those who try. We'd need more guards on the docks and ships patrolling the harbor. And what if the Consiglio mandated that each maker must serve under a House? We would each hire as many makers as we could afford."

Bell fought to swallow her outrage. "There aren't enough nobles to patronize them all."

"Merely the best would need to keep making. The goods and legitimate makers would remain limited. It would be much easier for us to control."

Her buried anger reared, and Bell shoved to her feet, shrugging off the powerlessness that always weighed her down in the presence of a Medoro. "You don't understand makers at all. We can't stop *making*. A law like that would only encourage makers to work outside the law. It wouldn't solve anything."

"Consider it, Bell." His eyes darkened, calculating the effect his words would have. His House already dominated so much of Bardia, and he wanted a tighter hold?

She curtseyed stiffly. "Good evening, Pater Medoro."

Roza spun toward their alcove, raining rose petals from her billowing skirt until the floor gleamed red. "There you two are. It's time for the family dance."

"What family dance?" Bell hissed as Roza dragged her away.

"Hush. I invented it." Roza strode out of the mock Bazaar and into lush Bardian-made music. Instruments made of Bardian wood played music sweeter and more poignant than regular pieces.

The marble ballroom floor gleamed with their reflections. Roza pushed Bell toward Father at the edge of a cleared space before the stage. "Dance, Bell."

Bell peeked back at the Bazaar. Pater Medoro followed close behind, and Roza turned to him.

Father moved toward her. "Are you all right, Blossom?" He took her hands.

The music swelled as he spun her out onto the floor, and Bell nodded. "Roza said we needed to dance. I think she was rescuing me from Pater Medoro."

His lips curved, and he pulled her smoothly into the dance pattern. Bell shuffled along for a few steps until she gave in to the tempo.

"Did you need rescuing?"

Roza and Pater Medoro swept into view, and Bell felt the Pater's gaze on her face. Father frowned.

"I can handle it."

The music slowed and quieted. Father's frown deepened. "I will speak to him, if needed."

"I said—"

"May I have this dance?" Garam's deep voice from behind her sent shivers up Bell's legs.

She shook her head quickly at Father, but he'd already stepped back. "Go on, Bell." He smiled encouragingly despite her glare.

"I—I'm feeling—" Bell stammered.

Garam grinned wryly, taking her hands. "I need to talk to you, Bell. I promise not to poison you during this dance in front of everyone."

Bell flushed. The music began, a stately basse danse, and Bell stepped woodenly after him.

When she stumbled, he raised a brow. "Am I so disturbing?"

"I haven't danced much." The goldenbell behind her ear crept down her neck, brushing her skin as if sensing her distress.

"That's not what your last dance looked like."

"What do you want, Garam?"

"I want to know what your intentions are. The rumors I've heard disturb me." He leaned down. "Are you fusing *permanenza* for her?"

She stopped, bumping into Grigor Salviati and his partner. "How dare you ask that?"

He pulled her back into the dance as other couples turned to look. Pater Medoro's face was a thundercloud. Heat swelled in Bell's head.

"So it's true," Garam said.

"No," she hissed. It wasn't. Not yet. She jerked her hands free as her voice rose. "How dare you accuse me." She'd never imagined Garam would accuse her of her crimes in front of every noble in Bardia. Was every person in the room looking? Everywhere she looked, calculating eyes watched for weakness. For several heartbeats, Garam and Bell stared each other down in the middle of the ballroom.

Piero appeared at her side. "Garam, you promised Father no scenes." Piero took Bell's arm and pulled her away.

"Go away." Bell pulled against his grip.

"Dancing with me might distract from your little outburst." Piero jerked her past Grigor, leaving Garam glowering behind her. Bell stiffened and Piero rolled his eyes. "One dance, Goldenbell."

Bell followed him dismally, her gaze darting over the crowd. Where was Father? She looked back at Piero's smug expression. "If you think you have a chance with me, you're insane. I'm not like my sister. I won't agree to a political marriage."

They fell into the steps of the dance. He glanced away, and Bell followed his gaze. Roza had swept Garam into a dance, but she was whispering angrily to him. Good. If Garam's bullying made her angry, maybe she'd stand up for herself. Roza released her partner and spun away, petals floating behind her. A slender, dark-haired man on the other side of Garam moved as if to follow her, but Garam grabbed his arm.

Piero turned Bell, and the other dancers hid Roza from view. "I'm not concerned about your opinion," he said, finally. The song ended, and he left her at the edge of the dance floor and strode toward the table of drinks. Party guests moved warily out of his path.

She rubbed her hands over the goosebumps covering her arms. *Is Piero going to try and marry me without my consent? Did Garam give him the Insidio to use on me?* She shuddered at the thought. Becoming a brain-washed slave to Piero would be a fate worse than death.

She clenched and unclenched her fists. What if she could find the Insidio in Garam's room? Then she would have proof and also pro-tect herself and her sister. If she could find it here, she wouldn't need the Seller. The guests watched her now, barely hiding their whispers behind their hands. She stepped into the mock Bazaar, escaping their gaze.

The Medoros had thought of everything. Thousands of yards of stone-textured cloth covered the floor. Clear gems filled with flame hung on strings from the ceiling, making it seem like the night sky was close enough to touch.

If she became Maestra as Agnella predicted, would the other Pat-ers pressure her into changing things in their favor? Being a Maestra was frightening enough without fending off slippery old men.

She forced Pater Medoro's smile from her mind by studying the stalls around her. She followed the smell of new paper to the wood-maker's stall that held a row of hardback books. Relief bloomed when she spotted a familiar halo of hair behind the counter.

"Carasti."

She looked up from the block of wood in her hands, blinking dra-matically at Bell's dress. "Well, look at you."

Bell slipped behind the table and pulled up a stool beside Carasti. "How did they get all these makers to come here?" she murmured. Was this Pater Medoro's first attempt to control the Night Bazaar?

Carasti grinned sweetly. "The Medoros asked us. We couldn't miss a chance to sell our wares rent free."

The stalls in sight all held one maker each. "No sellers to help you bargain?"

"No sellers allowed." Carasti shrugged.

Bell's fingers curled, longing for soil to bury themselves in. Everything was unraveling too fast. She stroked the goldenbell along her neck, and it unfolded into her hand, circling her wrist in soft yellow blooms. She pulled away before it could overextend itself.

"Is this going to be another book?" She jerked her elbow toward the wood in Carasti's lap.

When Carasti closed her eyes, her long, ruddy eyelashes sweeping her cheeks, she looked more like a living doll than ever. She traced her fingers slowly along the polished edges of the rectangular block. Hundreds of delicate lines formed on three sides, spidering out too fast to follow. Fine sparks rose like mist. The lines glowed for a moment, then blackened. With each sweep of her fingers, they deepened and multiplied until they cut the block into slivers. Carasti opened the book and whisper-thin pages fanned out as its spine crackled.

"You're so fast." Bell touched a smooth, empty page.

She shrugged. "It's not complicated. I'd be doing something else, but—" She pressed her lips together.

"But what?"

Carasti let out a long sigh between pursed lips. "He told me to make books."

"Pater Medoro?"

"It's his party."

Bell scowled. "It's Roza and Garam's, actually. What right does he have—"

"Oh, give it up." Carasti's eyes flashed.

Hurt crawled inside Bell. "I—"

"Sorry." Carasti laid her hand on Bell's. "I'm tired of it all, but I shouldn't take it out on you. I'll escape one of these days." Carasti set another finished book on the table. Bell gaped at her, but a boy came up and shyly thumbed through at least three empty books, sneaking glances at Bell the whole while, before buying two of them and meandering on.

"What do you mean, escape?"

Carasti flicked a hand in the general direction of Santa Croce. "There's a whole mainland out there to explore."

"But the *attuale* current doesn't let makers pass." Bell narrowed her eyes to slits. "You're not scheming to try."

Carasti shrugged.

"Carasti! You're the one who told me about the *Bardian Star* exploding as it crossed—in gory detail."

She grinned. "That was fifty years ago. And it's a story."

Bell gasped. "A *story*? The Consiglio has laws for a—"

"Oh, never mind." Carasti flapped her hand. "Have you been thinking about what we talked about before?"

Bell took a deep breath. Carasti's wild schemes would have to wait. The acrid poisonous scent from Roza's room swelled in her mind. "Someone tried to poison Roza. They got Elena instead."

Carasti glowered, the deadly glint looking peculiar in her eyes. "This is getting out of hand. What did your parents say?"

"Father's home, but he won't do anything. Garam was *there*, Carasti. He showed up right after I found Elena. He said he'd left Roza in the Piazza, and I found her there, but even if he wasn't involved, someone was targeting her."

"When did this happen?"

"Yesterday morning, right after I left you."

Carasti nodded slowly. "I was there for a few more minutes. I didn't see anyone."

"I think it had to be a Spy. The window was open, and Garam's too heavy to climb the lattice."

"You mean a Spy walked right past me?" Carasti sounded disgusted.

Bell watched two noble girls stroll by arm in arm trailing expensive perfume.

She let out a slow breath. "I confronted Garam. When I accused him of using Insidio on Roza, he flinched. Whether a Spy was working with him or not, he's guilty, Carasti. I *know* it. Maybe he planted the poison to warn me off." Glancing swiftly to make sure the girls had passed, she turned toward the back and pulled the map from her wrist bag. "The Spy was waiting for me in the woods." Her belly swooped nervously, remembering his half smile.

Carasti made a surprised squeak and tapped the labyrinth below the Bazaar. "This is the Sotto."

Bell's voice dropped to a whisper. "I know. I'm going to the Seller of Secrets."

Carasti nodded. "If you get proof Garam is using Insidio on another noble, Medoro will lose its standing with the other Houses, with the Consiglio—everyone would be against them."

"Agnella warned me to stay away from the Seller. Even the Spy said to be careful around him. What do you think?"

Carasti tapped her chin. "If you want to save your sister, you need proof." Carasti's eyes narrowed. "The Seller works for himself. If you want his help, you'll have to offer him something valuable." She nudged Bell with her elbow. "But he would probably love to have the future Maestra of Scents owe him a favor."

Bell bit her lip.

"You should ask the Seller if one of his spies tried to poison Roza," Carasti said.

"It wasn't the Spy I met," Bell said quickly.

Carasti tilted her head in birdlike fashion. "Why not?"

Bell hesitated. "He seemed too sincere. Like he didn't want me in danger. But there's at least one other Spy. A woman. She was glaring at me in the Piazza last night." Bell shuddered.

"The plot deepens," Carasti muttered. "Now there are two to watch out for."

Bell tucked the map away. "I'm going to sneak into Garam's room first to try and find the Insidio."

Carasti's lips made an excited *o*. "I want to sneak around in a noble's bedroom!"

"No. If they catch me, I'll only get scolded. You, on the other hand—"

Carasti harrumphed. "Fine. If you still want to go find the Seller, I'll be at the woodmaker's stall across from the fountain tomorrow night."

Bell stood and shook out her skirt. She thought about telling Carasti about Piero and Pater Medoro, but she was still shaken by the veiled threats they had made. Besides, it wasn't like Carasti could do anything about them.

"Look out for spies," Carasti said.

"Here, in House Medoro?" Sure, the Spy had found Bell's secret passage, but the thought of them infiltrating a fortress like House Medoro was ridiculous.

Carasti nodded, huge eyes sparkling like she'd been given the keys to a treasure chest. "Part of the Night Bazaar's charm, apparently. They even have a purple tent set up at the back."

Bell braced a hand on the stool. "The Seller can't be here."

"I doubt it. But these people love to pretend."

Bell straightened her spine. She'd stay out of dark corners and avoid anyone in masks—even someone in a half mask with kohl-rimmed eyes.

Fourteen

DESPITE HER DETERMINATION TO SLIP out of the mock Bazaar quickly and find Garam's room, Bell went a little deeper to watch the watermaker shade a fountain into a vivid thunderstorm. The watermaker's *attuale* power poured from his fingertips like blue-green paint. The lightning was so realistic, she jumped every time it blazed.

She glimpsed Roza surrounded by her courtiers and hurried on. She knew she'd lost her way when a velvet amaranth-colored tent appeared. Dim purple lanterns hung on poles lining the way to the tent's entrance. Two cloaked figures lounged in the shadows, one on either side of the tent opening.

Spies. She spun and retraced her steps, trying to find a servant's exit out of the ballroom. When she glanced back, one of the spies had edged half into the purple light, watching her.

"I don't think they will bother you, not here."

Bell spun toward a woman tucked into an alcove behind a beaded curtain, a glass of something iced tinkling in her hand. She beckoned and Bell froze. The curtain shadowed the woman's face, but she wore a glimmering green gown of Bardian cloth.

"Sit with me, if you please, Miss Asbury."

If only she had Roza's flair for rudeness. Cautiously, she slid through the curtain, the beads tinkling. What excuse could she give to leave quickly?

"You don't remember me?"

101

Bell's vision adjusted, picking out a broad face and dark eyes framed by thick black hair. "Have I met you, Matrona?"

The woman smiled. "You may call me Maestra Anna."

Bell's shoulders sagged. Now she knew why those dark, studying eyes made her shift. She dipped her head to hide a wince. "A pleasure to speak with the Maestra of Carpets. How may I help you?"

"It is I who wishes to help you. I have heard from good sources you are Bardia's most powerful scentmaker."

Bell bit her lip to keep from groaning.

Maestra Anna swirled the ice in her glass. "The things I've heard about your talents are fascinating." She glanced at Bell's neck, and Bell was fervently glad she'd tucked the goldenbell vial into her bodice.

Maestra Anna leaned forward suddenly. "The Consiglio is no place for children, Miss Asbury. Can you prove you are not a child?"

"Maestra Anna, whatever your sources say, I'm not—"

"The Maestra of Scents herself has made her position clear. I speak in your interest and that of the Consiglio."

Bell took a deep, steadying breath. "What do you want from me, Maestra Anna?"

"I want proof you will not weaken the Consiglio. That you are a suitable replacement for Agnella."

"I have no idea if the *attuale*—"

"A Maestra is chosen for skill and by need. If Agnella's gift is fading, our need is great. I will stand for you before the others if you can show me a valuable contribution. More than *protezi*." She gestured at Bell's neck. "We need something powerful, something that will shape Bardia for the future. Permanently." Her gaze bored into Bell's. "When you succeed, speak to me first. Do you understand?"

Bell frowned. Was she asking Bell to break the law and fuse *permanenza*? "I'm not sure what you mean, Maestra Anna."

Maestra Anna sat back. "That is all. Now go, please. I must return to watching the other guests."

Bell stood, dipped her head briefly, and tried to glide gracefully around the corner without glancing back at the spies.

She paused before a metalmaker's stall. Was Maestra Anna trying to get her disqualified? The Consiglio would never allow her to experiment with Magia. The metalmaker smiled expectantly as he sculpted a hand-sized ball of metal into a gleaming silver chalice. Bell stared past him before she realized he was waiting for her to speak. She spun away.

Maestra Anna could have been sent by the Consiglio to gather evidence. What if the Consiglio wanted a reason to get Bell into trouble? Why did everyone know she was thinking about fusing *permanenza*?

She smoothed her fingers over her temples as if she could push all thoughts of the Consiglio away. This was her chance to prove Garam's guilt and get the Insidio out of Piero's reach.

At the edge of the mock Bazaar, gilt curtains half buried a servant's entrance. As the guests swept into another dance, Bell eased into the corner and slipped through the door.

After the brilliant ballroom, the rest of the ornate house seemed dim. The paintings, the thick carpet, the realistic lions carved on the doorframes, the gilded mirrors that startled her as she came around corners—it all felt unbearably gaudy. The Medoros' power had been passed down since Bardia's beginning, and now it was like a presence, a beast waiting in shadow down dark halls. She hurried from one doorway to the next, opening each a crack to peek through. Where were the stairs up to the bedrooms?

If House Medoro was designed like most, Garam's bedroom would be upstairs. The last door in the hall opened to reveal a narrow ascending staircase. Even this railing was covered with intricate carvings of creatures she didn't recognize. Bell held her breath and tiptoed through.

Please let all the servants be busy downstairs.

The servants' staircase led to a maroon carpeted hall lined with dozens of walnut doors. Bell worked her way from the end, looking through all of them. Most of them were guest quarters. One near the middle was locked, and her heart sank. The next door was slightly ajar, and a burgundy cape was thrown over a desk chair. Garam's cape. She slipped inside.

Where to begin? The four-poster bed, massive, rumpled, and rimmed in gold, was swallowed by the huge room. A wardrobe bordered by windows was bigger than Bell's entire bathroom. Its doors hung open, and tailored clothes spilled in puddles on the floor.

At least he and Roza have one thing in common.

Dusk shrouded the abandoned tower outside the windows. It sat above the nobles' borough like the ghost of a guard.

She shivered and closed the door behind her. An open rolltop desk, its surface clear, with dozens of tiny drawers filled one corner. Bell crossed the room, opened one drawer after another, and rifled through business notes and silk handkerchiefs. She couldn't help but pause to admire a Bardian-made pen with eternally flowing ink. Footsteps sounded far down the hall, and she dropped the pen in its place. Reaching into the last drawer, she found a velvet bag. A tiny note lay curled inside.

"This is a surprise," a man said from behind her.

She whirled, crushing the note in her palm. How did he get in without her hearing?

He lounged against the window beside the desk, slim arms crossed. His thick dark hair was long enough to brush the collar of his white shirt. "I didn't think Garam was the type to receive lady visitors during his own engagement party."

Bell's face flamed. "That's not—I'm his fiancée's sister."

"Ah." He straightened. "You must be Bell, then."

"How do you—" What had Roza said? Dark hair? "Are you his cousin?" Garam had been standing with a dark-haired young man earlier. He'd looked taller across the dance floor.

He dipped his head and stepped forward. "Pleased to meet you."

His eyelashes curled around dark, fathomless eyes. Bell blinked. How long had he been holding out his hand? She stuck out her hand for him to take.

He brushed a brief kiss to her knuckles and released her.

"What are you doing up here?" she asked.

"I should ask you the same." His voice was solemn, but his eyes twinkled.

"I—" She bit her lip. What to tell him? "I don't know Garam very well. And he is marrying my sister. So I thought—" Her gaze flicked to the desk.

"You thought you'd make sure he's a trustworthy fellow?"

"I've—I've heard things."

He rubbed his chin. "What kind of things?"

"I shouldn't say." What was she thinking, talking to his cousin about this? Mother would be furious.

"I understand. For what it's worth, Garam is not as dishonest as you seem to think he is."

Bell furrowed her brow. "You don't know what he's done."

He spread his hands. "Enlighten me."

Bell's eyes narrowed. *He has Insidio and intends to use it.* Bell stepped back. "Thank you for your concern, but I should get back to the party. I would appreciate if you didn't mention this to him."

His smile spread like clouds on a gusty day. "I would never. That would spoil the intrigue."

"Thank you. Good evening, sir." She closed the door and darted toward the servant's stairway. Garam's door stayed closed, and she paused by a glow lamp to unfold the note.

Black Insidio—unknown to Consiglio?

That was all? Teeth gritted, she strode on. Mentioning a Magia wasn't enough to prove Garam's guilt. If she hadn't been interrupted, she might have found something better.

But part of her knew Garam wouldn't be careless enough to leave out damning evidence. Whatever game he was playing, it was deep and deceptive.

What if she couldn't prove his guilt?

Forehead tight, she hurried downstairs and along the hallway toward the muffled ballroom music. If she could get back to Carasti without the Medoros seeing her, perhaps she would get away with her snooping.

The heavy carpet buried her steps. Its musty scent mixed with something sharp. What was it? The sharpness strengthened as she passed a long narrow hall, and she stopped.

105

Her brain picked apart the scent—Aronil, Princess Seed, and something viscous that made her uneasy. The first two were ordinary, but the way they were woven was inelegantly forceful...and familiar.

Piero?

The carpet turned to wood in the narrow hall, and Bell tiptoed. The scent throbbed in her head, and she opened her goldenbell vial. A door on the left spilled a line of glow gem light across the floor.

Was he inside now?

She shouldn't risk this. But if he was fusing Magia, how could she pass this chance? He could be fusing something to use on Roza—or herself—right now. If she could discern what it was, she'd have a better chance at an antidote.

She laid her hand on the door—footsteps ran up behind her—a hand slapped over her mouth. She thrashed as the door opened and she was shoved inside. Piero slammed the door behind them before he brightened the glow lamp, revealing a small room half filled with a worktable and hundreds of vials. Dark gray and purple blossoms grew in pots of black, rocky soil. Hazy remnants of disturbing scent clouds drifted in the air.

He was fusing Magia.

She scrambled up, coughing as fumes hit her lungs. "I'll scream."

He sneered as he stalked forward. "No one is in this wing."

"Your cousin is."

His gaze flicked to the door. "I just saw him dancing with Miss Salviati."

"What are you fusing with the Magia?" She peered around the room. A vial full of a green-blue elixir lay in the center of the worktable.

He slammed her against the wall, making the vials tinkle. "Doesn't matter."

Bell gasped at the pain in her back and tried to shove him off.

"I should be the new Maestro of Scents, not you." He dug his fingers into her shoulders.

If they'd been discussing any other subject, she'd have agreed just to make him stop, but words flowed out of her. "You don't use your gift properly."

He shook her, banging her head against wood. Fear rattled through her. He was too strong.

"I have all I need. The mind for it, endless fioré, and means to get more. You wouldn't know what to do with such power. How can you fuse without fioré?" He glanced back at the green-blue elixir as if he was going to reach for it.

Bell blinked slowly. The back of her head pulsed painfully, but anger surged. "How do you know about my fioré?"

His lip curled. "Heard about it."

Rage swelled until she thought she'd burst with its heat. Her fury made her a giant. She slammed her fist up into his jaw. He staggered back, looking shocked. She darted around him and opened the door.

She looked back. "*You* destroyed my fioré." He'd probably walked right in and done it while she was out. How could the guards refuse to admit a Medoro? Had he paid them to keep it secret?

Piero rubbed his jaw and said nothing, his eyes coldly calculating the distance between.

"You are no scentmaker," she snarled. "The Saint ought to strip your gift. The fioré are blessed, *never* to be destroyed." Bell spat on the ground by his feet. "If I do become the Maestra of Scents, I'll make sure you never fuse again." She slammed the door in his face.

Fifteen

"WHERE WERE YOU HIDING? I NEVER got a chance to introduce you to Alessander." Roza, eyes closed, lay flat on the other carriage bench with her bare feet braced against the wall. Her rose skirt was mostly empty of petals, revealing tangled stems and buds. Her face looked pale as milk. Bell cracked the window to let in the cool night air.

"There was a lot to explore." Would Roza laugh if she knew Bell had hidden in an entryway parlor until her legs stopped shaking? All that risk—searching Garam's room, finding Piero's workshop—and barely anything to show for it. Could she have taken Piero's vial as proof?

"Wasn't it fantastic?" Roza's tired smile deepened Bell's scowl.

"Rather extreme, if you ask me. You shouldn't have danced so much."

"If I needed a nursemaid, I wouldn't hire you." Roza closed her eyes.

Bell clenched her jaw. "It's common sense, not nursemaiding."

Roza fluttered a hand. "Never mind. Now, about Aless. He's coming for dinner tomorrow night."

Bell let her head thump against the cushion. The trembling had finally stopped, leaving her limp. Her anger faded to resignation. "Really?"

"You'll find him interesting. He has his own opinions about makers."

"I thought he was noble."

Roza swung her feet down. She winced, and her hand went to her

108

side, but her face quickly cleared. "If he marries you, perhaps. Regardless, he's absurdly wealthy. His father owns all the ships in Bardia's docks."

"What don't the Medoros own?" Bell flipped her palm face out. "Don't answer that." Something had been different about the man in Garam's room. He might be extraordinarily wealthy, but he didn't carry himself like Piero or Pater Medoro. She hugged herself at the thought of his deep eyes on hers. He had been so calm and collected, unfazed by her intrusion. She was almost looking forward to meeting him again. But at a dinner with Mother looking on?

"I'm not ready to get married."

"Won't stop Mother from scheming."

"I'm surprised she'd consider a commoner, wealthy or not."

Roza raised her eyebrows. "Father was a merchant."

"That was different."

"Yes, it was."

"Why do you say it like that? Didn't they fall in love?"

Roza shrugged. "Aless is a first son, so one day you could be Matrona of his House."

"I want to be a scentmaker."

"If only life were so simple."

Arriving home, Bell felt weak with relief when Mother wasn't waiting in the entry for them. She half expected Roza to stop and forage in the kitchen, but she climbed the stairs ahead of Bell, her steps slow and measured.

"Are you feeling all right?" Bell asked.

Roza waved a hand before silently shutting herself into her bedroom.

As Bell's vision adjusted to her own dim room, she froze. A figure stood before the mirror on her wall.

"Close the door, Bell."

Bell's chest tightened. "What are you doing in here, Mother?"

"I need to talk with you." She brightened the glow lamp on the wall. "About your future."

"I'm tired."

"So am I," Mother snapped. "Tiredness doesn't matter to a Matrona."

Bell swallowed. "I won't be Matrona, Mother. What first son would marry me?"

Mother's heels clicked as she stalked closer. "I can think of several who would consider it, if you could lay aside the things that detract from your character." She gestured to the empty raised beds between the windows. "Give up your scentmaking, and you will have a long, happy, and *powerful* life."

"I don't want power. I want—"

"Well, I do. Do you know why? Because power is the thing that keeps us alive. You were born a noble. We must act the noble, or we will be destroyed."

Bell shook her head. "You think my marriage will affect House Asbury so much? Isn't marrying Roza to Garam enough?" She didn't try to strip her words of bitterness.

"It can never be enough. We must always strive for more power. The most powerful are truly safe."

Bell's stomach twisted. "I don't need to marry into a wealthy family. Agnella wants me to become the next Maestra of Scents. If I agree, I'll have the power to protect us all. I'll be a part of the Consiglio."

"What?" She grabbed Bell's arms, and Bell forced herself not to flinch. Mother's voice rasped as she turned pale. "You must refuse. You can't be a scentmaker. I forbid it."

Bell's mouth opened and closed. She examined her mother's stricken expression.

"Why are you so afraid?" Bell asked softly.

Mother smoothed her face. "Think of giving it up, Bell. For your family's sake." She dropped Bell's arms and fled.

Bell stared at her own weary face in the mirror, her mind tracing thoughts like roots of weeds. The goldenbell behind her ear had fallen out in the scuffle with Piero. She pulled her black velvet kit from the cabinet. She ran her hands through the bag, fingering the vials and sachets of dried fioré tucked into tiny pockets. What if she threw this all from the balcony, let the glass smash and the fioré fragments filter into the wind?

She found herself longing to run after Mother and tell her everything, but giving up her scentmaking would be like draining the blood in her veins, tearing her soul out by the roots. She shook her head. If Mother wasn't going to confide in Bell, then Bell wouldn't confide in her.

She sank onto the grass-woven rug by her bed, breathing in the dusty scent of fioré. Her gift stirred, eager to be let out.

Something tickled her knees, and she jumped. Lush grass ringed her bare legs, sprouting between her toes. Wherever her skin touched the carpet, life erupted.

Even if she could, giving up scentmaking wouldn't stop Garam from deceiving Roza. It wouldn't stop Roza from losing herself in the morass of the Medoro family. It wouldn't keep Piero from whatever he was planning.

She had to do something before they lost everything.

Thoughts shuddered through her head. She needed to steady her mind.

From her window, she could barely see the lights of the Piazza gleaming against the darkness. She grabbed her cloak.

The first *Infiorata* Night had already begun when she reached the Piazza. She wore her brightest yellow dress, one with a smocked bodice and puffed sleeves, leaving the peach one in a heap on the bedroom floor.

Descending the path to the Piazza felt like falling after balancing on the edge for too long—inevitable, terrifying, relieving.

The *infioratore* teams gathered along the La Festa parade route, meticulously chalking their flower carpet designs onto the cobblestones. The route commenced in the small square on the edge of Santa Maria

Novella and followed the length of Via dei Calzaiuoli to finish at the foot of the Rotunda. The Consiglio Maestris, dressed in white robes to signify unity with their people, would walk the route as the ones permitted to trample the beautiful *infiorata* carpets first.

The finest artists sketched the face of San Giovanni in front of the Rotunda. This carpet alone would be created from fioré. Agnella had already asked Bell to take her place on the final *Infiorata* Night in arranging the blossoms and sealing them with *attuale* so they would remain perfect until the parade.

Thoughts of dangerous secrets and deadly elixirs circled in her head like the endless flight of birds. When she raised her weary eyes, Signor Strozzi stood across the carpet, staring at her in the dim light.

She looked in the direction of the Bazaar. An inchoate pull to its secret keeper was morphing into need. It was beginning to feel like she was meant to go to the Seller all along. Resisting the temptation to toss aside caution and hunt for him tonight, she turned toward home. She whispered a prayer to San Giovanni that when she finally did find him, the Seller would not ask for the impossible.

Sixteen

THE NEXT MORNING, BELL WOKE FEELING grim. She tried to tiptoe past Father's open study door, but he was staring into the hall with his fingers steepled beneath his chin.

"Bell, come in and shut the door, please."

She felt as if her feet were mud. His frown meant he'd found a puzzle. He turned to the oak sideboard and poured her an inch of something brown.

"I brought back some Bardian cider. Don't tell your mother." His smile was a shadow.

She sat down and sipped. Bubbles exploded on her tongue. A laugh burst out at the sensation.

"Your mother was disappointed you didn't meet Alessander last evening."

Her smile faded.

Father's eyes held fond amusement. "I spoke with Pater Medoro later." Bell took another drink to hide a grimace. Father's frown deepened. "I don't like it, but you did very well. He's mentioned before that you aren't flighty like some other young noblewomen."

"He's talked about me?" She didn't bother to hide her face.

"He knows of your talent, Bell." Father reached for her hand, but she pulled away.

"I want nothing to do with him. Or his son."

Father jerked back. "Piero? He proposed marriage between you?"

113

"Vaguely. I made it clear I'm not interested."

"Good. I don't like that boy."

Bell set her glass down harder than she intended. "That *boy* destroyed my fioré. He admitted it."

"He what?" Father's voice turned to a low growl.

"He accosted me in the hallway and told me I can't become the Maestra of Scents because he'd destroyed my fioré." Bell hesitated. If she told him about Piero's elixir, she would have to confess to sneaking around. She pressed her lips together.

Father's fingers whitened around his glass. "Why didn't you come to me immediately?"

Anger bubbled up. "He's a Medoro. I have no proof."

He stood, aghast. "Goldenbell. If he attacked you physically—"

"I have no proof. Mother told me we wouldn't even investigate if it was someone from House Medoro. House Asbury comes before your daughters' well-being."

"You misunderstand your mother. She meant you and Roza *are* House Asbury, and we must provide for your future. It's not about money, Bell. It's about freedom."

"You didn't believe me about Garam getting Insidio. Why should I think you would believe me about Piero destroying my fioré and attacking me?" Bell's voice rose until she was shouting. "You and I must have different definitions of freedom." She spun for the door.

"Bell, please, I do believe you. I will speak to Pater Medoro, and Piero will never—"

She gripped the doorframe until her fingers ached. "He will never touch me again, because I'll never see him again. That family is…is *evil*, Father, and I'm going to save Roza from them."

Father said something, but the slamming door killed it.

Bell stormed into the hall, then out into the garden. The air hung heavy and wet outside. The humidity would increase until the Solstice rain, and today it thickened her frustration. Even now, Father was going to *talk* to Pater Medoro? After the wedding, most likely.

How long before it became essential to her parents for Bell to accept engagement to Piero? The sight of her bare fioré beds deepened her scowl.

"Is there anything I can do, miss?" Elena's voice came from behind her on the path.

"What are you doing out here?" The words came out hard as rocks, but she didn't care.

"I—you seemed troubled."

"I'd like to be alone right now."

Elena hesitated, seeming torn. "Of course. I wanted to make sure you knew I'm here to help."

Bell watched until she'd disappeared toward the house. The maid seemed to have recovered, but there was something broken about her.

Bell walked to her workshop. Burying her fear, she parted the curtain of vines and breathed deeply. The air inside tingled with the fused elixirs, ever-present soil the foundation of their scents. Her mind drifted to the problem of *permanenza*. Where should she start?

Without Agnella's help, going to the Seller seemed a better solution than tampering with the Magia from the black package. Bell brushed her hands onto her skirt and turned her attention back to what little first-level fioré she had left.

She was deep in nurturing the Princess Seed shoot's roots when Mother called from across the garden.

"Bell, would you come in? I need your help."

She ducked outside, the sun making her wince after the soothing dimness of her workshop. Bell followed Mother's regal strides inside and into the dining room. Golden plates gleamed at each setting, and silverware, goblets, and napkins were precisely arranged next to them. Roses embossed the gold wallpaper, but the table's middle looked stark without its usual flower arrangements.

Mother stood beside her ornate buffet. The carved Bardian wood gleamed under piles of red roses, white lilies, and silvery greens. "My dear, this has been hard for you."

"Of course it has." Bell laced her fingers together behind her back. Another lecture on appropriate pastimes for noblewomen?

Mother sighed. "*I* have been hard on you, and I'm sorry. Every girl has dreams, and I'm afraid I trample on yours."

Bell's lips parted, and she resisted an urge to rub her ears. Had Mother said she was sorry?

"But I do it because I care about your future, Bell." Mother glided forward. "You do have a charming gift. You did well with Roza's gown at the engagement party." She took a deep breath. "I would like you to arrange the flowers for this evening."

"Me?"

Mother smiled, for once all warmth. "Yes, you. Use your gift and make us something truly special."

"I thought you wanted me to give up scentmaking?"

"I want you to give up the dangerous meddling Agnella is pushing you into. This is merely an artful pastime." Mother cupped Bell's face, her fingers soft over Bell's hair.

Bell leaned into the touch.

"Your gift does matter, but it's time you changed it into an asset. These aren't fioré, of course. Using ordinary flowers will show the young Medoro your gift isn't a threat."

Bell opened her eyes, her skin tingling as Mother's polished nail brushed her neck. The young Medoro—it all came back to that *cursed* family. Mother squeezed Bell's hands, not seeming to notice Bell's smile was forced.

"I'll make something special," Bell murmured.

"Of course you will." She turned toward the kitchen. "I'll leave you to it, then."

Bell stared at the doorway until her footsteps faded. At least Mother understood Bell's gift tangled around her soul now. It seemed if Bell would give up serious scentmaking—using the full breadth of her gift—her *attuale* became an asset to House Asbury. As disparagingly as Mother spoke about Bell's gift, Bardian magic *was* highly sought after by Bardia's nobility.

Mother saw it as frivolous, but Pater Medoro wanted makers tied to noble houses, like indentured servants or...or pampered slaves? The rest of the nobles would jump at the chance to secure makers for themselves.

Even Mother.

Bell plucked a rose and spun it between her fingers. Was this all she was destined to be? A flower weaver? She groaned and slumped against the wall.

What if she gave up scentmaking and accepted her lot as a noble's daughter? Let Piero try for Maestro of Scents?

She laughed to herself. No. She clenched her fingers against the wallpaper, and rustling filled her ears.

She would stop the Medoros from controlling Bardia's makers. She would save Roza, even if she didn't want to be saved.

Save her from herself.

The thought swelled in her mind as silky petals rose beneath her hands. Deep in her gift, surrounded by scents and dusty life turned green, she didn't hear Mother return.

"Bell, what have you done?"

Bell looked up. The roses had come out of the wallpaper, making living golden walls. The cut flowers—which she hadn't touched—hung in deep scarlet garlands from the ceiling. She'd deepened every shade of red, slashing them together like streaks of blood. The white lilies laced the table in an intricate braid.

Bell cleared her throat. "They used real flower pigments in the wallpaper dye."

Mother ran a hand over the golden wall. "This is certainly dramatic."

Bell eyed her. It felt dramatic. It felt wild, uncontained. She half wished Mother would order it taken down. How had she woven the flowers without touching them? And so quickly?

Something was wrong with her, with her gift.

Mother nodded firmly. "Well done. It suits Roza's temperament. The Medoros will have to be impressed."

An hour later, a carriage pulled up to the door, and Bell hurried to join the others in the large front parlor. At least Mother had let her wear one of her own comfortable dresses. Facing Garam and his cousin in another whisper-thin silk overgown would have driven her mad.

"Garam and Alessander of Medoro," the housekeeper announced.

Father smiled. "Show them in."

The footsteps in the hall felt like they were tapping on Bell's chest. Louder and louder. Had Aless broken his promise not to tell Garam about her snooping?

Garam entered first, and they all rose. "Pater and Matrona Asbury." He bowed and stepped aside. His cousin approached, mirroring Garam.

Bell stilled mid-curtsy, her gaze caught on Alessander's. His eyes were blue, his face narrow and striking—and he was most definitely *not* the man from Garam's room.

"Bell," Roza whispered beside her.

Cheeks burning, she jerked through the curtsy.

Father welcomed them and led the way to the dining room. Mother glared icily at Bell until she followed Roza toward their guests and took Alessander's proffered arm. She couldn't resist glancing at him, but meeting his gaze and seeing his furrowed brow deepened her embarrassment. If she couldn't get herself together, he was sure to ask what was wrong, and what explanation could she give?

After Mother subtly attributed the floral decorations to her, Garam and Alessander exclaimed over Bell's handiwork. Garam's eyes turned keen, seeking hers whenever she looked his way. Was he waiting to see if she'd accuse him again?

Alessander asked polite questions during the meal, but Bell couldn't manage a multiword answer until he mentioned her scentmaking. She described her process for nurturing Princess Seed buds until she caught Garam listening.

She tightened her lips. Did he know what Piero had done?

"I wonder if you might show me around."

Bell blinked. Alessander's words puddled like oil spilled on rainwater. "Your garden?"

The words sank. "Oh."

118

Mother prodded her with a warning look. Had Father told her about their discussion? Perhaps the entire house had heard her shouting.

"It's not—"

"Wonderful." Alessander rose and dipped his head to the company. "Please excuse us."

He wanted to go *now*? Bell stood and Alessander took her elbow.

"Lead the way, Miss Asbury."

As the garden door shut behind them, his fingers suddenly felt too warm. She pulled away instinctively, then bent to pluck a lily to hide her reaction.

"Is everything all right, Miss Asbury?"

He was so much less intense than Garam. She'd never have imagined they were related. His gaze was soft and confused as he watched her twirl the lily between her fingers. "Please, call me Bell. Miss Asbury makes me feel old."

"Then please call me Aless. Bell, I can't help but think something has upset you." Everything he said in his deep voice sounded carefully chosen, as if he thought of nothing but her while he was speaking.

"It's not your fault." She took a slow breath. "It's hard to explain."

She tensed as he stroked a white lily petal, but he let it spring back unplucked.

"I have time."

She stared at him. "You're not like your cousins."

His lips curved and he met her gaze. "Perhaps not."

His thoughts sat plain on his face, eyebrows furrowed in sincerity. Aless was entirely different from the dusky-skinned man with his dark-sky eyes and sculpted lips of whispers and magic.

Must not think of him, not now. The lily curled around her hand as she focused her gift. He raised his eyebrows as she wove it into a star and held it out.

"Thank you." His voice was reverent as he took it.

"Why aren't you like them?" Bell fought a temptation to close her eyes as they stepped onto the fountain patio. The sound of splashing water soothed, even if the air felt stale without her fioré.

"I don't know. I've lived a different sort of life, I suppose."

The undergardener had cleared all traces of the fioré destruction, and to a stranger, empty raised beds and a bare fountain were merely subtle signs anything was amiss.

"Have you planted seeds here?" Aless finally asked when she didn't speak. He turned to survey each patch of bare dirt.

Bell studied the side of his face. How could she know so much of his family and so little of him? She knew he was the son of the wealthiest merchant in Bardia. He took after his mother in looks. Was that all?

Abruptly, irritation dug into her mind. "Not everyone can afford fioré, Aless."

He raised a gentle eyebrow. "This is where you would plant it?"

"Myrtle Leaf and Sciver here." She gestured at each bed in turn, describing the plants that still existed there in her imagination.

He nodded as she finished, his casual acceptance of her explanation making her grit her teeth. "I think I could have them here by next week."

She froze. "Oh. Oh no, I didn't mean—"

He broke into the following pained silence. "I know not everyone can afford fioré, Bell. Consider it my gift to you."

Her mouth dropped open. Was he serious? Did he actually think…?

"If we are to…to begin courting." He was beginning to look bewildered. "It's no sacrifice, I assure you."

"Courting," she whispered. There were wise and gracious words somewhere but not inside her. She traced fingers down her forehead and turned away. "Who told you we were courting, Mr. Medoro?"

"Did they not tell you?" Horror was dawning in his voice.

She spun back. "What are you talking about?"

"Your father…he spoke to me at the engagement party. I simply wanted to know you better," he said hastily, seeing her face.

Father's face, concerned and warm, filled her mind. Bell swallowed a wave of helplessness. Had he seen her distaste for Piero and not realized that distaste extended to the entire Medoro family?

"I've heard of you, of your work, so often. I…admire what you're doing with your gift. With my wealth and your gift, together we could do so much."

Bell tilted her head. His wealth? "Aless. I'm afraid I am not interested in courting at this time."

Aless slipped one hand into his pocket. The other still cradled the lily star. "Ah. I see." His mouth worked for a moment. "I had hoped…I know your father's debt has been a burden."

"You—" Rage flashed through her for a second, gone the next. Father was in debt? "You hoped to *buy* me by paying off my father's debt?"

"Of course not." His eyes flashed back. "I *hoped* to make your life easier."

"Let's go back inside," she ground out. One more arrogant word and she would send a thorn into his backside.

"Bell…"

She kept walking.

"Is it my family? Do you hate my cousins so much?"

Bell spun back. "Your cousins are ruining my and my sister's lives, so forgive me if I don't believe you wouldn't do the same."

His brow furrowed. "But Garam loves Roza. He's mad about her. I don't think she could do anything to make him leave her."

"Perhaps that's the problem," Bell muttered. She took a long breath, focusing on the scent of earth, the promise of green growth to come. "You, all the Medoros, you're used to taking whatever you like and never letting it go. That's the kind of life you've led, Aless. It's not the life I want."

She left him standing on the garden path with the rumpled lily star, his gaze still quizzical.

Bell rejoined the family in the large parlor for caffè once her angry flush had faded. She perched woodenly on the settee farthest from the garden door and barely looked up when Aless reentered, frowning. Mother looked exasperated, Roza tiredly amused, and Father had concerned wrinkles around his eyes.

121

Garam remained smooth as marble, reminding Bell of his mother.

She sipped her caffè from a slender-rimmed cup that gleamed in the flickering light of a dozen candles along the mantle.

Father was in debt—to the Medoros.

We are in debt.

Did they own this exquisite caffè service? Bell's new dress? Perhaps marrying Aless was the only way she'd ever get her fioré replaced.

She forced her jaw to relax. At least now marriage to Piero was off the table.

Garam and Roza sat together on the sofa, exchanging polite words, but their bodies spoke a different, sharper language.

Father was telling Aless a story about his life as a wine and spice merchant before he married Mother. Aless seemed to be enthralled by the surge of demand for black currant wine once it was discovered that scentmakers could infuse it with elixirs.

She let it all wash over her, meaningless words that changed nothing. Debt or not, she knew what she must do.

Seventeen

THAT NIGHT, AT THE EDGE OF THE WOOD stall in the Night Bazaar, Bell fingered an exquisitely carved statuette of a dancing woman, scanning the table like any Bazaar shopper.

"Carasti," she hissed. The statuette shifted under her hand, a living carving, and she reflexively dropped it.

Carasti glanced up, her eyes narrowed. The hum of the evening Night Bazaar cocooned Bell, feeling safe compared to the place she intended to go.

It seemed impossible that a week ago she'd been too afraid to step inside the market this close to Solstice. How could her life have changed so much? She was still frightened, but other things frightened her more.

Bell tugged her hood back an inch. When Carasti pulled on a short blue cape and stepped her way, Bell moved into the shadows between stalls.

"Look at you wearing black," Carasti said wryly.

Bell wrapped the borrowed cloak tighter, covering a sliver of her butter-yellow skirt. "My wardrobe is too well-known, apparently."

"You're ready now?"

"Let's go." She handed Carasti a blue vial necklace of *protezi* elixir and opened her own.

Though Bell had tried to memorize the map, she had to pull it out of her bag to check several of the dozen turns. Other shadowy stairways had been marked *The Sotto*, but the one the Spy had shown her was closest to the Seller's stall. The less time they spent below, the better.

Carasti hurried silently beside her, but her eyes practically fizzed as they peered out of her cape's hood. At least one of them was enjoying this. Bell's stomach tightened. Were spies already watching them?

I should tell Carasti to go back.

That knowledge warred with the chills scraping her spine every time she glanced into a dark stairway. As brave as she wanted to be, her feet would not take her down there by herself. For once, she was deeply grateful for Carasti's endless thirst for adventure.

As they passed the fountain where she'd first spoken with the Spy, she studied the dark patch by the bench. Was this what he had wanted since the beginning? Even though he'd warned her against it, it was too likely she was walking into a complicated snare.

Spies manipulated everyone for their own gain—for the Seller's gain—and she was no exception. She'd fallen into this one as easily as anything—no.

She took a deep breath. She wasn't a fool. She could take care of herself.

"Is this the one?" Carasti whispered as they passed the silk stall.

Bell nodded. "Carasti, are you sure…" Carasti swept past her. The cold air of the staircase enveloped them as they descended. Bell's neck prickled despite the cloak's warm folds.

A heavy scent-filled draft seemed to grime her exposed skin as they reached the damp, narrow alley waiting at the bottom. The Sotto was dim compared to the Night Bazaar, like a dirty moon next to the sun. Cold, flickering candles lit each muted stall. Gloomy curtains framed the stalls in dried-blood maroon, nightshade, and nevermore gray. Darkness and silence oppressed the air. Makers hid deep within their stalls, faces shadowed, waiting for the right customers.

Her skin crawled as she looked at their wares. At first, they seemed like dimmer versions of Bazaar goods—rippling gowns of Bardian fabric, metal purified until it looked like water, rugs that warmed or cooled the room they lay in.

She slowed by the carpetmaker's stall. Would a dream carpet from the Sotto give nightmares instead? The maker lounged against the stall's curtains, threads flashing around his tattooed fingers, his gaze piercing her. His lips parted to reveal sharp teeth, and he flicked his hands. The rug's fibers shot toward his own throat, winding tight like a choking vine, cutting off his breath.

Bell gasped and the threads loosened. He laughed, the sound cutting through the heavy air. A dark haze hovered around his hands as he returned to weaving.

"Don't look," Carasti ordered as she yanked Bell away.

She stumbled on. Was everything in the Sotto so deadly? She imagined sleeping peacefully above one of his rugs and waking to strangling fibers around her neck.

They followed the first right turn the map indicated. Carasti gripped her elbow through the cloak, but Bell wasn't sure if it was for her sake or Carasti's. Here, the alley was even darker, the stalls farther apart and spaced by thick shadows. Bell forced herself not to crumple the map in her fist.

A hand snatched Carasti's and yanked her toward the corner of a stall with obsidian curtains. Bell grabbed for her other arm, but Carasti staggered against her as the hand released. A man in midnight velvet that glimmered without light stepped into their path. His sleeves were rolled up to his elbows to display black vine tattoos twisting up his hands and arms. He had slapped a silver bracelet onto Carasti's wrist.

"And where might you fine ladies be headed?"

Words drained to the bottom of Bell's stomach. Should they run?

"That would be our secret and none of your business." Carasti pulled Bell around the man.

He turned so he was facing them and lifted a silver bracelet. Carasti froze. "I am afraid you will have to pay for the one on your wrist."

"What did you do?" Carasti looked down and tugged at the matching band on her wrist, but it was seamless.

"Give me something valuable enough, and I'll give you the pair."

"Take it off, now." Carasti slammed her hand on the wooden table in his stall. When nothing happened, she staggered back as if shocked.

He showed white teeth. "Too late. As long as I have this one, you cannot use your gift."

Bell took a deep breath, scanning the dark beyond the metalmaker. "What do you want?"

The metalmaker grinned at Bell. "Finally, someone with sense. I want a vial of whatever you're carrying, Scentmaker."

"I'm not—" Bell bit her tongue. How could he know?

Carasti turned to her. "He can have mine," she said under her breath.

All scentmakers knew the three rules of the Consiglio. No fusing Magia. No fusing *permanenza*. No selling or trading for wares that had not been approved.

What rule hadn't she broken? Bell pulled Carasti's vial over her head and dangled it. "Release her, and you can have this vial."

He tilted his head. "A protection elixir?"

She steadied her voice and filled it with confidence. "The strongest."

He stroked the silver bracelet, and the matching band on Carasti's wrist clicked open. She snatched his out of his hand as he took the vial and stepped back to let them go. "Stay for wine next time," he called as they strode away. Carasti shuddered as she shoved the pair of bracelets deep into her pocket.

They didn't slow until they'd rounded the next corner, staying in the center, away from the stalls.

"This was such a bad idea," Bell whispered.

"Act confident. They can tell if you're afraid."

They descended three steps into a short tunnel.

Bell froze. On the other side of the tunnel, a black-cloaked Spy leaned against the alley wall, backlit by amaranth lamps. Even from here she saw the half mask and kohl-rimmed eyes.

"That's him," she whispered.

Behind him rose a curtained entrance twice as high as the other stalls, reaching all the way to the stone Sotto ceiling. Four amaranth lampstands flickered across the front.

The Seller of Secrets' stall.

As if in answer, the Spy pushed off the wall in one lithe movement and slipped behind the curtains without looking back.

Carasti snorted, the sound delicate and comforting in the dimness. "How do you know it was the same Spy?"

"He moves like Bardian ink pouring into a pot," Bell murmured.

"Oh?" Carasti smiled. "Do we have a crush on our hands?"

Bell scoffed, pretending her stomach wasn't tingling. "Come on."

"Hey, it might go both ways. He's certainly seeking you out."

"Carasti, he's a *Spy*."

The curtains gapped in the middle, and beyond dim lights glowed within a large stone atrium. As they hesitated at the opening, a man inside wearing a purple tunic beckoned them.

Bell turned to Carasti. "Are you sure—"

"Stop asking."

They stepped inside, and Bell felt—or imagined—the covert gazes of dozens of masked or hooded people scattered throughout the globular atrium. Were they all here to see the Seller? Any conversation came from the servants offering goblets. Scents intensified, rising from a dozen bodies. Bell double-checked that her vial was all the way open. Her *protezi* might be weak against Insidio, but it was something. "Do you feel anything?"

Carasti shrugged. "How big is this place?" She scanned the smooth stone ceiling. Two wooden doors with rounded tops stood opposite the curtains, and dark magenta hangings embroidered with white thread covered the walls.

A servant with pale skin approached Bell with a goblet of wine. "Drink this to join the line," she murmured.

Bell frowned at the dark liquid. The scents in the room were so strong she couldn't make out the wine's magical components. "What does it do?"

127

"The Entrance Wine. It determines your place in line."

Bell glanced at Carasti, who shrugged with her face. "How long will I have to wait?"

"That depends on what the Wine reveals."

She had come this far. She couldn't refuse and return home empty-handed. Besides, people had been coming to the Seller for decades. If he poisoned them with Bardian wine, no one would come.

Bell took the goblet. The Wine smelled warm and spicy with an undercurrent of dusty magic, like when she fused a bouquet. The tiniest sip burned her mouth and throat, and she coughed.

"That is enough." The servant took the cup back and dipped her head.

Bell gulped back a cough, eyes watering.

"What was it?" Carasti asked.

"I don't know. It's very strong."

Carasti's forehead creased. "Do you feel anything?"

Bell shook her head. "Definitely magical, but I don't feel it working."

"I don't like this."

"Miss." The servant was back and bowed this time. "The Seller will see you now."

"Already?" Bell murmured. Carasti moved to follow them, and the woman held up a hand.

"The one who has tasted the Wine."

"But—"

"I'll tell you all about it," Bell whispered. They couldn't attract notice, not when they were so close.

Carasti pouted and settled back against the wall, muttering to herself.

Bell tugged her hood all the way forward as she followed the servant through the waiting Bardians and out the doors at the back. She wasn't a first daughter, but someone still might recognize her.

The doors opened to a narrow hall that continued on either side. The ceiling rose sharply to the top of another pair of doors, carved with vines and pitted from top to bottom. They looked as old as the stone surrounding them. Hinges groaned as the servant pushed through and gestured her into a dim room.

"I will return to fetch you when you are finished. Do not deviate from the path." The servant reentered the atrium.

The Seller's chamber opened into a long cavern with a gem-studded ceiling. The cavern was some fifty feet high with ruggedly sheer walls. Bracketed candles every few feet lit water trickling down the walls. A walkway that looked wooden but echoed like stone led through a black pool. At the end of the cavern, thin waterfalls streamed from above, surrounding a narrow staircase.

Bell kept her cloak close. What was wrong with the water? It stirred the wrong way, swirling oddly as she passed. Were there creatures inside? Carasti had told stories of sea monsters with hundreds of mouths along their bodies. The heavy smells of mold and rust crawled up her neck. She swallowed a swelling scream and lengthened her stride. If people didn't survive even visiting the Seller, no one would try.

The metal stairway creaked as she climbed. At the top, inky water filled the stone ledge, forming a black pool, and a metal grid walkway led to the left door of an ornate wooden confessional set against the cavern wall.

The door opened smoothly when she turned the knob, and she paused at the small nook inside. A shallow stone bench lined the back wall.

"Welcome, Miss Asbury." Bell jumped at the male voice coming through a screen that blocked her view of the other side of the confessional. "You have come far to visit me deep in the Sotto. Come in and sit."

She stepped inside and the door swung closed behind her. She sat facing the way she'd come and peered through the screen. Dark shadows, thrown by circles of indistinct light, moved against it. Through the gap between the screen and the wall, she caught a glimpse of a raised bowl of dark liquid. Despite the darkness, it reflected a face rimmed in brown hair, too delicate to be a man....

"What secret do you seek, Miss Asbury?" The Seller's voice was masterfully soothing, and in that moment, she knew she'd tell him everything. Finally, someone who could untangle her life.

"Garam—House Medoro's first son—did he try to poison my sister? And Piero, his brother, what is he planning—" She sucked in a breath and hesitated. She probably couldn't bargain for all of that. She collected herself. "I want proof my sister's fiancé is going to deceive her with Insidio."

"Ah. And what do you offer in return?"

She looked down at her hands. She could promise him a favor as the future Maestra of Scents, but the idea of that disturbed her. She didn't even know if she wanted the position, and if she did, she wouldn't want anyone, especially not Pater Medoro or the Seller, having sway over a member of the Consiglio. So instead, she said the first thing she could think of. "What secret do *you* seek?"

The Seller's elegant hands came into view as he pressed them together above the bowl. "So bold, Goldenbell." He sounded amused, as if he guessed what she had been thinking. "Your family has long interested me."

Chills prickled her arms as dread replaced her hopeful confidence. Her fingers clamped down on her *protezi* vial. It was flimsy protection against the Seller's menacing aura.

"Here is the secret I seek: Who is Roza's blood father? Bring me the correct answer within three days, and I will give you your proof."

Bell's mouth soundlessly shaped the words he'd spoken. "What do you mean, Roza's blood father?" Her voice turned shrill at the end. "She's my *sister*."

"Half sister." The bowl shimmered, and another face appeared. "Find out the truth, and I will make the trade." The Seller slid the screen shut and the indistinct lights went out, closing her in darkness.

Her door opened and the bench moved forward, the floor shifting beneath her. The smell of hot stone filled the air as the bench tipped and dumped her outside the confessional. She scrambled to her feet.

Her breath exploded out of her, lungs tight with anxiety. Three days was too long. Garam could attack any moment.

"Please, that *is* the truth."

"I will send for you in three days." His voice was fading into the distance beyond the screen, into another passageway.

"Please—" She had to jump back to avoid the door as it swung shut.

Click.

She stood before the door a moment, steadying herself. She'd been expecting the Seller to ask about her gift. He might have asked her to steal information from Agnella or someone else on the Consiglio.

His demand felt more like a personal insult than payment. Her hand covered her mouth. *Had Mother been unfaithful? Was Roza adopted?* Bell frowned. Whatever it was, she was certain Roza knew. Perhaps this secret was what was making Roza so miserable.

The metal walkway groaned as she moved toward the staircase. The pool surrounding her brooded, but she kept her gaze away from it. At the bottom of the staircase, her stomach lurched at a splash in the waterfall behind her. Her rigid muscles screamed at her to run. She took two steps away and turned slowly.

What looked like an Insidio plant parted the thin streams of water beside the staircase. A raven-colored blossom with a purple center unfolded as she stepped closer. This Magia had the same shape and foliage as Insidio, but the colors were darker, and the center was purple rather than white.

Garam's note had said black Insidio. Did he mean this?

Bell slipped on her gloves and reached for the blossom. She jumped back as vines extended from the plant, growing straight down to the floor and then across and up again. When the vines met at the top, curiosity stirred her.

It was the shape of a door.

Dark blossoms budded and opened all at once along the length of the vine. It was as if they were responding to her gift. Their cloying scent swelled together, pressing into Bell's brain. Alarm shrieked inside her chest, but she leaned closer, trying to decipher the shadow rising above them. It looked like a net of black chains floating toward her. The edge of the net touched her outstretched fingers, and her brain flooded with wild longing to snatch every blossom and fuse them all, to let the elixir they created drench her arms, pour down her face, to drink...

Bell staggered back, fingers clamped over her nose and mouth. She spun and sprinted down the walkway. She didn't breathe until the sanctuary doors thudded closed behind her.

In the hallway, the atrium door opened as she reached up to pull her hood low. The pale-skinned servant entered, followed by someone in silver-heeled boots. Mother's boots.

Mother strode through the doorway.

Eighteen

MOTHER COULD *NOT* FIND HER HERE. Bell fled down a side passage without raising her head. *Did she see Carasti? How do I warn her?*

"Stop," the servant called. "You cannot go that way!" Heavier footsteps rushed Bell's way. *Lanzis.*

Bell sprinted around the corner as shouts grew closer. Amaranth-curtained doorways lined the hall. She yanked one aside to reveal a tiny storage closet and hurried on. The footsteps thundered, echoing against the rock. Bell ran to the next curtain, threw it open—and came face to face with a familiar man. His dark-sky eyes took in the hall behind her; then he grabbed her by the shoulders and pulled her inside. Gasping, she staggered against his chest as he dropped the curtain and silently shut a door behind it. He opened the door of a wardrobe and pointed inside. She stumbled in, pushing aside a row of Bardian silk and cotton shirts. He shut the door, leaving her in near pitch black. Shouts continued as cloth rustled and the faucet turned on. Someone pounded at the door as water splashed. The man turned off the water.

"Can't a man wash in peace?" Metal rattled as the door opened.

"Sorry, sir. A supplicant was seen running toward this hallway without permission."

He gave a sound of supreme irritation. "I haven't seen anyone coming in. Believe me, I would have noticed."

"Let us know if you hear anything, sir."

"Certainly." The door clicked shut.

Bell waited, her breath shaky. The man hummed. Bell reached out and pushed the door open a crack. Bare brown skin met her gaze. He'd taken off his shirt, and the lamplight warmed his lithe, tawny back. He smoothed thick hair with damp hands. Black vine tattoos curled around his wrists and tapered toward his elbows. His head turned and she pulled back.

Footsteps. The wardrobe doors opened wide, and she shrank behind the shirts, toes curling in her shoes as she averted her eyes.

"I can still see you." His voice held an amused edge.

Her cloak had fallen back, and her dress glowed like a sun in the lamplight.

"Perhaps you'd like to choose a shirt for me."

"What?" she said faintly.

"You're in my wardrobe."

She grabbed a cotton one hanging by her face and shoved it through the others without looking. "Here."

"It's a good thing I like white shirts." His fingers brushed hers as he took it. "Thank you. You may come out, if you like." He pulled the shirt around his shoulders, and she waited until he'd finished buttoning it before she moved.

She pushed aside the row of shirts. Dark hair framed velvety black eyes. His lips were made for whispering and magic and mysterious smiles. He brushed wet strands of hair out of his face. "I don't charge for looking."

"You." She stepped out and brushed off her skirt.

"Me?" he asked innocently.

"You lied about being Garam's cousin."

"You assumed that's who I was."

"The real Aless came for dinner this evening." She shuddered. "Mortifying."

"He's that bad, eh?" He leaned one hand against the wardrobe, half framing her, and she edged away. Her gaze caught on a black-sheeted bed filling one side of the room. She swallowed as indignation wrestled with embarrassment.

"He was…honest. And confused by my reaction." She scanned the room and saw a black cloak thrown over a chair. Bell slowly looked up and studied his features. She lifted her hand to block the top half of his face. "I recognize that chin." Her hand lowered. "You're the Spy who keeps following me."

"I apologize. I hope this will make up for it." He glanced at the door.

"I think I deserve to know what you were doing in Garam's room."

"You're not going to thank me before you interrogate?"

She tightened her lips. "Thank you."

"Protective of him, are you?"

"Answer the question. No lies."

"I didn't lie—"

Frustration welled up and she stabbed him with her finger. "It's called lying by omission."

"Ow." He rubbed the spot under his collarbone. "Remind me to never let you have anything sharp."

She crossed her arms and glared. "Answer."

"Your brother-in-law to-be has too many secrets for my liking. I was simply digging them out—with your help."

"I don't believe anything you say."

His expression became serious. "I never lie."

"Never?"

"The Seller takes truthtelling elixir when he sells secrets, but otherwise his words are untrustworthy. I never wanted to be like him, so I vowed to never lie at all."

"Except the lying by omission part."

A rueful grin tugged at his lips. "You're saying you never do?"

He motioned to the other side of the room where a polished wood table and chairs sat before a small hearth. A tiny copper kettle steamed on a grate over the coals. "Tea? You'll need to wait here a while for the search to die down."

A rush of anxiety made Bell bite her lip. Had she ruined everything? If her deal fell through because of her panicked reaction... despair washed through her. Her forehead creased. "I should go back and explain. I *had* to run."

"You fled down his private halls without permission. The Seller of Secrets is many things, but forgiving is not one of them." He pulled out a chair and shoved a small stack of faded books aside. "I promise I have good tea."

Knees suddenly weak, she crossed the room, pushed back her cloak, and sank down. "I can't believe I'm here." She laughed, but it caught in her throat. *I can't believe Mother is here. Did she recognize me?*

"What did he demand from you?"

She grimaced at him. "At least he offered a trade. You can't give me what I need." She pulled out the map and pressed it against the table. "I mean, besides this, which I'm returning to you." She looked up through half-lidded eyes, too nervous to ask what sort of payment he would demand of her.

He sat in the chair next to her and leaned on the table, chin resting on his hand. She studied the black leaves encircling his wrists. The metalmaker in the Sotto who'd accosted Carasti had the same markings. "I may not be able to help you with the Medoros, but I can make you a better offer than the Seller."

She scoffed.

"I'm serious." He was starting to look frustrated. "Whatever he asked of you now is nothing compared to what he has planned for you, Bell. I swear I'm trying to help you."

She shook her head. "I don't trust the Seller, and I don't trust you. You could be making this all up to manipulate me. Isn't that a Spy's job?"

He sighed. "It's not the only thing." He ticked off his fingers. "I try out his new tailors. Taste his imported teas. Entertain his pretty lady guests." He winked as his easy smile returned.

She stood abruptly, longing for soil to dig her fingers into. "I'm leaving."

"I won't stop you." He hooked his elbows around the back of his chair. His gaze flickered to the door. "But the Seller and I have different goals, I think."

"Why does he let you stay here, then?"

The kettle whistled. As if he had all the time in the world, he pulled the kettle from above the coals and filled a green painted metal teapot that sat between two stacks of books. "I know too much to be allowed to leave." His expression was suddenly bleak.

She hesitated, then sank back into the chair. "What do you mean?"

"Once he finds a maker he wants to use, there's no escape. He's immovable. He'll do anything to make you serve him. If you don't do what he wants, he'll threaten family, livelihood—he won't let you live a peaceful life. He might even try to kill you." He checked the teapot, then poured her a cup. Smoky fragrance wafted up. He chuckled bitterly, his velvet voice shivering up her spine. "And Bardia's an island. Even he can't find a boat strong enough to carry makers past the *attuale* current."

Bell wrapped her fingers around the cup. Heat soaked through the delicate porcelain. "Why are you telling me this?"

He leaned swiftly across the table, making her flinch. "He's been thinking about how to ensnare you, Bell. He wants you in his debt." He placed his long, elegant fingers over her hand. Her lungs filled with his scent, her gift busily dissecting it. He smelled of magic, smoke, and herbs. With the purest sincerity, he said, "I need your help."

Bell pulled her hand free. "That's obvious. Otherwise, you wouldn't be helping *me*." Her gaze narrowed.

He smiled wryly as he read the suspicion in her expression. "I assure you, my ambitions are much smaller, and less…insane."

Bell looked toward the door. Carasti would be going crazy by now.

She frowned. The Spy's words rang with truth, but those dark-sky eyes looked at her because she was useful to him. She turned back and considered him.

"What's your name?"

"Call me Rian."

137

"Is that your real name?"

He flicked his fingers. "Drink your tea."

She automatically picked up the cup and sniffed. It smelled strong, but not magical. Cautiously, she took a sip and winced at the smoky, bitter flavor. "What is this?"

"Lapsang souchong. From the mainland." He glanced away. "Next time I'll have mint and cream for you."

Bell lost her grip and dropped the teacup. It hit the table's edge and broke, blue and green porcelain splintering onto the ground. Tea splattered onto the books, and Bell pushed back her chair to avoid the hot liquid dribbling off the table.

"How do you know what kind of tea I like?" she asked, a shiver working its way up her spine. "How long have you been stalking me?"

He grabbed a cloth from across the table and blotted up the puddle. "I wouldn't say stalking—"

"How long?" she demanded.

He shrugged.

Her skin crawled. Had he watched through her window while she drank her morning tea? Had he crept into her house like he had snuck into House Medoro? Had he gone through her things or stared at her while she slept? She swallowed, remembering the cold feeling of finding him outside her garden door. Suddenly, those beguiling eyes lost their appeal, and she wanted to be very far away. She lurched to her feet.

"Thank you for the tea." Her words were clipped. She had to get out of here.

He looked up, guilty. "I gathered information about you because the Seller wanted me to." He ran a hand across his face and sighed. "It was only recently I realized you could help me."

Bell tilted her head. Despite her better judgment, her alarm was fading. He appeared genuinely remorseful. She glanced at the door, then back at him. He couldn't be as dangerous as the Seller, could he? "What do you want me to do for you?"

"Your Maestra Agnella mentioned that, theoretically, you could protect a maker using a scent cloud."

She frowned at him. "Scent cloud? Those are for deciphering elixirs. We can't do anything with them. Besides, she'd never have told you that."

He shrugged. "Well, she wasn't speaking *to* me."

"I can't do that."

"Surely you will, after you become Maestra of Scents. Now, shall we go?"

She tugged at her cloak fastenings and looked toward the door.

"Not that way." He walked to the hearth and pressed his hand to the wall beside it. The stone melted.

Nineteen

THE AROMA OF SUNBAKED STONE ROSE. So that was the magic she smelled on him—he was a stone-maker, and a powerful one. He'd melted a hole through the six-inch wall faster than the Maestro of Stone had during an exhibition in the square. His hands glowed slightly, the color of coals behind smoky glass. Did the heat actually emanate from his skin? She stepped forward, fascinated, and he spread his fingers out for her to examine. The glow was fading already, but his skin still radiated heat. She looked into the narrow passageway beyond the hole. Obsidian-flecked stone sparkled in firelight.

"How can your gift have the strength? The Consiglio won't share the Solstice gift with makers from the Sotto."

He grimaced. "Your Consiglio prefers to keep Bardia in the dark about many things."

She flushed with indignation. "Like what?"

His fingers had returned to their original dusky color. "You think all the Sotto makers have been weakening every year?"

She frowned. "The Maestris check everyone in the square. There's no way they'd overlook so many."

"You've never considered we might get our power somewhere else?"

"The current rises at the Solstice Spring," she said automatically as her gaze flicked to the markings on his wrists.

He looked past her to the door. "Time to make a choice. Follow me and I'll lead you out, or leave that way and let the Lanzis find you. Who knows, the Seller might even let you go back home tonight."

Before the dim opening, she hesitated. A moment ago, she had been terrified of trusting him. Was she really about to follow him into a black tunnel where she would be completely at his mercy?

He stepped into the tunnel and held out his hand to her, eyebrows raised.

The more she looked at him, the more sincere he seemed. Maybe he had been watching her, but it seemed all he'd done was watch. *Don't be so eager to jump to conclusions.* Her father's words echoed in her head. She straightened her back and placed her hand in his.

"I'll go with you. I might even try to create a protective scent cloud, but if we are going to be allies, this must be an equal exchange. I want information—starting with why my mother was here tonight."

His forehead creased as he drew her into the tunnel. "Your mother was here?"

"Yes, and I want you to find out what kind of secret she wanted to buy."

He squeezed her hand. "I'll keep an ear out."

A flush of nerves swept her, and she pulled her hand free. "Where does this go?" she asked as they walked into darkness.

"Outside the Seller's caverns."

"I have a friend waiting in the atrium." Would Carasti still be there?

"I'll inform her you were forced to abscond." His voice moved away, and she groped about with her hands until her knuckles hit a wall.

"Slow down." Her voice was strained.

"Put your hand on the wall. Let it guide you. The floor is smooth, but I can lead you by the hand if you like."

"No, thank you."

"Very brave."

"It's not bravery, I'm…"

"Too shy to hold my hand?"

"You wish," she muttered as she followed slowly. They walked in silence for several minutes as she ran her hand along the wall and tried to think of something clever to say. When he stopped, she bumped into his back.

"We'll have to be quiet for a moment. I'm going to make sure your friend is still waiting." He opened a tiny hole in the wall with his finger, and a line of light streamed in. He pressed his eye against it. "She's by the entrance."

"I want to see."

He stepped aside, and she stood on tiptoe to look through. The tasseled edges of a wall hanging framed her view. Carasti, tucked in her blue cape, stood a few feet from the amaranth curtains of the entrance. She was still, with her hooded face trained toward the doors at the back. A Lanzi lurked to Carasti's left. His head turned and Bell ducked.

"They can't see you here," he whispered. With a brush of his fingers, he closed the hole.

"What if he realizes Carasti came with me?"

"They know already. They'll stay with her, expecting you to come for her."

"There's more than one?"

"Hidden."

Bell curled her fingers around her vial. "Can you melt a hole behind her?"

"It would take too long. A new opening takes five times as long as one I've melted before."

She rolled her vial in her fingers, tracing the familiar goldenbell shape. She needed to get back to free air and the smell of dark soil, but Carasti had risked so much to come with her. "I can't leave her."

His shirt rustled. "If you're spotted in the Night Bazaar, they'll leave her alone. Then I can guide her out."

"Won't they know you helped me?"

"I like to keep things confusing for everyone."

"What about the Lanzis? Will they chase me?"

"Not if you're with me. They never interfere with our business."

She frowned. "Even if the Seller orders it?"

He made a noise in his throat. "Nothing is ever straightforward with him."

"And Carasti? I don't want her to go through the Sotto alone."

"Don't worry, Bell. As soon as you've reached the square, I'll deliver her safely to you as part of the *equal exchange*."

She half smiled. "Now you're catching on."

"This way." His voice faded, and she blindly hurried after him. "Careful, the stairs start here." His voice rose above her, and she felt around with her toe until she found the first step.

"Did you make all of this?"

"These tunnels are my life's work."

"So that's how the spies and Lanzis get everywhere," she murmured.

"No, no one else uses them."

"Why not?"

"They're afraid I'll change them while they're inside, and they'll never get out." He sounded wickedly amused.

"Would you?"

"Depends on my mood—the stairs end here. We're not friends. We're rivals."

"Rivals over what?"

The answering silence stretched out in darkness, and she followed him by the sound of his faint footsteps.

"Stop here." The stone beside her glowed dimly, then folded aside into an opening as tall as Rian. A fountain splashed on the other side. The Night Bazaar lights glimmered beyond. Rian's eyes sparkled as he gestured her through. "Ladies first."

Twenty

THEY ENTERED THE BAZAAR IN THE SHADowed alcove by the fountain where they'd first spoken. "So this is how you appeared," she said.

"I was waiting for you, actually."

"How did you—" She glared at him. "Now that we're allies, can you please stop stalking me?"

"Will do my best." He certainly didn't look chagrined enough. They strolled into the street. Bell scanned for Lanzis, but the shadows were consumed by vibrant colors and scents so thick she could taste them—cerise punch and damp sea salt and another, now more familiar—sunbaked stone. "You must have watched me with Roza and came here to wait."

"Yes. I was curious to see what would bring you into the Bazaar so close to Solstice. It was unusual for you."

"And you knew Garam would be meeting that Lanzi here? Is he working for the Seller?"

He glanced away. "No."

A pair of pretty merchant's girls spun by on each other's arms, giggling and peering at Rian through their lashes. His gaze swept over them, scanning the edges of the throng. They passed another fountain, but Bell was too wrapped in thought to marvel at its copper and orange tints. She scowled at him.

"What aren't you telling me? Do you know what Garam is planning?"

His gaze felt dark and heavy when he looked at her. He glanced over her shoulder for half a second. She turned but found a stream of Bazaar shoppers bustling past, some taking tight, impatient steps, others meandering, their faces open like sponges, soaking in the colors and smells. All of them knew what they were doing here. Did she?

Rian tugged her on toward a gelateria. His liquid stride had tightened almost imperceptibly.

"It's an equal exchange, Bell. So far I've given you the map and hidden you. I've told you personal secrets, and now I'm sneaking you out. All you've done so far is break my favorite teacup."

"Has a Lanzi seen me?"

"Almost." He turned to face a gelato seller and tossed a coin in his jar. "Two lime gelatos, please. Ah, you don't mind if I order for you, my dear Sunbeam?"

"Shouldn't you know my gelato order too, my dear stalker—"

His palm touched the small of her back. "We're not in my bedroom anymore, Sunbeam," he murmured. The gelato seller's gaze stayed on the lime gelato he was scooping, but he grew a tiny smirk.

"It's not what it sounds like," Bell said as the seller handed them their cups of gelato. "Rian—"

"Eat your gelato before it melts." His hand guided her away, back into the crowd.

She gave him a salty look but then looked down at the cup. Thick veins of cream swirled through the lime green. It even smelled sweet.

Her annoyance evaporated after she took a bite.

Wondrous yellow and green flavors burst on her tongue. Lemon and lime and smooth cream wove sour with sweet.

Rian was already halfway through his. He grinned around his spoon. "Bardian gelato."

She took another bite. "I forgot how delicious it was. Thanks." Sudden guilt for enjoying herself twisted through her. Carasti was going to plant splinters in her bed. "When will you get my friend?"

"When I'm sure no overeager Lanzi will try to drag you back to the Seller. I'll leave you at the Rotunda steps. They won't touch you there. I won't let them hurt you, Sunbeam."

Bell resisted the urge to roll her eyes. The Seller needed her. It wasn't like he would send his Lanzis to beat her up in an alley.

He tensed—then put an arm over her shoulder and spun her so she faced his chest, pulling her into a dark space between two stalls. Bell froze. The Bazaar colors seemed to dim at the dangerous glint in his eyes. His arm slid to her back as he leaned closer, close enough she could see the cleft right below his bottom lip. At the last second, he turned his face away and pressed his mouth into her hair.

By the time he let go, her face burned.

"What was that for?" she muttered.

"I saw someone, and I needed to hide you," he murmured. "They're gone now."

Ahead, a gemmaker's stall took in lamplight and spun it out in a hundred colors.

"Look." He gestured to a row of glass spheres. In their center tiny landscapes were formed from gems. The glint left his eyes, and he looked pleased with himself again. Rian pointed to a goldenbell field. "I thought of you when I saw this."

The gemmaker, grinning, plucked the sphere up and held it out over the counter.

Bell took it and held her breath as she leaned closer. The goldenbells, their yellow cups half the size of her smallest nail, rippled in an unseen wind. "How does it do that?" she whispered.

The gemmaker beamed. "You'll only find such gems here."

Small as it was, the field sang of open sky and freedom. Bell memorized it in silence as long as she dared. "Thank you for showing me," she said softly, and held it out.

The gemmaker looked at Rian. "Ten florins."

Rian passed him a fistful of gold coins.

"No, I'm not taking it."

Rian curled her fingers around the sphere. "These gems were born for you, Bell."

"Remember the equal exchange? I don't need to owe you anything else," she snapped.

He strolled past the gem stall. "You don't. It's a gift."

She scowled. What would he do if she dropped it and let it shatter? She tried to open her fingers but couldn't do it. Finally, she slipped the sphere into her pocket.

They turned onto the main thoroughfare, the entrance arch framing a corner of the night sky. The Piazza was fuller than ever. At the foot of the Rotunda stairs, Rian smiled down at her.

"Goodnight, my lady." He bowed at the waist, turned, and vanished into the crowd. Bell stared after him, wanting to call him back, yet relieved to be alone again.

By the time Carasti appeared, Bell was wound like a spring. She'd thrown away the rest of the gelato. The tartness increased the taste of acid in her mouth.

"I suppose I'll forgive you for leaving me, since I got to escape through a tunnel with your Spy." Carasti glanced back toward the Bazaar.

"He didn't say anything to you?" Bell searched the crowd for Rian's face.

"Come with me if you want to see your friend again—that was pretty much it." Carasti linked her arm with Bell's. "Let's get out of here."

They walked until they reached the wide, low wall of the Piazza and sat half hidden by the overhanging branches of a linden tree. The boughs were heavy with the fragrant cream blossoms. Bell stroked a soft petal, trying to soothe her rigid nerves.

Carasti rested her elbows on her knees. "So, you most definitely have a Spy on your side."

Bell paused. "He's my ally. In exchange, he wants me to make him a protective scent cloud."

Carasti whistled through her teeth. "Now you've gone and done it."

"I'm worried, Carasti. He was very nice, all things considered. I shouldn't trust him, but I want to." A huge blossom dropped on her neck, curling up against her ear. She sighed at the silken petals, resting her awareness on the green life within the tree. "Am I being gullible?"

"I wouldn't call you gullible." She patted Bell's shoulder. "But why exactly did you leave without me?"

Bell told her about Mother.

"Was she looking for you?" Carasti asked.

"I don't think so. She doesn't even know I've been in the Bazaar." What would take Mother to the place she hated most? Or was her animosity toward the Bazaar and scentmaking a cover for her own activities? Bell shuddered. She and Mother might not agree on much, but at least until now Mother had been predictable. The idea that she had been going to the Seller to make her own deal made a painful uncertainty rise in Bell's chest.

"What did the Seller ask for?"

Bell hesitated. "He—he asked for a secret I don't have. I don't know if he really wants to know or if he's trying to scare me."

"Mmhmm." Carasti crossed her arms.

"He asked who Roza's blood father is," she half whispered.

"What?" Carasti's right eyebrow disappeared into her hair.

"He said I have three days to find out the truth."

"I don't like it. Maybe you shouldn't go back." Carasti gave her an apprehensive look. "I've been asking around in Santa Croce, trying to find information on Garam. I've found something else."

"What?"

She glanced across the throng. "Did you know the Consiglio has never allowed anyone to cross the *attuale* current in a ship of Bardian wood?"

Bell bit back a groan. "So? It's dangerous."

"Dangerous for their positions, maybe. Crafted Bardian wood can be sealed against any *attuale* alchemy. It would make sense to try, is all I'm saying."

"Maybe they don't think taking Bardian gifts to the mainland would be good for Bardia."

Another look. "I suppose, but the things I'm hearing don't make me want to trust them." She popped up straight like a bent branch released. "Maybe your Spy would know more about it."

Bell tightened her lips. "Garam wants to hurt my sister. That's all I need to prove."

"If it's true, I hope you can."

"*If* it's true?"

"Maybe he was playing the Lanzi? Maybe he wanted the Seller to think he was going to use Insidio on Roza?"

Bell frowned. "Why wouldn't he tell me that when I accused him?"

"He doesn't trust you? I don't know. Who knows what these nobles are scheming? Bardian politics are——" Carasti grimaced.

"I'm a noble. We don't all scheme."

"I'm simply saying the motive might be different."

"Roza doesn't scare easily. She begged me to help her."

"There is another explanation." Carasti took a deep breath. "Roza is a complicated person."

"What are you saying?"

"There are rumors about her——"

"Rumors?"

Carasti was looking at her with huge, sympathetic eyes, and Bell would have preferred her usual mischievous sparkle. "She spends a *lot* of time in the Sotto, Bell."

Bell's stomach tightened. "Where did you hear this?"

She shrugged. "Other makers. If Roza is working for the Seller, Garam might have a reason to use Insidio."

Bell shook her head slowly. "Nothing justifies using Insidio on her."

Carasti took a deep breath. "Of course not. Just be careful with her, Bell."

"She's my sister, Carasti. And Garam is…"

"A Medoro?"

"He's hiding something."

Abruptly, Carasti stood up. "Never mind all this. Let's go home."

Bell was sneaking by her garden fountain in the dark when a slight figure stepped in front of her. Bell started. "Elena?"

"Miss Bell," Elena said.

"What are you doing out here?" she whispered, peering up at Mother's dark windows. Without the moonflowers, the moon left the garden heavy with shadows. "Is something wrong? Are you still ill?"

"You've been to the Night Bazaar."

Bell's breath caught in her throat. "What are you talking about?"

"I watched you go into the Sotto with your friend."

"Elena, you can't tell anyone—"

"I don't intend to."

Bell's shoulders lowered in relief. "What were you doing near the Sotto, anyway?"

"I wanted to know what you were doing." Elena stepped into a shard of moonlight. "You're looking for the Lymbodia cure, aren't you?" Bell hesitated, and Elena's face brightened in triumph. "There's a scentmaker who claims he's found it."

Bell's heart sank. "Don't get your hopes up, Elena. A cure is near impossible."

"He's searching for a *permanenza* elixir to go with his healing elixir. He can stave off the disease now, but with both he could make it permanent."

Bell's insides twisted. "*Permanenza* is illegal. Who is this scentmaker?"

"His identity is secret. But his patients have lived longer than the healers predicted."

Bell paced, her brow fierce with thought. "Scentmakers have always searched for a cure—since Firinacci. They've never come close." She stopped. "I've been experimenting for years, Elena. The most I've gotten is an elixir that targets the pain of Lymbodia."

"Because *permanenza* is not permitted."

"*Permanenza* would cause more damage than good. If the cure is the least bit wrong, the patient would die."

Elena's gaze sharpened on hers. "Then why are you trying to fuse it for your sister?"

Bell's stomach dropped away. "What...what do you mean?"

She moved closer. "I know about Garam. I can help stop him if you fuse the elixir."

Bell stepped back. "What do you know about Garam?"

"I've heard whispers."

Her criminal plan to fuse *permanenza* was already news among the maids? How long before the Consiglio learned of it and came to revoke her rights as a scentmaker? "I need to go."

"Think about it, Bell," Elena called softly as Bell slipped into the shadows.

Twenty-One

THE MORNING SUN CAME LIKE A BLOW TO the head. Bell rubbed gritty eyes, watching as Elena laid a white porcelain tea tray by the bed.

"Good morning, miss." Elena smiled brightly as if their midnight meeting had been nothing but a dream.

Bell scooted back against her pillows. "Are you sure you're well enough, Elena?"

Elena stirred cream and a spoonful of sugar into Bell's cup. "Thanks to you." There was no sign of the triumph in her face now. She looked soft...and vulnerable. "You saved my life."

"You shouldn't have been in danger."

Elena gave her a wry look. "I know where I live. Drink your tea before it gets cold."

Bell sipped and wrinkled her nose at the sweetness.

"I am sorry, Elena. We'll catch whoever is responsible."

Elena patted Bell's knee and turned to lay out a dress from the wardrobe.

"I want to know more about the scentmaker," Bell said softly. "How did you hear of him?"

Elena paused, an amber frock hanging from her hands. "Anyone who has Lymbodia has heard of him by now. He heals for free. Eduard..." She swallowed. "He was at the edge of death. He'd hidden it for so long, even I didn't know. Our neighbor in Santo Spirito sent some people to see us. They told us about the healer. They said they'd have to get Eduard down into the Sotto so the scentmaker could work on him. He can't risk working above ground where the Consiglio would hear of it. They...they took him, and he came back better. The disease was slowed." Elena met her gaze, defiance shining in them.

"If he works in the Sotto, he's a dark maker," Bell said, keeping her voice matter-of-fact. Who was she to judge after running to the Seller of Secrets to save Roza from a miserable life? If she knew this dark maker truly could heal Roza's Lymbodia, she'd hunt him down in the Sotto tonight.

"Yes." Elena kept her chin up. "Will you meet him?"

"I can't fuse *permanenza*, Elena," she said quietly.

Elena's face closed, and she turned to go.

"I would do it if I could." Bell reached out a hand. "Please believe me."

The door clicked shut, leaving heavy silence.

Bell drank the tea as quickly as she could without burning her tongue, listening for Mother's footsteps. Birds chirped and the fountain splashed in the garden. She buttoned herself into the dress Elena had laid out.

Elena had said she knew about Garam. What did she know? Could she have proof that passed through the network of servants?

Bell slipped from her room and tiptoed downstairs. Father sat behind his study desk and looked up as she passed. "Bell, step inside please."

Lips tight, Mother turned toward her from the window behind Father. Bell's throat seized.

"Goldenbell, is it true you've been to the Sotto?" Father asked quietly.

The garden was like a vivid Bardian painting through the windows. Surreal and distant.

"Who said this?" she asked finally.

"Elena, moments ago. Last night, she followed you. She was trying to look after you, but like a wise girl, she dared not follow you below."

Mother stepped forward. "I have told you, in clear words, never to enter the Sotto. You are not even supposed to be near the Bazaar at this time of year."

Elena had betrayed her? Without warning? Her lungs seemed half their usual size, and her voice came out small. "I'm seventeen, Mother. I can make my own decisions."

Mother cut her off with a hand. "I've been to see the Maestra of Scents this morning."

"Why?"

"To inform her your scentmaking career is over. I have had enough. You are not to see her again. You will remain *here* during La Festa."

The words smacked Bell's chest like a handful of mud. She couldn't open her mouth.

"It is too dangerous. You know nothing of the treachery of the Sotto. We cannot let you be so close to it anymore."

Father nodded and Bell stood stunned.

Mother closed her eyes, and they were marginally softer when she opened them. "You are too much like me, Bell."

"Even House Medoro has a son pursuing scentmaking. Why can't you accept who I *am*?" Bell's words became shrill at the end.

"I too was drawn in by the magic of the Night Bazaar, but I did not emerge unscathed. I want to keep you from such a fate."

"You'd keep me out, but let Roza marry a poisoner? Someone who dabbles in Insidio?"

Her face whitened. "You are never to speak of that again."

"Francesca…" Father reached for her, his brow furrowed.

"I'm going to prove it," Bell snapped. They hadn't even asked what she'd been doing in the Sotto. There didn't seem to be much point in telling them.

Mother lurched forward and grabbed Bell's arm. "You will stay here."

"I love Roza, even if you don't. I'm going to save her from that family."

Pain flashed through Mother's eyes. She released Bell. "*You* tell her," she whispered and strode out.

Bell glared at Father. "Tell me what?"

"You'd better sit." Father's shoulders drooped. Bell crossed her arms as she dropped onto the half sofa across his desk. "Do you know why your grandfather, Pater Ilia, disowned your mother?"

Bell shrugged. "She married you."

"No. In her seventeenth year, when they visited from the mainland during La Festa, Francesca went to the Night Bazaar and vanished. Pater Ilia was frantic. He searched the Sotto long after La Festa ended, but she was too well-hidden. When she returned months later, she confessed a common scentmaker had seduced her. She regained her senses and left the Sotto, but Pater Ilia was furious. He married her to me to try to hide their shame."

"Mother was seduced?" Bell asked doubtfully.

"I think that scentmaker manipulated her, perhaps with magic." His voice softened. "The Francesca I knew loved her noble life, loved living in the mainland cities. She wouldn't have given it up on a whim."

"You knew her before?"

He smiled. "I was in love with her. She was captivating, the daughter of a powerful mainland family. Unattainable for a middling wine merchant from Sante Croce like me. Back then, she was engaged to Pater Medoro."

Bell's mouth dropped open. "What?"

"Oh yes. That doubled the scandal. House Medoro was furious as well." Father leaned forward. "Francesca learned how deadly the Sotto can be. Now do you see why she seems so cold at times? She's ashamed of her past, and she's desperate to stop you from suffering the same." Father's forehead creased. "If the *attuale* current would allow you past, she would try to repair relations with her father—"

"She wants to leave?"

"She wants you to be safe."

A question cleared in Bell's mind, like fogged glass being wiped clean. Something was driving Roza to escape her own family. Roza thought their parents didn't love her.

Mother was ashamed of her past. Bell lifted her gaze. "Was the common scentmaker Roza's father?"

Father stared at her for a long moment. "It doesn't matter, Bell."

"Of course it does."

He pressed his hands to his eyes. "I love Roza as my own."

"Now it makes sense." Bell's voice rose. "You're making Roza marry into a dangerous family, to a man she doesn't love, to pay back *your* debts. And you don't care because she isn't truly your daughter."

Bell spun and ran out of the room. The ground seemed unsteady as she hurled herself down the hall and fled into the garden. Her family was made for Bardia after all. Secrets tangled among them like brambles beneath the surface, pricking until blood ran.

Twenty-Two

SHE PLUCKED A HANDFUL OF GOLDENBELL from the arbor, letting her gift shape it into a intricate braid, releasing her frustration.

"I see why your father calls you Blossom," said a husky voice.

Bell's hands convulsed, crushing the woven flowers against her chest.

Rian peeked out from behind a hedge with a tilted smile. "Sorry." He strode into the open wearing a rumpled white shirt.

"What—how—get out of my garden. I'm not in the mood."

His eyebrows came together. "Did you expect me to vanish entirely? I wanted to see you."

"Not *here* in the middle of the *day*. Do you have any idea what Mother would do if she saw you?" Bell glanced behind her. A bird called over the fountain's rush. Any other day she loved the water, but today it would muffle any approaching footsteps. "Leave. Now."

"But I came all this way. I walked, you know." He motioned vaguely behind him.

Bell smothered rising hysteria. If Mother came charging out here, she'd rip this garden up by the roots to punish Bell for harboring an unknown boy. Mother might even think Bell had a secret, common love. If Elena saw him, she'd use it as more leverage. She grabbed his hand and tugged. "Hide somewhere, please," she whispered.

Her desperation must have leaked into her voice. "Where?" he asked.

157

She spun, scanning the patio. There was one place no one else could go. "Come on." She kept a tight grip on his hand, half expecting him to bolt toward the house and announce his presence. Her fingers tingled as they stepped inside the workshop, and she closed the vines behind them. The deep breath she took stalled as she turned.

They stood mere inches apart. She let go of his hand and backed up as far as she could. He sprawled onto her stool. When she sat on her workbench, his knees brushed hers.

"So, this is a scentmaker's workshop." He tenderly touched a vial on a shelf behind him. She opened her mouth, but he gave her a wry look. "I know how to be careful. I'm a maker too."

She studied him. He wore the same black pants and white shirt as always, but his sleeves were rolled to his elbows, his hem untucked, and his hair ruffled. "Why are you here?"

"I think you should try to move a scent cloud."

"This isn't…" She blew a strand of hair off her face. "Before Solstice?"

He leaned forward, reaching for a vial on a shelf next to her head. The warmth from his bare skin made her face tingle.

She slapped his arm back down. "You can stop doing that."

"Doing what?"

"Trying to…seduce me. It won't work." Her face burned. "You should leave."

He picked up another vial and turned it to read the label. "I'll go, but I can't promise I'll behave out there. How about this one?"

She sighed and snatched the vial back. What else could go wrong about this day? "How did you get in?"

He wiggled his fingers.

"Do you have a tunnel right up to my house?" she asked in alarm.

"I walked up the hill and came through the wall, Sunbeam."

She bit her lip. "Can any stonemaker go through the wall?"

He shook his head, looking smug. "One as good as me."

She groaned. "How can I make you go away?"

He gestured to the crushed flowers in her hands. "You have a strong affinity for living things."

She shrugged. "I've always been that way." The broken goldenbell petals pinched her heart. She stroked them, the pain easing as the petals healed.

"It's beautiful." He met her gaze. "Like you."

She scowled to hide a disobedient blush.

"Aha! The seduction *is* working."

She cringed. "Please, please leave."

He flew to his feet and peered down at her through his long lashes. "And to further the seduction—may I say, you remind me of a poem I read recently about the morning." His voice took on a reverent lilt. She folded in on herself, dying of embarrassment.

"A walking sun, the world turns bright, darkness fading, dying in the light." He gestured as if performing. "The morning bell, a golden hue—"

"Miss Bell?" A distant female voice brought breath to her lungs. Relief swept through her as Rian ducked his head and closed his mouth.

"Did she hear me?"

"I hope not," Bell whispered, aghast. "Stay here—and be quiet." She skirted past him and out of the workshop.

Shortly after, Elena rounded the fountain, relaxing as she saw Bell.

"Miss Bell. Are you sick? Your face is—"

"I'm not sick. I'm angry." All thoughts of Rian fled as Bell glared at Elena. "You betrayed me."

Elena winced. "You refused my request."

Bell circled the fountain, moving out of earshot of the workshop. "I can't trust you anymore."

"Eduard will not last much longer." Elena's face was bright with desperation.

"You've ruined everything." She was suddenly filled with a sick despair. "They've forbidden me from scentmaking."

"He's fading fast. I need you to begin now."

She glared at Elena, trying to feel pity for her. Bell felt like a flower choked by weeds, all of them sucking moisture and life from her soil. "I can't fuse it for a scentmaker I don't know. If it gets into the wrong hands—"

Elena's voice shook. "You'll fuse *permanenza*, or I'll tell them you've been to see the Seller."

"I don't even have a fioré—"

Elena let out a little breath. "He'll give you all the fioré you need."

An image of her fioré beds verdant and full filled her mind. "Really?"

Elena moved toward the vegetable beds, beckoning her. Two potted fioré sat half hidden by the stone border, Princess Seed and Sciver. "A token."

Bell couldn't help herself and touched the small round white-and-yellow Princess blossoms.

"Come work with him to fuse a *permanenza* elixir, and more fioré are yours. If you fuse it before Midsummer Solstice, your supply will never fail."

"A week? That's too soon." It would be like searching for a certain pebble in a field of dirt.

"His cure will be most effective when the *attuale* is strongest, and so will your power."

"But that won't affect my gift unless I…become Maestra." All legitimate makers' gifts would be refreshed at the Solstice, but the main strength went to the Maestris.

"You'll see." Elena held out the pots. "You can save Eduard, Bell. You can save them all." A fervent glow lit her eyes.

The fioré rustled toward her, new green shoots straining for her hands. She took the pots before they overextended themselves. Could she possibly do it? Fuse *permanenza* and heal Lymbodia? A Lymbodia cure would be the find of the century, and it would also free her family from the Medoros' clutches. It would pay off her father's debt.

"You have until tomorrow to think it over." The fervency took on a threatening edge. The gentle, caring Elena she knew was gone, swallowed up by desperation.

Bell slowly turned to go. Her neck prickled with Elena's gaze until she passed between the hedges. She held her breath as she opened the workshop. The stool was empty.

Rian was gone.

Half an hour later, Bell leaned back on her stool. Princess Seed calmed and Sciver cleared the mind, and fused together in the right amounts, their potency doubled.

She'd spent long minutes holding the open vial, studying the slowly fading scent cloud that rose above the elixir. She should have been looking for the Lymbodia cure, but she had no Myrtle Leaf, which had always formed the base for her past experiments.

Over and over, she tried moving the cloud with her fingers, but it maintained its even rotation. The sharp silver zigzag of Princess Seed looked like lightning striking the white and brown tree of Sciver.

She huffed in irritation. Whenever she stopped working, her gaze slid to the stool where Rian had said such ridiculous things. Had he really quoted poetry at her? *About* her? The corner of her mouth turned up. It was laughable now, without his smoldering eyes on her. Was he actually trying to seduce her? Or make her think he was harmless? She chewed on a fingernail, then wrestled her focus back to her work.

She scanned her shelves of vials. Her supply was running low, and it was always best to experiment with fresh fioré for optimal strength.

The black package of Magia hid in shadow at the back of the shelf. Could the secret scentmaker have used Magia for his cure? If she could find the cure on her own, there'd be no need for *permanenza*.

When Bell returned promptly for luncheon, Mother said nothing. Father finished his courses quickly, keeping his eyes down, and Mother retired to her parlor before Bell was half done with her roast cod. The front bell rang, and Elena answered it, returning with a note for Bell.

"What's this?" Bell opened the coarse fiber paper.

"From Woodmaker Carasti, Miss Bell." She sounded perfectly

161

proper, but the tension between them stretched so Bell could practically hear its bands sing.

Bell frowned. "Why didn't she come in?"

"Had other business, she said."

The note read:

B,

Maestra Agnella wants to see you at midnight tonight.

C

Despite herself, Bell smiled. She met Elena's sharp gaze. "Thank you."

"Is everything—"

"Everything's fine."

She would sneak out to meet Agnella and hear what she had to say.

Twenty-Three

AGNELLA'S WORKSHOP WINDOWS GLOWED. Bell stood outside, ready to call out, when the thorny vines parted, revealing a door.

It opened and Agnella peered out. "Inside, quickly."

The workshop was warm, and Agnella's fioré were already awake. They stirred as Bell passed. Low voices came from the office at the back.

Bell tensed. "Who's here?"

"People you need to meet."

Two familiar people stood when Bell and Agnella entered.

"This is Carlo, Maestro of Wood, and Piccarda, Maestra of Water."

Piccarda's tiered cobalt dress rippled as she clasped Bell's hand. Her midnight hair fell in wild waves, framing a flawless white face with almond-shaped ink-blue eyes. "A pleasure, Miss Asbury."

Bell blushed. They were here to see her? "The pleasure is mine, Maestra Piccarda."

Maestro Carlo took his turn, kissing her hand and winking. His copper curls reminded Bell of Carasti's. His smile was a merry dash across his square face. "I'm looking forward to seeing more of your work, Miss Asbury."

Maestra Piccarda waved impatiently at his display. "We must return soon."

"Then we must not dawdle." Agnella directed Bell to a rickety wooden chair. "Our mission tonight is vital."

"Mission?" Bell frowned.

Agnella sat with the others. "I know you've been to the Seller of Secrets, Bell."

Bell smoothed her skirt, her chair creaking. "I needed proof."

Agnella sighed. "So does he."

"What do you mean?"

"The Seller of Secrets claims to have discovered a cure for Lymbodia. He's been searching for someone who can fuse a *permanenza* elixir. He believes you can, but he wants proof."

Bell's mouth dried. *He's* Elena's secret healer? Hope bloomed in her chest. Could the Seller heal Roza? "Why can't he fuse his own *permanenza* elixir?"

Agnella stared at her. "Because no scentmaker has ever been powerful enough."

"And he thinks *I* am?"

"That's why Roza has been asking you to fuse it. He's getting to you through her."

Bell shook her head, dismissing the words. They'd made a mistake. They didn't know of Roza's constant pain. "No, Roza wants it to protect herself from Garam."

Maestra Piccarda snorted. "Roza doesn't need protection—"

"You don't know what Garam is capable of," Bell insisted. She shook her head. "You can't expect me to believe Garam over Roza. She's *afraid* of him. Roza, who's never been afraid of anything. He's lying to you."

Agnella grunted. "Forget Garam. You cannot let the Seller get a *permanenza* elixir. No one would ever be safe."

"What if he wants to heal people suffering from Lymbodia?" What if he would heal Roza?

"No, Bell. He wants to brainwash them."

"How do you know this?"

"That's how he's slowed down some of their symptoms. He's fused an elixir called mindmeld. He tricks their brains into thinking their body is well."

Bell furrowed her brow. "That's rather clever. It sounds useful."

"If he can force their brains to heal their bodies, what else can he force them to do, hmm?"

Maestro Carlo leaned forward. "Think of it, Bell. He creates sympathy for his cause, saying he'll use it for healing. As soon as he finds someone able to fuse *permanenza*, he can combine it with the mindmeld to use on whomever he wishes. His victims would be puppets, with no chance to escape."

"Are you sure Roza is involved? What if she's a puppet too?" Bell shook her head. "Why involve me? If you have proof of the Seller's plans, tell the rest of the Consiglio."

Maestro Carlo sat back. "We don't have the proof yet. We can't present speculation as fact. There is a certain order to things—"

"That's what Garam is looking for," Agnella said.

"What does Garam have to do with it?"

Agnella breathed deeply. "Roza *is* deeply involved, Bell. Garam has been observing her for months, searching for proof of the Seller's plans. He wasn't sure he could trust you either—"

Bell's anger erupted. "He's going to use Insidio on her to get this *proof*, isn't he? Will he even need to marry her afterward, or simply discard her once she's served her purpose? How is that different from what you're accusing the Seller of?"

"The Insidio isn't for Roza. It's for you."

Her blood turned to ice. "What?"

"We need you to find an antidote for the mindmeld, and to do that, you'll need to study its ingredients by fusing them."

Bell leapt to her feet. "This is—this is crazy. I can't fuse *Magia*. You know what happened the last time I did."

Agnella spread her hands. "My gift is fading in preparation of the Solstice. You are the singular scentmaker who has a chance at succeeding."

Bell stumbled back a step. Suddenly, she was a little girl again, staring at Roza's empty, misty blue eyes. "I'm—I'm not strong enough. I don't have the control. Find some way to manage the Seller. Make a deal. Surely there's something he wants."

"You don't know him, Bell." Agnella spoke forcefully. "He doesn't need to make a deal with us. If you go to him, he'll brainwash you."

"I've already made a deal with him. He'll keep his word. He uses Aronil. Everyone knows he doesn't lie."

"He manipulates. He omits certain truths," Agnella said sharply.

"And you don't?" Bell huffed. "If he can heal Lymbodia, we *should* bargain with him."

Agnella exchanged glances with Piccarda. "Even a cure like that isn't worth the price we'd have to pay."

Bell pressed her lips together as she studied each of them. She would pay *anything* to cure Roza. If they were in her shoes, they would say the same. Bell straightened her shoulders, cool determination filling her now. "You don't want him to create a cure because it would be out of your control." She lifted her chin. "The last time I fused Magia, I sentenced my sister to death. I cannot destroy her chance at living. I will help the Seller make a cure that *I* can control."

Agnella called her name as Bell walked toward the door, but she didn't look back.

The moon fought free as Bell slipped down Agnella's lane. The timid white light deepened the shadows, and she wished the clouds had kept it captive.

No one understood Roza like she did. No one knew the mischievous, adventurous girl she used to be. They'd spent so many hours climbing fruit trees together and sneaking tarts from the kitchen to eat later in bed. No matter how angry Roza was at her parents, surely she wouldn't willingly work against the Consiglio. Against her own people.

I will find a way to heal her.

A whistle sounded and the moonlight faded as a shadow spilled toward her from the tree line. She staggered back, her heart thundering like a fist trapped in her chest.

166

"It's me," Rian said. He wore his half mask and kohl around his eyes.

She clutched her chest. "You nearly scared me to death."

The moon sailed clear, and Rian stood close enough to touch. His teeth caught the moonlight. "The whistle was meant to politely alert you to my presence."

She straightened. "Send a note next time."

His fingers brushed her side as he took her hand. "Inviting you to a romantic tryst in Grenwood? I like the sound of that."

She jerked her hand away as her frustration boiled over. "Stop this. I'm not going to fall for you." Every movement he made was calculated to charm her. To get her to perform for him. And when he tired of her? He'd vanish into the shadows.

He half-smiled. "Are you sure?"

"Yes," she said tightly. "And I'm insulted that you keep trying. I know what you're doing. I appreciate your help so far, but I can't give you what you want, and you have nothing more to offer me, so *stop following me.*"

He took a step back. An awkward silence hung between them. He cleared his throat. "You're wrong, Bell. You have something I want, and I can still help you."

She turned away, hugging herself. The Seller was the only one who could help her now. She had to save her foolhardy sister and find a cure. Then she'd worry about protecting them all from the Medoros' scheming.

Gravel crunched under their feet as she moved toward the forest, and Rian followed her.

"I must be losing my touch," he muttered. He took the lead as they crossed the road and appeared to know her path as well as she did. Drat him.

"Rian, I've tried, but I can't do what you're asking with a scent cloud. What I need right now are the ingredients to this cure, this *mindmeld.* I need to see if it works for Lymbodia."

He was silent for a long moment. "You should try again."

Under the trees' canopy, she stopped and turned. "Are you going to hound me until I do?" In the dark, his figure was a swath of black and white that smelled of magic dust.

"Believe me or not, I have not been trying to *seduce* you so you'll do what I want. Bardia isn't safe for you. You need to be able to protect yourself better." His figure shifted. "But yes, I'm going to continue *hounding* you until I run out of time."

Her forehead furrowed. "Run out of time?"

"If you could try, Bell, please. You might not succeed until after you become Maestra of Scents, but I can't wait forever for you to fulfill your bargain." He stepped closer. "The Seller knows I'm planning something, and it will be too dangerous for me soon. I'll have to force your hand."

"Are you threatening me?" Her mouth dried as she cringed back. "You can't make me use my gift."

He cupped her cheek, his fingers soft as loam, and she froze. "You don't want to see me try," he said, his voice barely above a whisper.

Then he was gone, consumed by the shadows under the trees.

Twenty-Four

"**M**OTHER'S NOT GOING TO GIVE IN."
Roza pursed her full red lips in the full-length mirror.
"I won't step into their house." Bell sat on the edge of her bed, her back stiff.

Roza rolled her eyes. "Garam can't—"

"It's Piero. He admitted he destroyed my fioré."

Roza turned slowly. Her black velvet gown swirled with the slightest movement. "What?"

"He wants to be Maestro of Scents. But even if the Saint doesn't choose me, the Saint won't choose him."

Roza's face whitened. "That idiot came into your garden and ripped out your fioré because he wants to be Maestro—" She spun to the door, then lurched to a stop with a gasp, her hand clasped to her side. "Stay here. Drink tea in bed." Her voice sounded pinched.

"Roza?"

Roza dropped her hand and slammed the door. Moments after her footsteps faded, the carriage rattled out of the driveway.

Bell frowned and poured another cup of tea from the white pot on her bedside table. All these parties were worsening Roza's health. It was all a sham, anyway. Neither of them truly wanted to marry the other.

She carried her cup out to the balcony, studying her garden in the dusk. Mother was immoveable. Bell was banished to her room until she agreed to join Roza at her dinner parties. She was also under strict

169

supervision so she couldn't sneak out to the Bazaar. Not during daylight, anyway.

She tipped her teacup until lukewarm liquid splattered on the gravel path below.

Rian. How would he *force her hand*?

Her hand drifted to her wrist bag where the glass sphere rested. She'd promised herself she wouldn't fall for him. So why did her cheek still burn with the memory of his touch, as if he'd left remnants of himself behind?

The sunset was raging orange when a knock came at the door.

"Come in," Bell called from the balcony.

Elena stepped in, carrying a potted Aronil in full bloom.

Suspicion reared. "Where did you get that?"

"Delivery just now, miss." She handed Bell an envelope engraved with a graceful *M*, the Medoro sigil. Bell's fingers tightened, crumpling the fine paper. "At least open it, miss."

She narrowed her eyes at Elena's guileless face. Perhaps it wasn't a forced apology from Piero. She opened it.

Dear Bell,

Wishing you a clear mind.

Yours, Aless

She took the plant carefully. "Hmm. It's from Alessander."

"Ah."

"He feels sorry for me, no doubt."

"No doubt."

Bell scowled. "We're not getting married."

170

Elena grinned. "No, miss." She dipped her head and moved to step out.

"Elena."

The maid paused, half facing her. "Yes, miss?"

Bell nestled the Aronil into the raised bed by the window.

"The Seller might be manipulating people into thinking he has a cure," Bell said finally. "I want it to be real, Elena. I need to be certain it is before I fuse *permanenza* for him."

Elena's face clouded with disappointment, but she nodded.

Night fell over the garden like a blanket, bringing a desire to work. If the Seller had created a cure, Bell had to try to recreate it.

She slipped down the trellis and into her workshop. Her own garden's shadows grated against her skin, and she was relieved to be sealed within the vine. She pulled on her gloves and opened the package of Magia. Her usual fear of the second-level fioré was dampened by the thought of Roza, healed. The dried fioré weren't as potent as the living, but she still held her breath while she studied them. Insidio deceived the mind. Taiga created pain. Smemor induced forgetfulness. She touched the pointed gray petals of the Smemor and shuddered.

Bell shoved the package away. She had to try the other fioré again first.

She started with the Aronil fioré she'd plucked from her new plant. She combined it with different measures of Sciver and Princess Seed, releasing her gift to race hot along her arms. She ended with a vial of deep green elixir that should make secrets burn on the victim's tongue. She lifted the vial and stared at the scent cloud floating above it. It wasn't anything close to what she wanted, but it could be useful.

She needed someone to test it on. With a bitter little twist to her lips, she wished for Rian to appear.

She tucked the vial into her pocket and left her workshop. She moved across the garden and climbed up the trellis, weaving her way between roses. The air was heavy with pent-up rain. On her balcony, she leaned against the rail, rolling the vial between her hands. She needed to study the Seller's cure in person so she could stop guessing.

Clouds filtered the stars, sickening the yellow moon. She straightened and turned as a hand clamped over her mouth, and she gasped and jerked. Her eyes met Rian's.

"It's me." His words hardly lessened her terror, but she pulled her nails out of his arm and he let go. "I needed you not to scream."

She hugged herself and looked at him warily. "If you don't leave now, I'll scream anyway." Her voice shook.

"What's the matter?" he asked. The half-moon barely revealed his rueful smile as he rubbed his arm.

"The last time I saw you, you threatened me. Now you show up in the dead of night like nothing happened."

He looked down and shifted his weight, looking sheepish.

"Go away." Bell took a couple steps around him toward her balcony door.

"I've been thinking more about what you said. About the mind-meld ingredients."

She paused. Hope gave a little kick inside her. "And?"

"If I get them for you, will you promise one thing?

"Maybe," Bell said slowly.

He took a deep breath. "You can't go to the Seller to fuse *permanenza*. He won't let you leave until you've done everything he asks, and believe me, you won't like what he asks."

She frowned at him. "Even if I have the ingredients, I don't know how to make the cure. I might still have to bargain with the Seller."

"Trust me in this."

She shook her head. "I need to know if the cure is genuine. If it's real but it needs *permanenza* to keep working, I'll have no choice..."

"The cure is authentic, Bell." This straightforward tone sounded strange in his crushed velvet voice.

Bell stared up at him. Hope swelled in her chest—and gave way to suspicion. She slipped her hand into the pocket with the vial, twisting off the cork as she spoke to cover her movements. "You're sure?"

"It works for a time. The illness comes back, sometimes worse. But healing isn't his main purpose—"

She took his hand and slid her fingers to his wrist. He stood utterly still, looking at her touching him. "What do these marks mean?" she asked, sliding his sleeve back to show the coiling vines.

He sucked in a breath at as her fingers moved along the vines. "They—"

She pressed the upturned vial to his bared wrist, where it would reach his veins quickly.

He yanked his hand away. "What was that?" His voice was sharp and angry, like its cover had been torn off.

"Is the cure real?" She stepped back from him and capped the vial. She'd made the elixir potent enough that he would be feeling the pressure in his mind to speak truth.

He looked thoughtful. "A truthtelling elixir? Very clever. Did you fuse it for me? Because I find that rather sexy, the thought of you thinking—"

She scoffed. "Tell me the cure is real again, so I can believe you."

"You know I could simply refuse to speak."

She held his gaze. "I don't think you will."

"Because I want you to trust me." He stepped closer to her. "I *need* you to trust me. Your trust is important to me. *You* are—" His throat bobbed.

"Then why would you threaten me?" Her voice grew small. "Were you bluffing?"

All the humor went out of his expression. His mouth opened, the moon revealing his struggle to decide which truth to share. "The cure is genuine, and I would never hurt you, Bell, but I need a way off this island."

With all her mental strength, Bell shoved her deep curiosity about his feelings away, away, away. She didn't care about what he thought of her. She needed facts. "What do you mean, a way off this island? What do you need a scent cloud for?"

"I think the scent cloud would keep us safe as we pass over the *attuale* current. I need you to help me escape to the mainland."

She stared at him. "You—you *think* it would keep us safe? You want *me* to—"

"We have to escape. Otherwise, I'll have no choice but—" His throat convulsed as he forced his mouth closed.

Bell tilted her head, watching him struggle to hold back words. "What are you trying not to say?"

"Nothing," he gasped.

He took a breath, then froze; his gaze locked on the door to her bedroom. He crouched, pulling her down beside him, and she followed his gaze. A glow gem flared in the bedroom, its blue light seen clearly through the glass door.

"Be very still," he whispered.

The glow gem lifted higher, revealing Roza's face. She scanned the room, staring at the undisturbed bed for a long moment. She stepped toward the balcony, lips pursed in the blue light. Finally, she turned and glided slowly out into the hall, her silk bathrobe flowing behind her.

Rian didn't move until the light was gone from under the door.

"Why did we hide from her?" Bell whispered. Part of her wanted to run in and drag Roza out so she could meet Rian. Maybe Roza would help them. Bell was trying to get the cure for her, after all.

"We can't trust her." His eyes barely glinted in the dim moonlight. "Remember the first time we met? By the fountain?"

As if she could forget that shadowy feeling of meeting a Spy. "Yes."

"Roza brought you in there planning to take you to the Sotto. She was going to trick you into meeting with the Seller of Secrets. He had promised to give her something if she got you to come to him and fuse *permanenza*. She made a bargain with him, Bell. I sent you after Garam instead, hoping you would uncover the truth about her."

Bell gripped the railing and looked down at the shadows of her garden. A phantom breeze stirred, bringing a steadying breath of rose and mulch. "You expect me to believe Roza was going to…to betray me to him?" But the words sounded hollow. Right now, Rian had to speak truth. Phrases Roza had muttered returned, her growing frustration with Bell. *She spends a lot of time in the Sotto.*

No. Bell couldn't believe it of her sister. Roza was under some kind of elixir. Deceived and manipulated into doing the Seller's work.

Rian grimaced. "The Seller ordered all of us to convince you to work for him. It was…a competition. We each desire something desperately." He swallowed. "If you can't help me escape the island, I will have no choice but to return—trick you into joining the Seller—" He gritted his teeth. "I hate this."

She arched an eyebrow. "What, telling the truth?"

"It's like dragging a cart without wheels. No subtlety, no art." He narrowed his eyes. "When will this elixir wear off?"

Bell stood up. "Even if I must give the Seller *permanenza*, I have to save Roza." Her voice broke at her sister's name. He was silent so long, she almost reached out and touched him. "Rian, you don't understand. It's my fault Roza is…" Bell bit her lip. "She's sick. She can't have much time left."

Rian looked up at her, his eyes white in the moonlight. "The Seller wants to rule Bardia using the mindmeld, and he can't do it without you. If you give him *permanenza*, you give him Bardia. Be certain you bargain for something of equal value."

Twenty-Five

BELL PRESSED HER FACE INTO HER HANDS. Was Roza ever going to warn her about the Seller's plans, or was Roza willing to trade Bell and Bardia's freedom for the cure? Didn't Roza know Bell wanted to help her?

They could have bargained with the Seller together.

They still could.

"I'll find a way to get the cure without giving him power over Bardia."

"Not possible," Rian said.

She scowled. "What should I do then, Rian?" He flinched at his name, half turned away. "Let her die?"

"Yes." The word came quickly and without hesitation, but the shape of his shoulders under the moonlight suddenly looked vulnerable.

She gaped at him.

He made a pained sound, as if the words scalded his mouth. "My mother is dead because of him. If you give him this power, everyone you love will suffer."

"Your mother? You never told me this."

"I don't tell anyone about it. I'm telling you now so you don't make the same mistake she did."

"What mistake?" She hugged her arms against her waist. It felt like her heart would rip in two, half held by Rian and the other by Roza.

He stepped closer, longing in every line of his body. She knew he wanted to reach out and pull her to him, take her away. Make her safe. "She trusted him. It cost her life, and I suffer for it."

She closed her eyes. "I can't let her die." She breathed out slowly, a decision cooling in her chest. "I won't let that happen," she whispered. She moved to the balcony door.

When he spoke again, his voice sounded worn thin. "The other Spy, Arabia, tried to poison Roza. She was trying to eliminate the competition."

Bell gripped the doorknob, a chill of fear racing through her. She took one shaky breath, then another.

"Arabia will do anything to gain a favor from the Seller." He spoke quickly, his gaze distant as the night sky. "Be careful of her, Bell." He turned and melted over the balcony railing.

She stared out into the night, blinking stinging eyes. Not a shadow appeared out of place. The Spy had vanished. Emptiness and confusion wound around her mind like the roots of weeds.

It was time to demand the truth from Roza.

Bell crept down the hall until she reached Roza's door. The rumpled bed inside disguised any sleeping shape. A shadow shifted by the window, and Bell froze. Roza's hair gleamed as she stepped into the moonlight.

"Where were you? Sneaking out again, little sister?"

Bell hesitated. The weight of everything pressed down upon her. "Roza." Her name held so much disappointment that Roza tilted her head curiously. "Are you working for the Seller?"

Roza jutted her chin. "Who told you that?"

Bell glanced past her through the window, out into the starry night.

Roza took a deep, furious breath. "You understand nothing."

"You bargained with the Seller, didn't you? You want him to cure you." Bell looked up earnestly and stepped forward. "I can help you. You don't need to deal with him alone."

"His cure works, Bell. It's kept me alive for years, but it loses effectiveness with each dose. Now it only lasts two days. He needs a scent-maker like you to fuse *permanenza*." Roza moved to meet her in the middle of the room, her gaze dark with hope. "Fuse it, and I will live."

"Why didn't you tell me all of this?" Bell's voice broke. "What kind of bargain did you have to make?"

"I did ask. I was afraid if I told you the truth, you would…" Roza hugged herself, looking cold. Bell moved forward and wrapped her arms around her sister. Bell could feel Roza's ribs through her skin.

"I'll help you," Bell whispered. "I'll go to the Seller. I'll try to fuse *permanenza*. But not for him. For you." Somehow, she would uncover the ingredients for mindmeld on her own, without Rian's help.

Roza met Bell's gaze, relief making her white face glow. She spun to her wardrobe and flung a narrow dress the color of nectarines across the bed. A smile curved her lips. "Let's leave now."

Bell hesitated at the head of the wine cellar stairs.

"Come on." Roza's sharp voice and a purple glow gem in her hand pierced the darkness.

Bell stepped carefully after her, the cool cellar air shuddering over her cloaked arms. "I thought we'd go through the Bazaar."

"This is faster."

When Bell reached the bottom, Roza turned to go on. The wine barrels and cabinets filled one side of the small, cave-like room. Unease twisted inside Bell as Roza rolled aside an empty barrel and pressed the glow gem to a barely visible dent in the rock. The rocks rumbled aside, leaving just enough room for them to squeeze through.

"Has this always been here?"

Roza had already stepped down into the polished tiled tunnel, her posture taut as she waited. As soon as Bell followed, Roza blew on a glow gem along the wall and a line of them lit up out of sight, glowing off black tiles. A narrow border of amaranth tiles trailed the gems, the ceramic carved with vines.

"The Vasari Corridor. All the noble houses connect to it. He told me where it was, and I opened it from this side."

Bell jogged to keep up. "I thought the Vasari Corridor collapsed during the Primo Terremoto."

"He lets them think that."

"But the Vasari Corridor was built by the first Pater Medoro, centuries ago...."

"And his stall is built beneath House Medoro. Try to keep up." Her heels echoed down the passage.

Rian had to know about this. Would he try to find her here, warn her one last time? She shrugged off a wish that he would. "Do the Seller's spies use these tunnels?"

Roza glanced back, her face milky in the blue light. "Rian didn't make this one, if that's what you're asking."

Bell flinched.

Roza's smile died. "I told you not to fall for him. I *warned* you."

"I didn't—I didn't mean to." Bell huffed. "I chose you over him, if you that's what you're worried about."

Roza shook her head, pulling a hard caramel from her pocket. "His full name is Florian, you know. He takes the truth and—" She twisted her hands, using the motion to unwrap the candy, and popped it in her mouth. "The Seller isn't trying to brainwash Bardia. I'm sure Rian told you he was, but he doesn't know the truth."

Bell narrowed her gaze. In her pocket, she touched the truthtelling elixir. She wished she could get close enough to Roza to use it without her noticing. But what if the Seller had brainwashed Roza already? The elixir forced her to speak what she *believed* was true.

"Nothing to say?"

Bell was silent.

"He cut your gloves so you'd need new ones. Clever, wasn't it?"

Bell frowned. The damp, underground air was suffusing her brain. A headache crept toward her temples.

Roza clicked her tongue. "If you weren't gifted, I would have left you out of this. So would Rian. He wasn't stalking you because you're pretty, Bell." She sobered, reaching out a hand to touch Bell's shoulder. "He doesn't want *you*, Bell. Rian already has a lover, and she's nothing like you."

179

Twenty-Six

BELL CLIMBED THE LAST STAIRCASE IN SIlence with Roza's words echoing in her head. *She's nothing like you.* Humiliation crawled in her stomach, burning across her skin. His starry-sky eyes mocked her now. The scorn filling her body was stronger because she'd known he would be like this. She'd been *warned*.

Held up against that, her own feelings stood out, stark and mortifying.

They followed a curving corridor with doors on the left. Carved into the wood of each was a design that shifted as they passed. One bore an Insidio blossom whose petals stretched wider as Bell stared at it.

Roza rapped at a door carved with a closed hand that opened to reveal a cylindrical vial. "Come in," a muffled voice said.

Bell took a shuddering breath as they entered a round glass-ceilinged chamber. Countless scents swarmed her senses. The clouds had moved on and stars hung thick, almost bright enough to outshine the reflected lamplight. They'd reached the surface? She'd never seen stars so bright. It felt like another world, and the rest of the room did nothing to lessen that feeling.

The dome's thick glass panes sparkled like an enormous diamond. Waist-high fioré beds circled the room in half rings, leaving raised wooden walkways between. Several walkways hung by ropes above their heads, dark vines streaming between them.

A vine brushed her neck as they crossed a walkway, but Roza

yanked her away from its touch. In that brief moment, she'd felt the whole vine as one, watchful and malevolent. Was this the Seller's version of a weaving vine?

A dusky-skinned man sat at a worktable in the center. A silver pen in his elegant fingers rested on an open book. An amaranth mask was molded to the top half of his face. A pencil beard framed sculpted lips. Leather-bound books were piled on the worktable, and hundreds more shelved beneath it. Were they journals?

"Welcome to my Conservatory." The Seller's dark eyes glimmered.

Bell pushed aside the scents crowding her mind and stepped into the center. To the right, two wooden doors nestled between fioré tables, an Insidio blossom inscribed on one and swirling black water on the other.

A woman stepped up beside the Seller, her long black cloak showing flashes of leather-clad legs. A banner of hair hung down her back, its candy red obscene next to the amaranth of her mask. Her perfect red lips twisted in a sneer. "So, you've finally brought her."

The Seller stood and braced his fingers on the desk. His exquisitely tailored charcoal suit had white gems sewn along every hem, sparkling whenever he shifted. A wide dark window loomed behind him. "Excellent. Well done, Roza. Thank you so much for coming, Bell. I've been searching for someone like you for years."

The masked woman's hair glowed when she turned to face him. "You can't let Roza take all the credit—"

"You tried to poison me." Roza bit off her words. "You could have killed Bell." Arabia snarled, closing the distance between them and filling it with heat. They glared, faces inches apart—Midsummer and Midwinter striving for preeminence. Bell reached to pull Roza back, and the heat emanating from Arabia made her jerk.

"Arabia, if you use your gift in here without permission, I will cut off one of your hands," the Seller said pleasantly.

A firemaker. No one else could exude such heat and survive. Arabia edged back a few inches, tendrils of smoke curling around her hands.

Bell's fists clenched. Rian's warning about Arabia sparked unease deep within her. She stared at the Seller. "She almost killed Elena."

"But I didn't," Arabia said.

He half frowned, leaning forward. "I apologize. I did not know the lengths they would go to get your attention."

Bell stared at him. His eyes dared her to question him further. She crossed her arms. "I won't fuse anything for you until I can see for myself that the mindmeld cure is real." If she could get him to demonstrate it, she'd have an idea what it was made of.

The Seller looked at her evenly. The silence stretched out like a living thing. Bell glanced away first. "I expected no less. No doubt all your allies have been warning you of my supposed motives." The Seller closed the book and crossed his charcoal-clad legs. "I am not a good man, but I am a fair one. Make me an offer. I will give you anything for *permanenza*."

Bell swallowed. "I haven't fused the *permanenza* elixir yet."

"She's afraid of the Magia." Roza inspected her fingernails.

"I approve. The Magia are not toys. But Bell, your mentor refuses to teach you about Magia?"

"Agnella said you gave Magia to Roza in order to test me as a child," Bell blurted. "Did you?"

The Seller laughed. "Agnella will say anything to keep you away from me." His gaze slid to Roza. "Your sister is dying. Will you not fuse Magia for her?" Bell hesitated. The Seller's teeth gleamed in a smile as he stood beside Roza. "I have been giving dear Roza my cure for years, ever since she first contracted the disease. She takes a dose every few days now. The more one uses it, the less effective it is. With *permanenza*, she will be healed permanently." He touched Roza's shoulder gently, and she leaned toward him almost imperceptibly. "You need not fear Magia," he said to Bell. "I will guide you. I know Magia much better than Agnella."

Bell turned to Roza. "After you are healed, will you still marry Garam?"

Roza crossed her arms, which she usually did to intimidate, but this time she looked smaller.

The Seller smiled. "My dear, when you have shown Bardia what a *permanenza* elixir can do, your sister's marriage will not matter anymore. You will be the most powerful Maestra of Scents in history—you can do what you like with Garam."

"I—" Bell glanced over at Arabia, who leaned against a fioré bench, scorn lining her body like the cloak.

"I will give you time to think about it." The Seller motioned toward the door. "Roza, take her to her room."

"My room?" Dread crept into Bell's stomach.

"Oh, and one more thing." The Seller's mouth tightened. "If Florian manages to find his way in here, I would advise against listening to him. He has turned against me and wishes to set himself up as his own Seller of Secrets. He will soon try to cast me from my sanctuary. With you at his side, under his control, he would be challenging to stop." The Seller clapped his hands and two Lanzis emerged from dark corners.

Bell spun to face them. "No."

"It is late. You must rest now so you can work tomorrow."

Roza touched her arm. "Come on."

"Escort her to the Gold Room, Roza. We will begin in the morning." The Seller picked up his pen. Roza tugged her away and the Lanzis fell in step behind them.

Bell jerked away from Roza. "No, no. I came here willingly. I won't be a prisoner."

The Seller sighed. "I always hoped you would see reason and join me. I would much prefer your willing help, but time is running out. You will be free to leave after you fuse *permanenza* for me, not a moment sooner."

"This isn't fair. I haven't agreed to the bargain yet," Bell shouted as Roza pulled her into the hall and the Lanzis followed.

"Don't be dramatic, Bell," Roza said.

Bell shook her off. "You knew this would happen," Bell hissed. *Rian knew this would happen, but at least he warned me.*

"I knew nothing of the sort," Roza said haughtily. Bell didn't have to use her truthtelling elixir to know she was lying.

Twenty-Seven

"AT LEAST LET ME SEND FATHER A NOTE," Bell said as she was ushered into the Gold Room.

"Give me your hand." Roza held out a pin.

"Why?" Bell stepped back but Roza followed swiftly.

"Do you want me to die?" Roza pleaded. "I have to do what he asks. His cure keeps me alive."

Bell lifted her hand slowly. Roza pricked her finger and squeezed a few drops of blood into a glass flask. "Trust me. This will help both of us."

Bell followed Roza to the door. Stone-faced Lanzis stood outside. "I can't stay here like this."

"You have no choice. Florian could get to you too easily anywhere else. Don't think he'll ask your opinion before he drags you away." Roza's voice faded as the latch clicked.

"Roza!"

Her voice came through the door, imperious. "Two of you watch her door at all times. Florian has turned against us. And don't let Piero anywhere near her."

Piero was here? Was he part of this plot? Sucking her pricked finger, Bell brushed her other hand along the round walls. Under different circumstances, so many shades of yellow and warm brown would have soothed her. Bardian limewood covered both the floor and walls, which were mostly hidden by rugs and tapestries.

Bardian limewood resisted instruments. Even if stone lay behind it, Rian couldn't get through to her.

She growled and covered her face. Even if he could, she couldn't go with him. She scrubbed her cheeks as if she could erase every word he'd ever spoken, every warm touch of his fingers, every glimmer of his eyes.

This was about Roza, not Rian.

She sank onto the wide, low bed. Roza was born mischievous. Sometimes dangerously rebellious, but beneath the rebellion was a passion for life that made something soar inside Bell. Roza was wild and free, and the thought of her wasting away with Lymbodia was like a doorway to emptiness.

She could not fall through that door.

And Rian…she had known all this time he was using her. The Seller was manipulating her too, but at least a true cure lay at the end of his game.

She hoped.

Exhaustion clamped her eyes closed. She curled up on the bed and kicked off her slippers.

"Time to go, Bell."

The words sounded far away. Bell opened her eyes to light through windows Roza had uncovered. They'd been hidden behind heavy brocade curtains last night. Somber rain clouds buried the sun.

Bell groaned and rubbed her face as Roza turned on the bathwater. The thought of hot water pulled Bell from bed.

She padded to the windows and gasped. Santa Maria Novella sprawled far below, House Medoro reduced to a cottage by distance. The dim sky darkened the House's stern face. She knew where she was. "The old tower. I thought it wasn't safe."

"He lets everyone believe that." Roza stepped beside her as the

Medoro carriage swept out of the lane, small as a fingertip. "Don't worry, no one can see us. The glass is one-sided."

"How can he keep this a secret?" *I used to think the Seller was buried in the Sotto. I thought I'd be safe if I stayed away. He can see so much from here.*

"Few of us may go beyond his sanctuary. Come on, your bath is ready."

Bell followed her to the washroom, watching her sister as she laid out a towel and salts. How had she become one of the Seller's few?

"How did you get here, Roza? Why are you with the Seller, helping him?"

Roza swished her hand through the water. "He promised to cure me. He spent years researching and studying Lymbodia, perfecting his cure. He's done more for me than 'House Asbury.'"

Bell flinched at her mocking tone.

Roza gave Bell a patient look. "Oh, Bell. I know you've always tried." She slung water off her hands. "Hurry. He'll be waiting."

Bell sank into the water as Roza let the door close after her. The heaviness of her situation made her want to slide beneath the surface and wash it all away.

After Roza called impatiently for her to hurry up, Bell finally dragged herself out. She dressed in a chemise, then Roza showed her the wardrobe of yellow dresses the Seller had provided. Every shade of yellow she'd ever seen—and some she hadn't. Bell couldn't meet Roza's gaze. "Why does he have these?"

Roza smiled. "You're predictable. And he likes to prepare for everything."

Bell put on a soft dress the color of dandelions with white embroidery covering the skirt. They left the room to walk down the spiral hallway with the Lanzis following silently. At every branching hallway, Bell tried to get her bearings, but everything was the same smooth, polished stone. Finally, Roza opened a door to reveal the Conservatory. The glass roof glittered in sunlight, and the fioré were splashes of color open to its warmth. The Seller waited at his table, and beyond him the distant Inchio Sea rolled in shades of indigo.

186

He smiled as her eyes widened. "This tower was meant to watch for ships from the mainland, you know." He walked with her to the window.

"It's so blue," Bell murmured.

"Beautiful, is it not? Do you see the darker line in the middle distance?"

"The *attuale* current?"

"Yes," he murmured. His face clouded. "Our prison and our source of power."

She looked at him. "Rian also thinks the island is a prison."

His gaze cut her, and she caught her breath. He spun to face the room. "Have you had time to think of my offer? Still of a mind to cure your sister?" He smiled as if he'd asked about fixing breakfast.

Bell narrowed her gaze. "Keeping me here has done nothing to improve my mood."

"No matter." He clapped his hands, and a waiting servant bustled over with a tray. "Have a pastry, and we will begin with cloud sensing."

"Cloud sensing?" The scents in the room were overwhelming, but she was starving, so she chose a chocolate cannolo and took a bite.

"If you are to fuse *permanenza*, you must learn more about Magia."

Bell glanced at the rows of dark-colored blossoms growing behind his desk. Working with Magia made fear tremble in her chest, but who else would dare teach her? She nodded.

"You see the clouds above elixirs?"

"Of course."

"I can teach you to control them."

She shook her head slowly. "I've tried to move them. I can't." Could the Seller teach her the technique to create the scent cloud Rian wanted?

"That is because you have not been taught." He gathered an Aronil bouquet and handed it to her with a vial. "Fuse this."

Her fingers formed a fusing position on their own. Her worries faded away. The Seller's gaze prickled her neck, but she looked away and

187

let her gift flow. The heat trickled down her wrists, the warm glow of *attuale* lingering after the silver drops had slid into the vial.

He took the resulting vial of truthtelling and dabbed some on his wrist. What was he trying to prove? "Extraordinary. Your gift shows perfect control of the Aronil." He met her gaze. "I want to make Bardia a better place." He held out the vial.

"Do you see the cloud?"

Aronil's glimmering white circle floated above the vial. "Yes."

He lifted a flat black stone from the bench behind him. It glowed dimly at his touch. "Do you know what this is?"

"A…black glow gem?"

"A scentstone. The last one in Bardia." He handed it to her. "Fuse it like you would a bouquet, and it will make tangible any scent cloud."

The stone nestled in her palm, filling most of her hand. At a touch of her gift, a blast of brilliant color made her stagger. She covered her eyes and let the stone clatter onto the bench. The tints dimmed but still blazed beyond her eyelids, as if the sun had turned to rainbow and descended through the glass ceiling.

"I said to fuse it, not draw the life from it."

She heard him pick up the stone, and the brightness faded.

"Open your eyes."

Vivid clouds floated all around the room. Through her eyelashes, she picked out individual colored shapes around each fioré. They pulsed, as if waiting for her to fuse them.

"Now, which of these can you feel? Reach toward them with your gift." He motioned toward a tray holding five open vials on the bench.

Bell hesitated, then stepped closer and let her gift out through her fingers. The row of clouds rippled like a stick had been drawn through water. "All of them."

He nodded. "Marvelous. Few scentmakers can touch them all without extensive training."

Bell glanced around the color-filled room. Did he know she could see the clouds above the unfused fioré? "I've never heard of a scentstone before."

"I did not expect the Maestra of Scents would have taught you of it." His velvety voice turned rough.

She squared her shoulders. Why would Agnella have kept this from her if she wanted Bell to be the new Maestra? "What am I supposed to do with the clouds?" The kaleidoscope around the room almost drowned the complicated rainbow above the tray.

"Focus on them, like you do when you fuse." He spread his fingers, and the leaf-shaped haze above the green Myrtle Leaf vial gathered into a rough mimic of his hand. He waved his fingers, and the cloud copied the movements.

She reached for the brash azure blossom-shaped cloud above the Hertes vial. She tried to feel the cloud between her fingers and make it gather into a shape. The cloud rippled like it had before. Her heart surged but nothing else happened.

"You must try harder," the Seller said.

She tightened her lips. Five tries later, she'd managed to repeat the flicker. It was like trying to shape water with a thin stick.

"Let go of yourself. Let your gift take you."

Unease stirred. Where would it take her if she let go?

She gritted her teeth and tried again. The ripple did not change.

"Disappointing." The Seller stalked over the walkway toward the door into the hall. "You will never save your sister if you do not try harder."

"I *am* trying, but I don't know what I'm trying to do. Why do I need to move the clouds, anyway?"

"I will explain when you need to know."

She glared at his back.

"When you can create a hand, I will have lunch sent in." The door slammed shut.

Bell stared at the door for a long moment. He'd left her alone? She dashed to the worktable, her fingers trembling with urgency as she shifted through the open leather-bound journals on its top. She scanned page after page of elegant handwriting. All she found were diagrams and descriptions of Magia and their growth. Empty vials lined the back of the desk. She rifled through the shelved journals, looking behind them for hidden compartments. A locked drawer beneath the worktable clattered when she shook it.

She slumped against the worktable. It seemed foolish now to think he would keep his mindmeld cure out in the open where she could find it.

Her frustrated gaze caught on a Jonga Lily as big as her head. How had he grown it so large? She reached for it, then drew back.

If she could control the clouds, she shouldn't need to touch the fioré to move them. Was this unique to scentmaking? If it was, scentmakers would have a huge advantage over other makers.

"Perhaps that's why Agnella never taught me," Bell murmured. Despite her best efforts, the fioré cloud shapes only jostled together when she stepped closer. The fused clouds seemed pale in comparison. Extending her gift through her hands, she grasped the Jonga Lily's topaz cloud. It swarmed toward her. She clenched her hand, and the cloud contracted to a tiny ball.

Twenty-Eight

BELL STARED, TRYING TO BREATHE EASILY. *Was this what Agnella had meant when she said growing things know me as their own?*

Regret spread roots in the back of her mind. Perhaps Agnella would have taught her this when Bell was ready.

She firmed her lips and turned back to the vials. He'd said to shape these clouds, and he didn't need to know she could do more.

By midafternoon, the sun beat through the glass, and drops of sweat trailed down her back. The door opened and Bell jumped, losing the tenuous hand shape she'd made of the Hertes.

The Seller moved toward her. "Good, some progress."

"I'm—I'm doing the best I can."

"Indeed." He squeezed her shoulder, and she tensed. "I was harsh with you before. I merely wanted to motivate you to use your whole gift. It grows stronger the more you give of yourself."

He sounded kind, as though he genuinely wanted to help. She smoothed back a strand of damp hair, unsure what to say. When she looked up, he was studying her.

"The scentstone will remain linked to you as long as it is in the room. If you let it rest too long, you will need to pour your gift into it again. Soon you'll start on the *permanenza* elixir."

She tensed, ready to demand she see the cure at work first. A Lanzi materialized and bent to whisper in the Seller's ear. The Seller gestured sharply for him to leave, then stared out at the sea for a long moment.

"Perhaps this evening. You have worked hard. You must return to your room for some rest." With his hand on her back, he pushed her across the walkway and into the hall where Lanzis took her elbows.

"But I'd rather—"

Without a word, the Seller turned and walked the other way. The Lanzis tugged her along. Where was he going? His stall must be deep below, or perhaps further along the Vasari Corridor. What other things did he have hidden in this tower? When she tried to look back, the hands on her elbows tightened.

Windows lined the stairwell, and far below she glimpsed a darkhaired man stepping out of House Medoro. Did Garam realize she was gone yet? She hadn't seen Roza since the morning. Had she gone back to their parents? What would she tell them?

Bell sighed when the Lanzis shut her inside her room.

Nothing was going according to plan, and she was no closer to getting hold of the mindmeld's ingredients.

A scratching sound woke Bell to a dark room. She'd eaten a tray of cold meats and cheeses left on her bedside table. With nothing else to do until the Seller called for her, she'd laid on the bed until sleepiness overcame her. She blew on the glow lamp by the bed, then sat up and swung her legs down as dust speckled the rug across the room.

Slowly, tiny letters scrawled *Bell?* into the wall.

Bell yanked her hand back, fingers stinging from the letters burned into the wood. Had Rian found a way to get through Bardian wood?

It's C

That would explain it. She suppressed a giddy sound. Of course, Carasti would work with Rian. She probably sought him out as soon as Bell went missing.

Get you out

Her giddiness faded. Rian had to be back there with Carasti.

She stared at the wall, but no more letters came. Voices sounded far down the hall. She brushed the dust beneath the rug and tried to move the dresser to cover the letters. Footsteps came closer. The dresser grated on the floor, nearly tipping as the corner caught the rug.

"Miss?" A Lanzi's low voice at the door.

She grabbed the bottom frame and dragged it. The door swung open, and she straightened.

The Lanzi frowned at the dresser, his eyebrows furrowed into one.

Bell peeked back. The letters were covered. "I like it better here."

He grunted. "You have a visitor."

Arabia swayed into the room, her irises black against the amaranth mask conforming to her upper face like skin.

"You may leave us, Lanzi."

Bell forced her mouth closed before she could beg him to stay. The door shut, leaving them in dimness.

"It's dark, isn't it?" Arabia flung out her hands and flame erupted, heat searing Bell's forehead. She staggered back, catching her side on the dresser.

Arabia's white teeth stretched in a smile. The flames left her hands and flew to the oil lamps beside the door at a flick of her fingers.

"What do you want?"

"Dropped in to say hello." Her voice was light as if they were meeting at a party. "When the Seller told us to befriend you, I didn't bother." Arabia paced a half circle, looking Bell up and down. "How such a...simple little thing could attract anyone's attention is beyond my ken." Arabia stroked her chin. "This isn't the first time Rian has run off to chase someone else. He's hard to tame, but make no mistake, he always comes back to me."

Bell summoned every bit of pride and loathing her soul contained. "I don't care what Rian does."

Arabia twisted her lips and stepped closer. "I want to make it very clear. He doesn't care about you. Actually, he's the one who told me which room was Roza's so I could plant the poison."

Bell's nails bit into her palms. "If you *ever* threaten her again—"

Arabia laughed. "What will you do, exactly? It's all part of the game. Even now, Rian is trying to reach you, to keep the game going a little longer. Nothing stops him when he wants to win. He'll take you away and use you, then bring you back before the Seller gets too angry. Remember, little scentmaker, he's *mine*. I'm the one who knows he can only sleep sitting up, that his favorite thing is to wind his fingers through my hair while he—"

"Enough. You deserve each other."

Arabia shook her fingers free of her own brilliant locks and grinned. "Oh yes, we do." She knocked on the door. "Remember that when he makes his next move." Her grin dropped as she stepped backward into the hall. *He's mine*, she mouthed.

The door slammed shut. Bell waited for the footsteps to fade, then spun to the dresser and shuffled it aside, tracing her fingers over the letters. Carasti had been *here*, on the other side of the wall. She knocked gently on the wood.

Silence.

Either the Lanzis had chased Carasti and Rian out of the tunnels, or they'd given up on freeing Bell tonight.

Dejected, Bell snuffed out her lamps and climbed into bed. Arabia's flame burned behind her eyelids. If Arabia was telling the truth, could she even trust Rian to free her?

She'd never felt so alone.

Twenty-Nine

THE NEXT MORNING, ROZA DIDN'T AP-
pear. A maid brought her breakfast and then lunch, murmuring something noncommittal when Bell asked about her
sister. Bell picked at the food and stood in front of the window, looking
for anything to still the tension within her. Where was Rian? Was he
still roaming the tunnels? And what about Carasti?

The sky was heavy with clouds. Finally, some hours after lunch,
Lanzis came and escorted her to the Conservatory where the Seller
waited at his desk, rolling a pen between his manicured fingers. "Did
you rest well, my dear?"

Bell regarded him warily. His eyes seemed weary, his eyelids baggy.
Did he know about the writing on her wall?

"Florian has been trying to reach you."

She said nothing. Her mouth felt like dry soil would spill if she
opened it.

"He broke through one of the tunnels during the night. My Lanzis
lost sight of him, which is why I sent you to your room. He cannot
break through there."

Bell shivered. Would Rian have tried yesterday if the Lanzi hadn't
knocked? "How did he get in? Weren't they watching for him?"

His expression flattened, then regained his usual assured mask. "He
has built many tunnels over his years here, and my Lanzis can't keep
track of them all."

His words held a hint of carelessness, snagging Bell's attention. A

195

thread of pride made a smile play at her lips, but she pushed it away. "If he tries to take me, I won't go with him. He doesn't have what I need." *And I've already given him too much.*

The Seller smiled slowly and walked to the windows facing the sea before resting one hand on the wide wooden frame. "Good. But we will not let him close enough to try. My Lanzis worked all night blocking off all the tunnels again."

"Good." Bell's voice sounded stronger than she expected. She followed him but stood on the other side of the window.

The Seller didn't seem to hear. The dimming light from the overcast sky made his mask look damp. "He is jealous of my power. He sincerely believes I will use mindmeld to brainwash Bardians. For someone so conniving as he, that is the logical conclusion. He thinks of power, not healing." He leaned forward. "Bell, with your *permanenza*, we could make a permanent cure for Lymbodia. We could cure all manner of ailments. We could make people the best versions of themselves. Long-lasting youth. Endless beauty."

Bell frowned. "We can't use *permanenza* on something as trivial as beauty."

His shoulders sagged. "Perhaps we shouldn't." He turned away from the window and strolled along the fioré beds. Bell followed slowly.

"Your designs are noble, but if he finds proof you have fused a *permanenza* elixir, do not think he will hesitate to sacrifice you with me."

"Me?" She gulped. "Sacrifice me how?"

"He will take my cure, and your elixir, and all my secrets to the Consiglio. In exchange, they will name him Maestro of Stone." The Seller looked at her knowingly. "Oh, I know he claims he wants freedom. And he does, of a sort. But Rian does not know how to tell the whole truth. I have taught him too well." He spoke with an immense sadness. For a moment he looked fragile, as if made of dust. "I raised him, you know."

Bell's breath caught. "What do you mean?"

"Did he not tell you? He is my son."

She pressed her fingers into the soil of the bed next to her. Small phrases Rian had said returned to her. Her heart twisted in a strange mixture of indignance and compassion. Why didn't he tell her? What would it be like to be raised by the man in front of her? She tried to imagine Rian as a small boy, learning how to live by watching the Seller.

She swallowed. "And his mother?"

The Seller said nothing, and she looked up to see him gazing out the window again. Tension swelled, and she stroked a delicate Sciver leaf, finding refuge in its smoothness. She had to move carefully. If she pressed him, accused him of killing Rian's mother, who knew how he would react? She cleared her throat, and the spell of silence broke. "Show me the mindmeld truly works as the cure and show me how to make it. Then I'll try to fuse *permanenza*."

He tilted his head. "Why?"

He had to have guessed already. "I want to create an antidote to it." Bell smiled tightly. "A precaution, of course."

One side of his mouth quirked. "Of course." He strode back to his paper-covered worktable. She watched as he scanned the desk and turned back to her. If he noticed anything out of place, she couldn't tell. "Before that, though, you must do one thing for the *permanenza* elixir."

"What is that?"

He lifted a dark plum-colored vial. "Insidio. Once you can shape this, your power will be endless."

It wasn't Smemor. Roza was safely away. Bell eyed the Seller. If she lost control of her gift, it was his choice to risk himself by being here. Besides, Insidio was undoubtedly included in the recipe for the mindmeld. To make an antidote, she would have to work with it.

"What of the risk?" If she contracted Lymbodia herself, she wouldn't be of much use to Roza.

He tossed her a pair of slender gloves and mask. "Wear these as a precaution. But there is little risk when you control the clouds. Avoid breathing it in or touching it with bare skin."

Slowly, she pulled on the gloves and mask. She picked up the scentstone with one hand and the vial of Insidio with the other. She fused the scentstone. Holding the plum-colored vial, she fed her gift slowly out through her hands, tensed to retreat at any loss of control. The murky cloud above the vial swirled, coalescing into a net of purple chains.

"Take hold of it. You are much stronger."

She stretched her gloved fingers and her gift toward the Insidio cloud. It spun toward her, its malevolent awareness swelling over her, and she gasped and ducked back, lifting her gift like a shield. Fine golden lines sprang up and held back the twisting chains of the Insidio cloud.

"Open your gift and subdue it."

The chains reached for her, circling closer, closer, pressing through the golden lines—

The Seller gripped her wrist. A black haze coiled around his head at his touch, and a pulsing, dark-laced light appeared anchored in his chest. Was that his gift?

"Do it now." The Seller pressed an open gray vial to her skin above the glove. She struggled, but several drops of elixir sank into her veins before he let go. Fuzzy pain spread through her head as the golden lines vanished and the Insidio descended. It was going to smother her—she grabbed the scent cloud of Myrtle Leaf floating beside them and flung it as a net. The net snapped around the Insidio cloud, enveloping it.

The Seller stepped back.

She stumbled away from him, panting, adrenaline still surging. "What happened? What did you put on me?" The fuzzy pain faded slowly.

"I took down your shield so you would act." He smiled and tucked the gray vial away. "And you did. Your gift has learned to control the Insidio. Using other scent clouds to contain it was certainly creative."

Bell looked away, swallowing nausea. How had he taken down her shield with an elixir? At least he hadn't noticed she'd used unfused fioré. "It was all I could think of."

"In the future, picture a large vial with a stopper. Drawing it out in small increments will be easier then, more controlled." He frowned as he flipped through a journal until he reached a scribbled diagram.

"Are you ready to begin?"

"*Permanenza?*" She stiffened her spine as her nausea grew. "The cure first."

He clapped his hands. "Bring in Mr. Medoro."

Bell froze as footsteps thumped over the walkway behind her. Piero strode toward them, scowling, flanked by Lanzis.

"What is he doing here?" She dug her nails into the table behind her.

"You said you needed to see the cure."

"I won't work with him. He destroyed my fioré."

Piero sneered, his face gaunt, his warm Medoro skin sallow.

"You will not be working with him. You will blend your gift with his."

"Gifts can never be blended. That's *fusione.*" A memory of Agnella's glaring black eyes shifting from one apprentice to another while telling them never to blend gifts. The result could kill both makers.

"The Consiglio wants you to think that. Two gifts would be too powerful for them to control." He stepped close. "The Consiglio are not San Giovanni—they did not give us the *attuale*. They have made rules to suit themselves, to maintain power. If they truly wanted to heal Lymbodia and other diseases, they would have done this years ago."

"But what if they're right?"

"They are afraid to try. They would rather people die than change their rules." A tendon clenched in his neck, shadowed by his beard.

Agnella and the others would let Roza die. Could she trust leaders who refused to help the sick?

"No one knows what happens during *fusione*." In all her futile attempts she'd never imagined this would be the solution. Her heart beat fast and shallow.

"I told you she didn't have the—"

The Seller held up his hand, silencing Piero. "I have studied *fusione* for decades, Bell. Once a generation, a scentmaker is powerful enough to do it. Firinacci himself was the first."

"How do you know it's me?"

"The way your gift calls to living organic things. And when I touched your wrist after you fused the scentstone, did you see my gift, here?" He tapped his chest.

Bell nodded slowly.

"Those who can see gifts have the power to remove them. *You* have the power."

Dread crept through her. Was this the price Rian had said she wouldn't want to pay? "Are you sure this is the way?"

"She might kill me. I don't think she can live with that." Piero's eyes cut at her.

"He destroyed your fioré, Bell," the Seller said quietly. "And there is no evidence he will be hurt at all. None of the *fusiones* recorded resulted in death."

Bell bit her lip. *Fusione* wasn't *permanenza*, but she still hadn't gotten what she had bargained for. "I want to see the cure first."

The Seller gestured to Piero, who unbuttoned his silk shirt to reveal a bony torso. Bruises wrapped his ribs.

Piero had Lymbodia? Bell pushed away a pang of sympathy. He'd most likely given it to himself, with all his Magia experiments.

Piero tensed as the Seller stepped closer and pulled a blue vial from his pocket with gloved hands. The Seller dripped elixir onto Piero's forehead and wrists, then removed his gloves and pressed his fingers to Piero's temples.

Bell's feet took her closer of their own accord, her mouth opening as the bruises faded slowly and Piero's skin warmed to its usual tint.

The Seller moved back and dropped the corked vial back into his pocket. "You see? I have removed the Lymbodia from his body."

Bell's forehead creased. "But for how long?"

"A few weeks."

Her heart sank. "That's all? But——"

The Seller's gaze flared. His hand clamped onto her shoulder. "Roza is alive because of this cure. You need no other proof than that.

Do this now or Roza will never be healed. She will die within months. Perhaps weeks."

Wide-eyed, Bell sucked in a breath.

His quiet concern vanished as his fingers dug into her skin. "I will leave you to rot, locked in that room until you agree."

Bell swallowed and looked at Piero. Even if she hated him, she didn't want to hurt him irrevocably. "Do you want this?" she asked.

Piero looked first at the Seller, then to her. He shrugged. "I have the Burning Blood, anyway. If I let you experiment on me, he'll give me the cure as long as I need it. Do it. I dare you."

Bell opened her gift to Piero, keeping it well back. Now that she'd seen the Seller's, Piero's gift was easy to find. It burned like a smoky lamp in his chest. It looked tainted. "Tell me how."

Piero bared his teeth as Bell followed the Seller's instructions, but he didn't move. She pressed her gift toward Piero's in long, glittering lines, like a hundred falling stars. As soon as they touched him, Piero sagged.

Bell faltered.

"Do it," Piero screamed.

Bell let the brilliant streaks envelop his gift. She tugged. Energy surged through her as his gift came free, jerked out by its shadowy roots. Eyes wide, she stepped forward as Piero convulsed and fell, his fingernails scrabbling at the floor as he tried to push back up.

"Is he all right?" The energy surge trembled in her knees. Her hands glowed as if made of a golden glow gem. She waited for the glow to fade, but it remained. One of the Lanzis stared at her as he lifted Piero to his feet, horror in his gaze. She blinked, and his face was stony once more.

"You completed *fusione*, and your gift is intact." The Seller touched her cheek with soft fingers.

She pulled away, stepping toward Piero, who hung limp between two Lanzis. "Someone help him!"

The Seller waved at the Lanzis, and they carried Piero out.

"Is he breathing?"

The Seller lifted her glowing hands and studied them. "A healer will tend him. Forget about him. Think of all the lives you will save."

"But I didn't want to—"

"You must learn to place the right value on lives, Bell." He squeezed her fingers gently. "Your gift makes you a treasure. Piero's was too unsteady...." He pulled a key from his neck and unlocked the drawer below his worktable. When he turned around, he held a handful of vials filled with glowing blue elixir.

Bell's stomach lurched. "*Every* life is valuable."

"But some must be sacrificed, for the good of others."

She shook her head. Her fingers trembled against the bench. Her whole arm was shaking now. What had she done? "How do you know who?"

"I would think it is obvious." He slammed the vials down. "My mother died of Lymbodia before I knew how to use my gift. I begged the Maestro of Scents to help me fuse mindmeld so I could heal her, but he refused. Because she was poor, and as far as he knew, I was ungifted."

"They don't fuse Magia for anyone."

"They could have healed her. Her sacrifice—" His words caught, and he cleared his throat. "Her sacrifice was for nothing. But now I finally have the chance to show them they were wrong."

"All these years, you've been searching..."

"Do you feel the *fusione*?"

Bell didn't have to focus to sense the hot power within her chest. The mention of it made it swell until she thought it would erupt from her hands. The Seller held out a vial of glowing blue liquid. "All you need to do is shape this mindmeld to be permanent, and it will be. Roza will receive the first dose."

This was the final step to *permanenza*. The power surged at the thought. It *wanted* to show its strength. If she didn't use it, Piero's sacrifice would be for nothing. Bell's head spun as she took the vial and rolled it between her glowing fingers.

The *fusione* pressed against her will. Her gift burned her fingers as she strained to hold it back. The Consiglio was right. This was too much power for one person, but it had already been done. This was Roza's chance of true healing. She focused on the mindmeld.

Be permanent.

The elixir boiled and the glass flashed so hot that she dropped it. The Seller dove to catch it with gloved hands as she staggered back and the heat vaporized. She felt bereft, like the leaves had been stripped from her gift. Closing her eyes, she examined the energy within her. Her hands were her own honey skin again.

The *fusione* power was gone.

Thirty

"AT LAST." HE HELD THE VIAL TO THE light. The liquid bubbled continuously. The cloud above it wove intricate braids. It was beautiful—and it made her skin crawl. He grabbed another vial of blue mindmeld. "Again."

"The *fusione* is gone." Relief bloomed within her, so fierce her knees weakened. It was done. He couldn't make her do it again.

"What? Look closer."

"I am. It's my ordinary gift." She lifted her hands.

He pressed the second vial into her hands. "Try."

She took the vial and willed it to be permanent, knowing it was useless. Its cloud circled around her, loose and flowing as before. A dark streak wound through it. "It's not there."

"One fusing took so much?" He turned back to his drawings, muttering.

"Give it to Roza now."

"It was supposed to be endless." He crumpled a paper as he pierced her with his gaze, scanning her as if she were for sale in the Sotto. She forced herself not to cringe against the fear sweeping away her relief. *Agnella was right. Rian was right. I forged him* permanenza, *and he will give me nothing in return.*

"No help for it. We will bring in more scentmakers."

"I—" She gripped the desk as his meaning sunk in. He would bring her more scentmakers to sacrifice their gifts—to her. She shook her head.

He dropped the mindmeld vials into the drawer, then strode for the door with the permanent vial clutched in his hand. "I will return soon."

"I won't take any more gifts." Panic pinched her voice.

"You will if you want your sister to live."

Bell glimpsed shadowed Lanzis in the hall, then the door slammed. *Oh Saint, what have I done?*

She paced, fists clenched in her skirt. Some lives are more valuable than others? All he'd said about the Consiglio…how could he think this was any better?

A thought made her freeze: What if he decided to use the permanent mindmeld on her?

She had to escape. She had to get to Agnella.

She ran to the drawer. He'd forgotten to lock it. She shoved the remaining four vials into her pockets. They clinked softly against each other as she spun around the room, searching for irregularities in the stone. Would Rian have created an entrance to the Conservatory? The walls looked hard and smooth. Footsteps sounded in the hall as she reached the other side.

She dove beneath a bench of fioré on the far wall, buried in its shadow. Something moved yards beyond her under the next bench of fioré. Long dusky fingers and a white sleeve reached into lamplight and beckoned her.

The door opened and the Seller's clipped stride moved across the room. Rian beckoned more urgently, and Bell scrambled along the wall.

The Seller stopped. "Goldenbell?" Menace sharpened his voice. "I have no time for games."

Her hand closed around Rian's before he yanked her through a small opening in the wall. She crashed into him, and they tumbled back, their limbs tangled.

She'd never been so glad for darkness.

"Goldenbell." The Seller spoke low as if he suspected.

"Hold still," Rian breathed against her ear. He reached past her.

She caught one glimpse of the Lanzis' feet sweeping the Conservatory as Rian closed the opening. A smell like sun on the Piazza filled the passage.

A howl of rage, barely recognizable as the Seller's, filtered through the stone.

Rian scooted out from under her, then pulled her up.

"Point me to the way out."

He chuckled. "Not to underestimate your directional skills, but I have to concentrate to find *my* way out."

She found the wall and hesitantly stood. So many questions flew through her that she couldn't utter any of them. Besides, she didn't trust his answers without the truthtelling elixir. She patted her pocket for the vial.

"We must move quickly—he'll have sent Lanzis to search the tunnels again." He grabbed her hand and pulled her into a jog down the dark passageway.

"Where's Carasti?"

"She went on ahead."

In a blind run, she almost yanked free, but navigating inclines and sudden turns at that speed was impossible without his touch to guide her. As it was, she stumbled often, and once he had to catch her around the waist before she tripped past him into a deep pit. They followed a series of natural caves and crevices as well as his tunnels. The walls turned jagged without warning, and her knuckles were thoroughly scraped before long.

A dim light appeared ahead, and Rian shoved her backward into a crevice, pressing himself in front of her and melting the wall closed with swift, sure movements. He left a slim, natural-looking crack to watch through. Bell took quick breaths as the glow gem of a Lanzi passed, trying not to think of the hard rock pressing into her spine and legs or of her face imprinted on Rian's warm back. His heartbeat was fast but steady as if carving caves to hide in was something he did every day.

Perhaps it was.

Finally, when the air grew heavy and stale, he reformed the opening, and they hurried on. She waited for some comment about their close-quartered hiding place, but he seemed hardly aware she was there, as if his focus was spread out through the tunnels.

Finally, after a long ascent, he slowed and stopped before a spyhole on the crowded Piazza. "This is as far as we can go."

"Let me out here." The noisy Bazaar goers would be good cover for her to reach the path through Grenwood, and, from there, Agnella's farm.

He looked down at her through his eyelashes, his eyes barely visible in the spyhole's light. "If you go out like this, I might as well have left you back in the Conservatory. The Seller has made his move. His Lanzis are everywhere, not just the Bazaar."

"I need to warn the other scentmakers. I fused him *permanenza*." Her voice dropped at the end.

"Agnella has already warned them. Most have gone into hiding."

"What? Why?"

"They are preparing for the Seller to begin brainwashing the city. He'll go after the most powerful scentmakers first. Some of them have already vanished. When you disappeared, I went to her and told her everything."

"And she believed you?" Bell asked in disbelief.

He snorted. "Not until I took a truthtelling elixir. I'm taking you to her now."

"She's not at her farm?"

He shook his head. "You need me to guide you."

She frowned. "Tell me where she is. Is Carasti with her?"

"Stubborn." He blew out a breath. "I'm not trying to force my way into your company. Do you *want* to row a boat halfway around the island to her hideout in the dark? Carasti and Agnella fled as soon as we realized the Seller was sending Lanzis out to capture more scentmakers. She should be safe on the coast by now. If we get separated, go to Santa Croce and wait. Someone will come and look for you there."

"Aren't there Lanzis waiting for us?"

207

"Never fear, my dear. I have disguises." He pulled a sinuous black cloak and an amaranth mask from his pocket. He slipped the mask over her face and delicately tied the ribbon in her hair.

"But won't people think I'm…"

"A Spy? Precisely. They'll think you're her. She's busy elsewhere, I happen to know."

She stared at him. He wanted her to pretend to be Arabia? "I don't know how to act—"

"Keep moving. You're shorter, but they won't question you, at least not right away. I'll meet you in the street beyond the Rotunda."

She studied him, reaching for the truthtelling elixir. "Give me your hand."

His lips curved. He brushed his fingers down her arm and took her hand. "Don't be scared."

She twisted the cork from the vial and pressed it against his wrist. "I want to trust you, Rian."

He paused. "This again."

"Is everything you said true?"

"Of course," he said without hesitating.

She half smiled in relief. Leaning forward, she rested her head against his chest. Even if everything else the Seller and Arabia had said about him was true, he was on her side. "Thank you for coming for me. I never should have gone with Roza."

He tucked a lock of her hair behind her ear and inhaled. "You smell good—Saint." He groaned. "When will this wear off? As much as I want to stay within reach of you, we need to go."

She took a deep breath. "All right."

He hummed, peering through the spyhole. "A group of nobles will pass in front of the Lanzi across from us in a moment. We need to enter the mob before he can see again. Keep down as we step out." The stone oozed open and he slipped out. Bell stepped after him, gathering her cloak close.

The colors and smells after so much darkness made her pause. Rian had already disappeared. A woman jumped as she caught sight of

Bell's mask. The crowd edged away from Bell. The fear in the people hurrying to get away startled her. Was this how Rian felt all the time?

Bell dropped her hand from adjusting her mask. A Spy wouldn't adjust anything—a Spy was pure confidence.

Act like Rian.

She strode toward the Rotunda, the throng rippling like water around her.

Thirty-One

A SHADOW PEELED AWAY FROM THE ALleyway wall beyond the Rotunda and matched her stride.

"Any trouble?" Rian murmured.

She took a deep, steadying breath. "It actually worked."

Releasing a breath, Bell moved to untie her mask. Rian reached for her fingers, then paused, his hand in the air. "Leave it. We have a ways to go."

"I don't like wearing it."

"I don't know where all the Lanzis are stationed."

They turned onto a smaller street leading down to Santa Croce. The houses here looked tall and sleek and businesslike—none of the heavy, ornamental touches that filled Santa Maria Novella. No moonlight, no starlight, merely a damp heaviness in the air. They found their way by the dim light from windows.

"You said Lanzis would be watching my house. Are my parents all right?"

Rian glanced back. "They would want you to be safe."

"I have to warn them."

"Bell…"

Bell pulled him into a dark doorway with potted topiaries on either side. "He has a *permanenza* elixir. He promised it was for Roza, but he was so angry when I couldn't make more. What if he uses it on my parents?"

"He'll use it on you if he catches you again."

"It's my fault they're in danger." She should be going to them now, not running to hide.

"The best thing you can do for them is to disappear and fuse the antidote. If he catches you now, we're all buried."

"He might hurt them."

Rian hesitated. "His focus is on you. You need to go somewhere safe and make a plan."

What wasn't he saying? The elixir should still be working, but it felt like he was holding something back. "Are you sure?"

"As sure as I can be." The rawness in his voice was unfamiliar, but Bell found it comforting.

She imagined Father pacing in his study while Lanzis crept through her garden.

Voices echoed in the distance, followed by a rattling carriage. A sluggish breeze tugged her hair as she took his hand in the dark. "Show me the way."

Santa Croce descended to the sea in terraces. Waterfront taverns cast a glow across the indigo water. They skirted the wealthy merchants' mansions and their hired guards. Rian guided Bell around drunks and beggars in the shadows. The docks came in sight. Music floated from ferries traveling to and from mainland ships. Lights dotted the bay like a watery constellation. Somewhere in the distance, the current writhed. Rian stopped at the edge of San Vito Osteria's light. "I need to go inside and acquire a boat. Stay here in the alley."

"I'm going with you." The vast, open water only reminded her of all the things she couldn't control.

"You'll draw too much attention. Stay against the wall, out of the light."

She scowled at his back until he disappeared through the heavy tavern door. Laughter echoed from further down the pier, coming closer. She focused on the sound of lapping waves. Her mask itched, and she tugged it off. How long could it take to hire a boat?

A large graceful ship at anchor glittered from stem to stern, wrapped in glow gems. She stepped closer. It was so big for such a small island.

"There she sits, lads. The prettiest merch in all of Bardia."

Bell jumped at the familiar voice. A group of wealthy merchant boys in slim tailored pants ambled into sight, their Bardian shirts open and sleeves rolled up in the Solstice storm mugginess. Aless's tapered face caught the pier's lamplight as he poured black Bardian wine into the tiny crystal goblets they held. They swallowed a toast and leaned over the pier rails. One of them told a joke about a seagull whose nest was full of money.

They were boys, sons raised on money and confidence, but the sight of them was like nails scraping her skin. Maybe it was because Aless had been the one to tell her of Father's debt. Maybe it was the memory of the pity in Aless's gaze.

Several things happened at once, then. The boys turned to approach the tavern door as it opened, and Rian appeared framed by warm light and the grassy smell of beer. She realized she had moved forward instinctively, drawing the gaze of the stocky one with sandy hair.

He grinned down at her as she froze. "Why, hello there."

Aless looked from Rian to Bell as Rian approached her. "Bell? What are you doing here?"

The other boys grinned and jostled Aless as they passed, but the one who'd spoken planted his feet. "Won't you introduce us, Aless?"

"Hello, Medoro." Rian's voice was cool as driving rain, looking past the one still eyeing Bell. He wrapped his fingers around Bell's elbow.

Shock and confusion opened Aless's face for a moment as he stared at the small space between Bell and Rian.

The stocky boy muttered something irritable.

"Go wait inside, Carmn." When Aless lifted his chin, his blue eyes glittering hard, he looked like someone else.

Carmn backed toward the door as Rian's gaze fell on him.

"Are you with him, Bell?" Aless stared at Rian.

"Yes, she's with me. Come, Bell. Let's leave him to complete his *ceremony*."

Bell frowned. Did everyone think they spoke for her?

Aless flushed. "It's our newest vessel, that's all. What are you doing with him?"

"That's your father's boat?" Bell asked.

"Well…it's…"

"Let's go." Rian pulled out his mask and twirled it around his finger, lip beginning to curl.

Aless stiffened. He stepped closer. His hands were tight at his sides as if he wanted to reach out and drag her free of Rian's touch. Which was supremely annoying, coming from him. "Do you know who this is, Bell?"

She couldn't help a haughty scoff. "Of course, I do." She turned to Rian, using the motion to get out of his grip. "You said we need a boat," she hissed. If he hadn't pulled out his mask right then, escaping this would have been much easier.

"I don't need—"

"I have a rowboat." Aless stared hard at Rian. "I can take you where you need to go, Bell."

Rian glowered. "I have this under control."

"The sooner we get there, the better." Bell muttered. "Rian can take me, but we do need a rowboat, Aless."

Aless firmed his lips. "Are you sure?" He leaned closer. "I'm afraid you're in—"

"I'm all right." She held out her hand in a soothing gesture. "Please, Aless. I'll explain everything later, but I need to leave now."

Aless studied them a second longer. "Alouer, bring that little rowboat over," he called down the dock.

A guard by the dock house door saluted and scurried away. In moments, he'd dragged a small boat by a rope and placed it in the water beside the pier.

"Thank you." Bell forced a smile at Aless.

He furrowed his brow at Rian. "Have a care, Bell."

"I will."

Getting in was easier than she expected with Rian holding the boat steady. Silently, Rian rowed them out into the bay. Aless stood by the tavern door and watched them. Bell awkwardly pulled the oar on one side, but her hands rubbed raw quickly, unused to the friction. Before she could say anything, Rian reached around and took it from her. She hugged the cloak closer despite the humid air, watching the glow-stone-lit vessel shrink. At the end of the pier the ribs of a dozen half-alive boats curved up, dark lines against Santa Croce's lights.

The smell of salt water felt heavy in her nostrils. "I've never seen a ship so big. And they own more than one?"

"The Medoros are the largest ship merchants, so they own most of the vessels in the harbor. This is their shipyard we're passing."

"No wonder Mother was so insistent...." Bell blushed.

He snorted. "Why don't you marry him and let him sweep you off to a golden mansion?" She considered grabbing the oar back and thumping him with it. "You'd probably be perfectly safe there." Bell pictured Aless standing on the dock, watching their boat row out of sight, his forehead narrowed. Her gaze drifted back to Rian.

His muscles pulled smoothly through his shirtsleeves, the white fabric a dim glow in the moonlight. Life certainly would have been easier if she had been content to be Aless's wife. Would she have thought differently about Aless if she had met him first instead of Rian?

Rian looked at her with a twisted expression. He was waiting for a response.

"I don't want to only be safe." Bell looked ahead. What would it be like to pack a boat full of fioré and sail to the mainland? Set herself up as her own Maestra of Scents, without the Consiglio hovering in the shadows, waiting for her first misstep?

To sail with *Rian*.

"That's not his father's boat, you know. It's his."

Bell pulled her gaze from the horizon. "But—he's barely older than me."

"He's a Medoro. *Their* fathers give them business shares for birthday presents."

She looked at him askance. The bitter twist in his mouth was barely visible, but she could feel it in the air. It didn't feel right to say she knew the Seller was his father. It was his secret to share. "It's not Bardian wood, is it?"

Rian glanced at her. "You've heard about that?"

"Carasti was helping too. When it's finished, she…she wanted me to go along."

The pier noise faded, replaced by lapping water, a constant reminder of the depth beneath them.

"Would you? If she was going?"

"I don't know." She took a deep breath. If there was a sure way to do it safely, once this was all over…

His voice became wistful. "If the ship is built and sails, I'll be on it."

"What about your gift? Won't it wither if you get too far away from Bardia?"

He shrugged. "I'll be back for Solstice."

"Aren't you scared?" The words slipped out, and she forged ahead before her face flushed further. "What if it's even more dangerous than here?"

His small smile felt encouraging rather than mocking. "Have you seen the tourists that come? Ungifted and ignorant. A gift like yours would shake the mainland, Bell."

"So would yours," Bell said.

His gaze grew more intense. "I am not afraid of the mainlanders, Bell. And neither would you need to be, if you were with me."

They looked at each other for a moment that stretched like fabric. The silence deepened, and she realized why. "Keep rowing," she said shortly.

The oars returned to their steady movement, murmuring through the water as they swept the boat forward, keeping along the dark shore.

Thirty-Two

MIST HUNG HEAVY AND OMINOUS BY THE time they reached Bardia's north end. Nothing could hold back the Solstice storm now. Agnella's cabin nestled in a row of pines half buried in a cleft in the cliffs. They ran aground on a pebbly beach in the shade of two boulders. Bell could hardly see her own feet until Rian pulled out a glow gem. Her shoes squelched as they climbed a path up and across the wet rocks. A crevice opened before them, water splashing and foaming far below. Surprised, Bell wavered on the edge and Rian grabbed her waist and tugged her back. She stiffened.

"It would take a while to fetch you if you fell," he said defensively.

"I wouldn't fall." She fought back disappointment when he let go. *Control yourself, Bell.*

He bent and placed his palms on the boulder's edge. His back tensed, and a narrow stone bridge oozed across the gap like thick liquid, melting into the other side. When he stood and offered his hand, Bell didn't hesitate. The bridge was hardly wider than her feet, and she found herself clutching his shirt as well.

"Sorry." On the other side, she tried to free her hand from his. The cabin's one dim window glowed yards away across a wide, wet rock.

"I could have carried you, I suppose."

She snorted, eyeing his slim shoulders.

They picked their way across the last boulder. She slipped on a patch of moss and grabbed his arm. His muscles tensed as he stabilized her

216

and his grin flashed in the window's light. She looked away, her face hot.

The door creaked. "Who goes there?" A deep familiar voice filled Bell's heart with ice, killing the flush in her cheeks. Garam stood framed in the doorway. He wore a simple shirt and pants, his hair mussed. No burgundy cape.

"One daring rescue accomplished." Rian grinned.

"Is she all right?"

"I'm standing right here. I'm fine."

Garam's face softened with relief. "Thank the Saint. You're our last chance, with Agnella's gift fading."

Piero's crumpled form filled her mind's eye.

Agnella pushed Garam aside. The firelight gleamed on the white streaks in her crown of braids. She pulled Bell into the small cabin. A wooden table and benches filled the wall across from the hearth. Dried sage and lavender hung in bunches in front of the two windows, their fragrances soothing. A door in the back corner led to a shadowed lean-to. "Come in and get dry."

She leaned into Agnella's hug. "I don't know what to do."

"We'll help you."

Bell stepped back and scanned the room. "Where's Carasti?"

Agnella's mouth tightened. "She's gone to fetch Maestra Piccarda and Maestro Carlo. We'll need their help."

Bell reached into her pocket, her stomach tight. Beside the truth-telling elixir lay the mindmeld vials. She pulled one out. "This is his mindmeld. If you can look at it, maybe see how it works…"

Agnella rolled the vial across her palm.

"I'm sorry about the confusion, Bell." Garam's broad shoulders blocked out half the room.

"Confusion?" she huffed, deeply gratified when he edged back-ward. "I went all the way to the Seller of Secrets to find out what you were doing. You could have told me."

A rueful twist of his lips was all that changed. "I was trying to pro-tect Roza. I didn't want you to find out the truth about her too soon, in case you frightened her into doing something dangerous."

She tilted her head. "How exactly did you find out what she was doing?"

"I work for Signor Strozzi, who works for the pope."

"The Signor Strozzi whose daughter I—"

"He brought her here as a cover. A plan we devised during my year on the mainland."

She crossed her arms. Could he be more pompous? The wealthiest Bardian families sent their first sons to experience the mainland before they settled down to their occupations as even wealthier heirs.

Garam didn't seem to notice her silent judgement. "Signor Strozzi had been hearing rumors of the Seller's plan to cure Lymbodia. The Seller dabbles in Magia too often. It was a matter of time before he created something truly dangerous, and it was inevitable that he would find a way past the current. Signor Strozzi recruited me, and as soon as I returned, I searched for proof. Of course, I discovered Roza's connection to the Seller of Secrets immediately."

"So you proposed to her right off," Bell said flatly.

He nodded, looking sheepish. "Yes, it was the best course. It gave me a chance to watch—I mean—to make sure you—" He flicked a hand as if she were supposed to take his meaning.

"So he could spy on you too," Rian supplied.

Garam glared at Rian, showing a first sign of being ruffled. "The *Spy* is not one who should talk."

"At least I'm honest about my intentions." Rian's voice was smooth as velvet.

Bell spun on Agnella and Rian. "Why didn't either of you tell me about Roza sooner?"

Rian spread his hands. "You didn't believe me. I decided to let her tell you herself."

"If I'd known sooner, I could have..." Bell shook her head. "Maybe I could have changed her mind."

Agnella grunted. "Your sister made up her mind many years ago." Her fingers, bony but strong, took Bell's shoulder and steered her toward a stool by the fire. "Sit yourself. You've had a long day." Agnella bent to pick up the kettle.

Bell froze as Garam placed his hand on her arm. "I didn't mean to sound so callous, Bell. I—I love your sister."

That was likely all the apology she would get from him. She forced herself to meet his gaze. It was so strange to see him like this, without the clothes that marked his power. "Garam, did you know Piero…"

His brows lowered, a bold, angry line across his face. "Rian told me. I should have known, the way he came after you. Did you see him in the Seller's sanctuary?"

Bell nodded. "The Seller wanted me to complete *fusione*, to fuse our gifts."

Agnella whirled to face her, hot water from the kettle splattering the floor. "You didn't do it."

"I'm sorry." Bell's voice rasped. "He threatened me—and Roza, but I still could have said no. I took Piero's gift. Piero said that's what he wanted. He…he has Lymbodia. The Seller promised him the cure if he let me do it." If only she could liquefy herself like Rian melted stone and dissolve between the floorboards.

Agnella broke the silence. "You still have Piero's gift?"

"No. When I made the mindmeld permanent, the *fusione* disappeared." Her voice dropped away.

Agnella's face whitened. The shock on their faces choked her like a vine around her throat, and she couldn't breathe under their gazes anymore. Bell turned and ran out the door.

Rian called her name, but she let the darkness outside swallow her.

"Have we drowned ourselves in pity yet?"

Bell spun back at the familiar voice, slipping on mossy roots. The glow from the windows behind Agnella's cabin caught on a head of wild curls. "Carasti."

"No one else thinks they're worthy to comfort the great scentmaker in her humiliation."

"They didn't say that."

"I did."

"You're certainly right about the humiliation."

"What were you thinking, going without me? I thought we agreed—"

"He would have caught you too."

"Then Rian would have gotten us both out."

Bell raised her eyebrows. "My point. Why make him rescue two?"

Carasti scowled. "We adventure together. That's the deal." Her sweet voice made the sharp words more painful.

Bell sighed. "I am sorry. I thought I was doing the right thing."

"*There's* your problem." Carasti stepped up and braced a dainty hand on the damp pine trunk between them.

"What?"

"You have such ideas about what the right thing is, and you panic if you can't do it."

Bell slid down until she nestled between the tree's roots. The unsettledness, the aching stirring within her—this was it. She wanted the right thing so, so badly, but she didn't know what it was. How could she know?

"I don't know what it is anymore," she muttered.

This was the reason fleeing the island with Rian and being accountable to no one was beginning to draw her like a blossom turning to sunlight. If there was no right way, she couldn't fail at it anymore.

Carasti trailed her fingers along a branch. "There's a merchant who has built a ship of Bardian wood. I've signed on as part of his crew."

"You *what?*"

"He's paying twice what I can make in a year at the Bazaar."

Bell's mouth dried. "If the Consiglio finds out, you'd lose your title."

"They can't stop me from making." Her mouth twisted. "Besides, I think we're a little beyond that now."

"But the Solstice—your gift needs to be renewed. They could bar you from it."

Carasti hesitated. "That's the other thing. You know how we have to line up and touch the Maestris' hands after the Solstice to receive our renewal?"

"Because there isn't room for everybody at the Spring."

Carasti bit her lip. "How do you think all those makers in the Sotto renew their gift every year? The Maestris wouldn't let them near."

Bell suddenly felt like she was on a boat again, swaying with the waves, about to tip. "What are you saying?"

"The Spring isn't the only place to receive the Solstice gift."

"But the dark makers…their gifts are different. I can feel it. Rotted somehow. I thought it was because they were fading."

"Their gifts may be dark, but they're as strong as we are. I know several makers who've been barred from the Spring for one infraction or another. What are they supposed to do, give up making entirely? Can you imagine?"

Bell squeezed her forehead. To trap the power within her while it slowly weakened would be torture. "If this is true, the Consiglio has driven them to join the Sotto."

"Close enough."

"How could they not see this happening? How could they not know there was another source?"

Carasti waved a hand. "Because the Seller of Secrets hid it."

"The Seller of Secrets…" Bell's eyes shot wide. "His sanctuary. The pools. The dark current must come through there." No wonder they'd felt so strange, so alive. "He passes it on to all the dark makers." Her forehead furrowed. "But it does something to them, doesn't it? There's something wrong with their gifts."

Carasti winced. "Like I said, I know makers who've gone dark. Have you seen the vines on their wrists? Their alchemy is slowly twisted until everything they make is dangerous, whether they like it or not. The darker their gifts, the more the vines creep over their bodies."

Bell closed her eyes, picturing the black leaves twining up Rian's arms. Was that part of why he so desperately wanted to escape the island? He had to refresh his gift through the Seller's dark current. His tunnels hadn't seemed dangerous, but perhaps they were only a small part of what he'd made over his lifetime.

"Bell?" Carasti nudged her, and Bell realized she'd said her name more than once.

"Hmm?"

"You should think about leaving for a while until this is over. You don't want to be caught between the Consiglio and the Seller. I'll save you a spot on that ship."

Bell went silent and Carasti humphed. "Remember, there can be more than one right thing." She stabbed a finger into Bell's arm. "Tell me about the rescue. Did your Spy lover do anything romantic?"

Bell remembered the relief she had felt when she saw him and sighed. "Not my lover."

Carasti eyed her. "He looks at you like you're made of Bardian glass and he intends to keep you forever. I think 'lover' is the appropriate term."

"He said he needs me to help him get to the mainland, and then I'm free to go. Does that sound like a lover to you?"

Carasti eyed her from beneath her curls. "I'd certainly choose that over being locked up in some rich man's house, ordering servants about. Wouldn't you?"

Bell frowned. "It doesn't matter now anyway. I need to figure out how to save Roza before I can do anything else. The Seller promised he'd heal her, but I can't trust him to do it."

Carasti shifted. "He knows you can't resist trying to save her. So does she, for that matter."

Bell scrubbed her face and recoiled. Moss gloved her hands, every finger perfectly covered. She hadn't even noticed. The damp green dripped down her arms, the life in it soothing her, but she urged it away. It smoothed back onto the tree, and she fisted her hands. "I don't know who to trust."

Carasti cleared her throat.

"You, of course. But even Agnella...part of me can't forget what the Seller said about her, and the other Maestris. Everyone has buried motives."

"Including you, I assume."

Bell stared at her. "What do you mean?"

Carasti faced her, the cabin's glow outlining her whole delicate figure. "Look, Bell. We're human. Being Bardian makers doesn't change that. If we had completely unmixed motives, we'd be one of those mainland machines. I'm loyal to you because you're my best friend, but that doesn't mean I don't also hope that if you become Maestra, you'll loosen up on the makers. Does that make me untrustworthy?"

Bell took a deep breath of damp sea air. "No."

"And you must admit, you don't just want Bardia to be free of the Seller. You want things to be back under control."

Bell opened her mouth and shut it.

"I'll take that as a yes. Wanting something doesn't make us bad people."

Bell hugged her knees to her chest. "Roza wouldn't have gone to the Seller if she wasn't sick. It's my fault."

"I know you blame yourself for Roza. But you were a child when you fused the Magia unprotected. She's responsible for her own choices now. Roza's betrayal wasn't your fault."

"But...Piero." Bell had a hard time saying his name.

"We all make mistakes, Bell." Carasti crouched and slid her fingers into Bell's, her skin comfortingly warm and dry. "But living in them will not protect you from making another mistake. You have to learn from them, and move on."

Bell groaned. "In my head, I know you're right. But my heart..."

"I'll say it as often as you need it. Now, are you coming back inside to get dry?" She tugged Bell toward the cabin. "Maestra Piccarda came with me to help plan our next move."

Agnella offered two steaming mugs of dark tea as they entered. "Feel better?"

223

Bell met her gaze. Maestra Piccarda raised her mug to her from beside the hearth. Rian lounged in the corner, looking coiled and relaxed at the same time, his eyes gleaming in the firelight.

Bell sank into a chair beside Agnella. She took a sip and let the black tea warm her throat. "Will you tell me the truth, Agnella?" she asked quietly.

Agnella lifted her head. "What do you want to know?"

"Does the Seller have a source for the *attuale* current in his sanctuary?"

She glanced at Rian. "We know of it now."

"How could you not guess, with so many dark makers in the Sotto?"

Agnella grunted. "We did guess." She gestured to Maestra Piccarda. "Piccarda was certain the Seller was receiving renewal somewhere, but the other Maestris would not believe it was possible. I didn't until Rian confirmed it."

Bell studied Rian. He nodded slightly.

"Maestra Anna and Maestra Lux refused to give another chance to anyone who showed signs of darkness, for fear it was too late. It wasn't logical, but they would not be moved."

Bell shuddered. Was that what Maestra Anna was looking for in her? If she'd shown signs of darkness, would she be refused renewal and sentenced to the Sotto?

"What about the *attuale* current? The Consiglio forbids going through it, but have they ever tried a Bardian wood boat?"

Agnella scowled at Carasti, who affected pure innocence over her mug. "They have not, and I hope they never will. Reaching the mainland would be the end of Bardian makers."

Bell narrowed her eyes. "But you say it's impossible, when you don't know it is."

"I regret the Consiglio's wording. We have not tested a Bardian wood craft, but we all recognize the danger of taking our wares off Bardia."

"Nearly all." Maestra Piccarda raised her eyebrows.

"Yes, Maestra Piccarda has roving eyes," Agnella muttered. "Are you satisfied, Bell? All this is beside the point. We are here to plan our next step." Agnella stood and rapped on the worn table jammed against the wall. Yellowed maps covered it now. "Let us begin."

Maestra Piccarda took the chair at the table's end. Rian slid in next to Carasti on the bench, and Garam and Agnella beat her to the bench on the other side. Gingerly, Bell perched beside Rian on the bench. At least she wasn't trapped in the middle.

It felt unbalanced to have him here, mingling with Agnella and Garam and Carasti.

"As I suspected, the Seller is kidnapping scentmakers. I witnessed a few being taken, but if others heeded my warnings, perhaps they managed to escape."

"Where will they go?" Bell asked. "Could they hide at the Rotunda?"

Agnella grunted. "The Seller is watching it too closely."

"He does not yet know we are helping you," Maestra Piccarda said. "But we must tread carefully. If the makers work together, we can defeat him."

"He has more Lanzis than we expected," Garam said. "At least a hundred. My contact inside disappeared before he could get me a final count."

"Gregory." Rian stared into the fire. "I meant to help him escape, but the Seller discovered him before I could."

Garam nodded slowly, his eyes thoughtful. "He may be imprisoned. Perhaps we can—"

Rian grunted. "The Seller keeps prisoners deep in a cavern below his sanctuary. To get there, we'd have to find a way through his Magia garden."

Bell pictured an entire garden full of live Smemor and Taiga and Insidio, the mingling of their scents washing over her. She shuddered.

Agnella winced. "A Magia garden?"

"We call it the Midnight Garden. It's full of Magia and all the dark makings he's collected over the years. Even he hardly dares to go through."

"Can we get to it?"

Rian shook his head. "Not without me. There's an entrance in the sanctuary, but getting inside his lair from the Sotto would be too difficult. He's blocked off all my surface tunnels, so the way to reach it undetected would be at the end of the Vasari Corridor, where it turns to catacombs. You don't want to try that without a stonemaker."

Bell covered her face for a long moment. Her failures felt like dirt scooped onto her own grave. Except this time, it was the grave of another's freedom. Rian had been absolutely right. The price was too high to pay. "I've been such a fool." Her voice was hoarse.

Carasti scowled. "I told you—"

"I've been a fool, but I *will* learn from my mistakes." She should be the wisest woman on Bardia if she earned wisdom in proportion to her blunders.

Rian squeezed her hand under the table, like a lifeline to pull her from under her burden, and she nearly grabbed his hand back when he withdrew.

Agnella nodded. "I'm glad to hear it." She gestured to the largest map on the table, a sketch of the Rotunda and the surrounding area: the Piazza, the barrier circling the Rotunda, the small entrance at the front and the even smaller one at the back. Diagrams showed the transparent gem wall surrounding the structure.

"We will rescue the scentmakers, but first we must get Bell to the Rotunda before the Midsummer Solstice. The wards and the Consiglio will protect her once she's inside, but we have to convince them of the danger."

"Will this help?" Carasti pulled a silver bracelet from her pocket.

"Is that the one…" Bell shuddered.

"A dark metalmaker forced it on me in the Sotto. It stilled my gift." Carasti nodded to Rian. "He said the Seller is making them to use on the Consiglio."

Agnella touched the bracelet's rim. "I've heard of these but never seen one."

"The Seller has been working with a metalmaker to have these made," Rian said. "He thought I didn't know."

"How could he hide anything from you?" Garam asked, his words half scorn, half grudging respect.

Rian looked at him.

"We'll work on a solution, but we don't know for sure that's what he's been making. For now, we plan our entrance." Agnella smacked the paper on the table.

Maestra Piccarda held out her hand. "I will take it to Maestra Lux. Perhaps then she will see the danger the dark makers present."

Carasti hesitated, then dropped it into Piccarda's hand.

The Maestris would lead La Festa parade along Via dei Calzaiuoli, and makers and other spectators would follow on the sidelines. They would finish in the Piazza, where the makers gathered alone. The Maestris would enter the Rotunda to await the Solstice.

The makers would line up according to their gift, waiting for the Maestris to descend the stairs after Solstice arrived. The moment the gifts were distributed, the rest of Bardia would sweep into the square for La Festa finale.

A rainbow of fireworks, hot *cioccolata* with cinnamon, pastries dripping with cream, and Bardian magic everywhere—it used to be paradise for Bell.

Carasti tapped the Rotunda entrance. "But won't he be expecting Bell to make for the Rotunda?"

"He'll have Lanzis and dark makers watching the entire area." Rian leaned his elbows on the table, blocking Bell's view.

She shoved him over. "I couldn't get in anyway."

"Pshaw." Piccarda hissed at a too hot sip. "Once you're in the Rotunda, you'll be under Consiglio protection."

"But what if they refuse me as Maestra?"

"I've already discussed your ascension with them," Agnella said. "Most of them agreed with me. When we present my waning gift coupled with your growing one, they'll have no choice. I'll take you into the Rotunda myself."

"Why don't you take her now?" Everyone turned to Garam. "Before he's expecting it."

"Not until we're sure he's used that permanent mindmeld on someone else," Agnella said. "If he's lying in wait, he could attack with that before we get close."

Bell stood and leaned her palms on the table. "Solstice isn't for two days. I can't leave my parents vulnerable for that long."

"We need you to receive the Maestra's gift. If you don't, it will lie dormant another year, and you'll have less chance to defeat him."

"But if he receives a gift as well…"

Agnella shook her head. "Your gift is more powerful than his, more natural, but you need more control to stop his elixirs."

Would the Maestra's gift give her more control, or would it break the little control she had? Her gift rumbled within her, wanting to tear life from the trees outside and make *something*. Anything.

"I have traced the current's path to the Seller's sanctuary." Maestra Piccarda made a long swallow of tea look elegant. "I may be able to control it by Solstice."

"You could redirect his source?" Bell asked.

"Perhaps. At least lessen it."

Bell nodded, but her brow remained furrowed like a plowed field in drought.

Rian laid a hand on hers. "I'll be with you." She turned her hand and entwined her fingers in his. The touch of his warm skin helped lessen her terror.

"Bell will enter alone with me." Agnella leaned back, arms crossed.

"I'm not leaving her—" Rian said.

"Piccarda will leave the gate ajar for you," Agnella interrupted.

"And what am I supposed to do once I'm inside?" Bell asked.

"You'll take the Maestra's gift in my place."

Bell took a heavy breath. She looked at the map, her vision unfocused. If this was the thing she was supposed to be doing—the right thing—why did it make her skin crawl? "The Seller is hunting scent-makers as we speak to use for *fusione*. If we bring them all together like this for the Solstice ceremony, we'll make it easier for him to capture them."

The map crinkled as Agnella smoothed it and laid the mindmeld vials Bell had given her on top. "That's why you're going to fuse an antidote now."

Thirty-Three

BELL LEANED AWAY FROM THE VIALS. "HOW—"
Agnella held her hand up, palm out. Her knobby fingers looked like talons. "You're young in the craft, and the deadliest manipulator in Bardia sank his claws into you. You think I don't know what he's like, hmm?" She stood to face Bell, her eyes black and angry. "The fact that you performed *fusione*, illegal or not, is a sign of your strength. When you receive the Maestra's gift at Solstice, you'll have more control as well as more strength."

Bell took a shaky breath but managed to meet Agnella's gaze. "How do we make an antidote? We have the mindmeld, but we don't know what counteracts it."

Agnella looked at Rian, who held up his hands. "I don't know."

Bell's breath shuddered. "But I won't *fusione* again, not even to create the antidote." She closed her eyes. *Will Piero's empty face always be there in my mind?* Was this learning from her mistakes or making another one? "I will try."

Agnella's bony shoulders relaxed.

"Once we have the antidote, we will hold it ready at the Piazza in case the Seller attacks." Garam spoke as if his own formidable will would bring this to pass. He traced a path along the map of the Rotunda's edge.

Bell studied their faces as they focused on the map. They had so much trust in her ability. She swung her feet off the bench and paced to the fire.

230

"Where will I get the fioré?"

"I have starts of everything here, so you can begin," Agnella said. "I knew this day would come."

Maestra Piccarda stood. "I must be getting back. Someone may notice my absence soon."

Agnella nodded. "You have everything you need at the Rotunda?"

"I will move my supplies to your suite, as you suggested," Maestra Piccarda said. Despite her protests that the Maestra of Water was above assistance concerning the ocean, Garam went out to help her into her boat.

Agnella stood in the doorway and watched them go. She closed it firmly, then turned and beckoned Bell. "Come."

Bell followed her to the lean-to on the end of the cabin. It was walled in with two large windows, creating a narrow workspace. Heavy curtains covered the windows now, and a waist-high shelf ran the length of the little room, full of young fioré plants, elixirs, and empty glass vials.

Bell took a deep breath and let the warm, loamy smells calm her. She sensed movement behind her and glanced back to see Rian leaning against the doorway. He smiled softly, then pulled on a scent blocking mask.

Agnella gently set the mindmeld elixirs in a row. She handed Bell gloves and a mask, then put on the same. They pulled out stools and settled in as Agnella held a blue vial between them.

"Have you studied its scent cloud yet?"

Bell pursed her lips. "I saw him use it on Piero, but I couldn't get a clear view."

Agnella took the cork in her fingers. "Ready?"

Bell resisted the urge to look back at Rian, to reach back for his reassuring hand. Then she felt warm fingers on her shoulder, and the panic in her belly eased. He was here. Agnella was here.

Agnella twisted the cork and pulled it free. The scent cloud rose immediately as the intense, cloying fragrance of mindmeld filtered through her mask. A fuzzy black net of chains twisted slowly around a deep blue fluttering mist. Other colored shapes flashed briefly as the cloud shifted, but she couldn't make them out.

The scent thickened, and panic lurched through Bell's chest. "Enough," she said hoarsely. Agnella corked it swiftly, setting the vial beside the others.

"All right?" Agnella's voice sounded muffled through the mask. A haze floated at the edges of Bell's vision.

She took slow, shallow breaths until the haze faded. Slowly, she registered Rian's tightened hold on her shoulder. She nodded.

Agnella's back relaxed. "Do you recognize the components?"

"It wasn't clear enough. The black chain is similar to Insidio, but it's different somehow." She took a shuddering breath as a memory burst into her mind. The black Magia forming the doorway in the Seller's sanctuary. Could that be it?

Rian's touch vanished for a moment, then he pressed her mug of tea into her hands. The liquid stirred as a green sprig emerged from the dried tea leaves and unfolded above the surface of the liquid. "Do you know of a black Insidio? I broke off a blossom from the one I saw in the Seller's sanctuary."

Agnella frowned. "I've heard whispers but never seen proof."

She twisted to look at Rian. "Is that one of the ingredients?"

He pulled down his mask. "I don't know for sure." The words seemed to pain him. "He keeps his mindmeld very secure. But the black Insidio is his most prized Magia."

"Do you still have the blossom?" Agnella stood. "If you could fuse it, we would know for sure and could start testing for its counteragent."

She grimaced at the thought. But what choice did she have? "It's in my kit. Which is in my workshop." A scentmaker never went far without her kit. How senseless of her to leave it behind, but at least she'd have a chance to check on her parents.

Agnella crooked a finger at Rian. "A job for you, Spy."

"It only opens for me," Bell said.

"He'll have Lanzis watching for you."

Rian rolled up his shirt sleeves. "I can sneak her inside."

"You're sure? The fate of free Bardia rests on her shoulders, and hence on yours."

"I will bring her safely back," Rian said gravely. He stood.

"We're going now?" Bell asked.

"Not a moment to lose," Agnella said, nodding in approval at Rian.

Bell followed her out of the lean-to and paused at the fire to take in its heat for one more moment. The adrenaline from studying the mindmeld was fading, leaving her chilled by her damp clothes.

"Here." Agnella shoved a soot-colored homespun dress into her hands.

Bell grimaced at the dress, then stepped back into the lean-to to change. When she came out, Rian held a black cloak for her. He gave her a crooked smile.

The mist had turned to soft rain, the cool air on the porch soothing her cheeks. She longed for it to wash away the weight on her shoulders.

He stepped off the porch and Bell hesitated. What was this tangle of frustration at Rian's presence and relief he was here? Was she really going to follow him through the dark woods? What if this was part of an elaborate plot to betray them all? Or to force her to flee the island with him? Of course, he probably would have done that back on the docks of Santa Croce....

Rian cleared his throat. "Bell..." His voice was warm magic. "First—so you can trust me." He held out his wrist.

Bell instinctively reached for the truthtelling vial in her pocket, but she was frightened of what he was going to say. She looked away.

The misty rain hid the whitecaps out at sea, but she stared into it as if the water would show her the answer.

He stepped back onto the porch, looking down at her. "I want to care for you, Bell." His velvet voice cracked, and her belly felt like a pool of stirring water as she turned to see his face. The window's glow lit his eyes with tenderness so deep, it didn't seem possible he could be pretending. He bent toward her, his long fingers soft on her shoulders.

"Will you let me?" he whispered.

In a moment of breathless clarity, she saw herself as an ancient tree

233

reaching for an age-old star, and the star bending down to regard her. His silver light wound among her branches, lighting her leaves with magic.

That was how long they'd been moving toward each other. Slowly, inevitably, gloriously.

As he leaned his face toward hers, she dropped the vial back into her pocket. Her arms wound around his shoulders. She shivered as his lips brushed hers, and his hands slid along her waist, pressing her closer. Her fingers wound into his hair on their own, the strands silky and thick.

He doesn't want you, *Bell.* Roza's words flashed in Bell's mind. All the softness in her body hardened. She jerked her hands free. "What are you doing?"

"Something magical?" He let go. "Shall we back up?"

She glared at him; her anger sharpened by the flush racing over her body. "I'm not a toy for you to play with."

"Of course not." His eyes were wide.

"You can't go from me to her and back and expect me to take you in."

His mouth worked. "Her?" he asked finally.

She flapped a hand. "Your lover."

"Lover?"

"Stop repeating my words. Yes, I know about your lover."

A tiny smile grew into a grin. "You do."

"I met her while I was with the Seller. She was not pleased with you, let me tell you—" Bell blinked as his amusement grew. "*What?*"

"I don't have a lover, Bell. Unless you wanted to volunteer."

She narrowed her gaze. "Of course you would say that."

He held out his wrist again. "Why don't you make certain I'm telling the truth?"

"Arabia knew things about you like—" She blushed and stepped back.

"Arabia is a fellow Spy, Bell. She's not my lover. She was the one playing you."

"It sure didn't sound like a game."

"She is very good at her job," he mused. "And...well, at the risk of sounding conceited, she has made it clear she would *like* to be my lover." He sighed and pursed his lips.

"What?"

"I may have encouraged her, in the past. That would be why she thinks she has a chance."

Bell studied him. He did look remorseful, but the Saint knew he was an actor. "So you were lovers in the past." She considered pulling out the truthtelling elixir again.

"Of a sort."

"Perhaps she still thinks you are."

"Perhaps." He spun toward the water, hands laced behind his head. "But I don't love her, Bell. I never did. We used each other. Back then, I still believed in the Seller's cause. I hadn't met *you* yet."

She took a deep breath, stepped back. "I've heard so many things, Rian. It's...it's hard to believe you." And it was certainly unwise to let him kiss her, since reality shifted when he looked at her so softly. He turned around, his gaze considering. She found herself leaning onto her toes, remembering his hands on her waist.

The door creaked. Agnella stuck her head out. "Why are you still here? Time's flying, lovebirds."

Bell bit back her irritation, shoving her longing into a distant corner of herself. "Let's go then. We might need to melt through the wall if they've found the secret door."

"Lovely to be useful. Shall we?" He gestured toward the forest.

Thirty-Four

RIAN LED HER IN A CIRCUITOUS ROUTE through Grenwood, keeping out of sight of the road. They followed no path, but Rian never paused to check their direction. The rain hid the moon and muffled the sounds they made in the damp leaves and bracken. He held a dim glow gem to guide them around the wettest spots.

"I think he'll assume you're in Santa Croce. The woods would be a little rough for someone like you."

Swathed in Agnella's dark dress and a black cloak, Bell frowned. "Someone like me?"

She sensed his smile. "Someone who owns nothing but yellow dresses."

"I have a peach one."

"But you hate it."

"Hush."

A sliver moon showed the wall of House Asbury. Rian halted and pulled her behind a tree. "Wait here." He cupped the back of her head and pressed a soft kiss to her forehead before she could react. "I'll scout the front." He flashed a knee-weakening smile and slipped away.

Bell dug her fingers into the shallow ridges of a cypress tree as he vanished over the wall. If he was caught, she could hardly find her way back to the cabin in the dark without a path. The minutes dragged by as her eyes strained for any movement.

She gasped silently as he reappeared. "Three watching the gates,

236

one in the garden. I don't think they've found your door yet, so they won't be expecting us that way."

"What about my father's guards?"

"Bribed or under the control of mindmeld."

She bit her cheek. "I hope they're all right." She led the way to the hidden door, hesitating before pulling aside the vines and opening the scentlock.

The door swung open with a small rustle. They waited in the arbor, scanning for the lone Lanzi.

He was a shadow on their side of the fountain, facing away. The water masked their footsteps. Rian led them to the workshop at a crouch in case the Lanzi turned. Bell's lungs softened as the workshop appeared, whole and healthy. It whisked open as if it knew she needed speed. Bell felt her way to her kit, tucked in a hidden drawer. It bulged in her cloak pocket, bumping her leg reassuringly as they stepped back out.

Dim lantern light glowed in Father's study. He was up late working. She slowed.

"Bell," Rian breathed. "The Seller won't hurt them. He's leaving them as a trap for you."

"What if you're wrong?" she whispered. "We're so close."

He frowned.

Her face lit up. "You could warn them. Couldn't you get through the wall without being seen?"

He looked uncertain, then met her anxious gaze—and softened. "Of course." His hands warmed her arms. "I'll be right back."

She crouched beside the workshop as he vanished into the shadows. Between the hedges lining the path to the house, she watched Father pacing back and forth in his study. The lantern light dimmed every time he passed it. He glanced out the window and stopped, then stepped closer, his shape growing in the glass. Had he seen something? Bell dug her nails into her palms, willing him to stay silent.

Father spun and grabbed the lantern. He disappeared into the hall, then flung open the door to the garden and charged out. "Guards," he shouted.

Three more Lanzis appeared at the edge of his lantern light. Father pulled a short blade from his pocket, swinging it in an arc.

"Guards," he roared again. A figure rose behind him, brandishing a rock.

"Father, behind you!" Bell screamed and ran toward him as the rock cracked against the back of his skull. He collapsed like a bag.

The figure tossed the rock aside and opened a flame in her palm, revealing a masked face and long red hair. Bell jerked to a halt at the beginning of the path.

Arabia grinned, her eyes glittering viciously. "Welcome home, Goldenbell."

Bell gritted her teeth. Where was Rian? She scanned the darkness beyond Arabia's light. The fountain splashed behind her, muffling everything. "You'll answer to Roza for this."

Arabia shook her head. "You poor duck." She beckoned forward. "Come back to the Seller, and we'll take good care of all of you. Otherwise…" She looked down at Father, lying motionless across the path. Arabia's gaze came back to Bell. The flame blazed above her hand. "Come here, Goldenbell, or I'll burn his ear off."

Bell's eyes flicked from Arabia to Father's unconscious face. Where was Rian when she needed him?

Arabia lowered her hand toward Father. Bell jammed her hands into her pockets, searching. Why hadn't she brought the mindmeld with her?

"Arabia." Rian's voice wound down the path, dark and dangerous. The cobbles beneath Arabia shivered. "Step away from Bell's father."

"Florian. I've been waiting for you." Arabia straightened, her flames curling higher. She nodded, and the Lanzis dispersed in the direction of Rian's voice. But for the rustle of leaves as the Lanzis searched garden beds and behind bushes, it was silent.

Bell had to buy time. She sucked in a bracing breath and stepped onto the path. She faltered forward until she was almost within Arabia's reach.

Near the house, something like running footsteps sounded against the gravel path, and the Lanzis darted toward the gate.

Arabia's lip curled as Bell's heart sank.

"It didn't take very long for him to abandon you." Arabia reached into her pocket and withdrew a glowing blue vial.

The hedges' leaves shivered and twisted as panic swelled in Bell's chest. She edged backward, toward the fountain patio.

Arabia followed, her eyebrows furrowed to a vicious V. "Trust me, I know the feeling."

"Oh, please." A familiar voice said from behind Bell. Rian stepped into the light's edge, eyes sharp like knives. "You were never mine to abandon."

Arabia's fingers tightened around the vial. "Do you know what I wanted from the Seller, more than anything? Roza wants the cure, and you want freedom, but what do I want? Come a little closer, Rian. Soon you'll remember how much you love me."

Rian stilled.

Arabia raised her voice above the fountain's gurgle. "All I need is to deliver one powerful scentmaker to him, and he'll give me permission to use this on you. You can't escape who you belong to, Florian, though you try so hard." The Lanzis would hear her and quickly return.

Bell edged back toward Rian as Arabia stalked closer. A few more steps, and she'd reach Rian, and then the workshop and the courtyard wall.

Tension sang in Rian's shoulders. "I'll be free of all this soon. Free of him."

Arabia grinned. "Free of him? You can't be free of blood, my love."

Rian's hand closed around Bell's, tugging lightly toward the wall. She steadied her breathing. They were going to run, but she'd never have time to open the scentlock. His hand jerked and she sprang after him. Arabia lunged forward and caught her cloak, but Bell reached up and ripped the clasp, kicking free and throwing herself out of the way of a blast of fire. Bell scrambled to her feet as Rian slammed his hands onto the ground.

Arabia stumbled as the stone softened beneath her. She struggled and screamed in rage as the cobblestones clung to her feet. Before

Arabia could muster more fire, Bell stretched her gift across the garden, calling to the weaving vine that felt like an extension of her body. The vine surged toward Arabia, winding around her. She cursed and threw fire at the vine circling her. The smell of burning leaves filled the air. Bell glowered, urging the vine to wrap tighter. The four Lanzis were running toward them, short swords raised.

Rian spun toward the wall and braced his palms against the stone. A crack splintered the wall, creating handholds.

Bell took his hand, and he boosted her to the crevice he'd made. Her skirts tangled about her, but she struggled to the top. She clung to the rough stone as lanterns blazed within the house and voices rang through the garden. Rian flew up the wall past her, jumping off and landing gracefully on the other side. He pressed a hand to the wall and it rippled as the side facing the Lanzis grew jagged spikes. He held out his arms to her. Her heart twisted as she looked back to her father's inert figure.

"Bell," Rian shouted. Grimacing, she jumped down. Rian staggered as he caught her. He set her on her feet and grabbed her hand. She stumbled after him on trembling legs.

Bell held the weaving vine around Arabia for as long as she could, but she had to release it when they got too far away for her to sense it. They were long gone by the time the Lanzis made it over the wall.

"Does Agnella know you can do that? You called the vine without touching it."

Bell winced. "It's a normal scentmaking skill. Agnella has a thorny vine to protect her workshop at the farm."

"Normal...it's extremely rare that a maker can use their gift without touch, Bell. You called it away from the workshop from yards away. How?"

Bell blinked. Like the flowers she'd woven in the dining room, it had come when she called it. "I don't know. I...I could feel it, and it could feel me."

He slowed and studied her. "Has anyone ever told you how incredible you are?"

She laughed to hide a blush. She wished the drizzle would return and cool her cheeks. "Is this part of your game?"

"Please forget everything she said."

"I don't think I can."

"She's very full of herself."

"Oh, I don't know anyone like that."

He grinned, but it faded to a frown. "I'm sorry about your father, Bell."

His frown remained, and her gaze softened, studying him. He'd had a chance to betray her and choose Arabia, and he hadn't taken it. Bell leaned into him as they walked.

Rian wrapped his arm around her shoulder, tugging her closer. "We'll free your parents. I promise."

She glanced back into the dark woods, her eyes stinging. The Seller might not kill her parents, but who would stop him from hurting them?

Agnella opened the door at their quiet knock. "You have it?"

Bell held up her black velvet kit.

Carasti stirred from the pallet she'd made in the corner, peering out of her mop of hair. The rain made it more unruly than ever. Bell's own hair was tangled in leaves and pine needles. "Any trouble?"

"Lanzis." Rian latched the door and peered out the window. "And a Spy. Bell saved us with her weaving vine."

Agnella tilted her head at Bell.

"I told it to wrap her up." Bell shrugged. The vine had always felt like an extension of her arms, but she'd never had a reason to pull it from the workshop framework.

"You told it."

"I raised that plant from a shoot. It ought to do what I say."

Agnella shook her head, a tiny grin on her lips.

"Where is Garam?" Bell asked.

241

"He went to see if there's any way through the guard around my farm. Saint knows how much fioré you'll need."

"They took Father. And Mother, I think." Bell picked leaves from her hair, her forehead creased with worry. "And they probably used the mindmeld on the staff."

Carasti squeezed her shoulder. "We'll get them back, Bell."

Bell firmed her jaw. "I need to start fusing."

"It's dawn. I think you should rest a few hours," Rian said.

Bell gave up on her hair and rubbed her forehead. "I can't rest until I have the antidote in my hands."

Thirty-Five

THE CLOUD ABOVE THE MINDMELD WAS too faint without a scentstone.

If only she'd thought to steal that too.

She sat on the stool again, masked and gloved, Agnella beside her. The mindmeld cloud turned slowly, murky flashes of colors showing between black chains. She groaned at the sight of vivid orange in the shape of flames.

Agnella's mouth was a grim line. "What do you see?"

"Jonquil. And the Seller knows I'm allergic." She glanced at Rian, who leaned against the doorframe. "Right?"

He hesitated. "You have me to thank for that, I'm afraid."

Bell nodded as if the thought of him betraying her weaknesses to the Seller didn't wrench her gut.

"He had us watch all potential scentmakers. If I hadn't told him, Roza would have."

"I know." The Seller had hardly needed spies to bring her to him, not when her own sister… She rubbed her gritty eyes. "I should have taken his scentstone. I can't see the other components clearly enough."

Agnella raised her eyebrows. "I thought the last scentstone vanished decades ago when Isablia Mor died."

"I don't know where he found it, but it worked. Better than he expected, I think. I never told him I could even control the unfused fioré."

"Unfused? Perhaps we can use that," Rian murmured.

"Did you recognize the black Insidio?" Agnella asked.

Bell hesitated. Her memory of the dark Magia's scent cloud was jumbled up with the panic that had risen in her in the Seller's sanctuary. "It's hard to be sure."

Agnella touched the black Insidio blossom Bell had laid on the shelf. "Fuse it and tell me what you see."

Bell put one petal in her palm and laid her other fingers across it. The petal grew heavier, and unease stirred. Roza's misty blue eyes flashed in her mind. Bell's breath shuddered. "I can't," she whispered.

Agnella's hand closed gently on her arm. "You can. I know it."

Bell straightened her mask and repositioned her fingers. She had to try. She let her gift warm her arms. Slowly, so slowly.

The black chains exploded into view, looming over her. The scent gathered, weighing down her hand. She gasped as panic burst in her chest.

"Bell?" Rian sounded distant, his hand on her shoulder a breath of wind.

She forced her eyes open as Agnella held the vial below her hands. The scent drops rolled heavily into the glass, the black Insidio petal withering to a husk as soon as the liquid left it. Her legs trembled as weakness washed over her. She tried to pick up the cork, but her fingers wouldn't respond. Agnella snatched it up and stoppered the vial.

Bell leaned back into Rian's arms. Feeling returned to her fingers, and the darkness cleared. "I'm all right. It was so small, I couldn't keep from fusing it all."

"It's too much for you." Rian smoothed a lock of hair back from her face, his touch cool and soothing.

Agnella shook her head. "She's tired. She can study the scent cloud later."

"I'll sleep a little now." Her muscles felt like mud. She didn't resist when Rian carried her inside and laid her on a pallet beside Carasti's.

The Magia had been strong, but she hadn't let it overtake her. She hadn't hurt anyone with it. If her eyes hadn't felt like lead, the victory surging through her would have made her eager to try again.

She heard Rian mention the scentstone to Agnella as her consciousness faded.

Bell woke at Carasti's uniquely delicate snort. In the porch window, the sky was darkening gray with rain. Was it afternoon already? Agnella looked up from slicing sourdough bread, steam rising from the loaf. A pot of potato soup bubbled on the fire. The potatoes' earthy scent mingled with the sharp smell of wood smoke.

"Why'd you let me sleep so long?"

"You need to focus to fuse. Get up and eat something," Agnella said.

Bell threw aside the blanket and stood to get a slice of warm buttered bread.

Carasti staggered up and took the next slice. "Is it my turn to do anything yet?"

"Not until the Solstice." Agnella peered out the window.

Bell moved behind her. "Where's Rian?"

"Getting you a scentstone."

Bell choked and Carasti whacked her back. "But it's in the Seller's Conservatory," she sputtered.

"Rian has been sneaking through that lair since he could walk. He's also looking for alternate routes to the prison where the scentmakers are being held."

"If he gets caught, they'll mindmeld him—"

"You'll finish the antidote," Carasti said around a mouthful.

Bell swallowed, trying to lose the lump in her throat. "Did Garam find a way into your farm?"

Agnella frowned. "He hasn't returned."

Bell paced. "We need to stop taking these risks."

"Tell me about the clouds. What did he teach you about them?"

"He showed me how to shape them with my gift. That's—that's how I took Piero's gift."

245

"And you can see the fioré clouds before they're fused?"

"I didn't tell him. That's one advantage." Bell ate another bite. She could barely taste the bread, though the warm yeasty smell was comforting. "He told me his mother died of Lymbodia, and the Maestro of Scents wouldn't help her."

Agnella grunted. "Years ago, he begged the Consiglio to legalize Magia. He thought that if scentmakers were allowed to experiment with Magia, a cure would be made. He's deluded, Bell."

"But what if he's found it now?"

Agnella pursed her lips. "Magia is the cause of Lymbodia. If the Sotto shut down, so would the trade of Magia. If no one grows it, no one can sell it, and Lymbodia would disappear."

Bell squashed a morsel of bread between her fingers. "I'll fuse an antidote for the mindmeld, but I'm not giving up on the cure. Maybe the mindmeld can really be used to cure Lymbodia." *I won't give up on Roza.*

"It still requires *fusione*, Bell. Whose gift would you take next?" Agnella's fingers tightened on the windowsill as her gaze focused on something outside.

A shadow in the pines formed a tall figure. Bell let out a long breath. Who would have thought she'd ever be glad to see Garam?

Agnella let him in, and he tracked mud onto the floor.

"I didn't see Lanzis anywhere. If we keep off the roads, I think we won't run into trouble."

Bell dropped her slice of bread on the table. "You can't all leave."

Agnella swung on her cloak. "We have no time to waste, Bell. You'll need plenty of Aronil to counteract the Insidio in the mindmeld." She gestured to a white bundle on the table. "This is my La Festa robe and a vial of my blood for your disguise. You'll need to fuse a mask elixir and use the blood as the base."

Bell reached out for Agnella's arm, fear creeping over her. "He'll brainwash you if he catches you."

"What do you think he'll do with you, hmm?" Agnella scowled, but she squeezed Bell's fingers before stalking off with a basket over her arm.

"Take care, Bell." Garam held out his hand, but she edged back instinctively. His eyes flickered and he lowered his hand. "Stay in the cabin. We'll return in a few hours."

Bell watched until they disappeared. Minutes passed before she realized how quickly her breaths came, and she forced her lungs to slow.

They will come back.

She recited the words silently like a mantra. Rian would find the scentstone and return safely. Agnella and Garam would bring back more Aronil to try to counteract the black Insidio. With the scentstone, she'd be able to decipher the rest of the mindmeld, and the antidote would be within her grasp.

As for the cure to Lymbodia, maybe the answer lay within the antidote. Perhaps the Seller's discovery of a temporary cure had blinded him to further possibilities.

There had to be another way, or she would be forced to choose between stealing a maker's gift and watching Roza die.

Nails digging into her palms, Bell paced between the windows, searching the tree line as if she could glare Rian and the others into existence.

"Come sit down. You need to eat more than bread." Carasti set a bowl of potato stew on the table.

"How can I, when everyone is out risking their—their sanity, if not their lives?"

Carasti eyed her. "You are too, working with the mindmeld. That might be the most dangerous part."

Bell scowled. "I'm the wrong person for all this responsibility. I could fail everyone."

"You're the perfect person. You're so concerned about failing that you won't."

Bell leaned her hands on the windowsill. "I already have."

"Please. Do you know what would happen if *I* was supposed to save everyone?"

Too anxious to smile at Carasti's wry expression, Bell dropped into a chair and took a bite of soup. "You'd be on a boat to the mainland."

"I'd be gone." Carasti made a *poof* motion.

"I was joking, Carasti. You might complain even more than I do, but you would do it."

Carasti wrinkled her nose. "No one knows for sure because they'd never risk asking me."

Bell ignored this and swallowed a potato chunk. "I should look at the mindmeld again."

"Shouldn't you wait for Agnella?"

"You heard her. We don't have time. If—if Rian gets caught, that antidote will be the last chance we have."

"I think it's the last chance regardless," Carasti muttered.

Appetite fading, Bell shoved the bowl aside and stood. "I can't rest until I hold the antidote in my hands."

Thirty-Six

BACK IN AGNELLA'S LEAN-TO WORKSHOP, Bell tied her mask securely and tugged on her gloves. The glowing blue vials of mindmeld elixir brightened as she sat in front of them. Like they were waiting for her. She picked one up, rolling it between her fingers.

"You should try it on me."

She turned back to Carasti. "What?"

Carasti jutted her chin toward the vial in Bell's hand. "The mindmeld. Try it on me. Maybe then you could see its components better."

"No."

"Why not? It's not like you'll hurt me. Besides, we can see how long it lasts." Carasti grabbed a mask and tied it tightly on her face.

Bell shook her head hard. "I can't."

"Bell." Carasti dropped into the other stool, hands braced on her knees. "I risk being brainwashed as soon as we leave this cabin. This is your chance to keep me safe from those who *do* want to hurt me."

Her stomach lurched. Carasti was right. The Seller was already using the mindmeld on anyone who stood in his way. If Bell wanted to explore its components and counteragents, one of the best ways to do that was to administer it and observe its effects.

She took a steadying breath, then twisted the mindmeld vial's cork once. "Are you sure you trust me to do this?"

Carasti gave her a bright smile. "More than anyone else on this island."

249

Bell softened. "I'll use a small amount to start with."

She removed the cork and dabbed Carasti's wrist with a single drop, her gaze on the scent cloud rising from the elixir. It swirled above Carasti, enveloping her in the now-familiar faded black chains. Carasti stood still, staring at her with wide, complacent eyes.

"Feel anything?"

Carasti shrugged. "Make me believe something."

"You hate woodmaking. You wish the gift would go away."

Her freckles stood out as her cheeks paled. "I hate woodmaking?"

Bell's stomach clenched like a fist. "You don't hate woodmaking," she said quickly. She gripped the table, her knees wobbling. "I'm sorry."

"Why are you sorry?"

"Never mind." Bell stepped closer to the scent cloud, pushing back the nausea rising at the scent of Jonquil leaking through the chains.

There. A thick braid of Jonquil, like a slash of orange, and twisted within it, a gold-white arch. Jonga Lily. She let out a sharp breath of relief. The cloud listed a few degrees to the right, and she caught a glimpse of a dim color. She edged still closer, her mask almost brushing the chains.

A soft triangle of nevermore gray. Smemor, the Magia that had given Roza the Burning Blood.

Suddenly the air was full of Jonquil, flooding through her mask like a slap of salt water. Nausea ripped through her, and she corked the vial. Carasti danced out of the way as Bell gagged and yanked off the mask. She let the vial drop onto the table and ran to the sink. As soon as she opened her mouth, she heaved, emptying her stomach.

"Oh, Bell." Carasti looked around frantically. "What do you need?"

"Myrtle," Bell groaned. "The green vial." Bell sank to the floor and closed her eyes, skin crawling with sweat and stomach churning. Quickly, Carasti found the Myrtle and dabbed Bell's wrists liberally, then pushed a towel under her head and a damp cloth on her forehead. When Bell opened her eyes, the grassy scent of Myrtle filled the room, its healing power soothing her nausea. Carasti leaned over her, peering into her face. Bell pushed herself up, ignoring Carasti's frown.

"I know the components I need now." She leaned heavily on the shelf while she reached for a Sciver plant in the back row. "Sciver to counteract Smemor. Princess Seed to counteract Jonquil. Aronil to counteract Jonga Lily." She hesitated over the single Aronil plant. "And more Aronil to counteract Insidio. This is black Insidio, but maybe it's similar enough to work the same way." She sank onto her stool, fingers shaking as she formed the bouquet and prepped a vial. Carasti stood quietly beside her, an eerie, complacent look in her normally mischievous eyes.

Bell shuddered. This had to work. She let her gift rush down her arms and into her fingers, pulling the fioré into a single effervescent elixir. The vial glowed the palest blue, the color of the sea's horizon on a summer afternoon. The elixir's scent cloud rose above the vial, the sharp silver zigzag of Sciver cutting through the soft circle of Aronil. Princess Seed floated above it, a yellow-brown tree with low, draping branches.

She turned to Carasti. "Give me your hand."

Carasti held out her wrist. Bell applied the elixir and waited a long moment.

"You don't have freckles," Bell said.

Carasti's hands flew to her cheeks. "Of course I don't."

Bell felt like she'd swallowed a thorn. Had she fused it wrong? Or was Aronil the incorrect counteragent to black Insidio?

The cabin door opened, slamming against a wall. "Bell, Carasti," someone shouted. Bell corked her attempted antidote and grabbed the mindmeld vials and her kit, stuffing them all into her pockets. They hurried to the door of the lean-to as Garam stumbled into the cabin. Blood left a dark trail on his forehead, and he held his left arm to his chest. Angry red burns marked the skin beneath his shredded left sleeve.

"You have to run, now." He stopped, panting.

"Where's Agnella?"

"They were inside her workshop, somehow. The firemaker and a dozen Lanzis. I escaped while Agnella held them off with her elixirs,

251

but there were too many of them. They'll use the mindmeld to get her to lead them here."

Bell grabbed Agnella's Maestra disguise off the table, pulling her mask down around her neck.

"Hurry," he hissed.

The three of them slipped and staggered across the rocks in the thickening rain. Bell and Carasti held hands with iron grips, keeping each other steady as they skidded down the path toward the water. Garam held the boat with one arm while they climbed inside, then kicked the boat out into the waves.

Carasti lost her balance and sat down hard. "What are you doing?"

"I'm useless with this arm. I'll lead them off. Go to the far end of the pier and find Aless."

"There's room, Garam," Bell shouted. He sprinted back toward the cabin. The dark woods behind it absorbed his towering form. A hard ball of guilt and worry grew in her chest. She had hated him so much.

"Cursed man. He expects us to row all the way to Santa Croce?" Carasti's worried eyes softened her bitter words. She grabbed one oar and tossed Bell the handle of the other.

Rain and wind churned the water, tossing the boat up and sideways. Their pained efforts soon pushed them around the point and out of sight of the path. In the murky distance, the smeared lights of the pier appeared. They crested a wave and plummeted down the other side. Wind whipped Bell's hair against her face.

Bell's arms were already cramping. She blinked rain from her eyes. "We'll never make it." The rocks along the shore left no space to land the boat. They had to row all the way to the docks.

"We will." Carasti dug the paddle deep, grunting. Bell bent over as she labored, fighting the waves.

"See? The effects of the mindmeld are already gone," Carasti said between breaths. "No wonder the Seller wanted *permanenza*." Then, unbelievably, Carasti grinned. "It's not so hopeless."

"I used a drop, and it lasted for ten minutes. How long would it take to wear off if I had used the whole bottle?" Bell couldn't find the strength to say anything else for several laboring strokes. "What if I can't find a cure, Carasti? I'm sure he could create hundreds of doses, if not thousands. Even without *permanenza*, he'll do that to so many people."

"You'll find it. You're meant to." Carasti's grin turned teasing. "At least we get to see your almost betrothed." Bell bristled and Carasti laughed. "I, for one, will be glad to see Aless. Every girl knows about his pretty blue eyes, and he's as rich as a duke. Poor man. I heard he was torn up over you, Bell."

Bell poured her ire into rowing. "Oh, please." Her world narrowed to pull, lift, pull, lift, her palms burning. Her mind swarmed with worries for Garam, her parents, Agnella, and Rian. If only Rian had made it back with the scentstone. If only he was safe with them now.

"Please, let him not go back to the cabin," Bell murmured.

A wave slapped wood and water sloshed into the boat. Bell's feet sat in several inches of water. What if the boat filled up? She couldn't swim all the way to shore. Her chest tightened. Anxiety stirred.

"Bell, you were wrong about Garam."

Bell's attention snapped back to Carasti. Her sore hands tightened on the oar. "Well, he didn't exactly seem trustworthy."

"The crazy thing is, I think he still loves Roza. After all she's done."

Bell glared at her friend, using her shoulder to swipe wet hair from her face. "So do I." When had everything been turned upside down? Now Garam was her friend? Roza her enemy?

Halfway to the pier, the wind finally died down, and the pelting rain became a drizzle. An hour later, they reached a graveled stretch of shore several hundred feet from the pier. Too weary to row further, they beached the boat and walked.

Bell's wet skirt dragged at her ankles, and she envied Carasti's light tunic and pants. Beyond the pier rose several mansions where the masters of the boats lived. Bell scanned the houses, anxiety swelling. She had no idea where Aless lived.

"Let's ask for directions," Bell said when they stopped for breath at a low stone terrace stretching along the entire pier. The boardwalk was empty in the rain, a guard or two stationed in the guardhouses. They were there to watch the ships in the shipyard, not two bedraggled girls hurrying along the pier.

Carasti gave her an odd look. "Looking like this? Merchants' servants are even more uppity than yours."

"Elena and Bethesda are not uppity. Do you have a better idea?" She was trying desperately not to picture Aless's awkward face when she came begging.

"The Medoros are the last house." She gestured toward a huge stone castle with precipitous walls.

"How do you know that?" Bell narrowed her eyes. Thoughts connected in her head like grass roots. The Medoros were boat merchants. Carasti's recent obsession with ships of Bardian wood...

Carasti shrugged one shoulder, her gaze on the castle. "I've done some work for a Medoro."

Bell stared at her. "You're *working* for them? Are you helping them make the Bardian wood ships?"

"Is that a problem?"

Bell bit her lip, a sick feeling welling in her stomach. Carasti had heard Bell curse the Medoros over and over, and all this time she was working for them?

"You could leave now, if you want. You don't have to put yourself in danger for me," Bell said quietly as they walked.

Carasti's laugh sounded like glass bells. "Oh, Bell. Where would I go? There's nowhere to run, not from the Seller." Carasti pointed ahead. "There's a gap in the hedge on the seaward side of the house."

"Can't we knock on the front door?"

Carasti shook her head. "I don't work for the Medoros. I work for Aless. I was sworn to utmost secrecy, Bell. That's why I never told you who it was. But he's not like the rest of the family. He actually cares about makers."

Bell's lip curled. "Or maybe he wants more power over them."

Carasti sighed. "Look, you'll have to trust me. Garam didn't turn out to be so bad, right?"

Bell looked out to the sea.

Carasti turned back to face the house. "We can't knock at the front because we don't want to alert his parents. They don't know what Aless does with his time and money. Come on."

They circled the house and squeezed through the gap in the hedge. The back garden was cloaked in shadow. Light from the broad windows above them lit the path and the servant's door. "Aless usually meets me out here, so I don't know how to get past the servants," Carasti whispered.

Bell bit her lip. "We'll tell the servants we want to see him. Surely if we say it's urgent—"

"Looking like this?" Carasti ran her hands over her hair, and it sprang back exactly as it was—a wild, damp halo. "Two girls begging to see a merchant's son? They'll think we're both pregnant."

Bell gave a surprised laugh. "Well, that wouldn't do."

Carasti's face remained sober. "You'll have to use your mindmeld."

Bell blanched. Her hand slipped into her pocket and tightened around the vial. The idea left a sour taste in her mouth.

"You used it on me, and I was fine. It wears off quickly," Carasti said. "It's that or climb the wall and sneak in a window."

Bell sighed. The wall was bare stone, not even a clinging vine for her to work with. "Okay."

She held the vial ready as they approached the servants' door. Carasti knocked briskly. After what seemed forever, the door creaked open to reveal a dubious maid.

"We're not hiring." She started to close the door.

"Wait." Bell braced her foot against it and grabbed the maid's wrist. She dabbed a generous drop onto the girl's bare skin. The girl gasped and pulled back, then her muscles went slack.

Bell leaned closer and spoke quietly. "You must show us to Alessander Medoro. It's vital we speak with him and no one else immediately."

The maid blinked unfocused eyes. "Yes. I will show you."

Carasti made an impressed face as they followed her into the hallway. Ship's lanterns flickered everywhere, gleaming on polished wood paneling.

They lowered their heads as a large woman in black glided into their path, frowning. "Who is this, Maddie?"

Bell held her breath.

"They're to see young Master Medoro right away, Mistress Ina."

The housekeeper narrowed her gaze but let them pass. Bell had to force herself not to lift her chin. Who cared what the housekeeper thought?

They followed Maddie up a wide velvet-carpeted staircase and down a hall paneled in wood. Aless answered the maid's knock from behind a heavy door. He sat at a writing desk before a fire that was dwarfed by a huge hearth, scribbling in a notebook while bracing a thick book open with his other elbow.

He rose, eyes widening with recognition. Silence strained the air as he studied them. "Thank you, Maddie. That will be all," he said finally.

Maddie curtseyed to all of them but remained staring at Bell.

"That will be all, Maddie," Aless said, firmly.

"Go," Bell muttered, flustered.

Maddie curtseyed, gaze on Bell, as she backed out and shut the door.

Aless ran a hand through his hair, and it stood up in dark clumps. "What happened? What are you doing here, like this?" His horrified expression made it clear he meant their clothing, not their uninvited appearance.

Bell steeled herself. This was no time to preserve her pride. She leaned against the sofa across from him and lowered her voice. "We've run into some trouble, Aless." She glanced back to make sure the door was still sealed. "With the Seller."

"Ah. Something to do with the boat I lent you?" One of his eyebrows rose.

Her words tumbled out. "I borrowed the boat to get to Agnella's shelter. I was trying to fuse something…"

Aless frowned. "And?"

"Agnella was captured, and Garam sent us in the rowboat and went the other way to lead them off."

"Captured? You rowed here alone? In this weather?" He stepped toward them, gesturing to the sofa. "Please, sit. No wonder you look so ragged."

Carasti smirked at Bell as they dropped onto the pristine couch beside the hearth.

Bell reached toward the fire to warm her hands. Her palms, the skin red and raw, stung at the heat. Aless moved to the fire and grabbed a log from the basket beside the hearth. Sparks rose when he settled it into the flames. He turned back, looking them both over again, forehead crinkled with concern. Carasti smoothed her navy tunic over her leggings.

"Where is Rian? Did he abandon you?"

Bell and Carasti exchanged glances, and Bell took a deep breath. "The Seller plans to use his mindmeld elixir to brainwash Bardia."

His eyes widened. "I expected something of that nature, the way things have been stirred up."

"He's learned how to fuse a *permanenza* elixir, but it requires *fusione*, which means stealing—"

"I know what it means. I can read. It's my job to be familiar with the pitfalls of Bardian alchemy. So that's why all the scentmakers have gone missing." He paced before the fire. "What do you need from me?"

Carasti straightened. "You have fioré? Magia?"

"I deal in fioré, among other Bardian wares." He studied Bell. "And Magia. Are you trying to fuse an antidote?"

Bell nodded. "It contains Jonquil, and I can't work with the Jonquil until I have more control. I need the scentstone before I can fuse an antidote. If I can't get that…" She shook her head.

"Scentstone?" Aless asked.

"Didn't Maestra Agnella say the Solstice would strengthen your control?" Carasti asked.

Bell tilted her head, recalling Agnella's words. "She did."

"So you will be the next Maestra of Scents?" Aless asked excitedly.

"Then we need to get you to the Spring," Carasti said.

Aless dropped into his desk chair and leaned forward. "The Seller will be watching the Rotunda."

"I was planning to join La Festa parade in disguise as Agnella."

"If the Seller is watching, he'll know you're not her," Carasti muttered.

"What's he going to do? Attack the Maestris in the open?" Bell stood and drew closer to the hearth. She spread out her skirts, hoping they would dry soon. Otherwise, she would have to ask Aless for a dress. The awkwardness of it all turned her stomach.

"He'd have to admit he knows Agnella is gone if he tries to single you out." Carasti pointed one delicate finger at her. "But you'll be exposed, and the Seller has mindmeld. He could send someone else to grab you, and no one would know it was his doing."

Aless eyed them both.

A wave of despair crept over Bell. She had to do something. "What kind of Magia do you have?"

"All of them." He shrugged when she frowned at him. "We sell to all kinds of makers."

"Black Insidio?"

He smiled warily. "Promise you won't report me to the Consiglio?"

Heels clicked in the hall and Aless bolted up. "Behind the shelves, quickly." He flung a hand toward the far side of the library where rows of bookshelves slumped in shadow. Bell and Carasti hurled themselves into the corner as the door swung open.

"Alessander, what is this nonsense about two serving women?" Mistress Medoro's voice was thin, yet strong, like a delicate steel cable.

Aless's face melted into calm. He lifted a hand. "Oh. That was nothing. Merely asking for money. It seems their father is in dire straits and required their…assistance." His eyes never strayed from his mother's keen face, but Bell blushed regardless.

"I hope you sent them away quickly," she said.

"Yes, Mother. Was there anything else? I'm in the middle of Father's fioré logs." He gestured to the notebook sprawled on the side table.

She strode toward the door, hands clasped in front of her.

Aless's adam's apple bobbed. "Mother, has Father decided if he is willing to deal with the Seller? Did you tell him of the missing scent-makers and possible *fusione*?"

Mistress Medoro paused. "He is still considering. We must be very cautious, Alessander. It is too soon to decide one way or another."

Aless stepped toward her. "Mother, please."

She lifted her pointed chin. "My place is by his side. As is yours. Do you understand, Alessander? If he chooses to follow the Seller, we will follow him down."

Aless took a deep breath. "I will do my best."

She frowned. "See that you do. He will not return until late, but I am going to bed now."

"Good night, Mother."

Bell held her breath until Mistress Medoro's heels echoed into silence down the hall.

Aless turned toward them. "You can come out now."

The window behind him clicked and swung open, letting in a rush of night air. Bell gasped as a dark figure tumbled into the room.

Thirty-Seven

ALESS LOWERED HIS FISTS AS RIAN STOOD and swept his hood back. The kohl had been washed away, and his bare face looked fiercer somehow without it.

"Rian." Bell ran toward him.

The sight of his dark sky eyes opened relief within her, like a door bursting loose before a torrent of wind.

"Oh," she murmured. *I thought I'd never see you again.*

She cupped his face in her hands, and the feeling of his skin was home. He wound his fingers through her hair and pulled her to him. They kissed, fierce yet tender, eyes open like they were afraid the other would disappear.

He pulled away first and pressed his forehead to hers. "I'm glad to see you too…" His voice faded away, ragged.

Bell slipped her arms around his waist. "We're both all right." She leaned back. "How did you find me?" She glanced back at Carasti's smirk, too aglow with relief to blush. "Us?"

"Deductive reasoning. Your list of refuges grows thin. What happened at the cabin?"

Bell took a deep breath. The warmth of his touch pushed back her despair at the memory of their flight. "Agnella and Garam went to her farm to look for Aronil, but it was a trap and Agnella was taken. Garam came back to warn us and led them the other way so we could escape. I don't know if he—" She swallowed.

"He's resourceful," Aless said. He was staring disdainfully at Rian.

260

She gathered her courage and met Rian's gaze. "Did you see my parents? Or Agnella?"

His mouth tightened. "Your parents are imprisoned in the Midnight Garden, as I feared. I didn't see Agnella." Rian pulled out the flat scentstone. "Is this it?"

Her heart lifted. "How did you do it?"

His old grin returned. "Please."

She stroked the smooth stone. Hope stirred. If she could see the black Insidio clearly, it might give her a clue about its counteragent. "Maybe this will work." She could see the scent clouds so much more clearly with it.

Aless clapped his hands briskly. "I'll show you to the greenhouse. But first, you all need tea. And some new clothes?"

"I doubt anything of yours would fit," Carasti said drily.

Bell scowled at her.

Aless ignored her comment. "I was thinking of my sister's old things."

"What about your staff?" Rian said.

"I'll sneak everything we need in here or my quarters. Keep your voices down," Aless said acidly. "Hopefully, most of them have gone to bed."

"Are your parents in league with the Seller?" Rian asked.

"Wouldn't you know?" Aless's tone was hostile.

"I've been unsure, actually. Your father seems to be. Your mother is an unknown entity. Which is admirable, considering my vocation."

Bell took a slow, calming breath as Aless glared at Rian. She turned to dry the back of her dress. "Where is your greenhouse? If Rian could figure out where I am, surely the Seller will too, eventually."

"First, we need a new plan," Aless said firmly.

"*New* plan?" Rian arched a brow.

Bell and Carasti glanced at each other. Carasti spoke. "Her disguise as Agnella won't fool the Seller. He might send a mindmelded puppet to attack Bell or even get close enough himself to use the *permanenza* he has on her."

Rian tapped the windowsill, looking pained.

"You couldn't—you know—dig a tunnel into the Rotunda?" Carasti made a vague gesture.

Rian glowered. "I don't *dig* tunnels. I make them. And the Rotunda is built of an alloy using all the solid gifts, so as much as it pains me to admit, it would be extremely difficult for me to tunnel into it."

Aless grabbed a long piece of rolled parchment from a shelf below his desk and spread it out on his desk. It was a map of Bardia, every street neatly labeled in a swooping print. "La Festa parade begins here, at the head of Via dei Calzaiuoli." He tapped the small piazza between Santa Maria Novella and Santa Spirito.

"The Maestris will be wearing their white cloaks until they reach the Rotunda," Bell said. "Maybe I can get as close as possible through Rian's tunnels and then join the Maestris before Solstice. I'll have to leave the Seller as little time as possible to see me. We must hope the Solstice will make me strong enough to defeat him."

"Maestra Piccarda will know it's you," Rian said. "And I'll be with you, of course."

Carasti gave a tiny snort. "And how do you intend to do that without exposing her cover?"

He grinned sharply. "Leave that to me."

After devouring a plate of sandwiches, they changed clothes in another parlor. Bell's dress was slim and ivory and much too long. Carasti's sapphire and topaz dress fit snugly, nipped in around her waist and bust, giving her an entirely different silhouette than her usual tunics. Aless kept sneaking glances at Carasti, and Bell felt a small bit of relief. Perhaps watching her kiss Rian was enough to convince Aless to move on. Carasti completely ignored his attention and deftly knotted up Bell's skirt.

Bell's knot bobbed awkwardly around her calves, but at least she wasn't tripping every other step. When Rian saw her walk out of the parlor, he appeared to be swallowing laughter, undeterred by her icy glare.

They crept behind Aless down a back staircase and across a statue-lined courtyard. On the other side lay a greenhouse half as big as the house. Aless opened glass double doors, automatic glow gem lights bursting on to reveal rows of fioré stretching to the end of the room.

"Will this be enough?"

"Impressive," Bell said begrudgingly. Her heart reached tentatively for hope as the first fioré rustled and turned to face her.

Aless grinned. "We're the biggest wholesaler in Santa Croce. Father put me in charge this year, and when Garam warned me about the Seller, I doubled the stock."

Bell touched a budding Jonga Lily. She would need the illusion fioré to create the mask elixir to disguise her as Agnella. "Then Agnella got caught for nothing."

"Not nothing," Rian squeezed her fingers, glancing around. "But the Seller will send his Lanzis to hunt out every possible store of fioré. With the greenhouse lit up like this, we'll be visible from the pier. We have no idea how long we'll be safe here."

Aless rubbed his chin. "I wish there was a way to dim the lights, but they're automatic."

Pushing away thoughts of her parents and Agnella trapped in the Midnight Garden, she turned to Aless. "I'll work as quickly as I can. Do you have vials and a workspace?"

Aless turned to a doorway on the right. "Through here. Should be everything you need."

Their shoes echoed on the stone floor as Bell stepped into a smaller room with a wide table along the back wall. During the day, the glass roof and walls would let in warm sunlight, but cool air blew from fans built into the walls. Goldenbells bobbed in the breeze around the entire room, shifting their focus to her as she stepped closer. She cupped a yellow blossom and swallowed past a tight throat. The goldenbell wound around her hand without prompting, weaving an intricate braid around her shoulder and up into her hair. She giggled as a tendril tickled her ear.

When she turned to the others, Aless shifted awkwardly, and Rian looked amused at his discomfort. Was Aless thinking of her when he bought these? If she didn't feel such intense joy to be surrounded by flowers, she would find that idea mortifying.

Aless gestured to the row of vials and pairs of gloves and masks lining the table. "This is all our scentmaking equipment." He stepped back.

"Aless, thank you."

He paused, looking sheepish. "I hoped it would be of use to you."

"It's perfect. It's beautiful. They're my favorite." She suppressed more babbling words.

He cleared his throat. "Yes. Will you be needing Magia as well?"

Bell hesitated. The idea that black Insidio's counteragent lay within the Magia, or in a specific combination of Magia and fioré, had occurred to her. She pursed her lips. "Do you actually have black Insidio? I need to test for its counteragent, and it's best to use a pure elixir for that."

Aless nodded. "I'll unlock the dark room where we keep the Magia. We have three black Insidio plants at the moment. Will that be enough?"

"I hope so."

Aless showed her the windowless space at the end of the greenhouse where the Magia plants grew in darkness. They rustled as Bell stepped inside, her mask and gloves firmly in place. Rian held a tray, and she selected Magia until she had all the components of mindmeld. With relief, she backed out of the small musty room and closed the door. From the rest of the fioré, she gathered the counteragents she needed, then strode for the workroom.

Rian situated her stool and set out the plants while Aless lingered in the doorway. "I'll leave you to it, then."

Carasti glanced up at him, swirling her skirt. "Care to show me to your Bardian wood storage?"

How did she make her eyes glow like that?

"Certainly." Aless offered his arm, and Carasti flashed Bell a mischievous look as they strode away.

Bell turned back to the bench, and her pulse increased at the sight of the Magia plants waiting for her. She cupped another goldenbell and let it weave her a belt, humming a tune Elena often sang. She would get to work soon, but first, she'd let the goldenbell soothe her.

When Aless and Carasti's footsteps faded, Rian stepped closer to Bell. "You could have had all this." His voice was dangerously tender. He sounded regretful, as if it pained him that he could never give her as much as Aless.

She smiled. All of Bardia was in danger, but she couldn't keep from smiling, surrounded by these flowers that knew her so well. "Do you know why I love this flower? It's not even fioré. It's the—the soul of them I love. It's simple. I don't have to ask anything of it. I can simply enjoy them." He was silent as Bell turned to look at him. "Rian...I know your life hasn't been simple. But I'm beginning to see who you are. Your soul." She touched his hand. "I don't need to ask anything of you. I want *you*."

Were his eyes glistening? Time slowed as he cupped her cheek, his thumb at the corner of her lip. His velvety scent surrounded her. She slid her hands around the nape of his neck and pressed her lips against his. He made a noise deep in his throat and pulled her closer. For a moment, Bell was lost in the softness of his kiss and the rightness of his arms around her.

Finally, he pulled away and tucked her head under his chin.

"Saint help me. I wish we could leave all this behind," he said into her hair.

"This is my battle," she said, her voice muffled. "And yours too." She leaned back to look at him.

"Then I will fight at your side." He pulled the scentstone from his pocket and held it out. "Are you ready to begin?"

She set it carefully aside. "First, I need to prepare for La Festa."

In ten minutes, she'd fused an elixir using Agnella's blood and Blue Hertes, a few drops of which transformed her face into the Maestra's. Next, she filled a vial with Wings, in case things went wrong in La Festa parade and she needed to fly over the Rotunda's barrier.

Finally, she could put it off no longer.

Cradling the scentstone, she filled it with her *attuale*. The greenhouse burst into color, brilliant hues bubbling as they sensed her. The scentstone would hold her gift until she pulled it away, so she set it on the table and opened the mindmeld vial she'd used on Carasti. Its scent cloud sprang up. The black Insidio's chains were dark as a cavern, like strands of nothingness. Between them, she could finally see each shape of the other components clearly. The rough texture of the thick orange Jonquil braid. Jonga Lily's gold-white arch behind it. Smemor's nevermore gray mist was clearer from the corners of her eyes but faded whenever she looked at it directly.

It was the perfect elixir to bind a mind to someone else's. To meld it like molten metal.

Bell sank onto her stool.

"What is it?" Rian's voice was softened by the mask she'd ordered him to put on before she opened the mindmeld.

"It's beautiful." She forced herself to look up. "I hate everything about it, and yet it's beautiful."

"I understand. Some of the things I've crafted have been beautiful but had ugly uses."

"I'm beginning to see it's how we use things that makes them beautiful," she murmured, examining the cloud. This very thing could be used to heal, or to destroy. To free from disease or enslave to another's desires.

She cleared her throat. This idea was foolish, but it felt right. "Rian, will you…use the mindmeld on me?"

Wonder opened his face. "You trust me so well?"

"I need to know how it feels. Maybe, if I experience it, I'll be able to see what would counteract the black Insidio."

"Bell…"

She held out the vial. "If you're going with me to the Spring, I need to trust you."

He took it carefully. "I will be worthy of your trust."

The certainty that had filled her since his reappearance deepened. "I know."

What he saw in her eyes seemed to reassure him. He uncorked the mindmeld and let a drop fall on her wrist, above her gloves. As the elixir sank into her skin, she waited for a pit of panic to open in her. Instead, she felt warm, like she could walk into a sea storm and still feel safe. Her mind felt distant and cloudy. She couldn't seem to gather a complex thought.

"Do I need to test it?"

"Whatever you like." Her voice was husky.

His mouth twitched. "You have blonde hair."

Her subconscious tried to cling to her previous memory, but it leapt from her mind. In its place, she realized her hair was golden, like Roza's. "Yes."

He nodded. "It's working."

She felt distant, as if watching herself through a glass. It was a relief. She wasn't worried anymore. She had no decisions to make.

"And you want to marry me." His words all strung together.

She beamed at the thought of holding his hand and saying their vows before an official.

"Sorry, I couldn't resist." He looked half amused, half guilty.

"I do want to marry you. Can I?" She'd wear a gown with lace sleeves to the wrists.

He suppressed a laugh now, his eyes sparkling. "You don't want to marry me. Not yet, anyway."

She nodded. Of course, how silly to think she could marry him now. She gazed while he shifted awkwardly.

"So, ah." He rubbed the back of his neck. "How long does this last?"

"Around ten minutes," she said.

"I wonder." He paused to consider something. "Are you afraid of Magia anymore?"

"I don't think so?" Bell couldn't remember. All she felt was expectation for whatever he would say next.

He waved at the table. "Could you make me an antidote for the mindmeld?"

267

"Of course." She would make anything for him. Rian handed her an empty vial.

Her mind came into focus. Her fingers were sure and steady as they reached for the Aronil and plucked a blossom low on its stem. Next, Sciver and Princess Seed. Her hand hovered over the Magia, then dipped down and picked one black Insidio bloom. Rian watched with wide eyes as she formed the bouquet and eased her gift down her arms. The elixir shimmered as it spilled into the vial. She sealed it with a cork, then held it out like an offering to Rian.

He hesitated, then took it. "Bell, you still want to marry me, right?"

"I—" Anxiety flickered through her, then vanished. "Yes."

"You're still under the mindmeld." Rian opened the vial. "Shall we try the antidote?"

Black chains streamed out of it, and Bell jerked back. "Cork it," she spat out. How had black Insidio broken free?

Rian jammed the cork back into the vial's mouth, but the chains of darkness had already escaped and lunged toward her. She staggered against the goldenbell beds. A blossom caught in her fingers as she raised her hands to focus her gift. A fine gold net spread before her, its glittering strands cutting off the black Insidio's heavy chains. The net shifted as Bell moved her hands closer together. The goldenbell blossom between her fingers withered and scattered in dust.

"What happened?" Rian held the corked vial before him like it was on fire. "What is that shimmery dust?"

"The black Insidio escaped the vial, somehow. It must react with one of the components I used." Bell studied the sparkling gold net that dimmed the darkness. "You can't see the gold net?"

He shook his head. "It looks like dust specks in the sun."

"I've made a...a shield of sorts with the goldenbell, somehow." Wonder warmed over her. "I've never heard of fusing a non-fioré like this."

The black Insidio chains sought the edges of the net, probing its surface. When the goldenbell net turned to a sphere, sealing Bell inside, the black chains retreated. They lurched toward Rian, and Bell gasped. "It's coming for you."

Rian staggered as the dark chains wound around his throat and enveloped him. She tried to push the goldenbell net toward him. "Go. Go! Protect him instead." The net shimmered and tightened around her.

Bell closed her eyes, to shut out the sight of Rian choking in the dark. She reached for the unfamiliar and yet comforting goldenbell scent cloud. She pulled it toward her, gathered it into a ball, flung it into the black Insidio cloud—and the darkness consumed it.

Released from the net, Bell stumbled toward Rian. The black Insidio cloud whirled, shoving her back when she touched it. Its chains spun faster and faster until its gale knocked Bell to the ground. When she lowered her arms from their protective cage around her head, the cloud was gone. Rian lay still on the stone floor.

She lunged toward him and took his face in her hands. "Rian."

His eyelids fluttered.

"The clouds are gone. Can you hear me?" His cheeks felt rough with stubble.

"I—I couldn't breathe." He coughed.

"The black Insidio was trying to kill you." The fuzzy weight of mindmeld was gone from her mind. Why had she fused black Insidio?

"Ah. Hence the strangling effect. Is it still here?" His voice rasped like gravel poured into a pan.

"No, it's—" Bell reached out with her gift to feel the scents in the room. An echo of darkness, wrapped in a net of golden light, filled her mind, then vanished.

Her mind was empty. Eyes wide, Bell grabbed the scentstone. She hurried out into the greenhouse and plucked Myrtle Leaf, waiting for the deep green to fill her senses until she tasted grass. She pushed her gift at the scentstone, scanning the air above the fioré for colors.

Nothing.

"What are you doing?" Rian rose, brushing pebbles off his pants.

"My gift," she whispered.

"What's happened?" He hurried to her and slipped his hands around her elbows.

"My gift is—" She met his gaze, chilled. "It's gone."

269

"And you've never heard of an elixir taking away a scentmaker's gift before?" Carasti asked.

Bell slumped forward on the sofa. The scentstone tipped off her lap, and she snatched it before it hit the ground. "It wasn't an elixir; it was a non-fioré scent. But I've never heard of a making taking away *any* maker's gift." She turned to Rian, who sat next to her. "Why did the mindmeld make me fuse black Insidio? It's not like you asked me to."

He shook his head. "I never even thought it until you reached for it. I almost said no, actually, because I was afraid you wouldn't be prepared while under mindmeld."

Carasti frowned. "Did you learn anything about it? Maybe that was a step in the process you needed."

"All I did was lose my gift," Bell muttered.

Rian squeezed her knee. "We'll figure this out."

"How? I can't even sense the dried Myrtle Leaf on the mantle. I can't fuse a scent unless I can sense it." She waved the scentstone. "I can't sense *anything*, even with this."

"Your teacher never said anything about this?" Aless took the scentstone from her and paced to the sea-facing window. Dawn streaked the horizon like golden chains.

"Not that I remember. I need her." Bell rubbed her forehead.

Carasti pursed her lips. "Are you sure you need to sense them? Maybe the gift would work on its own."

"Yes, I'm sure." Bell jerked to her feet and paced. "Working blind like that is impossible." Her voice rose at the last word.

Aless pressed his finger to his lips. "The cooks will be awake by now."

Bell nodded at the scentstone in his hands. "You might as well put that somewhere safe. It's useless to me now."

"Did you sense the—whatever it is—in the goldenbell?" Rian asked softly. "When you made the net?"

Bell paused, lowering her voice. "I don't remember. It happened so fast, practically on its own. I think my gift was defending me."

270

"Maybe it would do it again. If you tried to fuse," Carasti said.

Bell shook her head. "I don't know how it worked."

"Try. That's all we're asking." Rian's dark eyes prodded her.

Bell sighed. The ground felt unsteady. Her gift had been part of her life. Her self. Without it, who was she? Certainly no one useful to her captive parents. "What if it doesn't work?"

"Then we'll figure something else out. Please, Bell." Rian touched her cheek. "I believe in you," he whispered.

"Perhaps if we all sleep a few hours." Aless straightened his jacket.

"But Solstice is so soon," Bell whispered. La Festa parade began tomorrow. Weariness and loss weighted her eyelids. Her body ignored her and curled against the armrest.

"I meant in beds," Aless said distantly.

Rian laid a blanket over her and rested his hand on her back. The mindmeld had faded, but he still made her warm. Whatever he said next was lost in a fog of sleep.

She woke to warmth against her face, the smell of fresh biscuits, and the sound of pages turning.

"I thought it was this one, but I'm not seeing it." A heavy thump on the floor.

Bell cracked an eye.

"We have twenty more to go through." Carasti sat beside Aless, her arm brushing his as she turned the pages of a huge tome. Rian sprawled asleep beside Bell, his head on her back, and his arm draped over her hips. Ignoring the pleasant heat rising in her, she blinked to clear her vision.

"What are you looking for?" she croaked.

"Information on historical fusings," Carasti said without looking up.

Bell lurched upright. Rian's arm slid off and he startled. She stared at the pile of dusty books on the floor. "Where did you get those?"

271

"My mother enjoys knowledge." Aless tossed another book aside with a sigh. "I remember her bringing in a book on early scentmaking, and I thought maybe you could find something to help." He snatched another volume. "Ah." He turned the spine toward Bell.

"I can't make it out."

"*Legends of Ancient Fioré*," Aless read.

Bell took the book from him, then sank to the rug. Rian slid down beside her, his eyes puffy with sleep. She brushed her hair back and opened to the front, coughing at the dust. "Doesn't she read these?"

Aless shrugged. "What does it say?"

Bell squinted to make out the faded signature at the end of the introduction. "Firinacci," she said. "He was the first scentmaker." She turned to the index and ran her finger along the section titles. "*Spineto, Afibia*—these are in the old language."

"Let me see." Aless tugged the book onto his lap. "*Princessa* would be Princess Seed. *Afibia*...Aronil?"

Bell gaped at him. Carasti's eyebrows raised speculatively.

"What? My mother made me learn." He bent over the index. "Here. *Gliorobella*. That would be goldenbell, right?"

Bell stared at him for a moment before his words registered. "Goldenbell is in there? What page?" She yanked the book back and found the title herself. The main text was in Old Bardian, but written in flowing script in the margin was this line:

Attuale blocked when Gliorobella fused in proximity to strong Magia. Block permanent ſ

Permanent? Bell's stomach dropped and she slammed the book shut. There it was, in print. Her gift was gone.

Thirty-Eight

"I DON'T THINK YOU SHOULD GIVE UP SO easily." Aless smoothed the page. "There's a squiggle after "permanent." It could be a question mark."

"Even if it was, whoever wrote that didn't experience it. I can feel it's gone." Bell traced the goldenbell blossoms hanging limp around her wrist. "Look at them." The Myrtle Leaf Aless had brought for her to fuse lay whole on the caffè table. It felt like her mind's eye had been blinded, like she should walk around with her hands out or risk falling.

She needed Agnella to tell her what to do.

Rian fixed his dark gaze on her. "We don't know for sure. The loss may be temporary."

Bell balled her dress in her fists. "I need it now," she growled.

"That's the spirit," Carasti said around a bite of biscuit. She licked a drop of honey off her finger. "I say we go on with the original plan."

"You think I should go to Solstice?"

"Why not? If your gift is trapped inside, another dose of power should knock it loose, right?"

Bell blinked, a tendril of hope worming through her despair. Could her gift be trapped somehow?

"I don't like her going there unprotected by her gift." Rian paced behind her.

"But I'll have you. If you're still willing to go."

"Unless you're admitting you can't protect her." Carasti's eyes twinkled. Aless studied Rian, as close to smirking as Bell had seen.

273

"Of course—" Rian was silent for so long that Bell turned to look at him. "It was her gift that saved us from the Lanzis in her garden." He squeezed her shoulder, and she leaned back into his touch. Normally, the reminder of Arabia would have her easing away, but right now, she needed all the warmth she could get.

"I need to take this chance. I must have my gift to save the others."

He kneaded her shoulders. "So. The original plan. We sneak into the Rotunda and convince the Maestris she must join them."

"What if they sense my gift is gone?"

"It's not gone." Carasti said staunchly, brushing crumbs off her fingers. "It'll come back when you get close to the Spring. Besides, who else can be Maestra now that Agnella is captured?"

"What if they don't believe she is?" Aless frowned. "No offense, Bell, but you're young. What if they think this is all a ploy to become Maestra?"

"They have to believe me. They know what the Seller is capable of. And besides, Maestra Piccarda will back me."

Rian's hands had stilled, but he quickly continued, working tightness from her neck. "I'll be there as witness."

"And I'll take the rest of the mindmeld." They had to believe her once they saw the illegal elixir.

Aless nodded, but his frown didn't fade. "And after you've received the Maestra gift?"

Bell breathed in slowly. "If—when—my gift returns, Rian will take me to the closest tunnel, and we'll sneak into the Midnight Garden from the Vasari Corridor."

Carasti reached for the empty biscuit plate on the caffè table and made a disappointed sound.

Aless frowned and tugged the bell by the door. "I don't know what's wrong with the staff this morning. I haven't even seen Maddie yet."

Bell met Carasti's gaze and cleared her throat lightly.

"Don't tell him," Carasti murmured.

When Aless came back to sit beside Carasti, Bell rose to pace by the empty hearth. Her guilt felt like a rash across her cheeks. She'd done the very thing the Seller had—for a good reason in her opinion—but still, she was acting like him. For Roza's cure, how much was she willing to sacrifice?

Carasti gave a discreet cough. Bell frowned at her.

"I was thinking, maybe Aless and I should stay here." She looked over at Aless. "We need a backup plan, in case…" She made a pained expression. "We should finish the boat. If the Seller gets ahold of you, Bell, that may be our only escape."

Bell stepped closer and squeezed Carasti's hand. "Of course," she said through an aching throat.

By ten that evening, they were in place within the crowd gathering at the piazza of Via dei Calzaiuoli. Carasti had spent the afternoon and early evening streaking Bell's hair with white dye and braiding it in a crown to match Agnella's. The less work the disguise elixir had to do, the more convincing it would be.

Her face felt tight in unfamiliar places and loose in others.

Bell's white Maestra's cloak was smothered in one of Aless's black ones. The heavy storm air hadn't cooled with nightfall. A drop of sweat slid between her shoulder blades. She positioned herself against an arch at the edge of the piazza, near the head of the parade, waiting until the other Maestris appeared. Rian, who had somehow acquired the green and gold livery of a Rotunda knight, had whispered he'd be right behind her, then vanished.

More than anything, she wanted him close enough to touch.

Finally, she spotted the first white cloak moving slowly through the crowd. Whispers spread as she slid Aless's cloak to the ground and stepped forward to join the other Maestris. Bardians and mainlanders parted for her, their faces lowered.

Her heart beat like a fist against her chest.

I am Agnella.

The Maestris nodded solemnly to each other, their hoods far enough

275

forward to conceal most of their faces, then stood in a single line at the head of the parade. Bell kept her back straight, resisting the urge to check her own hood. The disguise had been working when she'd left Aless's house thirty minutes ago, but how much longer would it hold?

There was no announcement to begin. The Maestris stepped forward—unprepared, Bell half-stumbled—and the rest of the parade followed behind.

Musicians following along played their lutes, and children called and ran, tossing flowers in among the paraders who laughed and flipped small coins back. The joyous noise grew until it carried them like a current. Bell glanced furtively back at the feet of the Rotunda knight behind her.

The *infiorata* carpets were soft as moss beneath Bell's feet. Without thinking, she reached out with her gift to touch the green life within them and gasped at the numbness meeting her in return. The Maestra next to her—Maestra Anna, judging by her build—turned to look at her. Inside her pocket, Bell kept her hand tight around the vial of Wings, tensed for an accusation, a shout to ring out through the parade noise.

It didn't come.

Then they spilled into the far end of the Piazza, where the rest of the tourists and Bardians waited.

Seven chairs had been placed at the foot of the Rotunda stairs before the barrier. Bell glanced at the sky. The moon was in position.

One chair was aflame—orange, red, blue-white undulating, licking the air. One of golden threads, weaving and reweaving fantastic images. Another chair was an ink blue wave continually cresting, curling in on itself. One was a tree swaying in the wind, branches full of birds, another glittering metal. Another was of stone and gems that appeared and vanished in a rainbow.

And near the center was a delicate weave of green vapor and glass. Maestra Agnella's chair.

Murmuring grew along the sidelines, soured by a twang of off-key music. Bell glanced at the bystanders as a musician stumbled to his knees. A Lanzi shoved past him, his hooded gaze fixed on her.

Thirty-Nine

FOR A LONG MOMENT, DREAD PARALYZED her. The Lanzis were here. Rian appeared suddenly between her and the approaching Lanzi.

"Fly," he hissed.

His voice shook her into motion. She ripped open the vial as an outraged cry sounded from one of the Maestris. Maestra Anna lunged for her, grabbing her shoulder as Bell spilled the elixir on her wrist and dropped the vial. Anna tightened her grip, pulling Bell against her, but Bell's wings exploded behind her, knocking the Maestra away.

She beat them hard, rising yards above the chaos in seconds. Hoods fell off masked faces as they gaped up at her. The street fell into chaos as dozens of Lanzis swarmed toward her. Half the Maestris drew on defensive *attuale*, while the other half looked around in confusion.

Bell searched frantically for Rian. He and the Lanzi attacking him had vanished into the screaming crowd.

She turned to face the Rotunda as thunder roared, drowning out the noise of the fight.

Solstice was coming any moment. If the Maestris didn't reach the Spring in time, someone had to be there to receive the *attuale*.

She flew for the barrier.

When she sailed above it and landed on the top of the stairs, Rotunda knights poured out, hands on their swords. She landed slowly with her hands up.

"An attack by Lanzis," she panted.

277

They flowed around her, flooding down the stairs and out the barrier, beating back the Lanzis forming a circle around the Consiglio. She hurried on into the Rotunda. Thunder rolled, rattling in her chest. Solstice was nearly here.

The stained-glass dome roofed three stories, each with a balcony of ivory jutting out. Gems textured the walls and ceiling, but the floor was utterly smooth.

Below the first balcony, a rainbow of gems glimmered in intricate patterns, marking a round opening leading to stone steps, descending into darkness to the Spring. Behind her she heard the crowd reach the steps.

Thunder rolled once more, then the rain fell. At the end of an ordinary La Festa, the festivalgoers outside would be dancing in it, water drenching their clothes and streaking their face paint. In ten minutes, it would stop, leaving clean night air behind.

Bell ran for the Spring, ignoring shouted orders from the Maestris entering after her. Half flying, half sprinting, she shot down the ancient stone steps that were slick with damp and moss.

The Spring pool was lit by glow gems beneath, glimmering blue and black and bubbling at the center. Below, the sound of rain and thunder faded, but the ground around the pool was beginning to vibrate. Was that the *attuale* approaching? Bell was too early. The Solstice was not yet upon them. Footsteps scraped on the stairs behind her. The ceiling was low and she folded her wings. She circled the pool, looking across it as the Consiglio and their guards streamed out of the staircase and into the chamber.

"What is the meaning of this?" Maestra Lux glowered at Bell. The Consiglio split and surrounded the pool, blocking her exit. Behind them, Rian came down the stairs, still dressed as a knight. Maestra Anna hurried behind him, slipping into the circle.

Maestra Lux pointed at Bell. "Explain yourself, imposter."

Bell was grateful her disguise had faded. She wanted to meet them as herself.

She steeled herself. "Maestris, Maestra Agnella sent me to join La

Festa parade because she was not able to bring me with her."

"Why did she not come with you?" Maestra Anna probed.

Maestra Lux frowned at her. "Miss Asbury. Regardless of what Agnella told you, this is most unorthodox."

"Please, Maestra Lux, the Seller has taken her captive. I must receive her gift so I can get her back. He has my parents, and—"

A familiar voice spoke. "Be careful, Maestris. This scentmaker is extremely dangerous."

Bell's stomach lurched as she and the Consiglio spun as one toward the stairway.

The Seller's black eyes gleamed, sharp and knowing. He had one hand in his pocket. Was he holding an elixir? Bell's heart sank. She couldn't run from him here.

Maestra Lux's angry cheeks shone like beacons on her ivory face. "Knights!"

"Now, now, Lux. I thought I would receive a better welcome after all this time."

"The Seller of Secrets," Maestra Piccarda breathed.

"You are not welcome here, Salieri." Maestra Lux chipped off each word.

"And yet you welcome this…impostor?"

The Maestris split their gazes between the Seller and Bell. Maestra Piccarda stepped forward. "She is no imposter—"

Lux cut Piccarda off. "Neither of you are welcome. Now remove yourselves before the Solstice arrives, or we will have you removed."

Bell stepped forward. "Maestra Lux—"

The Seller cut her off. "I came to bring you information. One thing I'm still permitted to do, no?" Metal poured down Maestra Lux's outstretched arms, streaking toward the Seller's neck. "She's fused a brainwashing elixir."

The metal froze, shards like swords quivering in the air before the Seller's face.

"She's the cause of Agnella's disappearance. She needed the former Maestra out of the way so she could take the scentmaking gift."

Maestra Piccarda gasped. "How *dare* you—"

"You *liar*." Rian stepped out of the row of knights gathered near the stairs. The Seller turned to see who had spoken and smiled. Maestra Lux cast Rian an irritated glance.

"Why should we believe you over her?" Maestro Carlo asked. "Bell is a promising scentmaker from a well-known house. You are the most dreaded man in the Sotto."

"I have proof." He lifted a hand toward the stairs. "Maddie."

The words reverberated across the bleak landscape that was Bell's mind.

A servant girl in black hurried down the stairs behind him.

"What is this?" Confusion tinged Maestra Lux's angry voice. Bell's mouth dried when the girl came close enough for Maddie's brown gaze to fix on her.

"Yes, sirs, she used something on me to make me do what she wanted." Maddie glared at Bell. "I'd never have let her near the young master if she hadn't."

Bell tried to take a deep breath.

"But this is not proof," Maestra Piccarda said. "He could pay any serving girl to say this. He could use the elixir on anyone to *make* them say it."

"A scentmaker can check her mind and see that it's been tampered with, and by whom. The remnants remain." The Seller glanced at Bell. He withdrew his hand from his pocket. "This is a truthtelling elixir, Maestra Lux." He opened a vial and dabbed some on both his wrists. Bell stared at the vial, trying to see the scent cloud. Silver flashed, then vanished.

"We have no time for this." The Spring's rising gurgle half drowned Maestra Lux's words. "The Solstice will soon reach full strength."

The Seller dipped his head. "It is with regret that I bring forth another victim. Of a deeper crime I have not yet mentioned. He also is a witness to the scentmakers' kidnapping." The Consiglio stirred.

"No. You can't believe this," Bell shouted.

Maestra Lux waved a hand for him to bring the victim forward.

Bell knew who it would be before the light revealed his sallow face and burning eyes. Piero hung between two Lanzis, his head trembling with the effort of holding it high.

"You all know Piero of Medoro had a scentmaking gift in days past. Test him now and see if you sense his gift."

"I sense nothing," Maestra Lux said. "Are you suggesting—"

"She took his gift with *fusione*."

Maestra Lux's eyes flashed. "Impossible. That is a fortunately lost art."

"I do not deny Goldenbell is highly gifted."

The Consiglio exploded in shouts and gesticulations until the cave reverberated with noise.

Maestra Lux raised her hands and they quieted. "You mentioned kidnapping of scentmakers?" she asked the Seller.

"Piero is willing to testify, despite personal stakes—" Piero lowered his head when the Seller said this, but he continued to glare at Bell. "His brother, Garam, has been taking scentmakers to a hideout on the north shore of Bardia."

"This is preposterous—" Maestra Piccarda's protest sputtered out as Maestra Lux gestured sharply.

"How do you defend yourself, Goldenbell of Asbury?"

Bell flinched. How could this have gone so wrong? "How can you believe him? His Lanzis attacked you and disrupted the parade."

"They were trying to get to you," the Seller said to Bell. He held out the silvery white elixir. Maestra Lux hesitantly took it. She looked at Bell. Bell stepped back, edging closer to the cavern wall. The scent cloud was invisible to her, and there was no way she'd let them put an unknown elixir on her.

"I—I used mindmeld to influence Maddie, but he fused it." She stabbed a finger at the Seller. "Everything he said is true, but I did it all at his direction."

Maestra Lux's chin rose slowly. "You performed *fusione* with Piero's gift?"

The air stilled, the burbling Spring the only motion.

"I did."

Silence. Maestra Piccarda and Maestri Carlo exchanged worried glances.

"I fused *permanenza*." Bell yanked the nearly empty mindmeld vial from her dress and held it out for all to see. "He told me it would cure Lymbodia."

Stunned silence. All of Bell's hopes and fears flashed across their faces.

Piccarda and Carlo's faces remained smooth, like a flower bed already tilled. They'd already wrestled with the hope of a cure and refused to sacrifice Bardia's freedom for it.

"I will gladly pay for my crime." She forced herself to meet the Seller's gaze. "But please believe me, he will use the mindmeld for revenge and control, not to heal. I've heard it from his own lips."

"What is your goal, Bell?" Bell's stomach turned at the Seller's smooth voice. Still, after all this, something in his words pulled her toward him. "To make history? To mold Bardia to your will? Or are you a tool in my son's hand to achieve his freedom?"

"Bell." Rian stood beside her now, his knight's helm gone.

The Seller's brow was furrowed, but his eyes remained sharp. "I have many regrets in my past. The greatest of them is teaching my son to take on my trade."

Rian squeezed her hand tightly. Bell gritted her teeth, her anger growing.

The Spring's rumble rose until it drowned their breathing.

"The Solstice approaches, bringing with it the *attuale*." Maestra Lux raised her voice. "Maestra Agnella has not appeared, and we have no time to find her. We must go on without a Maestra of Scents. Leave us now, Salieri. Go back to your lair."

The Seller pointed at Bell. "I will leave as soon as you send her from here. You cannot let her become the next Maestra of Scents."

He stepped closer as he spoke, and the Maestris' hands rose defensively. Tension sparked in the air.

"Go, Bell," Maestra Lux said.

"I can't," Bell said.

The Seller's teeth bared. "I will not leave without her."

Maestra Lux scoffed. "You'll fight us here? Where we are the strongest?"

"I'd hoped it would not come to this." The Seller retreated partway up the steps. Lanzis and dark makers flooded down past him, swarming the room with shadowy figures. Within moments, the Consiglio was outnumbered.

The Maestris fought with waves of fire and gem blades, but the dark makers were too many, and they carried blue vials and the glistening silver cuffs that stilled the gifts of those whose wrists were forcibly encased. As the battle swelled around them, Rian dragged Bell back to the cavern wall. He pressed his hands against the stone, and it glowed.

The Spring roared now, covering Maestra Lux's howls of anger as two dark makers melted her streams of metal with black fire while another held a vial under her nose and cuffed her wrist.

The Seller approached the Spring. A blue-black pillar rose, flashing, toward the ceiling. The battle slowed as dark makers stilled to look at the Spring, their faces ravenous. Blue vapor and black flames funneled within, so intense Bell could almost feel her gift return. This was it. She stepped away from the hollow Rian was melting in the cavern wall.

The Seller's hand trembled in the light of the Solstice as he approached the pool. He reached into his pocket, gaze fixed on Bell, and lunged for her. Rian sprang forward, grabbing the Seller by the waist and hauling him into the hollow in the wall. The hollow began to close as thick bands of stone cocooned father and son.

"Touch the water, Bell," Rian's scream pierced the roar as the cave wall sealed them in.

Forty

THE PILLAR BEGAN TO PULSE, THE BLUE-black *attuale* draining into the empty air.

Three steps to the Spring felt like rowing to the horizon. Her feet splashed the shallows as her fingers reached out and brushed liquid—she stiffened.

Light exploded within her—the sun, the stars, and every gift poured into her soul. Fire, and the water to quench it, gems that glittered until they stung her skin. The smell of a field freshly tilled, the taste of a mountain of hay dust. She strained to hold it in as it burned away the wet air. If she let go, the Solstice gift would float away and fade into the cave ceiling. The light flowed on, turning her senses numb one by one. She screamed, clawing at her chest with her other hand. She was going to explode. Her skin would shatter into sand. For an instant she glimpsed her *attuale* swelling within her, the glittering goldenbell net growing with it. Delight fizzed in her stomach. Her gift was still there.

Whoosh.

She flew into the air and landed, breathless, on her back. Someone stumbled over her ankle, and she huddled against the wall.

The vision of her gift was gone. She was blind.

No, a dim glow came from the stairs to the Rotunda. The Spring had gone dark and still, and a few Maestris and dark makers still fought. Fire gashed the air, stone slammed up dust. Light flared, revealing Piccarda leading a group of men and women charging down the stairs,

284

hurling themselves into dark makers and freeing cuffed Maestris. The first wave of mindmeld elixirs had worn off, and the rest of the Consiglio fought back again.

"Bell." Someone with broad shoulders bent over her, blocking the room.

"Garam? How did you get here?" Her voice rasped liked she'd gulped fire.

"We have to go. Can you walk?"

She pushed to her trembling knees, tracing the hump in the wall. Was Rian trapped somewhere inside, unable to use his gift fast enough to find air?

The bleak landscape in her mind stretched out of sight.

Garam swept his arms beneath her knees and shoulders and picked her up. He shouldered his way through the mob and across the Rotunda floor toward the front entrance.

The Solstice storm didn't hide the Lanzis swarming across the Piazza, battling makers and commoners. Blue elixirs flashed, and it was impossible to tell friend from foe.

They reached the first pine tree at the edge of the Piazza, and a Lanzi sprang at them. Garam tossed her to the side, and Bell tumbled to the ground, cracking her elbow against a root. She bit back the pain, staring at the root as Garam warded off the Lanzi's blows. If she had a Maestra's gift now, the tree should follow her. Bracing her hands on the wet bark, she reached for her gift.

Nothing.

Her scream echoed through the pines. The Lanzi glanced at her. Garam's fist smacked his jaw, and he flew back into a trunk and slid to the ground, limp.

"What is it?"

"My gift is still gone," she said with half a voice. Rian was gone, everyone she loved was in the Seller's clutches, and she could do nothing.

Garam's mouth thinned. "Your gift—we'll find it later. We must get to Aless's before we're seen."

The rain lessened the further they ventured from the Rotunda.

Lanzis stalked Santa Croce. There were too many of them with mind-meld elixirs, and they all had glistening silver handcuffs for when the mindmeld wore off.

The Seller had won. He would force all these makers to work for him. If he didn't take their gifts first.

If only the Solstice had freed hers. This had all been a waste.

No, she'd kept the Seller from receiving it. If she was giftless, she could never fuse *permanenza* for him again.

They crouched behind a raised bed of flowers in a street corner park, eyeing the six Lanzis lining the street ahead. Bell shivered as a breeze touched her sopping shoulders.

"We need another way," Garam hissed.

"We have to sneak into the Seller's lair," she whispered.

"You need a safe place to find your gift."

"I don't know how to get my gift back." Bell brushed back hair pasted to her cheek. "I need Agnella."

"She's locked away in his dungeon."

"Then let's go."

He gave her a disbelieving look. "Don't be foolish."

Bell's face lit up. "Garam, this is the perfect opportunity. The Seller and the Lanzis are probably all out in the streets looking for me. He thinks I have a Maestra's gift now. He'll want to use it."

"Don't you? I saw you take it in."

"How did you get inside the barrier?"

"Piccarda opened it. What happened to Rian?"

"He pulled the Seller with him into the cave wall. I don't know if he..."

There, the real question. Had Rian sacrificed himself for nothing? The Lanzis were still here. Surely that meant the Seller managed to escape from Rian.

Garam rubbed his chin. "We can't walk into the Sotto. And Rian's tunnels aboveground are blocked."

"We'll have to use the Vasari Corridor."

"Rian said not to try it without him. And how are we going to get into the Corridor unseen?"

"I can help you with that."

They spun at the low female voice. A cloaked woman bent beside them. Bell's alarm faded into hope.

"Maestra Piccarda, how did you—are any of the others free?"

Maestra Piccarda glanced past them. "I followed you out. They got the others with the cuffs—and the mindmeld. Anna has turned against us. She let the Seller in."

"You know the entrances?" Garam whispered.

"Follow me." She drifted back into the shadows of the street behind them and around the corner. Bell tiptoed after her. A Lanzi watched the next street. They waited until he turned the other way. Maestra Piccarda ducked under an arch at the street corner, and they followed. When she reached the wall, she slid out of sight. Bell touched the stones and felt the jagged edge of a cunning opening. The tiny stairway could only be seen from one angle.

Maestra Piccarda rubbed a glow gem in the wall until they could see the floor. "There are three entrances hidden in the streets of Santa Croce. Most nobles don't know of them."

"How did you find them?"

Her teeth flashed as she glanced back. "I'm never far from the water. I can sense the path the tunnels make deep beneath the island. I know where the rain flows and puddles gather." The glow gem softened the edge of a thicker darkness. The Maestra swept her hand toward it. "The Corridor. I'll leave you here."

"What? Why?" Bell said.

Maestra Piccarda gave her an even look. "I'm going to find any watermakers who have escaped. We'll flood the tunnels and drown Salieri out. The Consiglio has tolerated him and his dark makers for far too long."

"How do we get through the catacombs? Rian said we need a stonemaker, but maybe you know—"

"The Lanzis take their prisoners that way. Hide in the Corridor until you see them, then follow. And follow closely. You don't want to lose your way." She turned, then paused, her face softening. "Good luck, Bell."

She ascended the stairs, her ink-blue cloak swallowing her.

Garam tugged on Bell's arm. "Not a moment to lose."

Bell barely heard him as Piccarda's words echoed in her head. *We'll drown Salieri out. Salieri…*

Suddenly, she remembered where she'd seen that name.

Forty-One

Dear Francesca,

I have been thinking of you lately. Every waking moment, it seems, and sometimes in my dreams. Do you dream of me?

I think it is time we met again. Do you not think so? I can hear your protests, but remember, I know the truth about your daughter.

I regard you always,

Salieri

Salieri, Roza's blood father, had demanded Mother come and meet him. This was why Mother had been in the Seller's sanctuary.

Mother had been desperate to protect—Roza. That alone could explain why Francesca would return to the place she hated most. Mother must have tried to make a bargain for Roza's safety, perhaps not knowing Roza was already working for the Seller.

A well of pain and sympathy rose from within. Mother might have known the truth about Roza all along, but she'd risked herself for her firstborn.

"Bell?" Garam laid his hand on her shoulder. "Bell." He shook her,

289

his fingers hard. "We need to keep moving." She followed numbly, thoughts still aching. They trailed their fingers along the wall to stay oriented. The tiny scratching echoed.

The darkness pressed around her head. When a glow gem flared far ahead, her first feeling was relief. Even if Lanzis were coming for them, at least there was light. They pressed themselves against the wall as Pater and Matrona Medoro stepped into the light of the glow gem, surrounded by Lanzis.

Pater Medoro tried to shake off the Lanzi's hand on his arm. "Release me. The Seller knows of our loyalty, and I know the way. There is no need—" The Pater stumbled forward as a Lanzi shoved him.

When they vanished into the depths of the Corridor, Bell took a breath and realized she was standing inches from Garam's back and peering around him. He hurried forward, beckoning her.

"Your parents," she whispered, hoping the sound wouldn't carry too far.

"I knew," he said hoarsely.

They followed a ghostly trail of dying glow gems, walking on tiptoe to keep their steps from echoing. Pater Medoro's voice carried back to them occasionally but fell silent after they reached the end of the glow gems and the walls grew rough and damp. The Lanzis carried their own gems, blowing on them frequently to keep them bright. The light made the hovering shadows of the catacombs seem more foreboding. Narrow passageways led off on both sides, and several times the Lanzis' lights vanished to the right or left. Bell and Garam hurried to follow, their breathing ragged and footsteps louder as they worried more about catching up than being caught.

Finally, when Bell had begun to shiver in the damp air, the Lanzis halted the Medoros at a narrow ascending staircase.

Bell and Garam waited around a corner as the others climbed the stairs single file. A door squealed open, then thundered shut after them. Bell held her breath, waiting for the crunch of a lock.

Nothing.

Unable to stand the darkness one moment longer, she grabbed Garam's arm and hurried forward, holding the image of the staircase firmly in her mind. Its wall appeared beneath her hand, slick with mold, and they climbed.

Garam waited behind her as Bell pressed her ear against the wood and held her breath to listen. After a few silent moments, she cracked the door and peered out. It was the hall outside the Seller's sanctuary. Purple curtains marked the doors. Footsteps sounded down the hall to the left, coming closer. She eased the stairway door shut again until the steps passed.

Silence returned.

"We're close to Rian's room," she whispered to Garam. "If it's unlocked, we could hide there for a bit."

"All right."

They stepped into the hall quickly, and Bell led the way to the third door from the right. Its curtain was emblazoned in her memory as the last thing she'd seen before Rian had grabbed her shoulders. She bit her lip as she pulled aside the fabric and tried the door.

Click.

They rushed into the dim space. Bell fumbled to the sink and blew on the glow gem there. Rian's room looked more eerie by its dim blue light, without the warmth of the fire and the candles by his bed. Without him. She let out a sharp breath.

Garam stood stiffly by the door.

"I'm sure they're keeping him somewhere secure. If he's here," she muttered.

He stepped closer, frowning. "How will we reach the Garden from here?"

"There's an entrance through the sanctuary. It might not be guarded, with the Lanzis scattered."

He shook his head slowly. "You want to walk into—"

The door rattled, and Bell's heart plunged into her stomach. She glanced at the open wardrobe, and then the door swung wide.

Arabia stood there, Rian at her heels.

They stared at each other for a long moment. Bell took one second to register the utter shock on Arabia's face before Bell's gaze flew to Rian's.

Relief spiraled within her, its wings clipped by the lifelessness in his eyes.

He was alive—but under mindmeld.

It couldn't be permanent. She stepped closer instinctively, longing to rip him away from Arabia's clutch on his arm.

Arabia flicked a hand, her guttural chuckle smothered by the sound of her angry flames coming to life. "Not so fast, little scentmaker. He's mine."

Bell bared her teeth. "He's never been yours, and he never will be. Get your hands off him."

Arabia's flames grew as she moved into the room, Rian in tow. "Show her, my love, how much I own you now. Call the Lanzis to come and get our little invader." Her gaze flicked to Garam, who stood to the side, eyeing the space between her and the door. "And her handsome friend."

Bell's heart thundered as Rian nodded and stepped back toward the hall. "Rian, stop." He froze.

"Do as I say, love. Call the guards." Arabia's voice trembled with anger.

Rian cupped his hands around his mouth and shouted. A moment passed before footsteps sounded far down the hall, but it was long enough for an idea to sprout in Bell's mind. Arabia had let her fire die and turned to grab Rian's arm again, and Bell whispered to Garam, "Distract her."

Garam blinked, then stepped forward. "Arabia, I've brought the scentmaker to you. What will you give me in return?"

Arabia's gaze narrowed, but her red lips curved in a satisfied smile. "And here I thought you were friends."

Garam smirked, edging closer, his eyes sweeping her leather-clad legs. "She's not my type. Now you, on the other hand...I would love to be *your* friend."

Bell watched as Arabia's grip loosened on Rian's arm. Arabia tilted her head and turned to fully face Garam. "And what about your fiancée? Is she still your type?"

Bell ignored Arabia's purring and stared deep into Rian's unfocused eyes, willing him to *see her*. He squinted and gave his head a tiny shake.

"Bell?" he mouthed. Hope exploded in her chest. The mindmeld was fading.

Footsteps thundered outside, approaching the door. "Rian, take me out of here."

Arabia's head whipped toward Bell. She grabbed for Rian, but he darted out of reach. He grabbed Bell's arm and pulled her to the wall beside the table. The smell of hot stone filled the room as he melted the hole into his tunnel and shoved Bell inside.

"You will obey me, Florian," Arabia howled. She lunged toward them, then staggered back, Garam gripping both her arms.

Rian's step hitched, confusion flashing across his face. Bell took his hands and yanked him inside. Her touch seemed to settle his mind. He pressed his hands on either side of the opening and it melted closed, shutting out the sight of Arabia's bright red flames.

"They'll be in the tunnels in minutes." His voice was hoarse.

"Take me to the Midnight Garden."

He pressed his fingers to her cheek. "Are you sure? Is your gift...?"

"I think I still have it *and* the Solstice gift. It's bound by the golden-bell net somehow. Agnella is there. I need her help to release it."

"All right." He took her hand. "We can enter through the sanctuary."

He led her at a jog around a corner and up an incline. He stopped and melted a narrow opening in the wall. On the other side glimmered the black pool of the sanctuary, too far to jump across.

Bell made a disappointed noise. "How do we——"

He bent and laid his hands on the floor of the opening. A narrow bridge grew beneath his fingers, stretching across the pool. They crossed the bridge and hurried to the foot of the stairs. Frigid droplets from the waterfall spattered her face and hands. The waterfall rushed on, its flow uninterrupted by black Insidio this time.

"It's here," Rian murmured in her ear. He indicated the spot she had seen the door shape last time.

"Can you open it?" she whispered back. Rian slipped behind the waterfall and out of sight.

The doors behind them burst open. Bell spun to see Roza sprinting down the walkway.

"Don't go in, Bell." Roza wore a fitted black tunic over leggings. Her hair was a tangle around her face.

Bell stepped back, away from her. "I have to get Agnella and the others out."

"You don't understand." Roza panted for breath. "It's full of dark makings. The Magia...they'll twist your gift. You won't be able to fuse a cure anymore."

Bell stared at her. It felt like an audible crack should have sounded as her heart broke. She wanted to stay and save Roza. She had to go. "I'm sorry, Roza." She turned to the doorway, reaching for the water to feel behind it.

"Not so quickly, my dear." The Seller's voice was followed by the stairway creaking as he descended. Lanzis came behind him—then Agnella. Two long scratches marred her face, and her braided hair was plastered to her skull. Her eyes bore a dull sheen, and she wore silver cuffs on her wrists. She shuffled quietly behind the Seller until they reached the bottom of the stairs.

If Agnella was under mindmeld, who would help her release her gift? Despair and guilt surged at once, weakening Bell's legs. She staggered. The food she'd devoured at Aless's house had turned to vapor, and her limbs shook with weariness.

"He's going to use mindmeld on me, Roza," Bell hissed. "Is that what you want?"

Roza frowned.

"I know you don't think of us as family anymore." Bell winced. "But how can you let him brainwash us?"

She snorted. "I'm nothing to our parents. So they are nothing to me." She stepped forward. "But you're still my sister. You can still heal me, for good."

Bell shook her head. "No, Roza. I can't. Your so-called father already has a permanent mindmeld. If he wanted to cure you, he would have already."

"She is right." Bell shuddered at the Seller's voice. The Seller wore a faint air of regret. His hands slid deep in his pockets. "I know I promised Roza the first *permanenza* cure, but—" He withdrew a vial full of a gold-laced blue liquid. "I must use this on you first."

"He's using you, Roza." She forced herself to meet his black eyes. "From the moment he put Magia in your hands, he's been using you to get to me."

Roza scoffed. "Not everything is about you, Goldenbell."

Rage struck like a snake. "You were a *child* playing in the woods, and he gave you *Magia*. I don't care if he thinks he's your father or has some greater purpose. No real father would *ever* give their child something so deadly. Besides, where has he been all your life? The Seller accepted you once he realized he had something to gain from you."

Something unsteady flickered across Roza's face.

The Seller tsked. "I wanted to work with you as equals, Bell." He uncorked the vial.

"Roza?" Bell pleaded, pressing back until the waterfall misted on her shoulders.

"Say goodbye, Roza." The Seller came forward.

Roza caught the Seller's arm. "Is there no other way? If using that on her will make her like Agnella..." They both glanced back at Agnella's lifeless gaze. "What if she can't fuse with the same complexity?"

"You raise a good point." He stoppered the vial, studying Bell like a problem to be solved. "You misunderstand my mindmeld and my intentions. My mindmeld is merely used to give you what you truly desire. For a Lymbodia sufferer—it brings health. For a deceived lover—it brings true love." He spread his hands. "I gave Francesca the choice to be with me, and she refused. If I truly cared nothing about freedom of choice, I would have made her think she loved me."

"Don't talk about my mother," Bell said.

"Your mother, your father, Agnella, I will let them all go. If you simply join me, your loved ones can go on their merry way. Otherwise, you will work for me under the influence of the mindmeld, and I'll keep them all."

The faintest smell of hot stone reached Bell's nose. She shifted her feet as if considering the Seller's proposal. "It is a hard choice."

The Seller's face softened. He stepped closer, a few strides away now. "I know. I wish it did not have to be so, but you must choose."

She studied Roza's expression. Her sister's uncertainty had vanished, and she stood resolute beside the Seller.

Had Bell given Rian enough time? The waterfall distorted as Rian's arm slid around her waist. "No," she said. Rian jerked her beneath the water and into the wall.

Forty-Two

RIAN SLAMMED THE OPENING SHUT AS they staggered back and the Seller's snarl cut off. Dusky light revealed black vines stretched everywhere. The scent of black Insidio choked out the smell of water and Rian's melted stone. Their legs tangled, and they fell onto dry grass. Hedges surrounded them, growing in haphazard shapes. A horned statue shifted above them, a noose of Jonga Lilies around its neck. Rian rolled them away from the statue as it swung its fist low into the hedges. Scrambling up, they dashed around a line of low trees. Branches crackled as a stone hand shoved through the trees. The statue stomped closer, shaking the ground.

Rian spun back, diving at the statue's feet. Bell's scream strangled her throat as heat blasted, and the statue's legs melted into a molten pile. Rian danced away, then sprinted toward her as a wave of Jonga Lilies wriggled toward him. The Lilies' throats were black and their vines thick and hungry looking as they swarmed over the ground.

"Run." He grabbed her arm and half dragged her along the path. The Lilies buried the melted statue and swept toward them. The path narrowed until it opened on a clearing full of spindly bushes. The smell of damp and mold made her shiver.

Bell glanced back at the retreating Lilies. "Why did they stop?"

He pulled her tight against him. "Their roots only stretch so far."

Bell stared at his sculpted face, wanting to memorize every line. "How did you escape from the wall of the Solstice pool with the Seller?"

297

He smiled and cupped her cheeks. "Sheer determination. I never said it couldn't be done, but that it would be difficult. I had to get him away from you. As soon as we were free, though, he used mindmeld on me."

She searched his burning eyes as she laid her hands over his. "I was afraid I would never see you again. I couldn't bear it, if…"

His face softened. "I'm sorry, love." He kissed her so gently her chest ached.

"Will he follow us here?" she murmured.

"He'll want to gather more Lanzis and elixirs to protect himself. He rarely enters the Garden personally."

Bell worried her lip. "My gift is still bound, Rian. I won't be much help to escape."

He leaned his forehead against hers. "You'll find a way."

"You should have taken freedom when you had the chance."

His grip on her shoulders tightened. "I've never had a chance when it came to you, Sunbeam. In fact, I think it was love at first sight."

Her smile wobbled. "And look where that got you. Trapped underground with angry stone statues."

"I could say the same to you. This is my fault—"

She laid her fingers over his lips. "Shh. We're together now."

He took her hand and pressed a kiss to her palm. "I want to be wherever you are, Bell."

She cupped his cheeks, felt his dusky skin warm beneath her touch. He leaned close and she wove her fingers through his silky hair and pulled his face to hers. His soft lips turned hungry, and she gasped as they parted hers. His arms wrapped the small of her back and crushed her to him. The unsteadiness within her faded. She belonged here, her heart woven with his.

He smiled against her lips. "I guess I should get captured more often."

She shuddered, the flush of his nearness dampened by the memory of his deadened eyes. "Never again."

A thud echoed in the distance. He pulled away. "We should go."

He reached for her hand.

"Wait." She pulled out the mask and gloves she had shoved into her pocket and donned them. She slid her fingers into his and they hurried across the clearing. The path on the other side cut deeper into darkness, the wall of the Garden lost to shadow. Another statue staggered into a clearing ahead, its hands glowing like molten lava.

"We'll have to run past. Ready...now." They sprinted across the opening, and the statue spun with startling speed. "Get down!"

Bell dropped as Rian shoved her. He dove in the other direction, beneath the statue's outstretched arm. Bell screamed as the statue clutched at the air above him. Then it dropped to its knees, its feet glowing brighter and brighter until they went out. The smell of stones thrown in the fire filled the clearing.

She staggered up as Rian jogged toward her, wringing his hands. "Are you all right?"

"Me?" She glared. "Are you going to dive at every dangerous thing in here?"

"The stone ones." He blew on his palms. "Whew, that stings."

She turned his hands over, frowning at the angry red skin. "If I had some Myrtle..." And could fuse. She'd never felt so useless.

"I'll be fine. Come on."

"Do we have to go on the path? Couldn't we try to sneak around?" She gestured at the hedges.

"They're too thick. We'd be cut to ribbons by the thorns."

Bell scowled at the hedges. She needed her gift.

"There aren't many more statues anyway." They stepped into a grove of fruit trees.

"How do you know so much about this place?"

"The Seller doesn't come inside much, so he sends his spies instead."

She squeezed his arm, her heart aching. "I'm sorry."

"It's all right. I've always known he wasn't much of a father."

They ducked as rotten orange-shaped fruits fell around them. "Dark makers made all of this?"

He nodded and pulled her out from under the trees. "Their gifts begin to turn dark when they receive the Seller's Solstice gift. Some of their creations are too dangerous to sell in the Sotto, so he puts them here."

The path turned squishy beneath their feet. "Is this moss?"

A familiar scream pierced the air ahead of them.

"Mother." Bell pitched backward as the moss jerked beneath her.

Forty-Three

RIAN'S FINGERS BRUSHED HER HAIR AS the rippling moss tossed her off her feet and swept her around a corner and into a clearing surrounded by hedges. The hedges closed behind her and all was still.

She pushed herself up onto her hands, and the clearing erupted, glow gems casting amaranth light. The hedges morphed, and across from her a perfect replica of Roza lay crumpled, dark bruises covering her naked body. Blood poured from her slack mouth. Beside her, Father clutched his head, hoarse yells echoing, face twisted in pain.

"No." Bell crawled toward Father and the scene changed. Mother screamed, tearing her hair out until it lay in long blonde piles around her. Blood plunged down her forehead. Bell struggled forward but the moss pulled her back, always back. Mother's screams rose, and Bell covered her ears, clutching her own hair.

Warm hands circled her waist and jerked her back. The clearing went silent and dark as Bell and Rian fell out of an opening between the hedges and into the path. Bell's sobs filled the damp air.

"The Scentmakers' clearing," Rian said.

The moss lay lifeless beneath her now. "What?"

"I heard about this. He uses it to drive scentmakers mad because they cause the bushes to come to life."

Bell shuddered "It was so real."

Rian took her shoulders. "Don't you see, Bell? Only scentmakers. That means you're still a scentmaker."

"Are you sure?"

"I'll show you." He stepped through the opening.

"Don't—" The clearing was silent. Dark. No screaming, bleeding faces. Nothing happened.

His eyes glowed as he returned. "You're still gifted, Bell. I know it."

He helped her up and pulled her tightly against his chest. She caught her breath, trying to stifle the images that still filled her mind.

Silence blanketed the air.

"We have to keep going," Rian said softly. Bell nodded and took his hand. They walked on until they came to the guardian of the moss lying in a pile of molten stone, emanating a suffocating heat. They crept around it and along the path.

Rian sniffed. "Can you smell that?"

"If it's a Bardian scent, I can't." The air smelled damp and heavy and musty. That was all. With time, perhaps she could train her ordinary nose, but she didn't *have* time.

"I think it's—" He put out his hand to stop them. A steady, distant roar came when their footsteps stopped. "What is that?"

"The fountain?" Bell hugged herself.

Rian stepped forward, sniffing hard.

"Insidio."

"You can smell it from here?" Her mouth was dry. "How is that possible?"

"I think he's filled the fountain with it."

"That much Insidio would…" She shook her head. "How did he get so much?"

"He's been growing his own down here for decades. The prison is on the other side, and nearby there's a door that opens from this side."

She pursed her lips. "We can't get too close."

They took the path leading away from the splashing rumble. Bell didn't see the huge structure until it blocked half the air above them. The vines covering it rustled as they approached as if aware of them. "I don't think—"

"Bell." A familiar half-muffled voice came from inside the structure.

"Mother!"

Rian grabbed her arm. "Wait."

Something snapped out of the dark, and Rian jerked away, knocking Bell down and soaring into the air. He dangled by one leg from a vine.

A dark weaving vine, of course.

He cursed under his breath, fumbling in his pockets.

"Can you cut yourself down?" She edged forward. She saw a flash of white skin through the vines on the building. They were so close.

"Get back." The vine crept down his leg as Rian fumbled in his pockets. "I have a piece of glass here somewhere." The vine reached his waist and sent out feelers to his arms. It found his right arm and pulled it fast. He lost his grip on the glass, and it dropped. "Saint," he cursed.

Bell lurched for the glass and snatched it up from the grass. Something rustled and she froze in a crouch. A vine swung above her head, feeling the air.

"Don't move," Rian wheezed. Bell's knees trembled with the effort of holding still.

The vine lowered, like a snake searching for prey. It brushed the top of her head, and she gasped involuntarily. The vine pounced upon her, winding around her shoulders and neck.

She rushed through the air, the vine painfully tight around her chest, her neck. Her breathless scream strangled in her throat. How *dare* a plant treat her this way. She slammed into the structure, rattling against a window and feeling the whole malevolent life of it. It was so big she *had* to feel it.

"Bell," Rian's voice was a whisper, nearly choked by the vines squeezing his neck. In the dim reflection of the window, she saw him hanging behind her. Vines tightened over his entire body, slowly covering his face with black leaves.

Desperation flooded her, and she strained her senses, seeking the gift she *knew* was there. The window's reflection—was that a flash of gold in her chest? Yes! The goldenbell net was still with her. Then it

303

struck her—goldenbell couldn't be a non-fioré. *Gliorobella* had been included in *Legends of Ancient Fiore.* It must be a lost fioré that she'd always subconsciously known. Her lungs throbbed for air, and she stared hard at herself in the reflection, searching for the glittering net and the light of her gift. The goldenbell was not her enemy; it was a protective fioré.

Please, release me.

Something sparkled at the edge of her awareness. *I've been waiting for you to find me,* it murmured. Slowly the image in her reflection grew clearer. A fine golden net surrounded the light of her gift in her chest, protecting and trapping it. She imagined her fingers reaching beneath the net and tugging.

Nothing happened.

And then, like a flower opening into the sun, the net unfolded. Her gift blossomed from it, but the glittering strands of the goldenbell net still drifted beneath it.

Her heart felt too big for her chest.

She placed her hands on the vine, reaching out clumsily with her gift. "Release me," she croaked, pressing the words into the vine. The vine tightened like a petulant child. She reached again, more forcefully. "Release me. Now." The vine shied back and abruptly pulled away. She landed in the leaves with a grunt. Her mask had been wrenched down to her neck, but luckily, it was still there.

Rian's vine had completed its circuit around his neck. Standing on her tiptoes, she could reach the vine wrapping his ankles. Digging her fingers into its strands, she ordered it to flee, throwing the command like a sharp weapon. Rian dropped onto her, and she collapsed under his weight. He rolled off her, gasping for air. The workshop rustled and then stilled.

"Your gift came back," he rasped.

Bell nodded. The full, swelling feeling within her made it difficult to speak. Her throat felt thick and bruised, but she could breathe. She pushed to her feet and staggered to the edge of the structure, placed her hands on the vines, and *ripped* them apart with her gift. They came reluctantly, like tough fabric, and her fingers burned with the strength of her gift. The vines parted to reveal a doorway opening into blackness. Mother appeared on the other side, then Father, then half a dozen scentmakers stumbled out into the open.

The vine stirred and pulled back against her. As the last person ran through, her grip slipped, and the vines snapped shut like the mouth of a carnivorous plant. Bell turned, and Mother's arms wound around her like a warm blanket. Bell let herself be held for a moment.

"We need to go," Bell said reluctantly. Her words burned through her windpipe. Mother loosened her grip but slid her hand into Bell's. Bell squeezed her fingers.

The group tiptoed down the path, following Rian and pressing close to the hedges. From behind them, the structure sent feelers out, licking the air above them. Bell let go of Mother's hand to guard the rear.

"I don't know if I can defend us all," Bell murmured. A vine spun toward her, and she batted it away, but there were hundreds more reaching for them. "How close are we to the exit, Rian?"

"Close," he croaked. "I think."

The group rounded the corner into a cobbled circle, and the fountain rose before them, a vertical torrent of black liquid. Bell staggered to a halt.

Rian pointed to a hedged path across the clearing. "The door is right there, under that arbor."

Bell squinted. Beyond the thundering Insidio fountain, the cavern wall cast an endless shadow. Tall hedges on either side of the path would force them down a narrow lane. At the end of the path, she glimpsed an arbor covered in blossoms that looked bright against the cavern wall. Hope stirred. They were so close to the end. She grimaced at the fountain. "I wish we had masks for everyone."

Something scraped her ankle, and she spun back. "The vines." Long strands crept toward them, reaching for their legs.

"This is the closest door out. Hold your breath and stay together." Rian took her hand, and she took Mother's. She nodded to the other scentmakers. They sprinted across the wide cobbled circle in a tight group, holding their breaths. Purple Insidio spilled out of raised beds along the edges, turning toward her as if sensing her weakness. Mist rose around the fountain. The water churned and flung droplets at their feet. A bead narrowly missed her ankle, and she half turned to look. The fountain water was black as starless night, sucking her in, pulling her....

A low chuckle made her stumble. The Seller seeped out of the spray, a shade with glowing amaranth eyes and mask. He lifted his hands and streams of darkness wound around her legs. Mad thoughts exploded in her mind. She suddenly longed to jump into the fountain and drink the Insidio until it filled her veins.

The mask wasn't enough protection. She held her breath until her lungs screamed. She tried to force her legs to *move faster*, but the darkness felt like sludge around her feet. Mother and Rian pulled ahead and her grip on their hands loosened.

This wasn't the Seller—it was a scent cloud. It drifted around them, shuddering against her consciousness.

Bell snapped her hands out, her gift already pouring from her fingers. The cloud shrank back, howling, melting into the fountain. She sucked in a breath through her sore throat.

"Bell, hurry." Rian beckoned from the edge of the clearing. Black fog filled the air, but the Insidio remained in the fountain as she had commanded it.

"It's okay. I'm holding it. Everyone, get across." Bell stood still, straining against the scent cloud as the group rushed past her until Rian remained alone.

She backed out of the clearing after Rian. They entered the narrow path, which seemed to lengthen the farther they went. Finally, they reached the arbor, and she released her control over the Insidio. The scent cloud sprang back out of the fountain, swirling and searching for its prey.

With a sinking heart, Bell touched a yellow-orange blossom. The petals were thicker than goldenbell, the foliage too rough. "This isn't goldenbell."

"What is it?" Rian stepped closer, squinting.

She sighed. "Jonquil."

"Oh no." Rian moved to the back of the arbor. "It used to be an ordinary door…" He pulled vines aside, revealing a solid wooden door with a glass knob that opened at the top.

She shook her head. "It's a scentlock."

Rian grimaced. "It must be a fail-safe in case you made it in here. Perhaps one of the others—"

"Hurry," one of the scentmakers hissed behind them.

Bell glanced back. The scentmakers crowded closer, holding scraps of cloth over their noses. Their faces were pale with the strain of resisting the Insidio. Bell shook her head. "They're too weakened already. It has to be me."

Rian cupped her masked face. "You're the strongest scentmaker I've ever known, Bell. Haven't I told you that? The way you fuse…it's like you're breathing." He stroked his thumbs over the cloth and her lips parted. "Nothing could change that. It's not only your gift that's strong. It's you. You can pull beauty from the shadows."

"But if I fail…"

"You won't. I am here with you." Rian's smile grew until his eyes crinkled—then he swayed, catching himself on the arbor. Mother bumped into Father and giggled, a sound Bell could barely remember hearing. She stared at them for a long moment. The truth dawned—this much Jonquil, even unfused, was making them drunk.

Bell spun toward the scentlock as Mother's arms closed around her shoulders, her weight making Bell stumble into Rian's legs. She grabbed the doorknob, pushing out from under Mother's grip. Father lost his balance and slumped back against the arbor. He sank to the ground, muttering to himself.

Bell reached for her gift, trying to shove back the scent. It was like catching falling sand. Her mask blocked most of it, but she felt the edges of her mind brightening with an eerie lightness.

Her hands shook as she reached for her gift again. She snatched a blossom. *I was born to do this. San Giovanni will give me the strength I need. Jonquil will not defeat me.*

307

She closed her eyes, let everything go black. She centered her intentions on the Jonquil, prepared for nausea to knock her to her knees. Her hands moved into a fusing position over the scentlock's opening.

I am Bardia's strongest scentmaker.

A slow dribble of orange liquid fell into the scentlock. The lock clicked, and the door swung open on a dark room.

Forty-Four

BELL SHOVED MOTHER THROUGH THE open door first. Father drifted through after her. Bell darted back down the path to grab the others, then herded them all into the dark space. Rian still lay sleepily against the arbor, a soft grin on his face. She grabbed his arm and yanked. He was immovable.

"What's the hurry?" he asked, drowsily.

"I need you to stand up."

He mumbled something, his eyelids sagging.

She grabbed his shoulders and leaned close. "Kiss me, Rian."

His eyes opened, and he reached for her, but she pulled back. She took his hands, coaxing him to his feet. He staggered against her, cupping her face clumsily. She guided him through the door and shut it behind them. Darkness enveloped them. Something clattered across the room, followed by a startled curse.

"Antonio?" Mother called from a few feet away, her voice trembling.

Rian pulled the mask off her face and bent closer, his warm lips landing on Bell's nose. She grabbed his hands and tugged them down. "Rian," she hissed.

His breathing slowed. "What happened?" he whispered.

"Jonquil," she whispered. "Do you know where we are? We need to find a light and—"

Twin flames burst to life, glittering on the glass panes of the Conservatory. Between the rows of raised beds stood Arabia with a dozen Lanzis. Her eyes glittered like metal in the light of her fiery hands.

309

"Thanks, but I'm rather hot from our exertions," Rian muttered.

Mother straightened as she caught sight of Father held by two Lanzis, his arms twisted behind him. "The Consiglio won't stand for this. Lead us out of here immediately."

Arabia didn't take her deadly gaze from Rian.

"Of course, Matrona. This way." Behind Arabia, a glow gem flared to light in someone's hand.

The Seller stood at his desk, lips curved. Beside him, Agnella was bound to a chair and gagged with a cloth. Roza lounged against the side of his desk, arms crossed and her gaze stony. Maestra Lux and Maestro Carlo lay bound to the fioré bench behind Roza, their heads slumped. Maestra Anna stood over them. Piero leaned against the wall at the edge of the light, looking sullen.

"I am pleased, Bell. I was beginning to think I would have to fetch you myself." The Seller's fingers flicked, and Lanzis lunged for Rian. He shoved Bell back and knelt to press his hands against the stone floor. The floor rippled and two of the Lanzis sank to their waists in the stone before the rest reached him. Three grabbed Rian, holding him away from the stone floor while they snapped a silver gift-blocking bracelet on his wrist. The other scentmakers, still weak from the Jonquil, were quickly subdued with bracelets. The Seller lifted his hand, and the Lanzis left Mother standing and stalked warily toward Bell. The half-buried Lanzis strained against the stone surrounding their legs, their eyes white-rimmed.

Bell opened herself to her gift and the blossoms along the walls curled toward her, dazzling her with their light. She steadied her hands and gathered every fioré cloud, sending them streaking toward the Lanzis and the Seller. His smile froze, and he raised a vial swirling with blue light. Was that the permanent mindmeld she had made for him? In his other hand, he held a tiny dipper of something red. "Not so hasty."

Is that my blood?

She halted the clouds, and they hovered around him. The Magia jostled the fioré, longing to suck the life out of him. "Give that to me."

310

He eyed the clouds. "You have kept your own secrets, I see."

"How dare you treat us this way?" Francesca strode toward him, still looking formidable despite the tattered state of her purple skirt. "A Matrona is not your plaything."

"Francesca." His smiled softened. "Have you tired of your role?"

"Get back, Mother. He has mindmeld."

"Oh, do not fear for her. This is for you."

Mother stopped a few feet away from the Seller, casting a desperate glance back at Bell.

"You won't be touching me with that," Bell snapped.

"My methods have advanced, Bell. If I put your blood into this vial, the mindmeld will seek you out from any distance."

Bell frowned and glanced at Rian.

He furrowed his brow. "I don't know, Bell." He grunted as a Lanzi threw an elbow into his ribs. Bell flicked a tiny stream of Princess Seed and Smemor at the guard's face, and he fell to his knees, gagging.

The Seller smirked. "Do you think you can defend against all of us and keep the mindmeld from reaching you?"

"You will release us all, or I will take your gift from you." Her own burned within her, longing for the power of *fusione*. But that wasn't why she would do it.

Was it?

Mother lunged the remaining step between her and the Seller, her fingers closing on his wrist that held the vial of mindmeld. He cursed, wrenching free and flinging her to the floor.

Bell lurched forward. "Mother."

The Seller studied Francesca as she pushed herself up, head still high. When he spoke, his voice was soft and complicated. "I will make one more bargain with you, my dear. Choose to stay with me, and I will let your pathetic husband go."

"Leave her alone. Whatever you had with her, it's gone," Bell said.

"I hardly think so," he said. He offered his hand. When Mother ignored him, her gaze full of hate, he let it fall and turned his attention back to Bell. "But I will give her time to choose me. You, on the other hand, are too valuable to waste on choice." In one motion he smashed both vials into a gem-made bowl on his bench. The mindmeld consumed the blood and spun toward her, its intricate cloud seeking the blood within her veins.

She flung all the scent clouds she had gathered at it, trying to form a shield and contain it, but the mindmeld trickled through like water through gravel. The air lightened, taking on a blue tinge. She held her breath and sprinted across the room, throwing up shield after shield. Each one slowed the mindmeld, giving her another second to dodge it. The Seller spun to follow her. Was he still in control of the mindmeld?

The next time the mindmeld attacked, Bell split her shield and flung part of it over the Seller. He staggered back and snarled, but the mindmeld kept coming.

"It is too late. It has your blood now."

The mindmeld streaked for her like water from a geyser, and she dove beneath a table of fioré, rolling out at Arabia's feet. The Spy slammed her foot on Bell's chest and the mindmeld seeped into her pores, washing away her own thoughts and replacing them with the Seller's.

The Seller's consciousness surged through the mindmeld, wrapping Bell like a vine. Her awareness fused with his. Scent clouds tinted the amaranth lanterns with rainbows. Bell spread her arms. A lovely light filled her mind's landscape, shades of green and blue and silver. She was whole, as she'd never been before. Arabia moved back and let her sit up.

"How did you do this?" Bell said softly.

The Seller took a rapid breath. He gestured and Lanzis shoved Agnella forward. "Take her gift, Bell. It's the true way to heal Bardia."

Of course he was right. Bell moved forward and took Agnella's hands, feeling the dim glow within her. Agnella met her gaze, her eyes sad, but urgent. Why was she sad? Bell could use her power to help everyone. To make this beautiful mindmeld permanent.

She wrapped her gift around Agnella's, but it was already uprooted, waiting for her. Her thoughts flickered for a moment. Why was she doing this?

"Take it," Agnella whispered.

Take Agnella's gift? She could never—

"Finish it," the Seller said.

The haze thickened, and she pulled her gift back with Agnella's wrapped inside. Agnella crumpled.

Bell frowned.

"What happened to her?" Something about this was dreadfully familiar. She could almost bring it to the surface, but her thoughts were whirling too fast, full of this blue light.

"Forget her. Finish the task."

Bell turned inward, weaving her gift with Agnella's. The threads melted and light surged through her, forging her into a blazing column that pierced the sky. When the heat vanished, she gasped, and the scents of the whole Night Bazaar—the whole of Bardia—entered. The fioré in this room were a spark compared to the blazing sun of the whole. She staggered into the bench of fioré. The Seller followed, a dark, muddy scent writhing around him. What was it? Bell reached for him, and he recoiled.

"Don't touch me. What do you see?"

"I can smell everything. You are—" Had she felt this before? This power was deep, reaching into the sea that cradled Bardia. It felt like touching the Spring during Solstice, like becoming one with the *attuale* current, but this time her body was enough to hold it.

Agnella had *given* this to her.

"Stay there. Your gift is volatile."

Bell stilled. Darkness lay like ancient roots around the Seller. Roots that would kill.

He held out a vial and she took it. "Make me something permanent. Let me guide you."

She rolled it between her fingers. She ached to follow his words. She needed someone to show her how to use the Magia, but with Agnella's gift had come some other awareness, one she couldn't quite—

"You will never make a mistake again."

Ah, *that* was what she longed for. She let him direct her without

313

trying to understand what she was doing. A touch of her gift, and the vial flashed and bubbled. She twisted off the cork and coaxed the scent cloud out into her hands. Had this been hard before?

"Put it on yourself."

Something familiar caught her gaze. A golden thread, woven through the other shapes. She had seen it before…when the mindmeld was chasing her….

"Put it on." The Seller's teeth were gritted.

Bell looked at him and knew. The mindmeld held her blood, the golden streak. If she opened it, this haze would remain forever. And what would happen to the others?

She spun, taking in a room full of shadows. Where were they?

"Look at me. You can do nothing without me." The Seller's voice pulled her. Half her mind simply believed him, but the power of Agnella's gift in her was straining against his mindmeld.

Rian's words echoed within.

It's not only your gift that's strong. It's you. You can pull beauty from the shadows.

"You will hurt people, everyone you love, without me."

She let his voice draw her near, watched his shoulders relax.

"Good. Now open the vial."

Quickly, before he saw. She formed a finger with her mind and tugged the golden strand free. It rose, melting into her. Taking that finger, she pulled a strand from the Seller's cloud. His essence took the place of hers around the mindmeld.

He flinched. "What did you…" His eyes widened. She tossed the vial toward him. The mindmeld surged free, swarming toward his shield. The haze faded from her mind, replaced by bright clarity.

The shadows vanished, revealing Rian gripped between two Lanzis. He still wore the silver bracelet. She shot sharp streams of cloud to engulf the Lanzis. They collapsed, writhing. Rian pounced on the Lanzi with the twin of his bracelet and tore it off. Arabia's hands lifted as she aimed for Bell. Rian slammed his hands onto the ground. A stone shield sprang up, blocking her fire.

Jaw clenched, Bell pressed the mindmeld on the Seller with her gift. He writhed, fighting to keep his shield in place.

Roza stumbled toward her. "No, you'll brainwash him forever!"

"I have to." She wrapped her gift around him like chains, pressing against his shield. The Seller dropped to his knees. He deserved this, he—

Roza cursed. "Take his gift."

Bell hesitated. The Seller's face was purpling with effort. "I need to stop him." How could he fight so long? She gathered her strength to crush him.

"Bell." Rian's warm hands on her shoulders jolted her. "Take his gift instead."

His touch cleared her mind. She could take his gift and leave him an ordinary man. Could she get through his shield? Bell narrowed her gift to fine points, seeking a chink in his defense. The Seller howled, forcing her violently back. She shook her head, looking at Roza. "I'm sorry. I can't."

Roza held out a goldenbell blossom. The petals were crumpled from being crammed in her pocket, but the yellow flower glowed. "Fuse the goldenbell. It was meant for you to use."

The goldenbell. The powerful fioré that had been hiding in plain sight for centuries. She took it slowly, realization dawning within her like a sunrise. The *goldenbell* must be the counteragent to black Insidio. That must be why it reacted so strongly when she first fused it. *Could it be part of a true cure for Lymbodia?*

Heat billowed from Arabia's sputtering fire, and sweat dripped down Bell's neck. The darkness within the Seller scraped at her awareness, like malevolent roots. She looked into Roza's anguished face.

Bell released the craving to erase the Seller and fused.

A glittering net wafted from the golden flower, like a sphere of sunshine. Working quickly, she pulled the *permanenza* strand from the mindmeld cloud and wove it into the net instead. She dispersed the mindmeld, and the Seller staggered, then regained his balance. He stood poised, eyes glittering.

315

"So you weren't strong enough, in the end." He bared his teeth mirthlessly.

Bell shook her head. "I have always been strong enough, Salieri." She flung the net and enveloped him in golden light.

Forty-Five

THE NET SANK THROUGH HIS SHIELD LIKE it was nothing. She guided it around his gift and tugged, making sure every dark root was pulled from the soil of his soul. He convulsed as the gift left his body and his shield disappeared. "What have you done?" he rasped.

Rian handed her a vial, and she guided the goldenbell-wrapped gift into it.

It felt painfully similar to *fusione*, but this was the way to leave him alive and protect those she loved. The *permanenza* strand she'd woven into the goldenbell net would keep his gift safe from everyone, including herself. She knew now that *fusione* was never meant to be a true cure for Lymbodia.

The Seller's fists clenched. Was he seeking his gift? Bell corked the vial and pushed it deep into her pocket. Nothing happened.

"It's all right, Father." Roza reached out to touch his shoulder, and he smacked her away. She stepped back, blinking fast.

"How dare you." His face whitened with each word.

Bell's shoulders released. "It was the only way to save your life."

Arabia howled, and a stream of fire gashed toward Bell. The door to the tower slammed open and a rush of water spun the fire to steam that clouded the air. Maestra Piccarda strode inside, followed by Garam and Carasti, a line of makers close behind.

Agnella. Bell dashed to the limp figure in the chair.

317

Agnella stirred as Bell pushed her hair back. "Please, wake up, Agnella."

Roza screamed and a scuffle started across the room. The Seller fled through the water-printed door, and Piero had his arm around Roza's neck and a vial of something beneath her nose. Rian hesitated by the still-closing door. Bell froze, her gift at her fingertips.

"Let us go, or I'll poison her."

"Put it down, Piero." Bell stepped closer.

Roza's face was white with rage. "You fool. I could have gone with him."

"Roza, you don't have to go. I'll speak to the Consiglio—"

"I want no part of your Maestris. I belong with him." On the last word, she stomped on Piero's foot and spun out from under him. Rian dove for the vial and wrested it from Piero as Roza flung open the door and sprinted through.

"Roza, stop."

Bell followed, ignoring Rian's call to wait. Roza's discarded heels littered a stone stairway. A small door lay ajar, and Bell shoved herself through the gap. The black pool rippled beyond the Seller's sanctuary, casting strange shadows on Roza's figure descending the stairs.

Bell had to stop her this time.

Roza's long legs pulled ahead, nearing the double doors. Bell spread her gift, searching for green life, and found tiny algae deep in the pools. Green ropes swept out of the water, tangling like a net around Roza's ankles as she reached up to open the double doors to the atrium. Roza stumbled to her knees and screamed like a wounded animal.

Bell's breath was ragged as she left the last step. "Roza, *please*. Come back with me. Father and Mother love you. I love you. Garam loves—"

"Shut up. You know nothing about me."

Bell eased toward her. "I know you long for acceptance. I offer it to you. You don't have to do anything. We were children—I know it wasn't my fault or yours that I exposed you to the Smemor. Come home with me. I can heal you. The goldenbell is the answer, I know it is."

Roza used the doors to stand up. "He's already healed me, Bell. He used the permanent mindmeld to heal me." She spun, pulling her skirt aside to reveal a smooth, clear abdomen. "He's my father. I belong with him."

"But his cure requires *fusione*."

"He loves me more than you do." Roza's voice was raw.

Bell took a deep breath. Was she strong enough to do this? "I do love you. I love you enough to let you go." She released the algae, and it slithered back into the water. "You need to choose, Roza. I'm not like Salieri. For love to be real, it must be chosen."

Roza's hands fisted and loosened, over and over. Then she opened the doors and stepped through.

Bell stood blinking in the still darkness for a moment before footsteps thundered behind her. Garam half fell down the stairs, stopping dead as his vision adjusted and he saw her standing alone.

"Where is she?"

"She doesn't want to be found, Garam." Her voice cracked. Why did it have to feel so final?

"Tell me where—" He spotted the door ajar and strode toward it.

"Garam, be careful. I don't know where she's going."

He turned back, a hand on the doorframe. "I will find her, Bell. I *will* save her."

"Thank you," she whispered. His boots thundered down the hallway.

"Bell." Rian's relieved voice from behind her felt like a warm hand on her shoulder. "Agnella needs you."

Rian's hand never left hers as they dashed up the stairs and into the Conservatory. The pain in Bell's lungs felt distant, her heartbeat replaced with a plea to the Saint.

The Conservatory was full of grim activity. Lanzis were bound against the wall. Piero and Arabia were under watch by three Maestris. Makers hovered over Maestra Lux and Maestro Carlo, who were both sitting up and sipping water.

Agnella lay on a pallet near the center of the room. Mother gripped her hand. "I should have listened to you." Mother's voice broke. "I have no one to blame but myself."

Bell dropped to her knees beside Agnella.

Agnella's bloodless face made her dark irises glow. "We all make our choices, Francesca."

Bell took her other hand. "Agnella, I—I can fuse now. I might be able to heal you."

Agnella shook her head slowly. "Not even you are that strong."

Bell didn't have to reach with her gift to feel the life ebbing from her mentor. "But I—"

"Not one word about taking my gift. I gave it to you, girl." A cough rattled her chest. "You think any of us would still be our own if I hadn't, hmm?"

Tears dripped from Bell's chin, splattering their joined hands. "I'd give it back if I could."

Agnella smiled softly. "It was my choice, Bell. A free Bardia. But promise me one thing." Her voice threaded to a whisper and Bell leaned close.

"Anything."

"When that merchant finishes his ship, you'll go with him."

"Me?" An image of herself at the bow of a ship, hair flowing back in the wind, flashed in her mind.

"You're the one I trust to properly represent Bardia, girl." Agnella's lips flickered in a smile. "You're Bardian through and..." Her eyelids fluttered. "You'll be the one...find the cure...."

Bell choked on a sob. "Don't go, Agnella. Please."

"Promise..."

"I promise."

Agnella's face stilled.

A light went out in Bell's landscape, one color shade forever gone in the night.

When Bell became aware of hands on her shoulders, her head rested on Agnella's still chest. Agnella's hand was warmed by her own.

"I'm here, Blossom."

Bell gasped and lifted up. "Father?"

He tucked a blanket around her and pulled her close. "I'm so sorry, Bell."

"You're all right?"

His chin rubbed her head as he nodded. "The Insidio wore off when you shielded the Seller."

Tears rushed down her face until his tattered shirt stuck to her cheek. "Roza's gone, Father. She went after him."

"We will never give up on her." Father pulled back and cupped her face in his scratched hands. "She is family. Your sister, my daughter. She will always have a home with us." His gaze was steady as Bardian wood. Unsplinterable. Unbendable. The father she knew.

"Garam went after her."

His lips tightened. "And I owe him for it. He loves her." When Father laid his hand on Mother's knee, she startled from a blank gaze at Agnella's face. "The Saint knows I understand."

"Are you all right, Mother?" Bell sucked in a breath when Mother looked up. When had Francesca shown anything but control? Now agony pulsed in her eyes.

"She tried to warn me, so many years ago. I have brought this upon us all," she whispered.

Ah. No wonder the agony looked so familiar. Bell leaned across Father and took Mother's hand firmly, ignoring its iciness. "You are not allowed to carry it, Mother. No one may carry this alone."

"Except him," Rian murmured from Bell's other side. He'd been so silent Bell had forgotten he still knelt beside her. Now his gaze skittered past Bell's. Bell reached for him, but he had already risen and was flowing away toward the tower door, like a shadow fleeing at the first rays of the sun.

"Rian, where are you going?"

She scrambled up, stumbling after him on numb feet. Panic pulsed as the door shut before she reached it. What if he left her too?

He moved quickly, but she caught up with him outside the double doors leading to sanctuary. "Please, wait."

He slowed so she could walk with him, his lips tight. They followed a distantly familiar path to his room. Bell saw herself stumbling inside not so long ago, her heart full of fear when she learned who he was. So much had changed.

"Rian? What are you thinking?"

He braced his fingers on the wardrobe. "It's like your father said. You're a family. All my family has done is wreck yours."

"You're not to blame for his actions. You don't have a choice about your parents."

He shook his head. "I promised never to hurt you. But I don't know if I can trust myself not to. There's too much of *him* in me."

Bell's heart pinched. "I trust you not to. You sacrificed yourself to save me at the Solstice pool. You went into the Midnight Garden with me."

He met her gaze, his eyes pained. "When the Seller fled, part of me wanted to go with him. Part of me *considered* it." He grabbed a shirt and tossed it in the bag. "I need to get away. I'm going to the mainland. To start over."

She barked a laugh. "I thought you were smarter than this."

"You deserve someone better." He touched her chin.

She rolled her eyes. "I'll thank you to let me make my own decisions."

His face softened, wistful. "I wish it could be different." He turned and slung the bag over his arm.

"Florian, put that down." She grabbed his shirt and yanked him to eye level. "If you try to run to the mainland like a coward, I will find you and haunt you. Do you not understand? Our roots are tangled together. Where you go, I will go."

He remained wide-eyed for a long moment. "Is this one of your own decisions you speak of?"

He sounded wheezy, so she released the pressure a bit. "It is, and if you try to change my mind, I will rake you into my flower bed."

"At least I couldn't cause any trouble, then."

She grinned. "You'll always be trouble." She pulled his lips to hers. He wound his fingers through her hair, so gentle her eyes stung. The night sky descended and wrapped them in soft velvet. Soft and right and perfectly fitted, a night they could stay in forever.

The thorny vine lay lifeless, but Bell still felt its accusation.

"You don't have to do this now." Rian tightened his hand on her arm.

She cleared her throat. "Her fioré need tending." She laid her hand on the thorns, tugging at the life within it. It rose sluggishly, pulling back for a moment. Bell put aside her guilt. She had to win the vine to her side if she wanted to get inside without destroying it.

For the fioré. For Agnella.

She cleared her mind and took the vine with her gift, nudging it aside. At her touch, it melted into her consciousness, transferring its bond to her as the new Maestra of Scents.

Bell stepped inside the workshop, breathing in the humid fragrances of loam and rotting compost. The fioré clouds rushed toward her, a kaleidoscope of eager wind. She staggered, Rian's hands on her elbows holding her up.

"What's wrong?"

She gave a pained laugh. "I don't deserve this."

He snorted. "If anyone does, you do. But even if you didn't, you're the only one who can use it."

The clouds circled her, bubbling closer to her, their energy filling the air.

She took a deep breath. Rian stepped back, watching her walk between the tables. The fioré bent to follow, rustling for attention.

"What will you do first?" The plants and soil dampened Rian's voice from near the door.

Bell stroked a stunted Myrtle, feeding it life and coaxing it to the height of those beside it. "I'm going to fuse a true cure."

Forty-Six

PATER MEDORO SAT IN A PLUSH ARMCHAIR and dipped his head as she came into view. Apparently, the thick rugs and carved end tables and shelves of leather-bound books surrounding him made him forget the bars blocking his way to freedom. The cell in the Rotunda had been built for dark makers, and it was secure against any gift.

"Miss Asbury. I hope you will remember our Houses' continuing friendship. We would be honored if you would consider a future alliance…" He glanced at the farthest corner where Piero sat sprawled on a velvet sofa, staring vacantly at the wall. Matrona Medoro sat rigidly beside him, giving Bell no acknowledgement.

"You must be joking, Pater." What would he do if she laughed in his face? "I won't be entering an engagement anytime soon. I am busy." She held her breath, hoping he wouldn't move on to asking her to influence the Consiglio as the new Maestra of Scents.

"Ah yes, the young Maestra has much on her plate." His mouth twitched.

"What did you call me here for?"

He brushed off his spotless burgundy coat sleeve. "To remind you of where you came from. You were born a noble and will always remain so. As long as you remember that, you will have our support."

She stepped back, enjoying the swish of her new tawny-colored overdress against the floor. She'd yielded to Mother's pleas that she dress according to her new station as Maestra. That meant floor-sweeping skirts, dramatic sleeves, and wearing jewels in her hair. To her surprise, it made her feel capable rather than uncomfortable.

"I don't need your support, Pater Medoro."

He lifted his chin. "Foolish girl."

"I am the Maestra of Scents. Please remember that." She turned and gestured for the Consiglio's knight to let her out.

"You will come back to me, *Maestra*."

"To see if you're behaving, perhaps. Farewell, Pater." The door shut. Rian waited outside, eyebrows raised.

She shook her head. "He's still offering Piero, as if I'd ever want to ally myself with that family. I'm beginning to feel sorry for his son."

"He thinks you still need money."

"Why would I?" She stepped to the balcony overlooking the Rotunda's floor. Aless and Carasti waited below. Carasti was deep in a story complete with dramatic gestures that had Aless ducking. "I have Aless for that." She glanced up to catch Rian's dark expression. "I'm joking, Florian. I'm quite certain he's in love with my best friend."

"Don't call me that."

"You need to get over this rivalry."

"It's not a rivalry. It's distaste."

"You don't like wealth? Whose wealth bought me this?" She pulled the goldenbell field from her wrist bag. "I fell in love with you that day. I just didn't know it."

He pressed his forehead to hers. "And you know it now?"

"It's a little fuzzy—"

His lips silenced her, igniting warmth that traveled to her toes.

Several moments later, he pulled away. "You'll be late."

"I have five minutes yet," she protested.

He smiled mischievously. "Five minutes is not enough with you. Better to stop now."

She made a face, then descended the stairs slowly and walked across the floor to a double glass door that opened on a round table. The doors clicked shut and six Maestris looked up.

Maestra Lux cleared her throat. "Thank you for joining us, Maestra

Goldenbell."

She wasn't one minute late. "I've come from Pater Medoro, who requested a moment of my time, Maestra Lux." She lifted her chin.

Maestra Lux hmphed. "Well, sit down. We have much to discuss."

The first hour of her first Consiglio meeting consisted of painful details like how to reintegrate the Seller's employees into society. Maestra Lux could no longer deny that barring makers from the Solstice had driven them to the Sotto. With their source now blocked off by Rian and other stonemakers, the Consiglio finally agreed to allow all makers an interview to determine their worthiness to attend the next Solstice. Hardly any of the makers, dark or otherwise, had received a renewal this year after the chaos of the Seller's attack.

They would all need a fresh start.

"And you, Goldenbell? What have you brought to the table?"

Here it was, her opening. "Ah…"

"It's customary for a new Maestra to bring suggestions, as a sign of her value to the Consiglio," Maestra Lux said. The other Maestris leaned forward. Maestra Piccarda nodded, and Maestro Carlo winked.

She took a deep breath. "Actually, I have been considering something new. Bardia's wares have long been the heart of our island. But I think we can all agree the nobles have often taken advantage of the makers."

The Maestris exchanged surprised and speculative glances.

Bell leaned forward. "I propose we take our market further afield."

"Further afield?" Maestra Lux looked incredulous. "Where would this be?"

"The mainland, Maestra Lux."

"And they agreed to it?" Father spread another spoonful of fig jam on his toast.

"They agreed to consider it. But I think Maestra Lux was impressed with Aless's plan. Especially when I mentioned House Salviati would sponsor it. Of course, we'll have to convince the pope it's what San Giovanni wants." They also had yet to discuss Bell's promise to Agnella to travel on the first ship. The salt wind in her hair, Rian's fingers tangled with hers, Carasti beaming beside her...it was beginning to feel like an itch she wanted to scratch.

It would also be a chance to study the mainland's medicine and blend it with fioré.

"And the Medoros?" Mother asked. Bell had avoided Mother's gaze until now, and the glow she saw there soothed the knot in her chest.

"Pater Medoro...he will help if it's for his own gain."

"As I thought." Mother laid a hand on Father's. "Thank the Saint I didn't marry him."

Bell's mouth dropped open, and she took a quick sip of tea to cover her reaction.

"Bell, I have something for you." Mother stood, dabbing her lips with a napkin. She returned from the butler's pantry with a clay pot. Brilliant foliage spilled from it, and one bright white Jonga Lily bloomed.

Bell set down her tea before it sloshed on her knees.

"My daughter, I have wronged you." Mother's blue eyes were bright, and a tear hung at the corner of one. She held out the pot. "Will you...will you accept this gift as a token..."

Bell slid her hands around Mother's, feeling the cool comfort of her skin. "I forgive you, Mother. While it hurt me...you were trying to protect me."

Mother breathed out as if for the first time that morning and set the pot on the table. "I was foolish." Her eyes told stories of pain buried deep. "You are so much stronger than I was. I should have known that."

Bell scoffed. "You're the one who taught me strength, Mother. The Saint saw fit to give me a powerful gift, that's all."

"And you're doing wonderful things with it. We all have learned much wisdom, my dear." Father stood and wrapped his arm around Mother's shoulders.

Mother cleared her throat. "But, Bell, will you not consider Aless?"

Bell lifted a finger, scowling. Mother's mind was like the roots of a tree, all thoughts leading to the same place. "I'll forgive you, if you never mention my marrying him again. My heart is taken."

Mother smiled sheepishly. "I had to try once more. Not that your Rian isn't handsome, he's merely—"

"Penniless?" Rian strode into the dining room, grinning like a rogue.

"Oh, Florian—forgive me." Mother fumbled as Father laughed.

Rian dipped his head.

"I don't care if he *is* penniless, Mother, though I sincerely doubt it." Bell wound her fingers through Rian's. "Is Carasti finished?"

"Not yet. There's someone here to see you." He tugged her toward the hall.

"Bring our daughter back for supper," Father called.

"If he can stay too," Bell said, a grin taking over her face.

"Of course," Mother said. "Now, Antonio, shall we discuss what piece of *your* furniture we should sell for her next fioré? My sitting room is beginning to look bare."

"Didn't the Consiglio give her an entire workshop full?" Father asked.

Their voices sank to murmurs, but Bell could still hear Mother's smile as Rian opened the door to Bell's garden. They drifted toward the fountain.

"Mother's happy about selling the furniture." Bell shook her head. "I think they're delighted to have me out of the house these days. It's like they're newly married."

Rian laughed and kissed her cheek. "I think it's catching."

She blushed and wrinkled her nose. "Who's here to see me? It's not—" She froze as Garam pushed off the fountain. His eyes were bloodshot, his shoulders slumped. His body looked like a weight he could hardly lift. A lump swelled her throat. "Did you find her?"

He shook his head. "I lost her in the Sotto. Too many places to hide. I've heard whispers of where they're hiding though."

Bell's eyes stung. "Why would she want to hide in the Sotto?"

"He's deep into her mind, now." Garam shuffled closer. "I've been thinking. Your gift is much stronger now, right?"

"Yes."

"Then you could fuse an elixir to heal her mind."

"I'm not going to brainwash her, Garam. I vowed her that."

"Not brainwash. Just…clear her mind."

Bell chewed her lip. "I don't know."

"Just try. Please, Bell."

He looked so weary.

She let out a long breath. "I'd do anything for her too, Garam. Anything but force her. I'll try to come up with something that will help her see the truth."

"Thank you. I'm going back to look."

"You should rest."

"Not until she's safe." He backed away toward the house. "Help me save her, Bell."

"I'll do everything I can."

Rian let her stare into the fountain in silence for a long while.

"I asked the Consiglio to let you be on the first ship to the mainland."

Rian blinked. "Me?"

"Of course, you. You deserve your dreams."

He wrapped his arms around her waist from behind. "*You* are my dream, Bell."

She leaned back and smiled. "I know. That's why I asked to go along too."

His laugh shook her. "This seems a good time to give you a gift."

She turned, still in his arms. "I love gifts."

His smile was a touch nervous, but it filled her with affection. "I left it by your workshop."

A soft package tied with golden ribbon lay before the workshop door. As she bent down, the weaving vine wrapped a tendril around her neck, leaving a perfect necklace of white blooms. She fingered it as she glanced at Rian. "What is this for?"

"For opening."

She rolled her eyes, but her fingers itched to undo the ribbon. The wrapping fell away, and a swath of ink-blue Bardian velvet hung over her hands. "This is for a dress?"

"Do you like it?" He definitely sounded nervous.

Rich as a gloaming sky, it stirred her heart like a night bird calling. "It's perfect," she whispered. "It's you." She pulled him to her, crushing the magic fabric between them.

Epilogue

BELL SHIFTED FORWARD ON HER STOOL, trying to ignore the curious glances from the Night Bazaar crowd. A new Scentmaker stall run by the new Maestra of Scents was enough to attract attention—one across from the Sotto stairwell after recent events with the Seller of Secrets sent whispers through the entire Bazaar.

Finally, someone was brave enough to step up to her stall. Matrona Salviati, swathed in a green cloak, met Bell's gaze.

"Good evening, Matrona. May I interest you in a *protezi* elixir?"

Her chin lifted and she swept her cloak back. "Yes, Scentmaker."

"Maestra of Scents, now," Rian said from behind her.

Bell jumped, nearly toppling the neat row of vials. She glared at Rian. "Must you be so silent?"

"I spoke just now."

She rose and turned back to Matrona Salviati, who was eyeing Rian. "Excuse me." Snatching a vial of *protezi* elixir, she wrapped it in white paper. "Five florins, please."

The Matrona's eyes flashed to Rian as she counted out the florins.

Bell took the payment and dropped it into her purse. She waited until the Matrona had melted into the passersby. Grabbing Rian's elbow, she pulled him to the back of the stall. "I'd rather not force my status at this time."

"But that's who you are. People should know to respect you."

"It makes them uncomfortable to have such a young Maestra."

Rian grinned. "A little discomfort never hurt anyone, Bell."

She bit her lip. His grin was like hot water on her paper heart. "Fine. Maybe I'm the one uncomfortable."

He sobered. "Don't be. You're a natural."

"Thanks." She sighed. "I wish the Consiglio believed that."

"I think they do. They've granted your requests, haven't they?"

"I get the feeling they're humoring me. Because they feel guilty."

A blonde girl stopped and bought a vial of *protezi* elixir, her eyes wide as she took in Rian.

"They'll learn who you are, in time," Rian murmured as the girl backed away, white package clutched in her hand.

"And who am I?" Bell turned to face him.

He grinned. "Bardia's first Maestra to visit the mainland."

She tilted her head. "Are you saying…"

"Carasti is finished."

She bolted up. "Already?"

"Already? You've been complaining about how slow she is for weeks."

"It's—let's go see."

He took her hand. "Shouldn't you do something about your wares?"

"Oh yes." She plucked a goldenbell from the pot beside her table and fused a protective net from it, wrapping it over the table like a cloth. "This will keep all the scents in."

"I'm sure you could make a fortune selling this."

"Maybe one day." Bell cupped the goldenbell vial still dangling around her neck. She would sell what she could, but once she finalized the true cure for Lymbodia, she would be giving it away. She thought about Roza, Elena and her brother Eduard; they all had disappeared without a trace. Perhaps by the time she saw them again, she would have a cure ready.

People thronged the streets to Santa Croce. Aless's new Bardian-made ship was apparently enough to draw the city's attention. Gem garlands draped its sides, and white rose petals floated in the air above

332

it. Aless and Carasti stood on the bow, tossing petals and waving to the spectators.

"What are they, royals?" Rian's scowl looked forced.

"They are to me." She linked arms with him and pulled him to the front. Aless waved them to the gangway.

Bell stopped at the edge of the pier, watching the deep, ever-moving water. Far beyond, the blue-black current danced, calling her.

"Are you ready?"

She took a deep breath. "I want to see a new horizon." She wound her fingers into his, and together they walked the gangway and stepped onto the swaying ship.

Author's Note

Dear reader,

I once spent a week in Florence, Italy, with my sister and now sister-in-law. We arrived in the city intending to book a hotel for the evening. Unknown to us, the city was packed for a festival, which I believe was the Festa di San Lorenzo. Every hotel was booked, and we ended up spending the night in a hotel lobby, hosted by a charming and friendly hotelier who refused to let us stay on the street.

Despite what could have been a stressful beginning to our Florentine exploration, we found ourselves utterly charmed by this warm and magical city. The hotelier booked us a room before we even got to the desk in the morning and shooed us off to the hotel's breakfast room. Our room was near the rooftop gardens, and I could see the Duomo tower (which inspired the Consiglio) from my bed.

I knew I would write a story about this place. The artisans, the warm smell of the cobblestones, the gelato on every corner, the families roaming the streets in the cooling air after dark—I didn't know how to shape the magic of it into a novel, but I was going to try.

You are holding (or listening to) the results.

Bardia is inspired by Renaissance-era Florence, a time when the Medici family reigned supreme. While the Asburys and Salviatis are fictional, the Medoro family is based on the Medicis. Cosimo de Medici really was a patron of the arts and education and had his fingers in many areas of power.

335

Roza was inspired by Simonetta Vespucci, a girl who lived in the 1400s and was called the greatest beauty of her time. Nicknamed La Bella Simonetta, she was courted by nobles and artists alike, including the Medici sons. She died of consumption at twenty-one, which was the inspiration for Lymbodia. Her tragic end wouldn't leave my mind and I needed her to be in the story.

Although the real Vasari Corridor doesn't run beneath the great houses of Florence, it was an elevated passageway built as a way for the Medicis to travel unseen from the Palazzo Vecchio, their residence, to the Palazzo Pitti, the seat of government.

Historically the Guardia de' Lanzi were personal guards for the Medici, but having them as the Seller's guards fit the story better.

The city quarters really exist in Florence, and San Giovanni is the patron saint of the city. San Giovanni Day celebrates the saint with a parade that ends at the San Giovanni Baptistry. The Infiorata is a real Italian festival celebrated around the Summer Solstice. *Infiora-tore*—flower artists—spend days creating carpets out of real flowers. The priests and other religious figures lead the way, with the faithful following behind.

It is my dearest hope that this story transported you to a magical place where you discovered that you, like Bell, are far from ordinary.

Acknowledgments

Stories are a bit like flowers. The soil that produces them is complex, intricate, and a bit magical. Many people make up the soil that created *The Seller of Secrets*, and I will attempt to thank them here.

First, I wouldn't be a storyteller without someone to tell the story to. Thank you, dear reader, for picking up this book and giving my story space in your heart.

Thank you to my agent, Rebecca Lawrence, for working your editorial magic on the manuscript and making it a better story from the beginning. Thank you to Ashlyn Inman for loving this story so much and swooning over all the right parts. Thank you to Amanda Chiu, Jane Flautt, and the whole team at Turner Publishing for making this process so delightful for me. Thank you to Audrey Puente for a beautiful cover full of details my literal-cover-loving heart adores.

To Ted Dekker and Maggie Stiefvater, I learned most good things I know about story from you. Stephanie Garber and Margaret Rogerson, your novels are what I read when I need to be reminded of why I write YA Fantasy.

Nadine Brandes, you were the first YA Fantasy author I met in real life, and I will never forget how you pulled me out of the crowd and made me feel seen. You've been an inspiration ever since.

Emily Bain Murphy, your sweet friendship has enriched my life more than I can say. Emily Barnett, it feels like I've known you forever, and I can't imagine life without your encouragement. To my Whimsical Wednesdays: Jill Hackman, Jebraun Clifford, Laura Zimmerman, and Carrie Anne Noble, your support and advice has been so valuable over the years.

To the Cottage, thank you for your ever present support and for keeping me on my toes—I never know if I'll step into a food fight or a prayer meeting when I open our chat.

To the team at Spark Flash Fiction, I made many fond memories and learned to hone my fiction skills during my years working with you. I'm pretty sure I'll be back. Kim Duffy, you gave me "the speech" at Realm Makers one year and I never forgot it.

My Jerry Jenkins group, your endless enthusiasm and support for my writing has been such an encouragement.

Mary Weber and CJ Redwine, your mentorship through the Red Herring Society has been invaluable. Mary, I never would have found an agent without your fabulous editing skills. Thank you forever for banning the instalove and making Bell confident.

To my beta readers, Jordan Millsaps, Emily Barnett, Kristen Bazen, Norita Schrock, you helped make this story stronger and better in its early days.

Voces8, your ethereal voices have inspired many a writing session. Also thank you for making my husband so happy.

Titus & Daisy, Matt & Deborah, our conversations over the years have made me a more thoughtful, whole person. Someday I'll write a literary novel for you. <3

My church community, your enthusiasm and celebration of all my writing milestones has made me feel so supported and valued. Thank you.

To my family: I truly would not be an author without you. Your belief in me and your certainty that I'll achieve my goals is priceless. Mom and Dad, your consistent support of my writing dreams gave me the fuel I needed to keep going. Dorv, I think you're as proud of me as I am of you and that means the world. Miranda, thank you for using your artistry to bring my story to life. Sheila, you've been the best travel companion and you're there in all the memories that sparked this story. Let's go on another trip! Donovan, thank you for your endless support and brainstorming help. Sophia, thank you for being my honest and encouraging alpha reader, for letting me brainstorm and chatter on and on about plot problems and whether the boy is cute enough.

Dan, your unshakeable confidence in me has made me a better woman. I could not have done this without you. Of all the musicians in the world, you're my favorite. <3

Anika, Jasper, Finn, and Layla, thank you for being the sweetest kids and making me love my life as a mom. I think I've finally convinced you I'm a real writer and maybe, just maybe, I'm a better reader than you, Anika.

My Jesus, this story is all for you. I have so many more I want to write together.

About the Author

Sheri Yutzy lives in a small Ohio town in a nineteenth century Italianate home with her musician husband and four beautiful children. When she's not writing, she's tending her garden, baking something, or pulling her youngest children in their wagon. Find Sheri online at Instagram @sheriyutzyauthor, Facebook @sheriyutzy, or on her website at sheriyutzy.com

www.ingramcontent.com/pod-product-compliance
Lightning Source LLC
Chambersburg PA
CBHW020929260626
47169CB00006B/1643